Praise for

Send Me a Sign

"Touching and honest. . . . A moving and inspirational
novel that teen girls will love." —*VOYA*

"Schmidt's heroine believably vacillates between stoicism and
indignation as she learns to rely less on superstitious signals to
predict her future and more on herself, taking charge of the
matters within her control." —*Publishers Weekly*

"Girls who . . . enjoy romance and complex female
friendships will stick by Mia's side." —*Booklist*

"A fabulous and emotional read." —Cornucopia of Reviews

"Fun to read and difficult to put down." —Bookworm 1858

"If you like contemporary—get this, if you like
teen romance—get this, if you are a sucker for
sob stories—get this!" —Cover2Cover

D1023641

Books by Tiffany Schmidt

Send Me a Sign
Bright Before Sunrise

Send Me a Sign

TIFFANY SCHMIDT

WALKER BOOKS
AN IMPRINT OF BLOOMSBURY
NEW YORK   LONDON   NEW DELHI   SYDNEY

Copyright © 2012 by Tiffany Schmidt
All rights reserved. No part of this book may be reproduced or transmitted in any form
or by any means, electronic or mechanical, including photocopying, recording, or by any
information storage and retrieval system, without permission in writing from the publisher.

First published in the United States of America in October 2012
by Walker Books for Young Readers, an imprint of Bloomsbury Publishing, Inc.
Paperback edition published in January 2014
www.bloomsbury.com

Break Myself
Words and Music by Andrew Ross McMahon
Left Here Publishing (ASCAP)
All Rights Reserved   International Copyright Secured   Used by Permission
Reprinted by Permission of Andrew McMahon and Left Here Publishing

Superstition
Words and Music by Stevie Wonder
© 1972 (Renewed 2000) JOBETE MUSIC CO., INC. and BLACK BULL MUSIC
c/o EMI APRIL MUSIC INC.
All Rights Reserved   International Copyright Secured   Used by Permission

For information about permission to reproduce selections from this book, write to
Permissions, Walker BFYR, 1385 Broadway, New York, New York 10018
Bloomsbury books may be purchased for business or promotional use. For information on bulk
purchases please contact Macmillan Corporate and Premium Sales Department at
specialmarkets@macmillan.com

The Library of Congress has cataloged the hardcover edition as follows:
Schmidt, Tiffany.
Send Me a Sign / by Tiffany Schmidt.—1st ed.
p.   cm.
Summary: Superstitious before being diagnosed with leukemia, high school senior Mia becomes irrationally
dependent on horoscopes, good luck charms, and the like when her life shifts from cheerleading and parties
to chemotherapy and platelets, while her parents obsess and lifelong friend Gyver worries.
ISBN 978-0-8027-2840-1 (hardcover)
[1. Leukemia—Fiction. 2. Superstition—Fiction. 3. High schools—Fiction. 4. Schools—Fiction.
5. Family life—Pennsylvania—Fiction. 6. Secrets—Fiction. 7. Pennsylvania—Fiction.] I. Title.
PZ7.S3563Sen 2012   [Fic]—dc23   2012005070

ISBN 978-0-8027-3540-9 (paperback)

Book design by Nicole Gastonguay
Typeset by Westchester Book Composition
Printed and bound in the U.S.A. by Thomson-Shore Inc., Dexter, Michigan
2 4 6 8 10 9 7 5 3 1

All papers used by Bloomsbury Publishing, Inc., are natural, recyclable products
made from wood grown in well-managed forests. The manufacturing processes
conform to the environmental regulations of the country of origin.

For Morgan

I may have been your teacher,

but you taught me the true meanings of *grace* and *courage*

1

Hillary looked up from her phone, squinting at me in the afternoon sun before she pulled on the sunglasses perched on her head. "There is nothing happening tonight. Nothing."

Ally rolled onto her stomach and took a sip of Diet Coke. "There's a barn party coming up."

She had a streak of sunblock on her shoulder, which Hil leaned over and rubbed in. "That's still three days away—is there really nothing planned until then? Mia?"

"Not that I've heard," I answered. "But not that I've asked either. Do you want me to?" My cell phone was somewhere below my chaise and I made a halfhearted attempt to pick it up without looking.

She sighed. "Don't bother. But if the rest of this summer is as crappy as June has been, then let's just fast-forward to September." I couldn't see her eyes behind the dark lenses of her sunglasses, but I knew they'd look hurt; she'd had a rough week.

"Except for us, right?" Lauren asked. "We're not part of the crappiness."

I rolled my eyes and Hil poked me with a purple pedicured toe. "You guys know I love you—it's the rest of this suckfest of a summer I hate."

My phone kept beeping, but I didn't feel like checking it. It was one of those afternoons where the weather was too perfect to take anything seriously. I allowed myself some laziness— stretching my arms above my head, soaking up as much sun- shine and pool weather as possible. The summer was just beginning; I'd let it ramp up to excitement—there was plenty of time for parties and discovering if school-year flings would become summer ones. Plenty more afternoons just like this.

"Laur, you're turning really pink," I said, poking her arm gently and watching it transition from white to ouch-red.

"It's not fair. You're blond; I thought you're supposed to burn too." Lauren stated it like an accusation as she traded her spot at the end of our row of chaise longues for a chair beneath the shade of the patio table's umbrella.

"Nope, just redheads." I tossed her the bottle of sunblock. It was a bad throw, landing closer to the pool than to her hands. "But you'll be the only one of us without wrinkles when we're twenty, so it's almost fair."

"Who wants to come sit with me?"

Lauren was constantly asking questions like this. Yesterday I'd done the whole shade-time thing with her. Today I was too content to move, so I simply stared up at the deep and endlessly blue sky.

"You're, like, ten feet away. I think you're fine," Hil answered.

Shifting my shoulders to unstick them from the chair, I self-consciously adjusted the top of my bikini. Again. At the mall Ally had told me buying a smaller size would make my boobs look bigger. Hil had argued that I was asking for a wardrobe malfunction.

Hil was right—and, since she caught the gesture, she knew it. She raised an eyebrow and shook her head. "The green one looked better on you. We'll go this weekend and buy it."

"Plan," I agreed. I could maybe get away with this one while lying flat and tanning, but the thought of attempting to wear it while Gyver and I swam laps was enough to make me blush and look toward the fence separating his yard from mine. Laps often turned into races, and races turned into cheating, grabbing ankles, and dunking each other to get ahead. The winner was the person who didn't choke on pool water—swimming and laughter not being a great combination. And after we raced we floated side by side, hands, feet, legs, and arms bumping as we bobbed and talked. These scraps of fabric and sequins would never stay put through all that.

"What happened to your leg?" Hil asked, interrupting my thoughts. I'd been busy studying the house next door—something I found myself doing all too often lately.

"It's nothing. I banged it against the side in the game of chicken the other night." I shifted my leg so she couldn't see the bruise that wrapped around half my calf. It was the latest in a series of purple polka dots on my body.

Her eyes narrowed. "Ryan is such a klutz. He should've been more careful."

"Ryan? Careful?" I laughed. "I'm sorry, are we talking about the same person?"

"Ryan's never careful," added Ally. She liked to state the obvious, to make sure we were all on the same page.

"Speaking of Ryan," said Lauren. "Where are the boys? Let's call him and Chris and Kei—" She cut herself off, clapping a hand over her mouth.

Ally and I connected with "oh shit!" eyes.

"And no one," Ally finished, a weak attempt to cover Lauren's slip-up. Weak but sweet.

Hil was sitting so still, she looked like a statue—*Pixie in Red Bikini*. I dropped down next to her on the chaise and wrapped my arms around her. I could almost not blame Lauren; we were all used to including Hil's ex on the list of guys to invite, but Lauren tended to misspeak a little *too* often, and look a little too innocent afterward.

"Sorry, Hil," she said.

"It's fine." Her words were sharp. It was the tone that made freshmen flinch and made me buy cookie dough and schedule a girls' night for us—a voice she used only when she was hurting. Usually because her parents were involved in another custody hearing. Not because they were fighting over who got to keep her, but because neither wanted to.

"Mia, it's hot, stop hanging on me. I'm fine." Still the razor voice, but she was leaning into my hug. I didn't move. "Keith's an asshole. I don't need him."

She pulled her shoulders back, pulled away from me. In a fluid movement she rose from the chaise and dove into the pool, swimming a length before she surfaced and shook water out of her face. "Laur, Mia, Ally! Get your asses in here."

Potential sunburn forgotten, Lauren obeyed instantly—the pull to be included stronger than her sense of self-preservation.

My phone beeped again as I stood. I gathered my hair into a messy knot with one hand and pulled up the texts from my mother, placing the phone on my chair so I could read them while I secured the hair elastic.

Drs called. I moved your appt to today. 4 pm.

Leaving now. Be ready when I get home.

"Aren't you coming in?" Ally was already bobbing in the water, her toned arms wrapped around a pool noodle. "It feels amazing."

"My mom." I pointed to my phone. "Can't. We're going somewhere at four. If I'm not dressed and ready to go when she gets here . . ." There was no need to finish the sentence; we had years of friendship and my mom's dramatics in our collective history. "Stay. Swim. If you're gone before I get back, I'll call you later."

They were just bruises. It must have been a slow week at her advertising firm for Mom to make such a big deal about them. I probably had a low iron level or something—Lauren claimed she skewed anemic every time she went on a diet. I probably just needed to take a vitamin.

I paused before closing the door and shutting out the sounds of Ally's high giggle and Hil's throaty chuckle. Lauren shrieked,

"You guys!" I leaned out, plucked one of the flowers off Mom's bright-pink clematis from the trellis beside the door. Counting the petals as the door closed behind me:

One for sorrow
Two for joy
Three for a girl
Four for a boy
Five for silver
Six for gold
Seven for a secret, never to be told . . .
Seven petals.
I crushed the flower in my hand.

2

Coming tonight had been a mistake. I did a quick survey of the party: Hil mixing drinks on a makeshift bar made from hay bales; Ally and Lauren dancing; Ryan cocking his wrist to throw a Ping-Pong ball into a cup of beer. Since they were all occupied, I allowed my smile to slip, let my cup dangle loosely at my side, and stepped back into the shadows that formed along the wall beneath the hayloft.

"Drop the drink, Mia. We're leaving." It was Gyver's voice.

He didn't belong here. Not that the rest of us did, but we used the old Nathanson barn for parties more often than the East Lake Historical Society used it for their reenactments, so it felt like ours.

"What are you doing here?" I asked.

He grabbed the red plastic cup from my hand and threw it into the hay. "Seriously. I don't care if I have to carry you. We need to go. Now."

The action and the words clicked: he was the police chief's son. "I'm not drunk. I can walk."

"Then do. Quickly." He grabbed my wrist and began to pull me past the stalls containing couples mid–hook up. Past the blaring iPod-speaker combo set up on the ladder to the loft and the barn door balanced on hay bales, where one game of beer pong was ending and guys were fighting over who was next.

"But what about—" Twisting back toward the loudest part of the crowd, I tried to locate Ryan or the girls. I stepped in someone's knocked-over drink and slipped; my flip-flops had no traction on the dirt floor.

Gyver didn't answer, just steadied me and hurried me out the door, down the grass slope, and into his black Jeep, which was still running at the edge of the nearly empty parking lot. Most people parked on the other side of the woods, so they could escape out the back and run if needed. Gyver barely stopped for me to shut my door before he pulled out and sped away. I waited for him to speak. He didn't.

It was dark in his car. And quiet. The party lights and noise faded as we traveled around the lake and back toward town. It was too dark to see the titles of the CDs stored on the visor above my head. Too quiet for comfort. I couldn't handle silence; I'd gone to the party to escape, so I wouldn't have to think about what I learned today—and what would happen tomorrow. Not that I understood tomorrow's agenda. I still couldn't grasp what the doctor had told me. I understood the individual words, but strung together in a sentence they no longer made sense.

I wasn't sure I wanted to comprehend anything yet. I

wanted to hide from the truth for as long as possible. So while the doctor told my father about treatments and my mother sobbed on the shoulder of some supportive nurse, I'd tuned out and planned my outfit for the party we'd just left.

Parties and I were a predictable fit, like Gyver and his music. I reached up and grabbed one of his CDs—it could be any of his custom playlists: Songs for Studying, Rhythms for Rain, An Album for Algebra.

He liked alliterative titles. And names. Walt Whitman, Galileo Galilei, Harry Houdini, Arthur Ashe. And me, Mia Moore. Was that why we were so close? If I'd been named after Dad's mother instead of Mom's, would I be sitting in his car right now? Maybe my name was his sign.

But Gyver didn't look for signs the way I did, and he'd laugh if I suggested this.

He wasn't laughing now. He fixed his frown on the road, and I studied the CD I twirled on my finger. I wished, not for the first time, that his car had an iPod hookup so I could see the contents of his playlists.

It didn't matter; the first song that played would be a sign— and I needed something to point the way. Should I tell him? Could I tell him? I hadn't said the words out loud yet.

I slipped the disk into the CD player and pressed shuffle to add another layer of chance: track six.

A few notes floated out of the speakers and I leaned forward on the seat to catch them. The song began thin, a light piano repeating, fleshed out with the quietest tapping on a cymbal and a background layer of electric guitar.

Before the lyrics began, however, in the pause while I held my breath waiting for the first words, Gyver reached over and switched the stereo off.

"Let's talk," he said.

I twisted my fingers in my necklace, clutching the clover-shaped pendant.

Gyver glanced at me and sighed. "It's just a song, Mi. It doesn't mean anything. I don't want you looking for hidden meanings and all that crap."

He knew me too well. Hopefully well enough to know I couldn't let this go. "But what is it?"

"It's a bad CD selection." He pressed Eject, turned on the overhead light, held up the disk, then read the title while I squinted at his smudged lefty letters. "Anthems for Anger. You're already weirdly quiet and you're going to get all superstitious. What's up? Talk to me."

"I need to hear it." A tidal wave of panic battered against the blockades I'd reinforced all day. Something, anything, was liable to tear them down and leave me useless. "I picked it— I've got to hear it."

"Mia, it's just a stupid song." Gyver's voice was rough with frustration. He used his elbow to hit the window-down button and bent his wrist back to throw.

"Don't!" I snatched at his arm and we veered onto the dirt shoulder. My elbow slammed against my door as we jerked to a stop. A few feet from us was a blur of pine trees, and beyond that, water. The builders hadn't yet bulldozed nature on this side of East Lake, but unless there was a sudden drop in the number of couples moving from New York or Philly to raise their kids in our sleepy, postcard-perfect town, these trees had a limited life expectancy.

Life expectancy.

"Dammit, Mia! Do you want to kill us? What's wrong with you tonight?"

I was glad it was dark in the car—too dark to see the emotion I knew would be carved into his forehead, making his brown eyes blaze. Gyver was a master at intimidating stares, and his frown would be all it took for me to crack and spill everything. My fingers started to tremble. I untangled them from my necklace, sat on my hands, and waited him out—let him curse under his breath and squeeze the wheel with a one-handed death grip.

"Fine. You're not going to listen to anything I say until you've heard it, are you? It's 'Break Myself' by Something Corporate."

"I don't know it—I may need to hear it more than once." I rubbed my elbow. It was already bruising, a reminder of what I wasn't telling him.

"Be my guest." Gyver thrust the CD in, punched the Advance button, then twisted the volume to an uncomfortable level.

It was a male singer and he started quietly, but I knew I was in trouble before he'd finished the first verse. I was sniffing before the chorus. It was starting to be too real.

I'm willing to bleed for days . . . my reds and grays so you don't hurt so much

And crying before the refrain.

I'm willing to break myself. I'm not afraid.

I was afraid. Terrified.

"Do you need to hear it again?" Gyver growled as the final notes echoed through the SUV. I shook my head and he turned off the stereo. My ragged breathing was the only sound in the Jeep. "It's just a song. They aren't even a band anymore. What's going on with you?"

"It's been a long day," I whispered, then changed the subject before he could ask why. "Is the party going to be busted?"

"Yeah. I didn't think you'd want underage drinking on your perfect record right before college apps. You're lucky you're so bewitchingly gorgeous and I couldn't resist rescuing you." He poked my knee and smiled at me.

I rolled my eyes. "I wasn't drinking. I just needed a night out." A last night.

"You had a cup."

"Of water."

"And I'm sure The Jock's playing quarters with apple juice."

"Ryan! The girls! They're going to worry about me. Do you think they got caught? I've got to call." With everything else clamoring in my brain, I'd forgotten them.

"Why?" Gyver scoffed.

" 'Cause he's—"

"He's what? Your date when it's convenient for him? Your hook-up buddy? How exactly would you define it?"

"It's casual," I mumbled. "I'm not sleeping with him."

"He's an ass. You can do better."

"It's no big deal. And you should talk—either you have some impossible standard no East Lake girl can meet, or you get off on disappointing the ones who ask you out."

Gyver laughed and shrugged.

We were friends. Just friends. We'd been friends our whole lives. He'd seen me in footie pajamas and heard our mothers discuss my first training bra and the more embarrassing "milestones of womanhood." His mom made me a cake when I got my first period—there was no chance he'd ever see me that way. Besides, I had Ryan. Sort of. And my dating life wasn't a priority right now. I'd almost forgotten. My breath caught in a mangled sob.

"Calm down. I'm sure The Jock's fine. He's a fast runner. Your cheer-friends too."

"You should've warned everyone else." I wasn't too worried; we'd never gotten caught before.

"You're lucky I was allowed to get you. I begged for a ten-minute head start to pick you up. I had to pull the old Halloween photo of us dressed up as Sonny and Cher off the fridge and bring up how you chased down the sixth grader who stole my candy."

"Gyver, I just needed . . ." My voice was shaking. *I'm not afraid.*

"What? What do you need, Mi? I've been patient. Tears over a song? That's extreme, even for you. Even if you were drunk—"

"It was water." I wasn't sure yet. I wasn't ready to tell everyone. But he wasn't everyone. He was Gyver. I needed a sign. Or a distraction. "Why isn't that band together anymore?"

"Something Corporate? The lead singer wanted to pursue a solo project. Then he got leukemia. You've heard some of his new band's music. Jack's Mannequin?" He searched my face for recognition. "No? I've played it for you. You like it."

I gripped the seat with both hands. "What'd you say?"

"You like Jack's Mannequin?" Gyver reached toward his CDs, but I shook my head.

"Before that." I hadn't meant to whisper, but it was all the volume I could manage.

"He made a new band? He got leukemia? His original band was called Something Corporate? What part?"

Signs don't get much clearer than that. "I've got to tell you something."

3

"Can we stop somewhere? I hate talking in the car; I never know where to look. I know you have to watch the road, but I feel like I'm having a conversation with the side of your face and you're talking to the windshield."

Gyver eased his car into the parking lot for East Lake's "beach." It closed at sundown, and the only other things on the pavement were litter: sunblock bottles, deflated floaties, snack wrappers.

He raised an eyebrow, waiting for me to begin. I took a sip from the water bottle in his cup holder. It was out of a need to do something, not thirst. I choked it down with an awkward coughing noise.

He snorted. "You okay?"

I didn't want to tell him what was strangling me—saying the news aloud would make it real. I pulled my knees up and tucked them beneath my chin.

Gyver's hair looked blue black in the glow of the parking lot's lights. His face was a series of beautiful angles and shadows, but I could still see him as he'd been: the little boy who'd been bullied in elementary school for being named MacGyver after a cheesy eighties TV show about a guy who liked duct tape. I'd defended him then, and he'd been my best ally ever since. I needed him now.

"Remember about a week ago when you asked if Hil and I were cat fighting—because I had bruises?" I regretted my choice of openings; annoyance spilled across Gyver's features.

"I was joking. What's Hillary have to do with anything?"

"Nothing, but your comment made me notice how much I'm bruising." I held up my elbow as proof; showing him the purplish bull's-eye that marked the spot I'd just banged on the door.

Gyver touched it with two cool fingers. "Are you okay, Mi?"

"No." I swallowed against the tightness in my throat, the fear that piled like stones in my stomach. "I've also been really tired and I had a fever. Mom and I went to the doctor and he took some blood. He called me back the next day for more. We went to Lakeside Hospital for tests yesterday—they took a sample of bone marrow from my hip. Today we met with the head of oncology." I felt detached, as if narrating the details of someone else's life.

"What is it? Just tell me." His hand curled around my arm, hitting the bruise, making me wince.

"Leukemia," I whispered, the word sharp and acidic in my mouth.

"Leukemia?" His eyebrows had disappeared under tousled hair, and his face and voice were pleading.

I forced myself to continue. "It's called acute lymphoblastic leukemia. ALL for short. It's blood cancer; my body's making lots of bad white blood cells. They're called blasts—and they're crowding out all of my good cells." I parroted the words the doctor used that afternoon. My voice was emotionless, but my arms were trembling. I squeezed my knees tighter and tipped my head against the cool glass of the window in a last-ditch effort to blink back tears. I hadn't cried in the doctor's office. Hadn't on the drive home. Hadn't while getting ready. But with Gyver, it seemed like the only thing left to do.

"What do the doctors say? Mi?" He sounded little-boy lost, like the first time we'd watched *Bambi*.

I stared at the car's ceiling, speaking around the stutters in my breathing. "It's aggressive. That's the word they kept using. 'An aggressive form of cancer,' 'its spread is aggressive,' 'we need to start aggressive treatment immediately.'" I shut my eyes and tears traced salt lines down my face.

"That's why I went to the party tonight. I just needed to feel normal for a few more hours. Before my life becomes a mess of chemo and doctors and drugs." The last barrier between me and detachment fell, and the doctor's words hit with suffocating reality. "God . . . I have cancer."

He tugged on my elbow and pulled me toward him. I resisted at first; his sympathy would make it harder to stop crying. His other hand closed on my shoulder, and I surrendered, allowed him to draw my head to his chest and fold his arms around me.

I could feel the thud of his heart through his T-shirt, interrupted by the convulsions of my sobs and his unsteady breathing.

It grew hot in the car—late-June-in-Pennsylvania humid—and I couldn't tell tears from sweat. I needed to stop. To calm down. I couldn't go home blotchy and terrified. I unclenched my fingers from a fistful of his shirt, sat up, and focused on slowing my breathing and tears. I took another sip of his water and asked, "What are you thinking?"

"I'm mentally shouting every swear word I know." He rubbed his forehead with both palms, then leaned back against the seat and shut his eyes.

"Are you okay?" I asked.

"Am I okay? Am I okay? Of course not, but who cares? How are *you*? What does all this mean?"

"I don't really know . . . I haven't had much time to figure it out. We've got piles of brochures at home, and Dad's already ordered every book he can find." My fingers were at my throat, twirling my necklace in frenzied loops.

"So what do we do?"

His "we" filled my eyes again and I couldn't answer.

"Mi? What happens next?"

"I check into the hospital tomorrow for more tests. I'm not coming home for a while, like, at least a month. Probably not till August. Dr. Kevin—that's my doctor, my oncologist—said they'd keep me there so I don't pick up infections."

"A month! What about school? Are you going back in September?"

The mention of school sparked a different reaction. I put my feet on the floor and sat up straighter. "It's only been a day. I don't know. I haven't figured out all the details yet." I sounded angry, but the alternative was tears and I couldn't—I wouldn't—lose control again.

He sighed and squeezed my shoulder. "Mi, I can't believe this."

"Get this, my horoscope today was: *'Kick back and enjoy the flood of contentedness! It's a great day to appreciate what you've got and stop worrying about getting more.'*" I stared out at the litter-strewn parking lot. A lonely toddler-sized flip-flop. A cracked sand pail.

"I don't know why you read those. They're crap."

"Maybe. Or maybe the point is I should start appreciating my life, because this is as good as it's going to get." My words slipped from bitter to wistful.

"Don't," Gyver warned.

"Don't what?" I peeled my eyes away from the beach debris.

"Don't you dare start looking for pessimistic signs. You're going to be fine."

The windows were fogging, obscuring the lake from my view. "I need . . . I need air." I pushed the door open and stumbled into the humid night. Wiping my eyes, I crossed to a picnic table and sat facing the lake.

"Here. Drink." Gyver handed me his water bottle and sat on the tabletop.

We faced each other in a showdown of fear. I spoke first. "I don't want to go home yet."

"Understandable. How are your parents? I can't believe they let you go out tonight. Well, actually, I can." I looked away from the ripples on the lake and up at his disapproving frown.

"Dad's turned into Captain Cancer Facts—charts and spreadsheets in full force. And Mom? She's alternating between hysterics and a Prozac-fueled insistence that I'm going to be fine. When I left she was taking a bubble bath to 'calm herself down,' and Dad was cooking dinner with a spoon in one hand and a pamphlet in the other. There wasn't room for my reaction—I had to get out of there." I rolled the bottle between my hands and fussed with the sand at my feet, creating furrows with my toe and then smoothing them flat.

"Oh, Mi." Gyver, with his perfect parents, shouldn't be able to understand mine, but he'd spent enough time around my mom's melodrama and my dad's analytics to nod with comprehension. "You should've called me, or just come over."

"I should've. Is your mom going to make a big deal out of tonight?" My parents might accept that parties were a part of high school, but his mother—the chief of police—never would. Living next door to Chief Russo meant D.A.R.E. lectures at neighborhood barbecues. "I don't think I can handle her yelling right now."

"Don't worry about her. It's not a big deal," he reassured me.

"I guess not, comparatively." I kicked at the pile I'd built beneath the bench and watched the sand scatter into darkness.

Gyver reached out to touch my shoulder. "I'm here."

"Thanks." I leaned my cheek against his hand and took a deep breath. It stirred the faintest sense of comfort, the first flicker of reassurance. "You have your guitar with you, right?"

"I've got my acoustic in the car."

"Can you play me that song? Do you know it?" It had seemed scarily appropriate: "blood," "fear," words whose definitions had changed overnight. Knowing the singer had faced this too, I needed to look for more signs in the lyrics.

He'd already pulled a pick from his pocket and was twirling it as if this were any other night and this were any song request. Then he paused, "You really want to hear it again?"

"Please."

He squeezed my shoulder before backtracking to the car. After finishing the water, I fiddled with the empty bottle, spun it, and told myself if it stopped with the cap facing me, my friends would take the news well. If it stopped facing the lake they wouldn't. It twirled an irregular circuit across the table. I held my breath.

Before it finished rotating, Gyver plucked it off the sun-bleached boards and tossed it into the recycle can. "You want to play spin the bottle?" he joked, then saw my stricken face and gestured to the guitar. "You sure, Mi?"

I nodded.

No matter which singer he covered, I preferred his version to the original. A girl could fall in love with a voice like his and lose herself in his performance. Not tonight. His deep voice was unsteady—it cracked on the first line and broke the word "hopeless" in half. Normally his eye contact was electric, but tonight he looked away as he sang.

When he got to the chorus, his intensity was intimidating—until he choked and stopped playing. I wasn't surprised to find tears blurring my view of the lake, but I was shocked when he looked up and he was crying too.

I wanted to hug him—to remove the guitar strap from his neck and drape myself around it instead—but I couldn't move. I'd made Gyver cry. The knowledge reverberated somewhere beneath my rib cage with an ache too intense to name.

Gyver put the guitar on the tabletop and moved to sit on the bench next to me. I tilted my head against his shoulder. He slipped an arm around me and leaned his head against mine. We stared out at the water, united in our fear. The silence was filled with the chirps of crickets and the splash of fish surfacing to swallow mosquitoes.

"I think you're wrong," I whispered.

Gyver eased his head off mine and examined my face. He smiled, but it faded before erasing any of the pain from his eyes. "You usually do. What am I wrong about this time?"

"It's not an angry song. It's a sad, scared song. You've got it on the wrong playlist."

4

The next morning I deleted the drunken voice mails and beer-clumsy texts from Ryan, Hillary, Lauren, and Ally. Hil sounded annoyed. "So, you disappear for three days, show up at the party where you pout all night, and then you disappear again? What the hell, Mia? Is everything okay? If you're done being no fun, come meet us at Matherson's." There was a message from today too: plans for a hangover lunch.

I wandered into the kitchen and found my parents sitting with coffee and chemo books—a departure from their typical newspaper routine.

"Good morning, kiddo. How are you feeling?" Dad stuck a napkin in his book to mark his page. He believed that anything worth knowing could come from a book, chart, graph, or diagram. He made sense of the world through numbers and data—which was why he'd liked gymnastics more than cheerleading. He understood gymnastics' scoring: points added for difficulty,

deductions taken for not sticking a landing. Cheerleading competitions, with their unquantifiable categories like "crowd
appeal," baffled him. He sat in the stands with his clipboard,
trying to do the work of all the judges at once, until my mom
lost patience with him asking, "Did that girl bobble?" "Would
you say their voice quality is strong or barking?" "How
would you rate their tempo?" and finally told him, "Put that
away and just watch your daughter."

Yesterday's news had launched him into leukemia fact-
finding overdrive. His fingers twitched over the book's cover,
and he looked as if waiting for this conversation to be over so
he could resume his reading was causing him actual pain.

"I'm fine," I said.

Mom swept me with a head-to-toe gaze. "What happened
to your elbow? I'll get you some cover-up."

"It's no big deal. I banged it."

My dad nodded. I wondered if he was aware that he was
flipping the cover of his book open and shut. "We talked to
Nancy Russo this morning. It sounds like it was some party.
You're lucky she let Gyver come get you."

"I wasn't drinking." I grabbed the orange juice from the
fridge and expected that to be the end of the conversation.

Mom didn't believe in discipline and Dad didn't believe in
upsetting Mom. She had been an adored only child. She now
wanted to *be* adored by her only child. She didn't bother with
rules or punishment; she stuck with bragging about my accom-
plishments and making vague comments that teenagers were
"so difficult."

"Of course not," she agreed now. "Even so, you need to be careful. But you know this. I'm sure you were being safe."

"I'm going to meet everyone at Iggy's," I announced as I poured juice.

"Iggy's? Will Ryan be there? Oh, I bet he'll send you flowers in the hospital." She clapped her hands together and said, "How sweet!" like it had already happened. Choosing cheerful oblivion, a Mom trademark.

"Maybe." I kept my face blank. "I don't know if the hospital's really Ryan's scene. It's not exactly going to be fun."

"Kitten, I know that, but I'm sure you girls will still manage to create plenty of drama."

"The hospital isn't summer camp." I kept my annoyance carefully controlled. She'd been there when Dr. Kevin explained treatment: remission induction—a.k.a. a month's stay in the hospital so they could administer chemo and do other painful, awful things. "I don't know if I'm going to be up for girls' nights."

"Of course you are." But her smile weakened. She stood and brushed some hair out of my face, a transparent attempt to feel my forehead. Maybe she understood a little.

"I haven't even told them."

Mom touched my hair again, then frowned at my bruised arm. Her voice was slow, thoughtful. "What if you don't tell them just yet? Maybe you should wait and see how things go. Give it a few days—and if you feel up to visitors, then you could call them."

"Not tell them?" I was filled with sudden shame, like

cancer was my fault and something to hide. "Dad, what do you think?"

"It's your illness, Mia. You get to decide who you want to know." This was as close as he ever came to disagreeing with Mom.

"I already told Gyver."

Mom fluttered her fingers in dismissal. "Gyver's different. We told his parents this morning. But maybe hold off on your friends; you don't know how treatment's going to make you feel. You might want privacy."

"But you told the Russos?" I curled my fingers over my newest bruise, hiding it from sight as I realized how my mother saw it: a blemish and a dark sign of things to come.

"It couldn't be helped. I've decided to take a leave of absence from the firm until induction's done." She shifted her shoulders in a show of self-pride. "Vinny Russo would know something was up when all of a sudden I didn't carpool and wasn't at work."

"Maybe I won't tell the girls right now," I said, looking from Mom's nod of agreement to Dad. Hil would want to know everything. *Everything.* And I didn't have all the answers yet. Or the energy to sit through an interrogation.

Dad picked up a pamphlet off the table. "If you're not ready to tell people, that's okay. There's an article here comparing a diagnosis to mourning, because there are sta—"

Mom interrupted. "We'll beat this. Because, kitten, you can do anything. You are smart and brave and beautiful and you have friends and family who all love you very much." Her voice was chipper as ever—a throwback to her own days as a cheerleader—but her eyes were wet.

I did what was required when Mom gave one of her my-daughter-is-a-superhero pep talks; I smiled and agreed. Although I had to bite my tongue to keep from pointing out that none of the characteristics she named had magical anti-cancer properties. I couldn't think my way healthy, and despite her focus on cheerleading and beauty, leukemia isn't a popularity contest.

"I've got to get in the shower. I'm meeting the girls at noon."

"Don't be too long. We're leaving for the hospital at three," Dad reminded me.

Mom said, "And kitten, remember what we discussed." She put a finger to her lips and raised her eyebrows.

Was it even possible to keep my cancer a secret? I needed a sign.

5

My friends and I always ate at Iggy's. Not because the food was better than any other diner's, and not because the fifties décor of record albums and black-and-white-checkered floor tiles was anything special. We ate here because we always had—and the cheerleaders before us had too. We were guaranteed a booth with almost no wait, and they never kicked us out for spending too long gossiping over a basket of fries and Diet Cokes.

It was always the four of us—we called ourselves the Calendar Girls. Back in middle school we'd decided birthdays weren't enough, so we'd each chosen a season to be celebrated. Hillary Wagner's dark hair and icy attitude made her winter. Ally Wells's sunshine and frequent tear-showers made her spring. Lauren Connors's red hair and ghost-pale skin linked her to fall.

I was easygoing. I was carefree. I was summer. Technically it was my season; if I wanted the girls to spend the next month in my hospital room, they would. Just like we'd campaign to make sure Lauren would be Fall Ball queen, Hil would be crowned at the SnowBall, and Ally would wear the queen's sash at prom. My wish was their command until the first day of school—but what did I wish for?

"I have an idea," Hil announced once Lauren returned from visiting a group of boys in another booth. "But it won't work unless we all agree."

"Should we be nervous?" asked Ally.

"No," said Hil. "Well, maybe Lauren."

When Lauren squeaked, "Wait, me?" Hil laughed and said, "Joking." We each had our role within the group: Lauren's constant need for reassurance was balanced by Ally's need to be needed. Hil's outrageous schemes counteracted my pragmatism.

"What is it?" I asked, hoping her latest plan wasn't a reincarnation of last month's "Let's all get tattoos." I'd barely talked her out of it. Maybe in her new idea I could find a sign for how to proceed with my own announcement.

"It's the summer before we're seniors—our last year together—and I want to make it the best one yet."

"I already agree," interrupted Lauren.

"Last year I was so busy with Keith and all his stupid college drama. We spent so long obsessing about long-distance relationships and where he should apply. Now that we're broken up— thank God—I realized how much I missed out on and how much I missed you guys."

Ally gave Hil a hug. "We're glad to have you back. But you're doing okay with the breakup, right?"

Hil nodded. "I forgot how much fun it is to go to a party without a boyfriend to worry about. So here's my idea: we stay single for senior year. If we want to hook up, that's fine. Mia can continue on her path to heartbreak with Ryan, but nothing real or serious. No boyfriends. Thoughts?"

"I'm in," Ally said. "I'm bored with all the East Lake boys anyway."

"No boyfriends? Like, none?" Lauren's forehead was crinkled with horror.

"Oh, you can do it. You've gone through enough boys already," Hil said. "Mia? What's your verdict?"

"First, my heart is not in any danger. Second, I'm in." Giving up boyfriends would be easy; Ryan would never commit. It was giving up the rest of my life that worried me.

Lauren twirled a curl around her finger. "If you're all going to do it, I guess I'm in too."

"Excellent." Hil lifted her soda and we mirrored her action. "To us! To the Calendar Girls' Single Senior Year. It's going to be fab, wait and see. Drink up, buttercups."

We clinked glasses and sipped. Lauren waited about ten seconds to launch her first protest, "But it doesn't seem fair that Mia gets to keep Ryan."

"Keep Ryan?" Hil scoffed. "Don't let him hear you say that."

"Shh," Lauren said. "Here they come. Act natural."

I tried not to snort—nothing in my life seemed natural right now. Was Mom right? Should I keep this a secret? I tried to imagine doing pedicures in a hospital room or watching scary movies with machines beeping around us. I couldn't picture Ally reading *Cosmo* quizzes while I wore pajamas instead of a bikini. Hillary wouldn't be able to sunbathe topless, and I doubted there would be space to recreate the dance numbers from her favorite musicals. Scenes we watched over and over until we had all the steps mastered or collapsed into giggles. Lauren might mind less—she wouldn't have to worry about burning. Except she never could sit still. Being trapped in a room would drive her—and by extension us—crazy.

"Natural," Lauren repeated in a whisper before amping up her smile.

Hil rolled her eyes and asked, "Mia, are we still going to the mall later?" When I gave her a blank look, she added, "Remember? To get you a bikini that fits?"

"I can't." I pulled my fork through my salad, poking at things but not eating much.

"I'll go," Lauren offered as Ryan Winters, Chris Matherson, and Bill Samuels reached us. "Hey."

Chris and Bill sat by Hil, then commandeered Lauren's fries. Ryan waited next to me, his face a display of amusement framed by dimples.

"Any room for me?" he asked when I didn't get the hint. I blushed and moved down the bench.

Hil scoffed, "God, Mia, how much did you drink last night? I thought I was hungover, but you're a total space case today."

I forced a smile. "Too much."

Ryan acknowledged the lie by squeezing my knee under the table. He'd spent last night offering to switch my water for "something more interesting," and I'd declined each time. His blue eyes appraised me with a look that made me feel naked, both physically and emotionally. A dimple flickered onto his left cheek as he gave me his half grin—the one that made me want to find us a secluded corner.

"Where'd you go last night, anyway?" Chris asked.

"Yeah, and where have you been all week?" Lauren added. "You've been totally M.I.A. since that afternoon at your pool. Get it? M.I.A.? Mia?"

Ally laughed a little, the rest of us nodded and groaned. No matter how lame the joke, I was grateful it changed the focus of the conversation—no one seemed to remember I hadn't answered either question. The first one was innocent enough, but Gyver and my friends ran in different circles; it never went well when I tried to combine them.

"I thought I heard someone say bikini shopping? Can I come?" Ryan teased. His smile settled on me like whiskey, making me feel warm and tipsy.

"I can't. My mom wants to do something."

"So? Cancel," suggested Chris.

"Can't. You don't know how she gets if she feels ignored."

The girls nodded and Ally added, "Totally understand. It's fine."

Hil asked, "What time do you want us over tomorrow, Summer Girl? It's perfect pool weather."

I studied my salad, looking for clues among the lettuce and carrots, but the vegetables didn't give me any signs. "Sorry, I'm busy."

"It's summer! What are you doing, and why aren't we invited?" Lauren asked.

"What am I doing?" I couldn't look at her, so I gazed over her shoulder at the elderly couple in the next booth. "My mom and I are going to Connecticut to visit my grandparents."

"Lame," said Bill.

"Yeah. Sorry I can't play pool princess."

"When will you be back?" asked Ally.

"I don't know."

"But I leave for the shore tomorrow," Ryan protested.

"And you think you'd be Mia's priority, because . . . ?" Hil had hooked up with Ryan first, back in freshman year. She hated that we were together—well, not together—but she hated the idea of us. I couldn't tell if she was protective of me or territorial of him. Probably protective; Hil had Mama Bear down to an art form. Even at her bitchiest, Hil was unfailingly loyal.

"Watch the claws, Hil." Chris grinned across the table at Ryan. "This summer's gonna be off the hook. Beaches full of bikinis? I'll be practicing my mouth-to-mouth all day and all night."

I tried not to imagine Ryan's golden hair lightening in the sun as his abs and shoulders darkened, his blue eyes scoping bikinis, his oh-so-tempting lips pressed against someone else's.

Hil spun toward Chris. "You're disgusting. I can't believe you two were hired as lifeguards. I would not feel safe swimming on your beaches."

Ryan downed half my Diet Coke. "Then you don't have to come visit."

Chris added, "But there's plenty of room at Beach Casa Matherson for lovely ladies who are ready to party and have fun." He and Bill banged knuckles with self-satisfied nods.

"Be fair. You know Hil gets cranky when she's hungover. And we'll totally be there. Maybe we can drive down Friday," said Lauren. "You'll be back by then, right, Mia?"

"Probably not. Sorry."

Hil put down her fork and rubbed her forehead like she could erase my answer along with her hangover headache. "How long will you be gone? Tell me you'll be back when the squad goes to camp."

I studied the neon-pink stars embossed on the tabletop. There was no way I'd be out of the hospital before the squad left for cheer camp at Penn State. "Maybe."

"But—" Ally began, throwing her arms around me in one of her impulsive hugs.

"Ally, chill. Mia won't miss camp; it's still two weeks away. I can never stay long with my grandparents. Old people creep me out."

"Hil has grandparents? Who knew. I thought you were hatched or spawned in hell," teased Chris.

Bill choked on a fry and Hil whacked him on the back, then hit Chris. "You're. So. Not. Funny."

"Between visiting the elderly and cartwheel camp, you'll still come down and visit me—us—right?" Ryan asked me.

The banter. Their normal flirty, teasing banter was too

rapid for me to process today. They could joke and plan beach trips. Not me: I didn't belong.

"Right?" Ryan prompted again. The table had fallen silent and watchful as I suffocated from the weight of my secrets and lies.

"I'll try." I felt trapped in the booth and trapped by their questions. "My pops isn't doing well." I said a silent prayer I didn't jinx my active, healthy grandfather.

"Old and sick? Gross. Either one of those is bad enough, but together? Yuck! Come on, back me up—I'm not evil, right? Don't answer that, Chris." Hil wrinkled her nose in a way she knew looked adorable and looked around the table for support.

Lauren agreed—of course. "Yeah, yuck! I had to visit my gran at the hospital. It smelled weird and people kept shushing me."

"Hospitals are just creepy—period. Buildings full of sick people, ugh." Hil shuddered.

"Well, duh, they're where people go to die and stuff," added Chris.

As my friends nodded, I curled one hand around my necklace and covered my bruised elbow with the other. Hil's comment was an unmistakable sign. My cancer needed to be secret. Those grossed-out and disgusted faces would be for me. Ryan would be flinching, not rubbing my leg below the table.

I pushed his fingers off my thigh—too aggravated to be attracted. "I've got to go pack," I snapped. It wasn't fair I wouldn't have their support. They should be able to handle this.

I would have handled, it for them. Not that I'd wish this on them. Seventeen-year-olds shouldn't have cancer. "Let me out."

"Already? I thought we'd hang out a little," Ryan said. He didn't move, except for his hand, which was back on my thigh.

I needed to get away before I yelled, cried, or confessed everything.

"Can't. I'm leaving as soon as Mom gets home from work." I climbed over Ryan and stood at the end of the table, not sure what to say. "I'll call."

"Wait!" Ally pushed Ryan out of the way and gave me a hug. Lauren and Hil followed her.

"You are too good sometimes, Summer Girl. I would've told my parents no way. Don't let them waste your whole vacation. Get back to us ASAP and we'll make up for all the fun you miss," said Hil.

"Drunk shuffleboard?" I suggested. I left the restaurant while they were still laughing and making up rules.

"So? How'd it go?" Mom met me at the front door, swallowing me up in a tight embrace like I'd been gone for weeks instead of just an hour.

I slumped onto the bottom step and hugged my knees. "I didn't tell them. I just . . . I couldn't handle all the questions."

She hovered above me, smoothing my hair, patting my shoulder. "I understand, kitten. Maybe in a few days. We're all still adjusting to the idea."

"No. I don't want to tell them." This was all I'd thought about on the drive home—I'd asked for a sign and gotten one. I wasn't telling.

Mom's forehead puckered. "I guess that's best. We'll get through this and you'll go back to being the girl you were."

The girl I *was*? Had the diagnosis changed me that much already? I lowered my chin to my knees in defeat. She stroked my hair again, and I bit back the urge to jerk away and tell her to stop touching me.

Dad walked out from the kitchen, a book in one hand, a stack of printouts and a highlighter in his other. "All right, kiddo, I carried your suitcase down. It's time to go."

6

Admission was a mix of paperwork and waiting. Eventually I found myself in a hospital room with white walls, an antiseptic smell, and a view of the parking lot. I was put in a narrow bed, my parents perched in stuffed blue-vinyl chairs, worn shiny from too many passes with antibacterial cleaner. It became a blur after that. A whirl of blood counts, introductions, explanations, and tearful, lingering hugs from Mom. My parents decided to take turns staying overnight. Mom made a big show of volunteering for the first night and tucking me in like I was five before settling onto her cot. I pretended to sleep so she wouldn't know I heard her toss, turn, and cry in her pillow. I should've gotten out of bed and reassured her, but I'd faux smiled and done my no-worries dance all day. I didn't have enough energy to fake bravery. I was scared; her tears couldn't be a good sign.

The next morning I was wheeled off to my first surgery: the

insertion of a port in the right side of my chest a few inches above my heart. I wouldn't look at it, but it didn't feel like much: a small bump under a bandage with constant access to my veins so they could take blood and administer chemo.

I'd become the Summer Girl who couldn't wear a bikini top.

I spent hours with the oncologist as he explained my treatment, prognosis, and what to expect. I didn't feel like I understood a word, but when Gyver stopped by I regurgitated mostly coherent answers.

"They're going to be giving me a 'chemo cocktail': a mix of five different drugs I'll get every day for a week. The goal is to kill *all* white blood cells—the blasts and the normal ones—and then grow back new, cancer-free cells."

"When's this start?" he asked. He'd come with his parents, but they were in the hall consoling mine, which I was thankful for. I needed a break from the suffocating contradiction of their what-a-tragedy looks and we-can-do-this words.

"Day after tomorrow. Welcome to my home for at least the next month. You'll like my doctor. Everyone calls him Dr. Kevin—probably because his patients are usually younger. I'm the oldest one here." I swept a hand toward my door—where I'd had Dad hang my lucky horseshoe—and the rest of the pediatric oncology ward beyond. "His name is Kevin Kiplinger—alliterative, that's a good sign."

"Alliteration? Signs? Who cares? Is he a good doctor? I'm not doubting your parents' doctor-picking abilities, but an alliterative name?"

"I thought you liked alliteration."

"I only told you that . . . We were ten, Mia Moore." He reached out a slow hand and touched the bandages above my heart. "Did it hurt?"

"Not much; they used anesthesia. I guess it'll make things easier; all my IVs will go through there." I touched the bandage, then my necklace, twisting the gold four-leaf clover charm on the chain. "The worst part was they made me take this off. I felt so naked without it."

Gyver smiled. "Who knew you'd get so attached to that necklace?"

I rolled my eyes. "You've always picked out the best birthday presents." I let go of the shamrock and touched the bandage again.

"What will you miss the most about home?" he asked.

"Jinx. I brought my laptop and iPod and I can have as many pictures as I want, but they're not going to let me bring a cat. Will you visit her?"

"Sure. Can I come visit you after the chemo's started?"

"You'd better."

"Where is everyone? Your cheer friends? The Jock? Your mom told mine you're planning on keeping this secret, but that's just your mom being crazy, right?"

"No. They all think I'm in Connecticut with my grandparents." Hil's disdain for sick people still echoed and stung. "For now, that's what I want."

"Mi—" Gyver didn't need to say more than my nickname; he managed to cram disapproval and judgment into two letters.

"It's what I want," I repeated. "Besides, I thought you'd be thrilled; you hate them."

"I don't hate them, and if they're at least good at cheering you up, I won't call them useless anymore."

"I'm not ready to tell them. I have you—that's enough." I squeezed his hand and studied him. The haircut that drove his mother crazy because, while it wasn't truly long enough to be sloppy, it always looked like he should turn around and get back in the barber's chair. His T-shirts, worn in and soft without being ratty.

In a town where guys like Ryan and Chris wore polos with khakis or faded designer jeans, he stood out. His square-toed black shoes, where the other guys wore sneakers. His dark jeans that weren't loose or emo-tight, but fit him perfectly. These things set him apart from the typical male East Laker, but they were oddly comforting in the hospital. Familiar.

Besides, who needed visitors when I had a continual drip of hospital personnel flowing through my room? There were too many nurses to keep track of, so I started giving them code names. There was Mary Poppins Nurse, who had a singsong British accent. Business Nurse, who marched in, did her thing, and left. Nurse Hollywood, who left me copies of US Weekly and brimmed with celebrity gossip. Nurse Snoopy, who wore cartoon scrubs and stayed to talk if she had a minute. She was my favorite.

⊰◈⊱

Doctor Kevin wore gloves as he attached the bag to the pole, then connected it to my port. I stared at it, imagining it contained tiny soldiers—each one armed to attack and destroy my white blood cells.

"Well, Mia, now we start the process of getting you better. Are you ready?" Dr. Kevin was unwaveringly cheerful. If he were thirty years younger, thirty pounds thinner, and female, he'd make a great addition to the squad.

No, I wasn't ready to be filled with toxins. I was terrified of how I'd be affected. I twirled a blond strand of hair around my finger and prayed, please don't let it fall out. Tearing my eyes away from the orangey poison-slash-medicine, I looked from his optimistic face to my parents' determined smiles.

I flashed him my best cheerleader grin and gave the required answer: "Let's do this."

◈

Gyver was better at hiding his emotions than my parents, but I could read the tension in his rigid posture and attentive eyes. "Can I get you anything? How are you feeling?"

"I still don't need anything or feel different than five minutes ago. Promise I'll tell you if I think of something. It's not often you agree to be my slave; I plan to milk it." I poked his knee.

Business Nurse entered. Gyver startled and slid his chair backward a few inches. I was getting used to the zero privacy of the hospital. I didn't like it, but I'd come to expect every nearly normal moment would be interrupted by a blood test, meds delivery, or questions about how I was feeling. This time it was an IV change. The new bag was yellow orange and smaller than my typical fluids. I wasn't due for more chemo yet. The first dose hadn't been awful, but I'd been warned the effects didn't show up right away.

"What's that?" I asked as she flushed my port, cleaning and sanitizing it so she could stick in a new needle.

"Plasma. Your count was low." Her voice was business too.

"Blood?"

She nodded, oblivious to my stiffened posture and rapid breathing. Gyver wasn't; he leaned in and put a hand on my arm.

"But that's someone else's blood. I don't want it in me. It's not mine." My hand closed around my necklace, squeezing the clover charm.

"Doctor Kevin ordered it. Please move your hand so I can get to your port." Her voice wasn't as patient as her words.

"I don't want it." I looked at Gyver with tear-glazed eyes. He was the only one here. Mom had gone home for a "real" shower, and I'd sent Dad to get me a milkshake from Scoops, my favorite ice cream place.

"You need it, Mi. Look the other way and hold my hand."

Gyver's steady gaze eased my anxiety. I took a deep breath and gave him my hand.

I squeezed his fingers as the needle slid in; he squeezed back.

❖

There were other cancer patients in the pediatric ward, but I did everything I could not to meet them, acknowledge them, learn their names. I refused to participate in any of the groups or counseling—I didn't need to vent about how awful this was; I needed to endure it and move on. Besides, I didn't belong there.

The ones who were bald—not like me. The ones with transplant scars—not like me. The ones with radiation treatments—not like me. The ones who'd grown up on this floor, diagnosed at four and celebrating their birthdays and Christmases in the depressing lounge—not like me. The ones without visitors, the ones whose rooms overflowed with visitors, the ones who welcomed volunteers dressed as clowns and cartoon characters—not like me. The ones who played video games or watched movies in the lounge and laughed like they forgot the battles fought within their cells—not like me. The ones who died—not like me.

"Where've you been? I thought you were coming from work—didn't your shift end an hour ago?" I'd worried his tardiness was a sign he was tired of visiting.

Gyver laughed. "That's an intense greeting."

"Someone's a bit bored today." Nurse Snoopy smiled as she checked my chart.

"Very bored. I felt gross this morning, but I'm okay now and I've been dying for you to get here."

He leaned in to give me a hug, but I held him off. "What happened to your arm?" The crook of his elbow was iodine orange and bandaged.

"She's a perceptive little bug, isn't she?" The nurse patted my knee on her way out.

"I stopped to donate blood. You have to be nice to me today—see?" He pointed to a sticker on his shirt proclaiming the same fact.

"You did? Why?"

"Well, I am the universal donor: O-negative. What are you?" He looked at my hospital bracelet. "It figures, you're an A-plus. Do you ever do anything that's not perfect?"

"I've got about a billion mutant white blood cells."

"Yeah, the first nonperfect thing about you, and we've got to destroy it. I figured if you had to get blood, some of it might as well be mine."

"The song," I muttered, thinking out loud.

"What song? Do you need a new playlist? I'm working on Ballads for Battling Blasts. It's all eighties bands like Aerosmith, Danger*Us, Whitesnake, and Foreigner. I'll bring my laptop tomorrow and put it on your iPod."

"No, the song from that night. 'I'm willing to bleed for days . . . so you don't hurt so much.' It really was a sign."

"Mi!" Gyver groaned and slid his grip from my bracelet to my hand. "No more superstitious crap. I mean it."

Day four of chemo was worse. It hurt. Like frostbite in my veins. I writhed, but it didn't help. Lying still didn't help. Holding Gyver's hand didn't help. Prayed for sleep. It didn't come. Asked for sleep meds. Those helped.

⬥

My head was heavy. The room was bright. Shut eyes. "Mom?"

"Right here, kitten."

"Gyver?"

"I'm here, Mi."

"Okay."

Sleep.

Wake. Tired. Tried to eat. Too tired. Sleep.

⬥

"Where's your handsome boyfriend?" Nurse Hollywood attached another bag of chemo. I flinched, though this part didn't hurt.

"What?" Her words startled me. I'd been thinking about Ryan. My life was throwing up, sweating through stacks of the organic pajamas Mom bought me, and feeling too weak to get out of bed or focus on conversations. And I wasn't in the "bad" stage yet. I was grateful Ryan couldn't see what a mess I'd become.

"Gyver. Where's he today?"

"He's coming . . . after work." It took a long time for the words to move from my brain to my lips.

"Where's he work?" She was making polite conversation. I'd already failed to know any of the celebrity gossip she'd mentioned.

My mom sat at my bedside and flipped through a magazine—lately she couldn't look at me. And when she did, she couldn't look away. She'd always been a shopper, but now Dad was showing up with boxes nearly every day—the organic pajamas; chemical-free soap, shampoo, and body lotion; a white-noise machine; an air purifier. She ordered anything and everything she thought might help, and I did my best to sound enthusiastic whenever she unearthed another holistic whatever from bubble wrap and held it up to be admired.

"Me?" Dad asked from the doorway. Gyver was right behind him. He handed today's packages to Mom and then joined Gyver at the sink for the hand-scrubbing ritual. "I'm a Realtor. How are you doing, kiddo?"

I gave him a weak thumbs-up, not lifting my hand from the sheet. Dad kissed Mom's cheek and settled into a chair on my left.

Gyver took his usual edge-of-my-bed perch, pulled out his ubiquitous guitar pick, and began rolling it across the backs of his fingers. "Jinx is good, but she misses you."

"It's been a rough day," Nurse Hollywood informed them. To me, she asked, "Who's Jinx?"

"My cat." It was a Herculean effort to say the words.

"Gyver gave her to Mia years ago. Named her too." Dad chuckled.

Gyver shrugged. "I figured the best way to cure her of being superstitious was to give her a black cat named Jinx on a Friday the Thirteenth."

Nurse Hollywood smiled at him. "I was just asking Mia when her boyfriend would show up. She's lucky to have such a devoted guy."

Gyver dropped the pick and looked at me—eyebrows raised. Dad coughed and excused himself to go find water.

Mom paused with a page half-turned. "Mia and Gyver? They're practically brother and sister. Mia's dating Ryan, the captain of the soccer and basketball teams."

"Ryan's not . . ."

Gyver's words were sharp. "We're not dating. We're friends. Just friends."

"I'm sorry. I assumed . . ."

"It's okay," Gyver cut her off.

I shut my eyes, planning to pretend to sleep, but real sleep tumbled in.

Fevers.

Night sweats.

IV nutrition when I threw up too much.

Treatment continued. And continued to suck.

Without questions about cheerleading, my plans for the night, my friends, Ryan, or school, my parents were at a loss for conversation topics. "How was your day?" was out because we spent our days together—making my hospital room claustrophobically small.

Dad was on his third or fourth Sudoku puzzle, Mom was napping in a chair, and I was skimming a magazine while texting lies to Ally when a pair of shrieking girls scrambled through my door.

"What! What's going on?" Mom jerked awake, blustering and glaring at the tiny bald-headed pair. They were grinning and hiding giggles behind IV-bruised hands.

"Shh!" The taller one whispered, "It's hide and seek and Suzie's it. Don't give us away!"

Dad smiled indulgently and resumed his puzzle, but Mom opened the door and pointed into the hallway. "Out! This is a hospital, not a playground. Can't you see she's resting? Out!"

The girls looked at each other, at me, at Mom, and then left. I was glad the younger one stuck out her tongue and wasn't surprised when Mom followed up by paging Nurse Snoopy and complaining.

"Children shouldn't be running wild. It upset Mia—she has little enough privacy as it is. She should be able to nap without yelling and intrusions. That's unacceptable."

"Now, dear, to be fair, Mia wasn't napping," said Dad.

"Stay out of this! Couldn't *you* have told them to leave? You always make me play the bad guy."

Rather than argue, Dad excused himself to "go pick out something for dinner," and headed to the nurses' station to study the binder of take-out menus—though he probably had them memorized by now. I'd heard Mom and Dad's origin story a million times—how he'd been Mom's statistics tutor in college. "Forty-nine percent of me adored her, the other fifty-one was terrified of her," he liked to joke. Twenty years later, it didn't feel like those stats had changed.

The nurse turned to me. "I'm sorry if they disturbed you."

"It's okay. They were fine."

"No, it's not okay. We're paying for a private room for a reason," said Mom.

Nurse Snoopy nodded sympathetically. "Are you getting out of your room more? Have you met the other patients yet? You'd benefit from making some friends and getting involved."

"Why?" answered Mom. "Those kids were seven—what could they possibly have in common? Mia's not here to babysit. She's here to recover."

The nurse squeezed my arm. "Just think about it."

I did. About how Mom acted like the hospital was a spa and my stint here was supposed to be rejuvenating. How she didn't seem to get the scope of my treatment—this wasn't one month and done. And most of all, how she missed the big thing those seven-year-olds and I had in common: cancer.

But that didn't mean I wanted my room to be a stop on their scavenger hunts.

This was temporary. I knew it was more than a blip, but it wasn't permanent. I'd recover—then reclaim my life. There was no need to put down roots or make connections; these people wouldn't fit in my postleukemia world.

Hil called on a bad day. If my thoughts had been less muddled, I wouldn't have answered. Her voice sounded full of points and pinpricks; it hurt my head and distracted me from her words.

"So it happened. But I'm okay. Really. It wasn't as bad as I thought it'd be."

"What?" I asked, having comprehended nothing after hello.

"I saw Keith. At the grocery store, of all places. At least I wasn't buying something embarrassing like tampons. He was with his mom and she wanted to chat."

"Chat?"

"Yeah, like I could stand there and make small talk with the guy who dumped me the night he graduated."

"Oh."

"I said I had to go and walked out without the cookie dough I was supposed to bring to Lauren's. It was so strange to see him, Mia. He looked good, like he was still my Keith. I had to stop myself from hugging him . . ." Hil hiccuped and took a deep breath that ended in a whimper. "God, that sucked! But I'm okay. Really."

"Really?" My brain could only hold on to her last word and parrot it while I tried to process the rest of her rapid-fire speech.

"I think so. I will be. Please come home. We miss you. I need you."

"Okay," I agreed. "Love you, Hil." As I hung up, I felt vaguely like I'd failed her, but my body insisted sleep was more important than figuring out how.

"Are you excited? Last day of chemo." Nurse Hollywood smiled encouragement.

"Yeah." My lips were dry; the word made them split and bleed.

"Then what?" It was Gyver's voice; I turned and found him sitting in the chair to my left, flipping a pick between his fingers. He looked as exhausted as I felt.

"Then we wait for her white cells to grow back cancer free."

"And she'll start feeling better?"

The nurse busied herself checking the cups on my bedside table. She picked up two empties and answered as she exited, "Not right away, but in the long term."

Gyver looked from the nurse to me. "I made you a new playlist."

"What's it called?"

"Notes against Nausea. It's a good one."

I fiddled lethargically with my necklace. "I haven't listened to your last three. I try, but I fall asleep."

Gyver laughed. "That's kinda the point. They're called Sleep Songs. Like all good playlists, they progress toward a focus track. If you weren't asleep by the end, I failed."

"So I shouldn't play them on shuffle?" I teased. "What's on them? Iron and Wine? Coldplay?"

"Some Iron and Wine, Stars, The National. Not Coldplay."

"I like Coldplay. Are they not cool anymore?"

Gyver looked insulted. "When have I ever cared whether a band is considered cool? It's always about finding the perfect song for the moment."

"So then what's your issue with Coldplay?"

He shrugged. "It's not really an *issue*, just that a guy should never put Coldplay songs on a playlist for a girl. They're the ultimate surrender band."

"Surrender band?"

"As in, I surrender, I'm totally hopelessly in love. Not for friends." Gyver flushed and unhooked my iPod from his laptop.

"Is that an everyone rule, or just a you rule?"

"Probably just me." He passed me the iPod. "How about some Brothers K?" He pulled the book from his bag and returned his laptop. Since I was too nauseated to focus, he'd started reading our AP summer books aloud. Audiobooks couldn't compete with his deep, soothing voice. And they wouldn't summarize what I missed when I fell asleep.

I nodded and scooted over, making room beside me and

waiting for his voice to take us out of the hospital to nineteenth-century Russia.

"Aren't your friends even worried?" Gyver asked as he scrolled through e-mails on my laptop. He pulled up a photo of the girls sitting on the beach. There was a fourth chair between Ally and Hil, empty except for a plastic tiara. They all pouted at it.

"They don't know they should be." I pushed away my dinner tray. I had less than no appetite. Even the sight of food made me want to puke.

"How can they not suspect? You haven't answered half of these and you never turn on your phone."

"They probably don't think anything, because they're busy living their lives. I told them there's lousy reception and I respond when I feel up to it."

When I let myself think about it, the desire to claw my way out of this hospital room and back to my old life—the fourth beach chair, the parties, the lazy afternoons of laughter and chatter—was suffocatingly strong. But I wouldn't fit like this: broken and sickly. And if I forced myself upon them, I'd ruin all their fun too.

Gyver sat on the edge of my bed and picked up my hand. I was so used to holding his hand now—when I got shots, when they drew blood, when something hurt. We'd held hands constantly when we were little. When had it turned taboo? Why hadn't I missed it?

"You're not alone—you have to remember that. So many people care about you. Love you, even." Squeeze. "I'm here. Our moms are downstairs in the cafeteria. Your friends would come if you let them. You don't have to do this on your own."

But I did. When the thing you're fighting is your own body, you don't get tag-team allies. There's no "sitting out this round" or "taking a breather." I was at war with myself, and that's lonely.

"That woman!" Mom huffed as she stormed into my hospital room.

"Who? What happened?" I put my laptop on the side table and turned toward her.

"Nancy Russo crossed the line this time. She asked me who your counselor was."

"Same as Gyver's. Ms. Piper is the only guidance counselor at East Lake," I answered.

"No, like *therapist*." Mom spat out the word. "Like *you* need a therapist! You're popular and well adjusted. You're a cheerleader! If Nancy spent half as much time worrying about her own son, maybe Gyver wouldn't have turned out like that."

I gave myself half a second to be grateful Gyver had already left before asking, "Like what?"

"*Introverted*." Mom pronounced it like it was the worst possible swear word. In her mind it probably was. "And then she had the gall to suggest family counseling. Like I'm some crack mother she's arrested who can't take care of her own daughter. Family counseling!"

"You know she didn't mean it like that."

She tutted at me and went back to being offended. Their friendship was a one-sided competition and I knew from experience that my defending Mrs. Russo only made Mom feel more threatened.

I picked up my laptop and resumed the e-mail I was writing to the girls. I'd figured out it was easier to ask what they were doing than make up lies about all the old-people things I was supposed to be enduring.

The Calendar Girls didn't doubt me once—which made me feel worse.

I thought about telling them sometimes. When I opened a particularly sweet e-mail from Ally, or one of Hil's voice mails saying, "If you don't escape the elderly soon, I'm launching a rescue party," or when Lauren e-mailed me the rules she invented for drunk shuffleboard, or Chris and Ryan texted pictures from the shore.

Mom reassured me I was "doing the right thing," but I started looking for signs and made deals with myself. If I don't need a transfusion today, I'll tell them. If I throw up less than three times today, I'll tell them. If I stay awake until noon. If Nurse Snoopy's wearing her ladybug scrubs. If my numbers are . . . If the next person through the door is . . . If there's green Jell-O with lunch. I never got my "if."

I woke to laughter—a sound so foreign in my hospital room that I thought I must be dreaming. But no, Gyver and Dad were grinning and deep in conversation.

"What are you talking about?" I asked.

"Music," answered Gyver.

"Figures."

"Did you know your dad used to play the sax?"

I raised my eyebrows and turned to Dad, who looked sheepish. "For real? In the marching band or something?"

"That, and I was in a regular band too. Nothing serious, just a couple of guys who liked to jam and considered themselves the next Clapton and Kenny G."

"I can see it," said Gyver. I was glad he could, because I couldn't. The marching band, yes, but a *band* band? I couldn't imagine Dad being a Gyver—on a stage with people yelling and cheering his name. Mom loved to reminisce about how Dad had been the geekiest of geeks when they met, and how she'd taught him as much about being social and stylish as he'd taught her about statistics.

"We should play sometime," Gyver said.

"I'd love to jam . . . as soon as I figure out where Mia's mom hid my sax." Dad reached out for a fist bump. I wanted to laugh or put my pillow over my face and die from embarrassment. "So, kiddo, now that you're awake, what can I get you? Milkshake? Juice? How about some soup?"

I wasn't hungry but Gyver would eat it, so I said "sure," still staring at this stranger who looked like my father but was way more animated than I could remember seeing him.

"Be back in a jiff." He whistled on his way out the door. Whistled.

"Who was that and what have you done with my father?" I asked Gyver.

"What?" he answered, shifting out of his chair and onto my bedside. "Your dad's cool."

"Since when are you guys BFFs? And how'd you learn he played the sax when I've never even heard him mention it?" I tried not to sound jealous.

"Mi, we carpool most days. Spend enough time in a sedan with someone and you bond." He fiddled with the hospital bracelet around my wrist.

"What else do you know? What was his band called?"

Gyver laughed. "You can ask him, you know. He'd tell you."

"Yeah," I agreed, but part of me wondered if he would. It's not like he'd lacked opportunities over the past seventeen years. Maybe, and the thought made me a little ill, he thought I wouldn't care. Maybe, and this thought made me feel even worse, I wouldn't have. Our relationship had always been based on tasks, not talks—we could do puzzles, play board games, use his telescope to find shooting stars—but anything deeper than "how was your day?" resulted in awkward pauses.

When Dad came back, he was bearing a tray laden with soup, milkshakes, three different bottles of juice, and french fries and wearing a guilty grin. "I know your mom wants me to go on a diet, but the fries smelled good."

"I won't tell," I replied, breathing through my mouth because for me the fry smell was nauseating. "*If* you tell me more about your band." I stifled a yawn and hoped I could stay awake long enough to hear his answer.

My phone chirped. Gyver lifted it from the bedside table, flipped it over, and scowled. "I think you'd better answer this one."

"The cheering references too complicated for you?" I'd been here two weeks and the girls had left three days ago for Penn State. Their updates were prolific, silly, and bittersweet. Ally bawled when I told her I wouldn't be back for camp. Hil called my mom and complained. Lauren promised to document everything and had bombarded me with photos and video clips.

Gyver handed me the phone, then stood and paced.

I looked from him to the screen. Ryan. So? He'd texted plenty before, and Gyver begrudgingly handled it when I was too tired or queasy. What was the issue?

I opened the message: Miss u. Can I drve up tmw?

What? I fumbled with the keys. No. Sorry. Not a good idea. Miss you too.

I put the phone down and debated whether I felt sad

because I had to say no, disappointed because I wanted to see
him, or thrilled because he missed me. I hadn't decided or
responded to Gyver when my phone rang.

"Hello?"

"Hey, Mia. God, it's good to hear you." Ryan's smile warmed
his voice and my cheeks.

"You too."

"How 'bout I call in sick, borrow Chris's car, and come up
tomorrow. I don't have the address, but you said Bridgeport,
right? That's about four hours from here."

"Ryan—"

"If I left early, I could be there around lunch. I'd stay until
midnight—your grandparents go to bed early, right? And I'd
be back before work the next day. I'd be tired, but you're
worth it."

"Ryan—"

"I miss you. Don't you miss me?"

"Of course, but it's not a good time."

"C'mon. Your parents can't exile you to Connecticut. They
won't get mad if I visit. Your mom loves me. Or they don't
even have to know I came. We can be quiet."

My eyes stalked Gyver's back. I blushed. He was in the
room during what amounted to a booty call. How I felt about
Ryan booty-calling was irrelevant; there was no way I could say
yes, so there was no point in thinking about how good it felt to
kiss him. Or even if I still wanted to.

My door opened. It did all day, all night. I didn't turn and
look.

"I wish you could; it's just not a good time."

"What's that mean?" Ryan asked.

"How's my favorite patient today? Are you sick of the hospital yet?" Dr. Kevin's voice boomed. I rolled to face him; his eyes were on my chart.

I held up one finger and spoke into the phone, "I've got to go."

"The hospital? Did something happen to your grandfather?" Ryan asked.

"Yes." My voice radiated relief; he'd created the perfect alibi. And technically, unfortunately, it wasn't a lie. Pops had a nasty flu, which was why he and Gram hadn't visited me. I sent another prayer I hadn't jinxed his recovery.

"I've got to go. Bye, Ryan."

"Is Gyver here?" I asked Nurse Snoopy when I woke to see her adding a bag of fluids to my pole.

"Right here." His voice circled from my other side. He had a tired smile on his face. "Your mom's getting lunch."

Nurse Snoopy asked, "How are you feeling? I know you were uncomfortable this morning, but that shot of pain meds I gave you should have kicked in by now."

"I'm okay."

"That's a good friend you've got. I think he spends more time here than I do."

"Possibly," Gyver conceded.

"Gyver's the best," I cooed.

Nurse Snoopy smiled. "I've been meaning to ask you, what kind of name is Gyver?"

I giggled. The sound startled me and I giggled more. "Ask him what it's short for."

Gyver snorted. "What'd you give her? She sounds wasted."

"Morphine. What's Gyver short for?"

"MacGyver!" I crowed.

"Like the show? Say, if I gave you a paper clip and a stick of gum, could you build me a hang glider?"

"Uh-oh, Gyver doesn't like those jokes," I warned.

"I loved that show—or I loved Richard Dean Anderson. He was gorgeous." Nurse Snoopy fanned her face.

"My MacGyver's gorgeous too," I protested.

"Yes, he's very handsome," the nurse agreed. "Why don't you go by Mac?"

"There was a nickname in middle school," he explained, sucking air through his teeth.

"Mac 'n' cheese," I helped. "Gyver hated it."

"And Hillary loved it."

"I like Gyver better anyway. I don't care what Hil says. She's wrong, you're cool."

Gyver shook his head and laughed. "At least I'm cool."

"Very," I reassured him. "You always were. And then you got hot—"

"Baby girl," Nurse Snoopy interrupted, "why don't you save your confessions for when you're a little less medicated? How about you and Gyver watch TV?"

"Okay," I agreed. I handed a grinning Gyver the remote she'd given me.

"And I'll make a note on your chart that you're very sensitive to pain meds."

Ally called sobbing the day she got home from camp. "I heard!"

My heart raced—I wondered if I would set off a monitor. "What'd you hear?"

"I can't believe you didn't tell us!" Ally paused to blow her nose. I clawed at the blankets, sweaty and claustrophobic. "I shouldn't have had to hear it from Ryan."

"Ryan?" He knew too? My throat tightened.

"I am so sorry about your pops. Are you okay? When's the funeral?"

"Pops?" I was swept up in a flash flood of relief and confusion. "He didn't—he's not dead."

"But Ryan said—"

"Ryan's wrong. Pops is fine. *Fine.*" I repeated the word to reassure myself.

"So can you come home soon?"

"I hope so."

"What's your address there? We're sending you a care package."

"Ally, I've got to go." As the panic receded, it left me exhausted.

"Already? Well, text me the address for the box. My mom even made brownies."

Ally's mom's brownies were legendary, but they were sent to Connecticut. By the time the package was forwarded to me they were stale. Gyver and the nurses still enjoyed them and made me put on the plastic tiara included in the box.

"Can you eat those in the hall? The smell's making me nauseated," I lied. When the room was empty, I looked at the girls' cards and photos, covered my face, and cried.

"Mom?" I hated to wake her. Leukemia had changed her as much as it had me; she no longer wore business suits or heels or makeup. She wore frowns and creases between her eyes. An air of fear, desperation, and fragility clung to the threads of her cotton tops and pants—clothes intended for yoga or gardening and never before worn outside our house and yard.

"Mom?"

"Mia? What's the matter?" My mother's hands reached for me before her eyes opened.

"I can't sleep."

"What can I do? Do you want a sleeping pill?" She smoothed her hair and sat beside me.

"I guess."

She pressed the call button and took my hand. "Dr. Kevin said sleeplessness is normal."

I nodded. Her hand seemed so cold.

"Is there anything else I can do, kitten?"

"No. Thanks."

"You're sure?"

I looked up, alarmed; there were tears in her voice. "Mom?"

"I'm so sorry," she gasped.

"Sorry? For what?"

"This is all my fault! These cancer genes had to come from somewhere. Bad DNA your father and I passed on."

"It's not anyone's fault." I was shocked by her apology. "It's bad luck."

"But what would we do without you? You're all we've got, and I can't do anything to fix you. I feel so helpless!"

"I'm going to be okay."

"You're right, you're going to be fine. Of course you will be." She sniffed and tried to get herself under control.

Southern Nurse arrived. She was only on duty at night. The less I dealt with her, the better. Not because she was mean—she was pecan pie sweet—but because if I didn't see her, it meant I slept. She listened to Mom's request and came back with apple juice and a pill.

"Mom?" I whispered. The pill had started to pull me toward sleep and I needed to get this out. "Do you think I was stupid not to tell? I miss my friends."

"I know you do, but they'd just sit here feeling useless and uncomfortable. Do you want them to see you like this?"

The words hung in the air: guilt wrapped in a cocoon of maternal caresses and a gentle tone. I knew it was her projecting how *she* felt, but it didn't make it less true. She kissed my cheek and added, "Of course it's your decision, but things will be back to normal soon."

The sleep meds caused weird dreams. In a blurry, drugged subconscious, I dreamed of Gyver—on stage with his band, Empty Orchestra. In my dream, just like in real life, I marveled how Gyver's look—just off of normal in high school halls—worked on stage. Really worked. In a girls-in-the-audience-swoon sort of way. I was trying to convince the bouncer—Business Nurse—to keep all East Lake girls out. It wasn't because I didn't want them to see me in a hospital gown, it was because I didn't want them to see him on stage or hear him sing.

Dr. Kevin had replaced Gyver's drummer, and Business Nurse wouldn't be bribed, not even when I promised to let the volunteers make me latex-free balloon animals. Yes, even the lounge clown had a cameo in my dream.

I woke to find a pick on my pillow and Nurse Snoopy in the doorway. "Gyver was here all morning. You just missed him."

"I know," I whispered. My left hand was still warm from holding his. I'd missed him and I missed him. More than made sense. More than I should.

"I'm waiting at the airport for my parents. They're coming back from visiting Louisa and her new baby. I had a few minutes and figured I'd call." Lauren was an eleven-years-younger-than-her-sister oops.

"You didn't go?" I asked.

"Nope. It's all baby gushing and I'd worry about dropping him. I'll see him when he's bigger. Plus, no parents equals parties. I wish you'd been here, it was insane. So, how's Connecticut?"

"Fine. Boring."

"Yeah right. I'm totally convinced the reason you've stayed so long is you found some gorgeous preppy with his own yacht and you're acting out a Nicholas Sparks summer romance."

"What?" I laughed. Only Lauren. As long as I shut my eyes, I could pretend I wasn't in a hospital room with Mr. Russo and Dad discussing football a few feet away. Pretend this was a normal conversation.

"It would be a hundred percent okay if you met someone. It's not like you and Ryan are exclusive."

"I know that." This was a sore point and she knew it. Why would she bring it up, unless . . . "Wait, has he?"

"Not in front of me. He'd be crazy to do anything while we were at Chris's house—Hil would castrate him for you. But I think every girl on the beach knew his name. I mean, are you surprised? You disappear for a lifetime and you know he's a man-whore."

"Thanks, Laur." I smacked the bed in frustration—sick of being stuck and forgotten.

"What? Would you rather not know? Geez, shoot the messenger. He did ask about you, and if you'd been there, I'm sure it would've been the Mia-Ryan show."

I was teetering between hanging up and clinging to this bit of normal. I was angry: at myself for being here, at Lauren for prattling on about the "stupid no-boyfriends pact," at Ryan for being Ryan, at my life for not being what I'd planned and worked so hard for.

"Everything's falling apart." It was a whisper. A confession. If Lauren had pressed, I would've spilled everything.

"Okay, drama queen." I could practically hear the eye roll in her voice. "If you're sick of Ryan's games, move on. So anyway . . ."

I didn't hang up. Just sighed and half listened as she told me about the "mutiny-worthy guy" who worked at Scoops, launching into rhapsodies about his ability to make a frappe and complaining about the weight she'd put on drinking them. I tried to feel connected, tried to care, but it all felt so foreign. My contributions to the conversation were minimal and awkward.

"Oh, here are my parents. I've got to go. Come home soon!"

I said good-bye and opened my eyes. No parties. No cute ice cream scoopers. Just sterile white walls and stacks of photos of them having fun without me.

The pain became tolerable. The nausea bearable. The boredom wasn't. Gyver finished all our summer reading. I'd never known a month could feel so long; I'd run out of things to say to my parents weeks ago. Mom's refrain was: "I think you look better. Do you feel better?" Dad's was: "Can I get you anything? Want to play Go Fish?" There was never enough time for Gyver to visit or enough contact with the outside world. I missed the Calendar Girls. I missed Jinx. I missed Ryan, cheering, and my life. I could handle the shots, the bone marrow tests; it was the waiting that was the worst.

It had been an eternity. A shapeless eternity where days and nights blurred with pain, boredom, and repetition. Where my body belonged more to the doctors and blood counts than me. Where life outside the hospital seemed like another world, one I was no longer a part of.

Then, five weeks later, it ended. "Your numbers are looking good and holding steady. It's time we sent you home. Though we're not done with you just yet. We'll see you in late September for your first round of consolidation therapy. And, of course, sooner if you're feeling at all . . ." Dr. Kevin continued to lecture me on limitations, statistics; Dad took notes.

My mind locked on the word "home" and tuned out the rest.

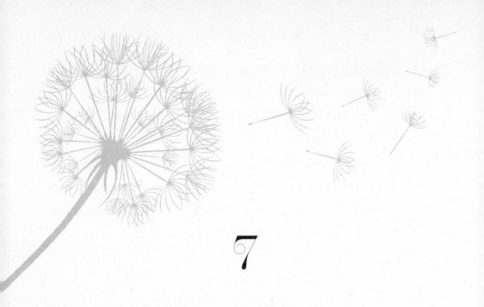

7

My parents were nervous about my homecoming. They tried to hide it, but there was an undercurrent of "now what?" in the looks they exchanged as they carried my bags from the car. Jinx was in cat bliss. She followed me like a puppy, twisted through my legs until I had no choice but to pick her up or trip.

"I think Gyver overfed Jinx. She feels heavier." Either that or I was weaker, because my arms began to shake pathetically.

Mom looked up from the grocery list she was writing for Dad. "You might want to shower and get dressed."

I looked at her notepad: quinoa, acai berries, salmon. "What is this stuff? Since when do we eat kale? What is kale?"

"It's a superfood. Your dad read about it," Mom answered defensively. "You'll like it. You're a healthy eater, but it couldn't hurt to eliminate some of the junk food."

Healthy eater? Had they seen Iggy's menu? But she looked so anxious, the pen in her hand was quivering. "I'm sure it's great."

"You'll love it. It's good to have you home. I've missed you so much."

I opened my mouth to ask how she could miss me when she'd spent almost every moment by my side, but she'd already turned away, opening the fridge and clucking at its contents. "I hope no one's expecting a gourmet dinner. There's nothing in here for me to work with."

"Do you want me to pick something up while I'm out?" Dad began listing options and Mom criticized each in turn.

I scratched Jinx below the chin. She purred and nuzzled closer. Mom had moved on to complaining about her neglected garden; Dad was scanning the grocery list. I slowly climbed the stairs, plopping Jinx on my bed before heading to the bathroom.

The shower felt amazing—real water pressure. I took my time, wrapped myself in cozy towels and rested before smoothing on lavender lotion to cover any lingering hospital smells. I twined my hair into two loose braids—pretending not to notice how much had stayed tangled on my fingers and in the drain while shampooing. Digging through my suitcase, I found my horseshoe and rehung it above the bedroom door, picked up Jinx, then headed downstairs.

Mom unloaded strange foods from Whole Foods bags. New diet, new grocery store: I might be home, but things had changed.

"Pajamas?" Her face tightened in disappointment. "I thought you might like to get dressed for a change."

"I'm not going anywhere today."

"But you're home now. And better. You don't have to go back there for seven weeks. You don't need to wear pajamas anymore. People don't wear pajamas in the middle of the day unless they're sick." A box of organic, whole-wheat crackers dented beneath her fingers.

Dad put a hand on her shoulder. "Relax. If Mia wants to wear pajamas it's okay. She's still healthy."

Mom inhaled a shaky breath. I noticed she wasn't dressed in her wrinkled gardening clothes today. She had on khaki capris and a button-down shirt. Her hair was smoothed in a twist and she had on makeup. She looked like Mom again. She needed me to look like Mia.

"You're right," I piped up with a silly-me smile. "What was I thinking? I'll go change."

Mom exhaled and placed the mangled crackers in the pantry. "Well, if that's what you want."

My bed felt too big and soft after so many nights on that thin mattress and stiff hospital sheets. The silence felt hollow, like the air was empty without the soft padding of nurses' shoes, the squeaky wheel on the meds cart, the giggles and shrieks of kids in the lounge, the falsely positive chatter of visitors stepping into the hallway to "get some air," the blip of machinery, the scream of alarms, and the buzz of the crash cart. I missed the noise. I'd become accustomed to it, even the annoying rattle of my hospital room's air conditioner. It was scary to have so much freedom and privacy.

I was alone for the first time in five weeks. I could breathe without them watching. I could sneeze without raising an alarm.

I could . . . cry.

I'd leaked a tear or two during excruciating moments in the hospital, but these were real tears. Real, pitiful, fear-saturated sobs that shook my bed until Jinx mewed in annoyance and moved. Until I started to feel motion sick and empty. Now-what? tears that had been forbidden during the heavy surveillance of hospital life. Can-I-do-this? tears that would shatter my mother. I'm-so-lonely tears dedicated to the Calendar Girls and the lies I'd told them. My face felt tight and raw. My nose streamed all over the pillowcase.

"Get a grip," I told myself in the dark, squeezing my necklace until I could feel a clover-shaped imprint on my palm. With one hand tangled in the chain and the other on Jinx, I fell into a dreamless sleep.

8

A salon appointment was my first trip out of the house since I'd left the hospital three days ago. I'd slept most of the first two days, grateful to wake up in my own room. Grateful my parents were settling back into hobbies other than watching me: Mom to her neglected gardening and Dad to the pool-shed-turned-astronomy-hideout, which he escaped to each night after dinner.

The August sunlight reflected off the salon's windows. My head felt lighter. I'd left more than a foot of blond hair on the salon floor—until my mom had it all gathered and bagged. "I heard about a program where they can make a wig out of your own hair. Just in case."

Nurse Snoopy had been right; the thinning wasn't as noticeable with shorter hair. My phone rang while Mom paid. I tucked a strand of my new bob behind my ear and ducked out the door. "Hey, Ryan."

"I hear you're back in town."

"I got home this morning," I lied.

"I heard from Chris, who heard it from Hil. How come I didn't hear it from you?" He sounded a little petulant and a lot sexy.

"Because I just got home. Are you in East Lake?"

"At the shore. Come down, we'll celebrate your escape from the elderly. I've got the day off tomorrow and Chris's mom is totally laid back about people staying over."

Mom walked a step away—could she hear? "You want to celebrate my return to PA in Jersey?" I tacked on a teasing laugh.

Mom heard that—and shook her head. I mouthed, "I know," and scowled.

"Well, your return to the Mid-Atlantic. C'mon—we'll throw a big party and have everyone down. I don't know anyone who deserves a party more than you, Saint Mia."

"I just spent three hours in the car, I don't want to spend the rest of the day fighting beach traffic." They were reluctant lies. I'd gleefully sit in traffic if it meant I could flirt, bask in sunshine and Ryan's smiles, and feel normal again.

"C'mon. You're overdue for a party."

"I just got home. Jinx'll never forgive me if I leave again."

"Ouch! I rate below your cat?" Ryan laughed. "Fine, if you won't come see me, I'll come to you. What are your plans for tomorrow?"

"I'm meeting the girls at Iggy's."

"I'll be there. But I want to see you afterward." His voice dropped into a husky tone that made me blush. "Alone."

"Okay," I managed.

"What time?"

"One thirty."

"Can't wait."

"Bye." I opened the car door.

"Ryan's coming to lunch tomorrow?" Mom asked as she climbed into the driver's seat.

"He's driving up from the shore."

"That's nice. He's such a handsome boy. How are you feeling?" She placed one hand on my forehead and fumbled in her purse with the other. She pulled out a thermometer in its plastic case.

"I can't believe you have that in your purse," I said. "What else is in there?"

"Dr. Kevin said you had to be careful. And that I needed to watch you closely for any signs of illness or infection."

"I'm fine."

"Humor me." She pressed it into my palm.

I did. Put the thermometer under my tongue and waited for it to beep. "Perfectly normal. See?" I held it out to her.

"Thank you." She took the thermometer back, handing me one of the bottles of antibacterial gel that were sprouting like a fungus around the house, in our cars, and inside all my purses.

"Do you think they'll guess? Do I look okay?" In the hospital everyone was sick so I blended in. In the real world I felt like a frail, pale-faced freak.

She leaned over and clasped my chin with her hand, forcing me to look at her. "You're beautiful. Always."

Her voice was too earnest to respond with an eye roll. "Thanks."

"It's true. Anyway, the haircut's adorable and with some makeup and strategic clothing choices, no one will suspect a thing."

I tugged the clasp of my necklace to the back and made a wish for acceptance. "I might tell them—now that I'm home. What do you think?"

Mom was quiet for a long time. She stared out the windshield at the parking meter. "I don't want you to regret anything, kitten. Once you tell, you can't take it back. They may not handle it well. You need to be prepared for their reactions."

"What do you think they'd do?" I asked.

"We know how Ally'll be. The others . . . I don't know. I love Lauren, but she's not very tolerant or patient. And Hillary? I can never guess how that girl is going to react."

I tried to picture telling Ryan and saw his *come here* look melt into *stay away*. "The hard part of treatment's over, so it'll get easier to hide, right?"

Mom hugged me. "I can't tell you what to do. It's got to be your choice. Whatever you decide will be right; do what you think is best."

"I just want things back to normal." Or I wanted a clear sign for how to proceed.

"They will be." She smoothed a strand of my hair and started the car. "Soon it will be like this all never happened."

9

After trying and rejecting a dozen outfits, I settled on white shorts and a navy-and-white-striped long-sleeved shirt. Mom helped with makeup, stepping forward to daub on color, stepping back to examine the effect. The result was more makeup than I usually wore, but I looked less pale and sickly. Once ready, I fretted and called Gyver. "Will you come with me?"

"Your goal's to pretend everything's normal, right?"

"Yes."

"Then my coming isn't going to help. I don't normally hang out with your cheer friends and The Jock."

"I guess." I frowned at the mirror.

"You're going to be okay. They're your friends. You miss them. Remember?"

"Yeah." I didn't sound enthusiastic.

"How about this? I'll call a friend. We'll grab a late lunch at Iggy's before my band rehearses. That won't be suspicious. But if you need me, I'll be there."

"Really?"

"Really. But you won't need me. You're going to be fine, Mi."

I was fifteen minutes late because I sat in my car and flipped through the radio for a song sign. The distance between my friends and me stretched from the month behind me to the parking lot in front of me. I should've been running through the diner's door, but the radio was being uncooperative and I was glued to my seat. One hand clenched my necklace, the other jabbed at the Scan button: an unintelligible rap, a commercial for laser eye surgery, a schmaltzy long-distance dedication. And then my sign: No Doubt's "Don't Speak" on one of Mom's easy-listening stations.

The lyrics taunted me, sucking the oxygen from my lungs and making my hand shake as it reached for the radio's Off button. The A/C felt too cold, the car too small. I gritted my teeth and opened the door.

Everyone was already seated in a corner booth. It was déjà vu of our last meeting, only they were the same and I wasn't.

The song was a sign, and my friends' appearances reinforced it; they looked . . . healthy. After a month of seeing hospital-pale patients, it hurt to take in Hillary's toasted-almond tan, Ally's new blonder-blond highlights, and the sunburn balanced across the bridge of her nose. Even fair-skinned Lauren was freckled and pink-cheeked.

Then Ryan stood up and my breath caught. His hair was bleached to the color of sunlit sand. His blue eyes glowed from within the faint outline of his Oakley's tan line. A jolt passed through his hand squeezing mine before it was ripped away by Hil's fierce hug.

"Miss me?" Her grip revealed her feelings.

Before I could answer, Ally chimed in, "Mia! You're never allowed to go away for that long again."

Hil's hug and musky perfume were replaced by Ally's grapefruit lotion, then Lauren's vanilla body splash. But all of these were erased when Ryan wrapped me in his arms—smelling of beach, sunshine, and . . . him. He swung my feet off the floor, twirled me once, then set me down. Casual, like he did so every day, he pressed his lips to my cheek and whispered the words I'd been thinking, "I forgot how good you smell."

Chris nodded his greeting from the booth, where Lauren was climbing across his lap to reclaim her Diet Coke. He was cute, but cute compared to Ryan's sexy. He smirked at Ryan's display and my shocked face. "Hey, Mia. Someone's either really horny or he missed you."

I'm sure Hil smacked him, but I was dizzily being tugged away from Ryan so Ally could grab a second hug before pulling me down into the booth beside her.

"What'd you do to your hair?" Lauren asked.

I forced a quick laugh. "I tried to get it cut and highlighted in Connecticut. Oops."

"Why? It was so long and gorgeous," Hil said. "You're supposed to call me before you make any big beauty decisions, remember? We pinky-promised after I dyed my hair with Jell-O in eighth grade."

I laughed. "I totally forgot about that. Your head smelled like lime for a week."

She grinned at me. "It wasn't my smartest decision—especially since I used my mom's good towels. Oh, before I forget, Cobb salad with fat-free Italian on the side, right? That's what I ordered you, so if you want something different, you need to grab the waitress."

"Actually, I kinda want a cheesesteak. You can't get a good one in Connecticut." I craved real, nonhospital food.

"Really?" Lauren asked. "But that's so fat—er, fried."

"And a vanilla milkshake." After a month of vomiting, I wasn't worried about calories.

"I'll go tell the waitress," Ryan offered, slipping out of the booth.

Hil was still studying me. "Where are the highlights?"

"I don't see any either," Lauren agreed, kneeling up on the booth and tipping her head to examine me like a lab specimen.

"It didn't take—my hair had a weird reaction and burned. It was a mess."

"Oh my God!" Ally squeezed my arm in sympathy. "I'm never getting my hair cut in Connecticut! Poor you."

"It'll grow back." Turning to Lauren and Hil I added, "It's just hair."

"I'd kill for your blond." Hil blew her perfect brown bangs

out of her eyes and reached out to take a lock of my hair. I scooted away, bumping into Ryan, who was sitting back down.

"If you want to sit in my lap, all you have to do is ask." He smiled but I was too overwhelmed to echo it or joke.

"How's your pops doing?" Ally asked. "And are you okay? That must've been so hard!"

"He's doing great. Really, really well. Thanks."

Hil continued her critique. "You don't look like our Summer Girl! Didn't your grandparents let you out in the sun? And I thought Lauren was pale."

I swallowed and tried to look casual, but Hil was circling. She could tell something was off—we'd been close for far too long for her not to pick up on whatever vibe I was projecting— and I knew she wouldn't rest until she'd figured it out.

"I'm a redhead. You know I don't tan, I burn and freckle," Lauren grumbled.

Ryan picked up my arm and compared it to his own. "You've got some serious catching up to do." He slipped both our hands under the table and didn't let go.

I forced myself to join in the laughter and smile at the Casper and albino jokes. So many lies needed to be remembered, topics avoided, questions dodged. Ryan and I didn't usually hold hands. Or we hadn't before. My palm sweated and I was sure he felt my pulse pounding.

"Hey, neighbor. Didn't know you were back. Hi, guys." Gyver's deep voice cut across the good-natured criticism. My racing heart slowed as he approached.

Hillary batted her eyelashes and Lauren smiled supersonically. Gyver didn't look at them.

"Hey." My tension melted. I poked Ryan and he stood to let me out of the booth.

Ryan gave Gyver a stiff nod.

I launched myself into his hug. "How are you? It's good to see you." Stepping out of his arms was hard, but I'd stayed there a beat too long already. I released him but stood close, breathing in his familiar safety.

Gyver picked up the conversation. "How was Connecticut? You cut your hair—it looks good."

"Are you blind? They destroyed her hair," Hillary growled. Her flirty smile was gone.

"I like it." He smiled at me without acknowledging Hil. Lauren leaned forward in a way that showed too much of her lace bra and cleavage.

"Thanks." I meant it to sound casual, but my desperation and appreciation snuck into the word. Out of habit and fear, I nearly laced my fingers through his, then overreacted and jerked my hand away.

"I like it too." Ryan's words and arms wrapped around me at the same time. He pulled me back into the booth, onto his lap. "Now that I'm used to it, I like it a lot."

Gyver's eyebrows went up. I shrugged off Ryan's arms so I could slide onto the bench beside him. Hil looked puzzled and annoyed. She'd always been dangerously observant. And opinionated.

I moved down to create more room between Ryan and me. "It was good to see you, Gyver. I guess I'll see you around."

The others gave halfhearted good-byes, but Gyver focused only on me. "Welcome back."

He was barely out of hearing when Hillary said, "I get that you guys were sandbox pals, but I don't see why you still hang out with him." Her eyes traced a blatant path between me, Gyver, and Ryan.

"Why wouldn't I? Am I supposed to reject him because he rejected you?" I challenged. Ally's mouth was a perfect lip-glossed O and Lauren's eyebrows were halfway up her forehead. "I mean, clearly he has bad taste, but he's still my friend."

Hil smiled icily. "I only asked him out because you were always going on and on about him, but he's such a loner."

"He's not a loner, he's here with . . ." I looked up to see who he *was* here with and the rest of the sentence died in my throat.

The girl was wearing a light-green sundress. It was the type of thing I'd had to retire to the back of my closet because the straps would showcase my port and bony shoulders and the color would make my pale skin look gray. She, of course, looked adorable. She was smiling and saying something that made him laugh. She was leaning toward him. She was touching his arm.

"Who is that?" asked Lauren.

"Meagan something." I barely knew her. I didn't know Gyver did. Well enough to have lunch, just the two of them. Then again, I didn't know how he'd spent his nights. Except for gigs and his work at the record store, we hadn't talked about how he'd spent the nonhospital part of his summer or with whom he'd spent it.

"She's a no one," Hil said, looking at me with concern. "*No one*, Mia."

I went into autopilot protective mode. Defending Gyver was what I did. "She's in our AP classes. And he's got his band and plenty of other friends—ask anyone who knows him and they'll tell you he's great."

Hil grinned and waved a dismissive hand. "But those classes are full of nerd types. I wasn't counting them."

"Nerd types? Thanks, Hil." I was probably being too defensive, and aggressively so, but after all he'd put up with this summer, I wasn't going to shrug this off or let Hil use him to create drama with Ryan. And why was that girl eating one of Gyver's fries? If she wanted some, she should've ordered her own.

"Mia? Seriously? You know I'm kidding." Hil reached across the table and poked my arm. I reluctantly looked away from Gyver and Meagan and at Hil's confused expression. "Geez, one month away and you lose your sense of humor. As long as Mac 'n' Cheese leaves me alone, I won't bother him."

Lauren glanced across the diner. "What a waste. He's OMG hot, don't you think?"

Ryan scoffed, "Did his shirt say pixies? Like, little fairy things?" He shifted his arm to the back of the booth and placed his hand on my shoulder.

"We're friends. I don't think of him that way." My voice was too loud. I was being too sensitive. I forced myself to shrug and added, "By the way, The Pixies is a band."

Ryan frowned. "What kind of band would name themselves after fairies?"

"As fascinating as this conversation is, here comes our food," Chris said.

Hil poked me again. "Want my cucumber?"

They were my favorite veggie, and she knew it. This was Hil's version of a peace offering. I nodded and she dropped the slices on my plate, snagging a fry as she did so. I laughed and she did too.

Ryan passed the ketchup across the booth to Chris, and I looked over their arms to Gyver's table. He faced me and caught my gaze. Cocking an eyebrow in a look that was half-quizzical and half-comical, he watched for my reaction. I smiled and gave him a discreet nod; he smiled back and waited for me to look away.

When I did, Hillary was watching me, her expression part puzzled and part intrigued.

10

I tore into my sandwich, wanting this reunion lunch over.

"Didn't they feed you in Connecticut?" Lauren joked.

I swallowed a sip of milkshake. "I haven't eaten anything with a taste all month."

"Old-people food—yuck!" Hil dipped the tines of her fork in fat-free dressing and speared a piece of lettuce.

"Help yourself to my fries too." Lauren pushed her plate toward me. "The last thing my butt needs is an excuse to get bigger."

Chris looked up from his cheeseburger. "Your summer really blew. You had to live with old people, your hair got fried, you're practically albino, and they didn't feed you. Sucks to be you, huh?"

"And she missed cheer camp!" Ally added.

"But I'm back now," I chimed in, twirling a finger in my necklace chain and maintaining my smile with an effort.

"We're not letting you out of our sight for the rest of the summer," said Hil.

"Tomorrow we'll do a pool day. Magazines, drinks, and lots of gossip," Ally soothed.

"Sounds perfect," I said. She described a typical day from any other summer.

"We'll catch you up on the choreography you missed at camp, so you're not clueless during tryouts," added Hil.

"You can have her tomorrow, but she's mine tonight." Ryan stood and offered his hand. "Ready, Mia?"

Ally gave a high-pitched squeak and smiled at Lauren. Chris groaned and rolled his eyes.

Hillary stood up too. "Wait! What? I thought we'd sleep over my house tonight."

"Sorry. I made plans with Ryan."

"But you haven't seen us in a month!" Hil glared at Ryan's hand on mine. "I can't think of a *single* reason you'd choose him over us."

I'd noticed her watching Ryan watch me and knew exactly what her emphasis referred to. "I promise I'll see you first thing tomorrow." My eyes pled with her to let it go.

She did, with a reluctant, "If it wasn't August and you weren't Summer Girl . . ."

"Relax, Hil. I go back to the shore tomorrow. It's one night," Ryan said.

Chris grinned and leaned toward Hil. "I'll sleep over."

Hil sneered, "You wish," and hid her smile behind a sip of Diet Coke.

I hugged them all. "It's so good to see you guys. I can't wait till tomorrow."

I followed Ryan across the restaurant, catching Gyver's eye as I passed. He nodded once and I nodded back, fighting an urge to interrupt his lunch so I could hug him too. I'd gotten used to seeing him every day; it'd be hard to readjust to the small doses we saw of each other in normal life. I needed to remember I wasn't usually the central person in his life, and he shouldn't be in mine.

Ryan was holding the door open for me. "Want one?" he asked, holding up one of the chocolate mint candies from the dish by the register.

"Sure."

Lauren always had a handful of these in her purse. "Kissing mints," she called them.

Kissing was exactly what I needed right now. Kissing Ryan— whose fingers were warm and strong around mine when he passed me the green-and-brown mint. Whose smile was an invitation.

I smiled back.

Ryan led me directly to his bedroom door.

"Am I allowed in here?" I asked.

"My mom's not home." He stepped into the room. I'd avoided situations like this before—limiting Ryan to party and parking-lot kisses—but it seemed too late to turn back, so I followed.

It was a shrine to sports: a collection of his trophies on shelves beside his bed, newspaper clippings tacked above his desk, his soccer jersey draped on a chair.

I stumbled over a duffel bag. Ryan caught me and kicked it to the side. "Dirty laundry. Mom offered to do it before I head back."

I nodded and examined the photographs on his dresser. Some of the soccer team, more of the basketball team, and a couple of the two of us from prom and parties last spring. Comparing my face in the photos to the gaunt, pale one in his mirror was painful. I put them down—facedown.

Ryan stepped behind me, kissed the back of my neck. I felt the afternoon's tension melt, along with my resolve. "When are you coming home from the shore for good?"

"Not until right before school." Ryan resumed his kisses. My hair had never been this short, so he'd never had access to so much of my neck before. The feel of his lips almost convinced me to leave it bobbed.

"Really? Not sooner?" My words were breathier than I expected.

"I make extra pay if I work after the college kids go back. And double for working Labor Day weekend. I need the money—I've saved enough for my car, but there's insurance and stuff. Wait till you see it. It's worth it."

"Hmm." I managed an almost word.

"You'll come visit, won't you? I don't want to wait another month to do this again." Ryan tipped my face back toward him, leaned over my shoulder, and covered my lips with his. I relaxed into the kiss, luxuriated in it.

I stopped relaxing when his hand began to drift down inside the collar of my shirt. Too close to my port, which hadn't been there the last time his hand had.

"Stop." I pulled away.

"What? Come on! We haven't seen each other in a month. Haven't you missed me?"

"Of course." I was tired and a little queasy. The greasy food wasn't settling well.

"Really?" He sat on the end of his bed.

"Ryan, you're the one with the commitment phobia. As for this"—I pointed to my shirt—"I've spent the past month living with old people. Give me a little while to catch up."

Ryan laughed. "You are a lesson in patience, Mia. I hope you know that."

I lay down next to him on the bed. "Just slow down a little. Tell me about your summer."

Ryan draped a hand across my stomach and started talking.

We'd never had a conversation like this before. We'd talked, but not about things that mattered: how he didn't like his mom's new boyfriend or his older brother's decision to stay at college all summer. It wasn't why he'd brought me here, but it was nice.

"Was it all bad at your grandparents' house? I'm glad your grandfather's doing better." He picked up my hand and kissed the palm.

I stroked his cheek, tracing the creases of his dimples as he smiled at me. "Thanks. I'm glad to be home. How's your job? Is it *Baywatch* come to life?"

"Hardly. For every hot girl there's three old men and five moms with insane kids. When are you coming down to make my *Baywatch* dreams come true?"

Each time he asked about me, I deflected. I relaxed under his stories and warmed under his fingers as they made slow circles on the skin below my belly button. Ever lower circles.

Finally he ran out of stories and I'd run out of questions. He lowered his lips to mine and rolled toward me, keeping his hand where it was: dipped below the waistband of my shorts and just brushing the top of my underwear. "Is this okay?" He pulled his lips off mine enough to breathe the words.

"Yes. So far." As long as he kept his hands away from my port and out of my fragile hair, I could pass for a thinner, paler version of the girl from June. Except his words had flavored the kisses: I wasn't hooking up with a hot guy from school; my lips were against Ryan's, the boy who missed his older brother and dreamed of his own escape to college.

His hand skimmed along the top of my shorts. It stopped at the button and unfastened it in a moment. He paused again—his pinky just edging down my fly—and looked in my eyes for confirmation. There was hesitation; he read it and moved his hand back up to my stomach.

Was he as frustrated with me as I was with myself? I couldn't figure out if I wanted *him* or wanted reassurance he still found me attractive. Was I hesitating because I wasn't ready? Or because I didn't want to reveal my illness? I needed a sign.

My cell rang. I looked away from Ryan and saw it on his bedside table beside his alarm clock. It was 5:13, my lucky number combined with the unluckiest number. What did that mean?

"It's my mom," I groaned and reached for the phone.

"Let it go to voice mail. You'll call her back."

"I can't." With the old me, that would've been fine. Now? She'd dispatch the police and an ambulance if I didn't pick up. The thought of Gyver's mother walking in motivated me to wiggle out from under Ryan and answer. "Hi, Mom."

"Are you okay? You sound out of breath."

"I'm fine."

"I want you home. Your dad read an article and he has me all freaked out about public places and germs. You've seen your friends. You can still see them tomorrow, but come home now so I can stop worrying."

"Okay." I would've been more annoyed if I wasn't so exhausted. I shut off the phone, slipped it in my pocket, and buttoned my shorts. "I've got to go."

He'd been watching me with heavy-lidded admiration, but his eyes blinked into sudden focus. "What?"

"Sorry."

"You'll come back over later though? After dinner?"

He looked so confused. It hurt to disappoint him. "I can't. I really can't."

"When did your parents get strict?"

"Long story."

"I liked it better when you had no curfew." He sat up and reached for my hand, pulling me to stand in front of him.

"Me too." I gave him a quick kiss. "I'll try and come see you at the beach. If you come home again, call me."

"Don't get mad, but can I ask you something?"

"Okay." I tugged my hand, not quite wanting him to release it.

Ryan stared at the floor. "If you don't want to have sex with me, what are we doing?"

"What?" The unexpected question had me flustered and blushing. "You think that's the only the reason I'd be here with you? Is that the only reason you wanted me here?"

"No." He squeezed my hand but didn't look up. "I like talking to you; you listen to me. And you're smart and nice and hot. But I do want to sleep with you."

I tried not to melt from embarrassment. Why couldn't I be confident about this stuff like Hil or tactless like Lauren? "Ryan, I like you. I'm just not ready for that."

"But you'll be ready eventually, right?" His blue eyes met mine and I felt equal parts mortified and attracted.

"I've got to go. We'll talk soon."

He quirked an eyebrow at me—did he know how sexy that was? "Talk or . . . ?"

He knew.

"Talk," I repeated. I leaned in and kissed him good-bye. The type of kiss he'd remember when he was in his lifeguard stand and a bikinied girl romped by. Then I pulled my hand free and ran for my car.

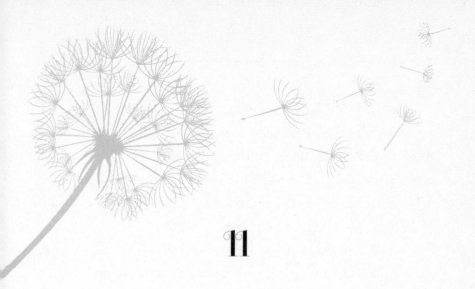

11

Lauren was the first to arrive the next morning. Her red curls fought against her green headband as she struggled to carry the essentials: a bag of Twizzlers, sunblock, and stacks of magazines. "You've got Diet Coke, right?"

"Yes." Although I wasn't allowed to drink it anymore—one of Mom's new obsessions was making sure that everything that passed my lips was natural and organic.

"Hil was getting out of the shower when I called and Ally was leaving to pick her up." Lauren breezed through the kitchen, greeting my dad on her way to the pool. He was "working from home" today, which translated to "babysitting Mia." Mom had left with Gyver's dad for her first day back in the office. She'd called four times.

I poured three sodas and a water and followed Lauren into the backyard. She turned the chaise longues to face the sun and stripped down to her bikini. "Aren't you going to change?

You've got to tell me what diet you're on. I feel like an elephant next to you."

"You're not! I'll change in a bit." Lauren would start to crisp in twenty minutes. I planned to point that out and we'd both move to the shade. She'd be thrilled to have company and I'd avoid bikini, port, and weight-loss exposure. She selected a magazine and handed me the stack. I'd read them all in the hospital. Thank you, Nurse Hollywood.

It didn't matter, because Lauren shut the magazine as soon as she opened it and turned to me with a confiding expression. "I really hated camp without you. Don't tell Hil and Ally because they did their best to make me feel included, but they had all these captain meetings and I couldn't go. I felt so lame and third wheelish."

"That sucks."

"They totally deserve to be captains—it's not that—and I missed you the whole time you were gone, but especially then."

"Sorry."

"It wasn't your fault. I'm sure you'd rather have been with us too." She flipped her magazine open again.

"Definitely." I pulled my feet up on the chair and thought. Of the Calendar Girls, Lauren was the best listener. Ally was too easily distracted and Hil was too opinionated. Lauren wasn't a Gyver give-advice type listener, but the kind you went to when you wanted someone to nod and agree.

"Why are you staring at me?" she asked self-consciously.

"Just spacing out. Sorry." I looked away, searching for a sign. Not finding anything obvious, I reached over and plucked a flower out of one of my mother's patio pots. Tell her. Tell her not. Tell her. Tell her not . . . Not.

I dropped the naked stem onto Lauren's open magazine. "So tell me about camp."

She launched into a play-by-play and was still talking when Ally and Hillary flopped onto the waiting chairs and added their commentary.

"I hate that you missed everything: camp, parties, our trips to the shore—you should see the Mathersons' shore house. And Ryan talked about you a lot," Ally said.

"Really?" I sat up.

"Really. And he was all touchy-feely at Iggy's," Ally said.

I nodded. Hil put down her magazine.

"And he wanted you alone last night," she added.

"So? Did you finally sleep together?" Lauren asked, since Ally wouldn't. Hillary sat up and turned toward me. Ally squeezed in next to me on my chaise.

"No. We didn't. We just talked. And kissed a little."

"Ryan? Talk?" Hil scoffed. "Not when we were hooking up."

" 'Fess up," teased Lauren. "We won't judge."

"He could talk to Mia." Ally leaned her head on my shoulder.

"Thank you, Ally. Sorry to disappoint, but that's all we did. I don't know, do you guys ever look at him and think . . . he's got so much potential?" I asked.

"I look at him and think, God, he's hot!" laughed Lauren. Ally gave me a puzzled smile.

"What do you mean?" Hil asked. "Boyfriend potential? Because you agreed."

I struggled with the words, wanting to explain why I was so attracted to Ryan, besides the obvious. "That's not what I mean. Like, he could be so much more than he is . . . if he wanted to. Does that make sense?"

"Um, not really. Sorry," said Ally.

"What did you two talk about?" Hil asked. She was studying me again, clearly on the cusp of some bigger question. One I probably didn't want to hear and probably couldn't answer.

"Lots of stuff. His job, living with Chris." I shrugged, frustrated I couldn't express it and they couldn't understand. My eyes darted over the fence to Gyver's house. He'd get it, but he wouldn't tolerate the topic.

"Hil hooked up with Chris," Ally exclaimed. "Did we tell you? It was when we visited."

"No way!" I turned to her in surprise. "So? How was it?"

Hil pulled a rhinestone flask out of her bag and began mixing its contents with Diet Coke. "I need a drink before I'm ready to relive that."

She distributed cups and toasted, "Drink up, buttercups."

I joined in the echo of "I will, daffodil," but only pretended to sip. I knocked the contents into the grass and drummed my fingers against the empty plastic while they rehashed the hookup, then some party, or a beach trip, or whatever from their summer full of: "so wasted," "oh my God, so funny," and "you should've been there."

I stood, mumbled "snacks," and walked into the house.

I took my time pouring popcorn into a bowl, watching out the window as Ally demonstrated a cheer move and almost fell in the pool.

They were laughing; I was gripping the countertop with white fingernails.

It was the same summer day we'd had for years—but it seemed trivial, boring.

I wanted them to leave as fiercely as I'd wanted to see them—anything to end this hollow feeling, like I was betraying our friendship by not being on the same page. Or like they were betraying me by being the same when I wasn't.

"Mia!" Hil was standing on her chair, yelling toward the house. "Where are you? Do you need help?"

"Coming." I picked up the popcorn and practiced my casual smile at the toaster until it felt less like a grimace. Pushing open the screen door, I called, "Hey, Laur, you're starting to burn. I can see it from here."

12

Gyver was my bridge between the hospital and real life; he made it impossible to separate the two or doubt the existence of either. We sat in his basement after cheerleading tryouts. All I'd done was demonstrate a few routines, but I was exhausted. Gyver was playing guitar and I was slipping into a doze when a thought blurbled into my mind.

"You were chatty in the hospital," I accused.

"One of us had to be." Gyver took off the guitar and sat on my side of the couch. I rested my sleepy head on his shoulder. "Luckily, you slept all the time so I never ran out of topics."

"What did you talk about?"

"You don't remember?"

"Some—but not a lot." My hospital memories were smudged a bit. Even my emotions were faded, like it had happened to someone else—a character in a book I'd read or a movie I'd seen. "It's all hazy. Like trying to take a test after pulling an all-nighter. I'd flunk if you quizzed me on my own life."

"Like you'd ever flunk anything."

"I got a C on a pop quiz in bio freshman year," I reminded him.

"And you cried for hours. You're crazy." He traced a lazy hand up and down my arm.

"I'm motivated," I corrected. "You should talk—isn't your GPA three hundredths higher than mine?"

"I don't know. Who keeps track of that?" Gyver leaned his head against mine.

"We talked about movies, didn't we?" I asked after a pause. "You were making a list of movies I needed to see. And music. You talked about bands I'd never heard of."

"Maybe that's why you kept falling asleep." Gyver pulled me closer and I nuzzled drowsily against his chest. "I made lots of lists. Bands, movies, things to do when you got out of the hospital."

"What're we going to do?" I wanted to stay awake and have this conversation—it felt important—but I was so sleepy and comfortable.

His voice hushed. "Anything. Everything. I want to do everything with you, Mi."

"Can I see these lists?" I murmured, an escapist yawn splitting the final word in two.

"Not tonight. We've got time."

❖

"Are you sure you're up to this?" Mrs. Russo fretted as she showed me where to stack the mail and how she'd gathered the plants on the kitchen table so I could water them while they were away for a week in Martha's Vineyard. The routine hadn't changed since I started plant sitting in second grade.

"I'll be fine."

"If you're feeling too tired, it's okay to miss a day."

This was proof I shouldn't tell people; Mrs. Russo doubted my ability to empty a mailbox and fill a watering can.

"I've managed to keep myself alive so far; I don't think a dozen plants will be too tricky." I smiled, she didn't.

"Dearest, take a seat. Do you have a minute?" She fussed in the fridge, serving me a large dish of tiramisu. "Can you eat this?"

I reached around the island and grabbed a fork from the drawer. "I can if you don't tell my mom."

She smiled, poured a glass of milk, and sat across from me. "I've wanted to talk to you since your diagnosis, but I haven't found a moment where you weren't guarded by my son or your mom."

I dragged my fork through the dessert, mixing the powdered top into the creamy layer. "About what?"

She put a hand on my shoulder. Her eyes were all sympathy with no trace of their police-chief sternness. "This hiding thing you're doing, it isn't good. You're sick. You've got leukemia. Hiding it, lying about it, those are forms of denial."

"I know I'm sick." The dessert curdled in my mouth.

"And I know your parents. I know you." She paused. "This

is your time to kick your feet and make a fuss. Cry, yell, do something. You're allowed. It'd be healthy."

The irony of the word "healthy" snapped me out of the pity cocoon I'd started to build. "Thanks, but I'm fine."

"Leukemia is not fine. Not accepting you're sick isn't fine. Your stoicism and the lies—Mia, you have to tell people."

"I don't have to do anything." I crossed my arms. "You think I don't know I'm sick? I couldn't forget if I wanted to! Whether or not other people know—that's my choice. I don't need or want people judging me."

"I'm not judging, but you need to focus on getting well, not waste energy pretending everything's okay for your parents or your friends." She pulled me close and I relented, clutching a handful of her sundress so she couldn't let go.

This comfort felt a bit like betrayal; Mom would hate this whole conversation. She'd say Mrs. Russo was meddling; that this wasn't sympathy, it was pity.

I let myself linger for another few seconds before I pulled away from the embrace and swallowed a sob. I couldn't go down that pathetic, sloppy, poor-me path. It wouldn't accomplish anything. I just needed to try little harder and do a better job of faking it until the pieces of my life fell back into place.

"I'm fine," I repeated.

"And I'm here. Whenever you need me. I believe you can beat this. I pray for it and I believe it." She kissed me on the forehead. "Now eat—you're far too skinny."

13

I tugged at my T-shirt and yoga pants; they didn't fit like mine anymore.

"Hil, I can't tumble." Dr. Kevin had forbidden it, and my secret backyard attempts were displayed in a blackish bruise across my butt and left thigh.

"What?" Her eyebrows arched and she crossed her arms.

I gritted my teeth and forced myself to meet her eyes. The old Mia didn't back down from Hil. Of course, she didn't have to lie as often either. But I'd prepped for this one. "I pulled something in my knee running in Connecticut. I can still cheer, but the doctor said no tumbling until it's healed."

Hil pressed her lips into a thin, shiny line and I braced myself, but a new girl spoke first. "So all of Ally's talk about Mia being the best tumbler ever and she can't even tumble?"

Hil spun around and the girl choked off midgiggle. "And you're so great, Sarah? Maybe if you'd spent all summer training instead of bitching, you'd be close to as good as Mia is. No, never mind, you wouldn't. And even when she's not tumbling, Mia's a more important part of this squad than you'll ever be."

Sarah blinked and backed away. I touched Hil's arm and she turned. "Get a doctor's note for Coach Lindsey and don't run if it will make your knee worse. I want you tumbling ASAP."

"Thanks." My eyes strayed to where Sarah whined to another freshman; Ally was headed over to do damage control.

Hil released a slow breath. "I meant it—we need you. You're the heart of this squad and camp wasn't the same without you."

I hugged her, but she brushed me off. "You might as well go home—the rest of the practice is tumbling; it's a waste of time for you to be here." Having dismissed me, Hil stomped off to critique a sophomore with bent elbows.

I drove a roundabout route home, then sat at the kitchen table and watched for the mail truck. It was just collecting mail, but I was glad to have something on my calendar that wasn't a trip to the doctors for endless blood work to test liver function, kidney function, and always, always white blood cell counts.

The only other things on the kitchen calendar were the first day of school, cheerleading, and a red circle around September 21. Mom, Dad, and I all knew what it meant, and none of us needed to have the words "chemo" or "hospital" staring down while we ate breakfast.

School would at least be something distracting. Right now cheerleading filled my mornings, but my afternoons were empty. The girls came over some days but were preoccupied with back-to-school shopping. I wasn't allowed at the mall—it was number eight on Dad's list of germiest places. Avoiding it required a complicated series of lies and excuses—made slightly easier by Mom's online shopping sprees. I could honestly say I had no need to buy any more new clothes.

I embraced the mail collecting and plant watering and tried to ignore how weird it was to be in Gyver's house without him. It was weird just to *be* without him, and I'd begun carrying one of his guitar picks in my pocket—something to hold on to when I was stressed or lonely.

The mailbox was nearly empty today, just a catalog, a bill from the cable company, and a red bug crawling across a college brochure. Were all ladybugs lucky, or did it need to have a certain number of spots? I tried to remember as I gently nudged it off the envelope and onto the mailbox post.

I tossed the mail and paper on the Russos' counter. The plants were still damp from yesterday. It occurred to me that Gyver'd been in my bedroom recently, but I hadn't seen his since elementary school. Would it be like Ryan's—the smell of sweat and a shrine to all things athletic? Not likely. Before I could talk myself out of it, I slipped off my flip-flops, stepped through the archway connecting the Russos' kitchen to their dining room, and crossed to the stairs.

The floor plan was identical to ours. I knew which door at the top of the stairs led to the bathroom and the master suite. I stood in front of the door that would've been mine if this were my house. In this house, it was his.

And it was just like him—slightly disheveled, but more attractive because it wasn't orderly. The walls were green beneath the music posters. I touched the corner of the Radiohead one from the concert we'd attended last year. Ticket stubs everywhere. There were spools of blank CDs on his desk and burned ones scattered about. Favorite and local bands were interspersed with Gaiman, Auster, and Bradbury novels in a wide bookcase that took up most of the space under the two windows facing his bed. A few photos were stuck on the corkboard and on his bureau. Some of the pictures were of Guyver and me; some were of family; most were from concerts he'd played in or attended. I resisted the urge to edit the photos, taking out the ones where I looked hideous or had braces. I couldn't look at his bed without imagining him on it and blushing, so I turned my attention to his desk.

More ticket stubs. Wristbands from clubs. His laptop with band stickers on the cover. An external hard drive to back up his music. There were sticky notes and paper scraps in his undecipherable handwriting. Sheet music—mostly printouts of songs he was learning, but also a few pages that were covered with pencil marks.

I picked up the top sheet, a smudged mess of notes that didn't make sense to me. The notes only reached the third line of music bars, and there was an angry slash across the page. The second sheet was full, not just of notes but lyrics as well. Lyrics that were incomprehensible, just a couple of legible words: sweet, soft, held, kiss, mine. A love song? By Gyver? I blushed and studied it, picking out additional words: the, for, first, now. Nothing revealing. At the top, in all capitals—which he used when he was trying to be neat—he'd printed: "FOR M.A."

For ma? Gyver didn't call his mother "ma." No, there were periods there; definitely M period, A period. My hand shook as I replaced the paper and backed out of the room. I closed the door and leaned on it. The hallway felt small, like the walls were tightening. Gyver—the boy who'd visited every day in the hospital, whose voice chased away my fear, and whose hands knew just when to hold me—wasn't mine. I couldn't swallow and I felt sick—but this time I couldn't blame it on the chemo. I couldn't blame it on anything but my own stupidity.

Back in my own room an hour later, I was still studying the yearbook. There were four girls with the initials M.A. attending East Lake. A fifth graduated last June, but Maggie Arturo had been on the squad and was a Hillary clone, definitely not Gyver's type.

Mindy Adler was attractive, but she smoked . . . and not just cigarettes. That wasn't Gyver's thing. Maddy Appiah made it clear she didn't like boys. Michaela Abbot was a cute soccer player, but she'd been a freshman last year; I doubted they'd met.

Not that I'd needed sixty minutes to figure this out. Or even sixty seconds. Meagan. Meagan *Andrews*. Her activities were listed beneath the yearbook photo with her glossy brown hair neatly tucked behind a headband and Lacoste polo shirt: student council, eco club, jazz band. She had a carefree smile on her face. The same smile she'd given Gyver at Iggy's. It felt like it was mocking me. I slammed the cover so I wouldn't have to look at her. I'd never realized how much I disliked her.

Stupid! I'd almost thought . . . He'd said, "We're just friends" to Nurse Hollywood; but I hadn't wanted to believe it. Though that was in the hospital, where I'd been drugged and delusional. This was real life. And there was Ryan to think about—though I really didn't want to right now.

And in real life, Gyver and I didn't make sense—not as a couple. What would the Calendar Girls say? Plus I'd agreed to Hil's stupid stay-single pact. And my mother, with her dreams of *Most Attractive Couple*, *Most Popular*, and all those other superficial superlatives she'd received her senior year! I couldn't expose him to their scrutiny.

Trade his friendship for something riskier? Could I even handle a relationship right now on top of everything else? He'd probably be better off with stupid Meagan; she didn't come with as much baggage.

And if I failed to be everything he deserved, I'd hurt him.

I had to get over this. This had to be another piece of home-from-hospital readjustment.

I took his pick from my pocket, gave it one last squeeze, then dropped it on top of the tear-soggy tissues in my trash can.

14

On Gyver's second-to-last day of vacation, the last Friday of summer, Mom and I went to a meeting at East Lake High. A meeting about me—and how to accommodate my leukemia.

I hadn't wanted to go. I wanted my hospital life and school life to stay separate from each other. I wanted to leave my illness at the hospital door and not deal with it until I returned in three weeks for my next round of chemo. I wanted to enter the lobby of East Lake High and be the same girl I'd been on the last day of school in June. I wanted the impossible.

After the meeting, Mom dropped me home on her way to work. Dad was waiting at the kitchen table, a notepad and pens all ready. "How'd it go?"

He'd had an open house that morning, and Mom was pissed he'd missed the meeting, but this worked out perfectly. Explaining it to Dad—logical, list-making Dad—would help it make sense to me. He was the perfect person to rehash this with.

Well, him or Gyver—but I needed to stop depending on Gyver so much. Hil would've been a good choice too; she'd get mama-bear protective and point out all the places Principal Baker's idea of East Lake didn't match the reality. But she clearly wasn't an option.

I sat in the chair across from Dad and started with the worst part. "Principal Baker wanted to make a cause out of me. He had all these plans to make me a poster child for leukemia awareness, with assemblies and fund-raisers."

Dad raised an eyebrow. "I assume your mom had some words to say about that."

I nodded. "He's probably already shredded all related documents."

"God love her, your mother is a force of nature." He laughed. "Then that's resolved. Let's focus on what's in place. Let me see the paperwork." Dad took the manila folder, *um-hmm*ing and nodding as he read through the provisions for extended absences, make-up work, and home care.

He took off his reading glasses and rubbed the bridge of his nose. "This all looks pretty standard. It's in line with what I've researched. Does it look good to you?"

"They wanted to change my schedule. Ms. Piper, the guidance counselor, suggested I drop my AP classes and take easier ones."

"I bet your mom had something to say about that too. What do you think?"

I told him the same thing I'd told Ms. Piper and Principal Baker. "There's nothing wrong with my brain."

Dad nodded, looking satisfied. "This looks good, and we can always revisit it later if it needs changes. How about some lunch? Grilled cheese?"

I wanted more from him. Less logic and more acknowledgment that my high school experience was never going to be the same. These sheets of paper were documentation of how much had changed.

If I couldn't have that, I needed a reprieve. A place to pretend this wasn't going on. "No, thanks. I'm going to go have lunch with Hil."

An hour at Iggy's with a Diet Coke, salad, and Hil chattering about Keith leaving for college and whether or not she should've called to wish him luck was exactly what I needed.

"Hey." There was a tap on my doorframe, and Gyver's voice floated through the crack.

"Welcome back! How was Martha's Vineyard?" My arms were full of clothes, so I nudged the door open with my foot. Jinx followed him into my room.

"Warm and beachy. Did you miss me?"

"Of course!" More than I'd admit; more than was acceptable. Dumping the clothes on my bed, I curled into a hug and inhaled his scent. When the embrace stretched to a length bordering on ridiculous, I stepped away and folded a shirt. "Look at your tan. I'm jealous."

Gyver shrugged his broad shoulders. "I'm Italian. Mom's pleased the plants are looking green and leafy. She says thanks. What's going on in here? Laundry?"

"Just picking out clothes."

"Ah yes, the all-important first-day-of-school outfit. Feel free to model for me." He spun my desk chair and sat.

I ignored him. "Jinx, get off the bed—I don't need cat hair on everything. Here, you take her." I passed the cat to Gyver. "It's my second-day outfit. Hil and Ally want the squad to wear our uniforms tomorrow."

"Because nothing makes a good first impression like a miniskirt in school colors."

I crossed my arms and snapped at him, "It's a spirit thing—you wouldn't understand."

Gyver tapped my foot with his. "Probably not, but I didn't come over to talk about your pompoms. I wanted to see who was driving tomorrow."

"Actually, Ryan's picking me up."

"Ryan? Still?"

"He's fun." I scooped Jinx out of his lap, wanting something to hold and hug. "I don't need a boyfriend right now."

"You need someone popular to take to parties? Or is that *your* role? You're the hot girl he gets to drive to school?"

I wanted to ask why he cared. Or explain that Ryan was what people expected of me, a distraction, and an antidote to thoughts of him and Meagan Andrews. Ryan wouldn't break my heart, and he'd never let me close enough to break his. He was safe.

"Don't be a jerk. He got a new car and wants to show me. Is it really a big deal?"

"Between the ride and your uniform, you're starting senior year off with class." He dug his elbows in his knees and interlocked his fingers.

"You are so judgmental sometimes!"

"I don't want you turning into one of those girls."

"What girls? The same ones you were telling me to call the whole time I was in the hospital?"

"Ally's fine, and some of the others too. But Hillary? That girl's the inspiration behind the evil-cheerleader stereotype." He peered up through the messy fringe of his dark hair.

"She's my best friend. Once you get to know her, she's not bad."

" 'Not bad' isn't exactly a glowing recommendation."

"I don't want to fight." I reached over to poke him, but he swiveled out of range.

I counted to seventeen—my other lucky number—then spun his shoulders to face me. "So, second day. Are you driving or am I?"

15

I wasn't ready when Ryan pulled his red sports car into my driveway at 6:40, but I didn't worry. Unlike Gyver, who couldn't string together a coherent sentence until after nine a.m. or his third cup of coffee, Ryan was a parent pleaser 24/7. I popped downstairs to tell him I'd be a few more minutes and found him sitting at the kitchen table with my dad. They were having bowls of organic corn flakes and a conversation about soccer.

"Basketball's my real sport, but soccer keeps me in shape during the fall, and the team has a good chance of making states."

I greeted him and pointed to my pajamas. He nodded. "We've got time."

I stood in my bathroom with a headband in one hand, a brush in the other, and considered my reflection. I think my hair was my initial pass to the in-crowd. It had been my best feature: long, shiny, and blond. Now it was short, duller, and thinning. The nurses told me the hair loss would stop in a few weeks—but there were only eighteen days until I'd be heading back in for more chemo, and the cycle would start all over again. How long until it would be unmistakable? My weak excuse about a bad salon wasn't going to last forever.

Mom had gotten overzealous at Sephora, and dozens of bottles and jars cluttered my sink space. I dabbed and smeared vitality on my face and tugged on my purple-and-gold uniform, frowning at how loose and sloppy it looked.

The last thing I did before leaving my room was flip over my Magic 8 Ball: "Will I have a good first day?" *Better not tell you now.* I shivered.

Putting on a smile, I went downstairs and tried to calm my parents while pretending for Ryan that today was a regular school day and I was a regular student.

Dad pressed me to eat. Mom fussed, fluttered, and stopped just short of taking my temperature (again). I couldn't talk her out of first-day photos: "It's tradition, kitten."

Tradition was Gyver and I hamming it up at our old bus stop. This was Mom with an agenda.

Ryan smiled tolerantly, posed with his backpack and a hand around my waist. I faux smiled through four flashes, then stopped her. "We need to go."

She gave me a kiss on the forehead—sneaking in a final temp check. "Seniors already? That makes me feel ancient. Where'd the time go?"

"We've got to go," I repeated, my hand on the doorknob.

Ryan opened the passenger door for me. His car smelled

new and beachy. A sprinkling of sand stood out like sugar on the gray surface of his floor mats.

"I like your car," I said once he'd gotten in his own seat.

"Thanks. Isn't it great?" He leaned toward me. "Now how about a real hello?"

"Welcome back." But I flinched when I saw my parents watching from the kitchen window. "We've got an audience."

Ryan groaned but started the car. "You're killing me." He filled the rest of the drive with chatter about the shore. I nodded and said *mm-hmm* at the appropriate times, but my mind raced ahead to identify potential obstacles and secret-exposing scenarios.

We only had time for a brief parking lot kiss before I suggested that being late on the first day probably wasn't a smart move.

"To be continued," Ryan said with a laugh as he opened his door.

I hesitated a moment at the top of the stairs and looked up at the wooden sign on the stone wall: EAST LAKE HIGH SCHOOL in gold letters on a purple background. The building hadn't changed—the same lockers with sticky doors and gym-sock smell, the same crowd of kids who pushed, called greetings, and discreetly checked their reflections in classroom windows as they passed.

School was exactly the same, but I felt like I didn't belong.

"I've got to pick up my schedule at the office—want me to get yours?" Ryan asked.

"I already have it." I'd gotten it during my medical meeting.

"Right. Of course you do. I forgot what a little nerd you are."

I frowned and he laughed. "Did I mention you're the hottest nerd?"

"That's better."

"I've got to run or I'll be late for . . . ha, I won't know what till I get my schedule."

"Thanks for the ride."

"Have fun. Play nice with the other nerds." He winked, a dimple tempting me when he nudged his shoulder against mine in farewell. I watched his blond head wind through the crowd, distributing greetings, hugs, and high-fives.

I adjusted my bag. With a quick shake to clear my head and smile frozen to my face, I melted into the hallway traffic.

I ran into Ryan between my first two classes. Literally ran into. I turned a corner in a preoccupied daze and he careened into me while catching something Chris threw from down the hall.

As he hit me, Ryan switched from trying to catch the Snickers bar, which crashed to the floor, to catching me. "Mia! Sorry. You okay?"

Chris's laugh and "sorry" boomed toward me, but he didn't stay to see if I was pissed.

"I'm fine."

"Figures I run over you. But seriously, you're okay?"

"I'm not that fragile." I was defensive—I hated being

asked how I was. Perhaps because it was all Mom said to me anymore.

"I'd better walk you to class, just to make sure," he teased.

"Then you'd better watch out," I answered with a flirty smile and prayer of gratitude for a normal moment. "Because if it gets me an escort, I might start staging hallway collisions before all my classes."

"You think I'd complain about slamming into you a few times a day?" Ryan followed me down the hall. I paused at the door to my calculus class. He leaned in and pecked my startled mouth before disappearing into the crowd.

I stood there, too shocked to do more than press fingers to my tingling lips.

"Miss Moore, if you wouldn't mind joining us in the classroom, I'd like to begin," the teacher suggested. I hadn't heard the bell or noticed the students shuffling past me.

"Choosing a seat might be helpful. Unless you plan on standing all period," Mr. Bonura joked before turning on his projector and launching into a well-worn introductory lecture about his love for mathematics.

I ducked into the desk beside Gyver. He flipped open his notebook, scrawled angry words, and pushed it toward me. I shrugged and gave him a clueless look.

Gyver rewrote his message in block letters—pausing to take a syllabus from the stack being passed around—then slid his notebook across the desk. This time I could read it: What was that about? I shook my head and shrugged again.

You ok?

I nodded.

"Please let me know if I mispronounce your names. I'd hate to be calling you Smith all year if it was really Smith-thay. Joyce Reynolds? Nice to meet you, Joyce. MacGyver Russo? Is it Mac-Guy-ver? Like the show?"

I winced and glanced to my right. He lifted a few fingers in response. "Gyver."

"I loved that show! Can you build stuff out of duct tape and tube socks and ballpoint pens?" Mr. Bonura was under the delusion he was funny. A delusion the rest of the class fed with sycophantic laughter.

"Clever," Gyver answered calmly. Only the muscle twitching in his jaw betrayed his feelings. I wanted to reach across the aisle and squeeze his hand, but that was impossible while I could taste Ryan's kiss and see the dark words Gyver had carved in his notebook in response. While M.A. sat in the desk in front of his, her lips pressed together in disapproval and her eyes full of sympathy.

So I made myself cough.

Mr. Bonura's laughter choked to a halt. He turned to me with a panicked expression.

I stopped coughing and gave him a reassuring smile. He mirrored it feebly and resumed taking attendance.

16

"Maybe we should be more than casual hookups," Ryan suggested. He was waiting at my locker when I stopped to grab my lunch.

"What?" I dropped my book. It landed half in my locker; I kicked it the rest of the way.

"We could go out. I can see myself as your boyfriend." He shrugged.

"What brought this on?" I leaned against the locker next to mine.

"Ally," he replied, placing his hands on the lockers on either side of my neck.

"Ally?" I echoed. How could I keep track of how I felt "compared to normal," when not-normal things kept happening?

"She told Chris about some deal you guys made to stay

single. I couldn't get it out of my head during math. I didn't hear a thing Mrs. Kim said." He grinned and leaned in, kissing close.

This would be the perfect place for one of my faux laughs. I could dismiss his suggestion and push things back to the status quo with one melodic giggle. I opened my mouth, but the sound that came out was a mutated squeak-gasp.

"So, can I be your deal breaker?" He brushed his lips across mine.

"No." My voice was small. I ducked under his arm and fled.

"No, you don't want to? Or no, because of Hil's pact?" Ryan grabbed my lunch and followed me toward the cafeteria, where superficial conversation about classes, teachers, and who had gotten hot—or not—over the summer waited to shift things back toward normal.

"I-I don't know. Let me think about it." My frantic fingers sought my necklace.

"Ouch! You need to think about it? You're breaking my heart." Ryan feigned a stagger and clutched his chest. When I didn't smile, his expression turned serious. And stormy. "Fine. Think about it and let me know what you decide."

He handed me my lunch and walked off to join Chris, Bill, and the rest of the soccer players. I scanned the cafeteria for some sort of sign and jumped when Ally linked her arm through mine.

"Hey! I haven't seen you all morning! How's your day? Anything exciting happen?"

I lied. "Just typical school stuff. Boring. How about you?"

"How'd you manage to domesticate Ryan?" The voice was Hillary's, and it wasn't happy. She looked like a doll—with her perfect, petite body and oversized eyes—but her current mood was anything but playful. She and Ally waited at my locker after the final bell.

"Why? What'd you hear?" I thought the afternoon had been uneventful. Apparently not.

Lauren joined us, clutching a bouquet of sunflowers that Hil or Ally must've given her to celebrate the first day of school— her first day as Autumn Girl. "What's up?" she asked.

"Ryan told Chris he asked Mia to be his girlfriend. Then Chris told Hil. Can you believe it?" Ally's eyes were bright with excitement and gossip.

"No," said Lauren, wide-eyed. "Really? Wow. Good job, Mia."

"Good job? We agreed! Single Senior Year," Hil accused. I remembered how crumpled she'd been after Keith tossed her away with the contents of his locker.

"It's only because he heard about the pact." I turned my lock absently. Part of me wished he'd meant it, or that the pact was my only reason for saying no.

"At least think about it!" Ally said.

"What happened to all of his potential?" Lauren teased.

"Who cares why he's doing it? You like him and he's hot. Anyway, did you guys see the new boy—"

"This is Ryan. He's not serious," Hil interrupted. "Do you know how many girls Chris says he hooked up with this summer?"

"Do you know how much Chris exaggerates?" I retorted.

"So explain it to me—if it's two girls instead of twelve, that's okay with you?" Hil turned to face me, edging Lauren and Ally out of the conversation.

"He hadn't asked me then. If he hooked up with someone now, it'd matter. I can't care what he did while we were in different states and single."

"*If* you were going to date someone, and you promised you wouldn't, you could do so much better than him!" Hil's fingers drummed against her bare arms. "Chris thinks—"

"Who cares? Why would I take dating advice from the guy who broke up with Maggie Arturo by changing his Facebook status to single? Besides, did I miss the part where I expressed any interest in saying yes or dating Ryan? Calm down."

"So anyway, the new guy?" Lauren persisted.

Ally stepped around Hil and grabbed my arm. "Good point, Laur. There's not another guy, is there?" She leaned in, eager for confidences she'd accidentally repeat within minutes.

"No, of course not."

"What about Gyver?" Hil demanded. "You've been hanging out a ton lately. Are you really going to tell me that you guys are just buddy-buddy?"

"What? No. We're just friends!" It was easy to be wrapped

up in this. I wanted to be the girl who'd left this school last June, the one who would've giggled, blushed, and eaten this up. The one who wasn't too exhausted to stand and had to slump against the lockers.

"Ryan can't be serious, right? I mean, why me?" I could be vulnerable about this, especially with them. I had handed out tissues to each Calendar Girl when they'd had breakups. It was why I'd vowed never to fall for a guy like him. Then, last spring, when I was two beers beyond buzzed at one of Lauren's hot tub parties, I'd seen him sling an arm around the shoulders of a shy sophomore being mocked by seniors. "Hank's my buddy," he'd said, and steered the shocked boy away and introduced him to a giggly girl. Ryan had paused to admire his matchmaking, and I'd pushed him into a corner and pressed my mouth to his.

I was already blushing from that memory when Hil answered, "Probably because you're the only girl who won't sleep with him."

Ally swatted her. "Be nice! Because you're you, Mia. I mean, he talks to you. Maybe that's it."

"Or maybe—" Lauren began.

"Does it really matter why if you're saying no?" Hil asked. "He'd hurt you, Mia. I know he would."

"Enough! It's fall. It's my season!" exclaimed Lauren. "Can't I just tell you to say yes or no and we can go back to celebrating me?"

Hil scoffed, "Power-tripping much, Lauren?"

Her face crumbled with the rebuke. "It's just, it's my day . . ."

Hil put her arm around Lauren's waist. "Come on, girly.

It's time for practice. I'll let you pick out the music and lead stretches."

Lauren perked up. "I've got a totally great mix of—"

The intercom buzzed. "Mia Moore, please report to the office."

They looked at me in surprise; I shrugged. "No clue. I'll be there as soon as I can."

17

Gyver was waiting in the hall outside the office when I left ten minutes later. "What was that about?"

I sighed, shrugged, too tired to recount Principal Baker's "How was your first day? We're all here for you" speech.

"Nothing, really."

Gyver touched my hand. "You okay?"

"I'm tired. It's been a long day. The first day of school always is."

"Why don't you go home? I'll take you."

I wanted to, but I couldn't give up that easily. "No, it's all right. Ally'll drop me off after practice."

"You sure? You look exhausted." He stepped in front of me, studying my face.

"Just overwhelmed. Lots to think about. Practice'll help clear my head. School stuff, friend stuff, that"—I nodded toward the office—"and . . . Ryan asked me out." He'd hear soon enough; it seemed like it should be from me.

At the mention of Ryan's name, he pulled his hand away and stepped back. I felt the weight of his disapproval on my empty palm and in the space between us. How could he be so supportive with cancer and so judgmental about who I kissed? Did I criticize the amount of history class he spent chatting with stupid M.A.?

"Am I supposed to go tell The Jock he's a lucky guy?" he asked in a quiet voice.

"No. I don't know. I haven't decided anything."

"Then you'd better get to practice and clear your head."

"Hurry up and change into your practice clothes," Hil called as I entered the gym.

"Everything okay?" Ally asked from atop a pyramid. Her form was perfect and her face didn't waver from its competition smile.

"Fine. It was stupid. I was late for calc. I'll be right out." The locker room revealed another challenge: How would I change without the team seeing my port? Maybe layers? I could wear a tank under my school clothing and put practice shirts over the top. All this deception was so tiring.

When I reentered the gym, Hil and Lauren were scrolling through an iPod. Ally was demonstrating something for a freshman. I nodded to Coach Lindsey and went over to the mats to stretch. With the other girls in tight tanks and bra tops, I felt self-conscious in a T-shirt. It used to be fitted, back when I had curves for it to fit against. I tugged at the extra fabric as I bent down to tie my sneakers.

Ally was calling out a formation when the whistling started. Hil turned with a fake-shocked smile—the soccer players did this every day, whistled and shouted as they ran through the gym and out to their field.

Maybe if I'd been tucked within the confines of the squad, Ryan would've continued running with his team. But I was alone on the warm-up mats. He ran over, a confident grin played on his lips as he watched the surprise on mine.

"Made up your mind yet?" He didn't look angry anymore, just amused—like my agreement was inevitable.

"No," I answered.

"Winters! Stop flirting and move your butt," his coach barked from across the gym.

"Coach Burne, control your players," called mine from her perch on the bleachers.

"Let me know when you do." Ryan laughed and kissed my cheek before sprinting to catch the rest of his team. I looked between the giggling squad and his retreating back.

"Focus, girls," said Coach Lindsey.

"If you're done with whatever you're doing, Mia, maybe you could join us?" ranted Hil.

I'd passed exhaustion and entered *what the hell!* As I found

my spot in formation, I smiled innocently and offered an insin-
cere apology. "Sorry, I don't know what's wrong with him—he
just won't leave me alone today!"

In the car Ally was quick to bring up my trip to the office.
"I can't believe Mr. Bonura had you sent to the office—it's the
first day! What if you'd gotten lost on the way to class?"

"I'm a senior. I know where classes are."

"But still. He's . . . he's such a tool!" Ally didn't swear or use
objectionable language. "Tool" was a major show of loyalty.

Before I could think up an innocent cheer question to keep
Ally chatting, she sucked on her lip and spoke slowly, "Hil's
pissy about it, but she'll get over the Ryan thing; this single-
seniors idea is totally a Keith reaction. You really should say
yes to Ryan."

"Why?"

"Why not? You like him! How many times have you told me
you felt slutty for hooking up with him? And, really, all you ever
did was make out, which is, like, nothing. I thought this is what
you wanted."

"Yeah, but . . ." I sighed and scratched a bug bite behind my
knee.

"But what? Last year every other week you were promising
if Ryan didn't ask you out, you were done with him. And then
every time you kissed, you beat yourself up. What changed?"

"Nothing." Everything.

"Did something happen in Connecticut?"

"What?" I stared at her blankly for a moment. "Oh. No, nothing."

"You're different since you came back. You sure nothing happened? I'd be the last one to judge you if you hooked up with someone. Don't get upset, but you know he did." Her face was a portrait of concern and sympathy.

"Different how?" Mine must've been painted with panic.

"Let go of your necklace and relax! That's what I mean; you're so tense all the time! But about weird things, like you don't drink . . . and Ryan. And you didn't flip about your haircut."

"I did when it happened." I touched my head self-consciously. Mom had sent the bagged hair to the wig maker. No one expected my fragile strands to endure my next round of chemo.

Ally shrugged and turned her lime-green VW Bug onto my street—a row of matching two-story, four-bedroom colonials in a line as straight as a Monopoly board. Gyver's house stood out because of the police cruiser in his driveway; mine for having the most overly landscaped yard—flowerbeds strategically scattered from the mailbox to the front door.

"This Ryan thing, though. How much time did we spend talking about him last year? Are you really going to say no because of Hil?"

"It's not that." My eyes filled. It wasn't just Hil's pact; it was leukemia, and Gyver, and twelve types of doubt about why Ryan really asked.

"Oh, don't cry. I'm sorry! Mia!"

I smeared my tears and makeup with the back of my hand.

"I think it's good he asked." She pulled into my driveway and fished a tissue out of her purse. "It shows he's got good taste. And maybe it's that potential thing you were talking about. If you're not into him anymore, then tell him no, but don't because of a silly agreement."

"I don't know what I want." I checked my makeup in her visor so Mom wouldn't pounce when I walked in the door.

"I'll tell Hil to back off, okay?"

"Thanks."

"Of course." She gave me an awkward seat belt hug. "Love ya, Mia! I'll call later in case you want to talk."

I was exhausted by the demands of the day, bruised from Ryan's collision and cheer practice. By the time she called, I was asleep.

18

"How're you feeling? You look good, considering . . ." The words were an ice bath; they left me shivering and gaping, because they hadn't been offered by a doctor, nurse, or one of my parents. Not even a teacher or Principal Baker. They'd come from Meagan Andrews. She'd said them in the middle of history class.

It was the second week of school, and I was finally relaxing into a routine. Granted it was a routine that included trips to guidance, two skipped practices because I'd been too tired, and I-want-you-to-know-I'm-here-for-you comments from my teachers. Each day felt like a magic trick, convincing people to look at one thing so they missed what was going on behind the curtain—but Meagan's question had shattered the illusion.

"What are you talking about?" My voice dropped to a razor-blade whisper. I pretended to be absorbed by the timeline of the Roman Empire on the board.

Meagan leaned across her desk, conquering the aisle between

us. "I know about your leukemia. I wanted to make sure you're okay."

"Gyver told you?" He was by the pencil sharpener but turned at the sound of his name. "You can't tell anyone," I hissed at her. Without waiting for a response, I walked up to Mr. Yusella. "I need to go to the nurse."

"Oh. Oh!" He swallowed a worried breath. "Do you want someone to walk you?"

I shook my head and hurried out the door. Before I'd made it past three classrooms, Gyver caught up. "What's going on? You okay?"

"I trusted you." I had to wrap my arms around my stomach to get the words out. Everything inside felt broken. I couldn't believe he had betrayed me—to *her*. But why wouldn't he? If he wrote her songs, why wouldn't he tell her secrets?

"What are you talking about, Mi?" He held open his arms to embrace me, but instead I rained weak fists against his chest.

"I can't believe you told her."

"Who?" He took both my fists in one of his hands, and with the other drew me into a hug. "I haven't told anyone."

"Who do you think? Meagan Andrews. She knows, Gyver, she knows." My face was slick with tears, which I wiped against his Velvet Underground T-shirt.

"I didn't tell her. You know I wouldn't." He rubbed my back and released my hands; they dropped to my sides.

"I need to go home." I couldn't be in school when Meagan told everyone. I couldn't face their scrutiny and overwhelming pity.

"Okay. Let's go." Gyver's hand around my shoulder supported and propelled me outside to his car. I couldn't do anything but bite my bottom lip and shake my head. All those weeks of hiding and lying and I was going to be exposed . . . by her? Would it change how Gyver felt? Would he go home and add a verse about M.A.'s life-ruining tendencies?

"It's going to be okay," he reassured me.

I shook my head and reached for him. He drove one-handed to my house.

"Your dad's home." He pointed to his car in my driveway. "I'll head back to school and let them know you weren't feeling well."

My eyes grew wet, but I nodded.

"Do I need to tell your cheer friends?" he asked.

I nodded again and continued to chew my lip.

"It's going to be okay." With one finger he reached out and touched my lower lip, easing it from the clutch of my teeth. "I promise. Try not to worry."

I got out and trudged up the steps.

"I'll stop by after school," Gyver called from half in, half out of his car. I waved a limp hand and resumed kneading my lip with my teeth.

It was a long afternoon. Dad was out of his depth once he confirmed I had no temp. "Mia, kiddo, people were bound to find out."

"No, they weren't!"

"Did you really think you could keep it a secret?"

"Yes," I gasped through a fresh tide of tears. "Mom thought I could too."

"Your mother means well, but she's . . ." He paused and passed me a box of tissues. "She's struggling with the reality of your illness. I've tried showing her some books and charts . . . Well, you know how sensitive she is. But this keeping your cancer a secret, it's not really a long-term solution."

"I'm not ready," I responded, annoyed he had higher expectations for me than Mom did.

He made me a cup of chamomile tea. When I ignored it and cried harder, he said, "Hang on," disappeared into his office, and reappeared with a pack of Oreos. "Don't tell your mother."

I smiled in spite of myself, took a cookie, and twisted it apart. I ate the creamy half and dunked the naked chocolate side in the milk Dad set on the table.

"Better?" he asked.

I nodded and stared at the crumbs floating on the surface of the milk.

"Good. Now let's look at this logically." He lifted my chin. "You can't control everything. If people find out, they find out. And sick or not, you're a person to be respected."

I gripped the cookie too tightly and it crumbled all over the table. How could I explain that my image was the only thing I could control? Only, thanks to Meagan, I couldn't.

The door opened, and both of us looked guiltily to the

cookies. "I'll take the heat," Dad reassured me. But it wasn't Mom, it was Gyver.

"They make health-food Oreos? Are they as awful as that tofu ice cream?" He hesitated before reaching for one.

"These are the all-processed kind. Don't tell her mom, but we needed some artificial flavoring today." Dad gave Gyver a sheepish grin.

"Sure." Gyver shoved a cookie in his mouth and dunked a second in my milk before he even took a seat. "I let the office know and told Ally you had a migraine."

"Thanks."

Gyver pointed to the box of tissues on the table and the discard pile in my lap. "Enough of that. I talked to Meagan. She won't tell anyone."

"Really?" I latched myself around his neck, scattering tissues on the floor and knocking the Oreo out of his hand.

"Easy there, Mi. It's no big deal." Gyver laughed at my awestruck expression and reached around my back to help himself to another cookie.

Dad cleared his throat. "Well, it looks like you're in good hands. I guess my work here is done." He gathered the cookie and tissues off the floor and poured Gyver his own glass of milk before leaving. "I'll be in my office."

"Thanks, Dad." I squeezed Gyver around the neck again.

"You're—choking—me." He laughed. I relinquished my stranglehold and returned to my own seat.

"Spill!" I ordered.

"It wasn't hard. Meagan's cool. I told her you didn't want

people to know and she apologized and promised she wouldn't say anything."

"You're the best!" I quashed the urge to hug him again—once he mentioned Meagan, I no longer felt like I had a right to.

"I know. But it's no biggie. After all, it's my mom's fault she knew. Mom works with Meagan's dad, did you know that?"

I shook my head. "So, you two, you've hung out a lot?"

"Well, yeah. Anyway, what I was going to say was Meagan's brother, Max, had leukemia too. When Mom first found out you were sick—before she knew it was a state secret—she asked Officer Andrews about treatments and stuff."

"Her brother?"

Gyver looked down and his dark hair obscured his eyes. "Yeah. It was years ago. Don't worry about him, worry about you. I hate seeing you upset like this, Mi. Just tell—"

I held up a hand to stop him. I didn't want a lecture. "She seems nice," I managed.

I was proud of myself for the effort, but unnerved by the way my insides twisted when he crunched a cookie and nodded. "She's great. You'd like her."

I highly doubted that. "Thanks again—for everything today."

"If I tell you it wasn't a big deal for the third time, will you believe me?"

"It's a big deal to me. I don't know how to show you how grateful I am."

"I can think of a few ideas." Gyver arched his eyebrows.

"Don't you have homework?"

He stood and grabbed another cookie. "I was just going to suggest you drive tomorrow. And maybe write my English essay."

"I'll drive, but you're on your own with Dostoyevsky. I've got my own essay to write."

"See you later, Mi." He squeezed my hand and left; leaving me alone with my relief, uneasy thoughts about M.A. and Gyver, fingers that tingled from touching his, and a renewed conviction that I really, truly needed to get over him.

19

I couldn't handle school today. Staying home, I texted.

After hunting for the stupid letters, I pressed Send and collapsed on my pillow. I was drifting off when my phone chirped. No, I didn't want a response; I wanted sleep.

I sighed and flipped it over: BRT.

Be right there? Which part of my two-word message had he interpreted as a request for visitors? I rubbed my eyes and began a response: You don't—

But I could already hear him in the kitchen, his morning voice rusty as he greeted my parents. "I'll take that up to Mi."

"Thanks. Quiet though, she might be asleep."

Wishful thinking. I kept my eyes open but didn't bother sitting up when he and Mom entered my room. "Kitten, look who I found in the kitchen."

"Hi."

Gyver filled my bedroom door, his eyes more alert than I'd

ever seen them before nine a.m. He balanced a kitchen tray and his mug of coffee. "Hey, Mi. Are you okay? Do you want this?" He nodded toward the tray. It was loaded with juice, fruit salad, toast, a bottle of water, organic cardboard toaster pastries, and granola bars: an arsenal of food for a patient who had no appetite.

I shook my head. Gyver placed it on the floor and sat on the corner of my bed. Mom hovered by my desk. Both of them stared at me like they were decoding a puzzle written on my face.

"I'm just tired. Dr. Kevin said I would be." I'd slept all weekend, bailing on cheering on Friday and Saturday's party with a weak excuse of food poisoning. I'd felt recharged enough for school Monday and Tuesday. Enough to feel jealous of everyone's party stories: Chris peed in a house plant; Lauren hooked up with Bill's older brother; a JV cheerleader broke up with her boyfriend, so Ally spent the night comforting her and Hil ordered the linebacker ex to leave—even though the party was at the house of one of his teammates. Ryan had, according to Hil, spent the night pouting and texting. While I doubted the first part, I had a half-dozen Saturday night texts from him—all clever variations of date me. I'd spent Sunday morning trying to come up with a response: trying, and failing, and avoiding him at school like some reverse game of hide and seek.

Today school seemed impossible.

"Just tired," Mom repeated. "Let's take your temperature."

"Again? You've taken it three times, and it hasn't been above 99.1."

"Just once more." I accepted the thermometer and returned it post-beep. "Okay, 98.9. So, a day in bed? But Mia, I can't stay home today. I've got client meetings. I've missed so much work and I'm taking next week off for your chemo. Mr. Russo will be here to get me any minute . . . But if you need me, I guess I could try to work something out." She twisted her hands and looked at me with tortured uncertainty.

"I'll be fine." I yawned.

Mom started to pace the room. "Your father already left—but I called him. He's got a showing this morning, then he'll come home. He'll be back by noon. Maybe I could go in late? Cancel my nine-thirty meeting?"

"I'll stay." Gyver tickled my foot through the blanket.

"Seriously, I don't need supervision. I'm just going to sleep."

"Then I'll sleep with you," Gyver blurted out.

I raised an eyebrow and Mom blinked rapidly.

"I mean, I won't sleep *with* you. But if you're sleeping . . ." Gyver ran a hand through his hair and took a gulp of coffee. "This is why I shouldn't speak before ten."

"We understood what you meant," Mom said. "And that's a kind offer, but you have school."

"My dad'll say it's okay. I can at least stay until Mr. Moore gets home. That way you'll have someone here if you need something—like, I don't know, what's not on your tray?—apple juice." This was directed at me, but he turned back to my mom. "Wouldn't you feel better knowing someone was here?"

"My nine-thirty meeting is important . . . ," Mom mused. "You'll call if you need anything?"

"Of course. I know the drill; I spent so much time at the hospital this summer, I'm practically an RN." He handed me a bottle of water. I obediently took a sip.

"I would feel better if you weren't alone, but I'm not saying yes. That's up to your dad."

"What's up to me? Is there a neighborhood meeting going on up there?" Mr. Russo's voice sounded from the bottom of the stairs. Gyver left to talk to him.

"You okay with this, kitten? Are you sure you don't need me?"

"Go to your meeting. If Gyver wants to stay, he's going to be bored. He should know by now that when I say I'm going to sleep I sleep."

"It can't be more boring than listening to you talk about cheerleading," Gyver said from the doorway. "My dad said it's fine. He's waiting in the car and says come out when you're ready."

My mom looked at her watch. "I've got to go or we'll sit in traffic. Call me if you need anything. Thank you, Gyver. Let her sleep as much as possible."

"Will do, Mrs. Moore." The scent of her perfume lingered as we listened to the front door close and then stared at each other.

"What do you want to do now?" Gyver asked.

"Sleep." How had I made it to seventeen without realizing my eyelids were so heavy?

"Right. You sleep. I'll . . ." Gyver retrieved a magazine from beneath a stack of clean laundry on my desk and sat next to me. "I'll read about 'Jen's Baby Drama' and 'Hot New Trends for Fall.' You know how hard I strive to be trendy."

I nodded and shut my eyes.

"Mia?" The whisper and hand on my arm were unwelcome.

I tried to keep irritation out of my voice. "Dad, I'm really tired."

"Shh, Gyver's sleeping." He crouched next to me, a hand resting on my bedside table for support. "Sorry to wake you, kiddo, but you need to take your meds. Then you can go back to sleep."

"What time is it?" I lowered my voice to match his. My room was bright and my eyes were crusty.

"After two."

I tried to sit up and take the bottle of juice Dad offered, but something anchored me in place. It was Gyver's arm, which he'd wrapped across me while I slept. His foot weighed down my calf. His face was inches from mine, his breath warm and steady on my cheek.

I blushed, wide awake. What had Dad thought when he walked in and saw Gyver wrapped around me like a hotdog bun? Granted, Gyver was on top of the covers and I was underneath. Still.

I took the thermometer, muffling its beep with a cupped hand. "98.7." Then lifted my head off the pillow enough to swallow the pills and juice. Oh so carefully, I lay down. "I'm going to sleep more," I lied in a whisper, hoping my blush would pass as just-woken flush.

Dad nodded, patted my shoulder, and tiptoed out of the room.

Gyver was half on my spare pillow, the one Jinx normally occupied, and half on mine. His exhales breezed over my cheek; if I turned my head in his direction, our noses would've brushed. I focused on the warmth and weight of his arm and leg and listening to him breathe.

Because I was paying attention to the rhythm of his inhales and exhales, I knew the moment he woke. Other than an instinctive tightening then relaxing of his arm, he didn't move right away either.

"You awake?" I whispered at the ceiling.

"Yeah."

I rolled to face him. His foot slid off my leg, but his arm remained around my waist. Only a few inches of pillowcase separated our eyes and lips. I was too aware of that fact.

"How'd you sleep?" Gyver whispered, though there was no one left to wake.

"Great." Whispering must be infectious, because I did too.

"Are you hungry?"

"Not really. I'll get something in a bit. Are you?"

"No, I helped myself to your breakfast tray."

"Good. Thanks for staying with me. Sorry I was so boring."

"I'll play hooky with you anytime. Not only did I get out of our history test, but I got to read about"—Gyver reached behind him for the magazine and flipped it open—"the best pants for my body type."

I smiled. "Which are?"

"No clue. I couldn't figure out if I'm a triangle, rectangle, circle, or sideways bow tie. How do girls know these things? What are you?"

"That's an hourglass, not a bow tie. I'm a rectangle, because I'm not super curvy, but an hourglass, too, since I have a waist." I felt stupid talking about my body—and self-conscious drawing attention to my waist, where his hand had just rested. A fact he was aware of too; his eyes flicked there before coming back to meet mine.

We were quiet for a heartbeat. Two. Then my heart sped up as my blood rushed to my cheeks and that was no longer an accurate way of counting.

My focus shifted from my racing pulse to an awareness of how good he smelled. My eyes drifted to his lips, and my thoughts? They drifted to our first kiss. Our only kiss.

It had taken place in his car—more than a year ago—on the night Gyver got his license. He'd taken me out to celebrate with ice cream.

We could've eaten at our usual picnic table. In fact, we could've walked home—Scoops is less than a mile from our houses. But that night we'd sat in his car and Gyver cranked the A/C to keep my cone from dripping. "Where should we go next, Mi?"

"Wherever. It's just nice to be parentless." I gave him a

cheesy high-five, but he grasped my hand instead, leaned in, and pressed his lips to mine.

It was the best kiss I'd had—until I knocked my ice cream off the cone and into his lap. There's no way to read that as anything but a bad sign. A very bad sign. He'd pulled back in surprise and banged his head on the window. I'd gone to retrieve the melting glob of chocolate fudge—until I realized where I'd be reaching and he stopped me with a sharp, "I've got it."

I'd darted out of the car to get napkins. By the time I'd returned, he'd wiped himself off with tissues from the glove box. The only evidence of our ill-fated kiss was a chocolate stain on the crotch of his khaki cargo shorts and my red cheeks. We never discussed it.

Was he thinking about it now too?

I willed my gaze from his lips to his eyes; they were dark, questioning.

My phone beeped on my nightstand. I blinked—how long had it been since I had blinked? In the instant my eyes were closed, something changed. When I opened them, the intensity was gone, the moment passed.

Gyver rolled away and sat up. "I bet that's The Jock."

I picked up my phone and read the screen. "Don't call him that. Not that it's any of your business, but it's my horoscope."

Gyver snorted. "You have your horoscope sent to your phone? So what's today's dire prediction?"

"It says: *'Things can't balance on a knife's edge. Make*

careful choices because once you decide, you can't go back.' I
guess it was a good day to hide in bed."

I flipped through the other texts. Ally: *U OK?* Lauren's:
Out again?! Hil: *Call me.* There were two from Ryan: *L8 or
sick?* Then, a few hours later: *RU contagious? Can I get a good
luck kiss b4 the game?*

I looked at Gyver. He was playing with his own phone, but
lifted his eyes to meet my gaze. "Meagan says hi and that the
test was easy."

She knew he was here. At some point today, Gyver had
checked in with her, which meant that while he'd had *my* full
attention, at least during the times I was awake, I hadn't had
his. I hit Reply and fumbled with the keys. I didn't feel lucky—I
felt a little queasy—but Ryan wanted me, which was more than
I could say about Gyver. And if he thought my kiss was good
luck, I wasn't going to jinx him.

"You're blushing." Gyver glanced over my shoulder. "Oh.
What are you telling The Jock?" he asked in a tight voice.

"I'm serious, stop calling him that!" When Gyver waited, I
added, "That I'm not contagious. He can stop by if he wants."

He stood up. "I better go then. School gets out in ten minutes. If *Ryan's*"—he overemphasized the name—"going to come
over before his game, he'll be here soon. I doubt he'd be happy
to find me here." He pointed at the bed and echoed his last
word, "*Here.*"

I nodded. He was right, but I didn't like the new attitude in
his voice. "Thanks again for staying with me."

He opened the door, and Jinx squeezed between his legs

and jumped on the bed, her tail twitching as she settled on the pillow he'd abandoned.

"I hate to say this, but your horoscope was right, Mi. You've got to make some decisions. Things can't stay like this." I looked down at Jinx and didn't reply. "I'll call you later."

20

I took a quick shower and changed into clean pajamas—regular clothes seemed pointless this late in the day. Mom would have to deal with it.

I was gently towel drying my hair when I heard Ryan's voice in the kitchen. "Hey, Mr. Moore."

"Hi, Ryan. Mia's in her room. Wash your hands before you go up, please."

I cringed, but Ryan's "sure" sounded fine.

Things had changed. I never had many rules, but my parents had drawn the line at boys in my bedroom. Maybe now they felt I was too sick to do anything, like having leukemia made me less of a teenager.

They were wrong. When Ryan stepped in the room, I forgot all about cancer. I studied his hair first—the natural highlights turning it gold—and then his summer-at-the-shore tan, dark-yellow hooded sweatshirt, and blue soccer shorts. Finally, I let myself focus on his face—bright blue eyes and brighter smile. He looked down at me with such concern and . . . attraction. This was why I never had any luck not kissing him. But maybe kissing was what I needed right now; a reminder that Gyver wasn't the only guy in the world.

"Hey, you. Are you skipping or really sick?" He crossed the room with athletic strides and sat next to me on the bed. His mouth was paused a breath from mine as he waited for my reply.

"Not contagious." I stretched to meet his lips and his arms curled around me. The summer sun seeped from his skin—warming mine where we touched. We lay down—annoying Jinx, who jumped off the bed, pawed the door open, and left.

"It'd be worth it to catch whatever," Ryan murmured against my neck, sliding his hand up the hem of my pajama camisole. He paused and glanced at the now-open door. "Your dad's downstairs. He's not going to come check on us, is he?" He moved his hand back to my waist.

"I don't think so." But his "catch whatever" felt like clouds on a sunny day. The words stole the warmth from my skin and all playfulness from the moment.

"I should go. Coach Burne'll kill me if I miss the bus." He sat up, then crashed back for another kiss. " 'Kay, I'm really going now. Wish me luck."

"Good luck." The words tasted uncertain.

He hesitated. "Mia, I know you've been avoiding me, but have you thought at all? About us?"

"Ryan . . . I can't." I played with the cuff of my pajama pants.

"Why not? At least tell me why. Is it Hil? Since when does she run your life?"

"I thought you had to go." On cue, his phone beeped. "See? That's probably Chris or Bill wondering where you are."

"I've got a minute." He put his hand on mine.

"Why can't we keep things like this?"

"Because it's not enough anymore. I want to get to know you, as much as I want to do this—" He kissed me until I was dizzy and breathless, then leaned back against my pillow with a look that was exactly as seductive as he intended. "If you really don't want to date me, let me know. I'm not going to ask again."

I stared at my hands and chewed my lip. His words were the second echo of my horoscope. "I can't."

"Why not?"

I looked at him, lying across my bed like he belonged there. "I'm sick." The words weren't as hard as I'd expected, but I waited for his reaction.

He grinned and stood up. "We don't have to go on a date this minute. I'm already going to be speeding to make the bus." He pulled out his phone.

"No. I'm . . . really sick." These words were harder. I choked them past my necklace, which I'd twisted strangulation-tight. "I've got leukemia."

Ryan continued to look at his phone, but he wasn't texting. He hit the Power button, shoved it in his pocket, and sat down.

Sank down. His face was gray beneath the tan and his mouth half-open. "What?"

I didn't repeat myself. He couldn't want to hear it again; I couldn't say it again. I reached for his hand. Tentative, because I wasn't sure how he felt about me anymore. Would he ever look at me like he had when entering my bedroom?

"When?" His eyes looked huge against his ashen face. He cradled my hand like it was breakable.

"I found out this summer."

"This summer? That's why . . . Connecticut? And cheer-leading?"

"Those aren't complete sentences, but probably."

"Leukemia?" He said it slow, like a tricky vocabulary word. "Are you going to be okay?"

"The doctors say everything's going well . . ." He was star-ing at my hand, but his eyes were unfocused. "Don't you have a game you need to get to?"

I wanted him to stay, to process this and want me anyway. But it had to be his choice.

"The game." He placed my hand back on my lap like he was putting away a delicate teacup. "Yeah, the game. We'll talk." He stood and turned away.

"Ryan, it's okay. I didn't expect . . ." My voice and heart were breaking a little.

"I can't . . . Shit! I don't—I've gotta go." He failed at smil-ing, then shut the door. His footsteps ran and his tires sped. He couldn't get away from my illness—from me—fast enough.

I buried my face in my pillow and sobbed. Mad at myself.

He wasn't worth it. I'd let myself hope. I'd known he'd react this way. Mom warned me. Telling him was a mistake. I couldn't take it back, though. Soon everyone would know. I ruined everything.

"Kiddo, you need anything?" Dad called from downstairs.

"No, thanks," I answered in a voice that almost sounded tear free. Not that he'd notice. "Doing homework."

"Sounds good."

I hugged the spare pillow. Tight. Pressed into it to muffle my sobs. It smelled of Gyver and Ryan until I drenched it and changed the scent to moisturizer and sadness.

There was a knock on my door. "Dad, I don't need anything."

"Mia, don't cry! Crap." Ryan stood at the foot of my bed. His hands curling the bottom of his soccer shirt, eyes red-rimmed, and hair disheveled. "I panicked. I had to think. I'm sorry."

"What about your game?" I rubbed my cheeks dry, but new tears wet them.

"Screw the game. You can't seriously think I'm going."

"But you left. And the coach . . ." I made a second futile attempt to wipe my face.

"I'll tell him something came up. Doesn't matter! Tell me what's going on. Leukemia?"

"You really want to know?" My breathing almost calmed, I almost hoped.

"I got halfway to school before I asked myself: What are you doing? Mia, this is where I want to be. Please tell me."

I told him: the bruising, testing, chemo, and hospital stay. I wanted to think it felt good to share, but I wouldn't know until he responded.

"God, Mia, I can't believe you didn't tell me. I could've . . . I don't know, done something. Who else knows? Anyone?"

"Not really. Gyver. My teachers. If I told the Calendar Girls, the whole school'd know."

Ryan flinched. "Russo knows? That's why he's been your shadow all year. I thought he wanted you."

"We're just friends." Right now, with Ryan's arm around me, I was honestly okay with that. "He lives next door and my mom works with his dad, there was no way to keep—"

"I'm glad you had someone." He tightened his grip. "It could've been me, though. God! And all I've done is talk about sex—you should've told me to go to hell."

"I think I did, once or twice." I leaned my head against his shoulder. "You didn't know. You were acting like any guy would."

I'd forgiven him, but Ryan wasn't ready to forgive himself. "Would 'any guy' have run away like an asshole when you told him? Is that what Gyver did when he found out? No wonder you said no to me."

I pulled away so I was facing him. "That's not why! You don't date—how many times did you tell me that last spring? If you hadn't heard about Hil's pact . . ."

"Okay, so Hil's stupid pact put the idea in my head—so what? I couldn't stop thinking about it—us. I don't want 'a girlfriend.' I want *you*."

Could Ryan handle this? Earlier with Gyver, had that meant anything? Did I want it to? Of course I did, but he didn't. And I wanted Ryan too. It was a knife's edge and I wasn't balanced. It was also ridiculous—how had we gotten from leukemia to crushes?

But crushes are normal and it felt good to worry about something normal. I wasn't thinking like a cancer patient, but just like me: I wanted this. I wanted Ryan.

But I was a cancer patient and I couldn't pretend this decision was as simple as what I wanted. Or what he thought he wanted. "You don't know what you'd be getting into."

Ryan reached across the bed, threaded his fingers through mine and let our hands rest on my knee. "So tell me."

Like it was that easy. "Ryan, no. My answer's no."

He looked crestfallen—for half a second. "You still don't think I'm serious."

"That's part of it."

He leaned toward me, dimples flashing in a smile that made my heart skip. "Let me prove you wrong. Fine, say no for now, but give me a chance."

I stood and stepped away from his touch. "I really don't think we'll work—not as more than a casual hookup."

"Maybe," he admitted. "Or maybe we'd be great together."

"I said no, Ryan." My voice was more stern than I'd intended, but the sternness was self-directed. I was not going to give in to charm and confidence and dimples. No matter how much my lips wanted me to.

Maybe Ryan would've accepted my answer and left. Maybe

he would've argued. Maybe kissed me. I don't know because Mom knocked. That was a sign—with Gyver I'd been interrupted before I did anything I'd regret. With Ryan, all distractions waited until after I'd decided.

Mom knocked again, then entered. "Hi, Ryan, it's good to see you. How are you feeling, kitten? Dad said you slept all day. You look—" She paused, noticing my splotchy face and disheveled hair. "A little flushed. Everything okay?"

"I told Ryan, Mom."

With a smile locked in place, she said, "Told him what?"

"About the leukemia." I recognized the warning signs in her posture; Mom was tensing for a tantrum. But she wouldn't do it in front of Ryan, so I met her eyes.

Her smile didn't waver. "Dinner's ready and we'd love to have you join us, Ryan. Why don't you go downstairs and call your mother? We'll be down in a minute."

He shot me a confused glance, but nodded. "Thanks. It smells great."

She waited until he'd left before whirling toward me. "Mia Ruth, what were you thinking? After we worked so hard for your privacy."

"I had to tell him."

"Why? I thought secrecy was what you wanted."

"But why is it a secret?" It had made sense at one point, now I wasn't sure.

"It's what you wanted: no one to know so they would treat you the same." Her voice was stern and I felt ashamed, like I'd done something wrong.

"I know. But I had to tell him. He asked me out. I had to explain."

"You and Ryan Winters?" The tension ebbed from her face and grasp. "That's great, kitten!"

"I said no."

"But why? It's *Ryan*, honey. You used to glow when he'd drop you off after a party, and you'd blush and run to your room if he called."

"That was last year."

"So? As you've gotten to know him better, you like him less?"

"No." I sighed. She'd never understand how I could turn him down. In her mind he was perfect—we were perfect together. "It just won't work."

"Because you won't give it a chance! This is exactly what you need right now: a distraction and someone who makes you happy."

This type of debate could go on all night, or at least until I gave in. I couldn't concede, but perhaps if I offered her a partial victory. "Maybe. I'll think about it."

Mom kissed my forehead, her face radiant with the same smile she'd worn when I first made the squad. She jumped up. "Oh no! We've left him alone with your father. He's probably filling Ryan's head with all sorts of cancer facts."

I followed my maternal hurricane down the stairs, praying dinner wouldn't be a disaster.

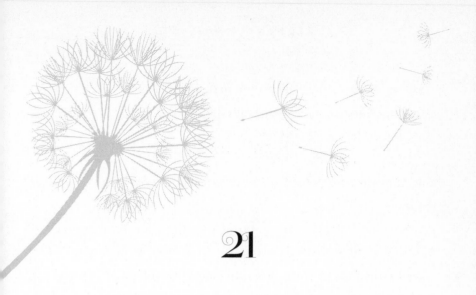

21

Over pork chops and mashed potatoes Ryan was fully indoctrinated into Team Cancer. Dad went into excruciating detail about treatments and warnings: keep Mia away from germs, wash your hands, stay away if you feel sick, don't get her too tired, absolutely no drinking because of the meds . . .

Mom beamed at Ryan and repeated, "But she's going to be fine. All the doctors say so. Don't worry." I could practically see the thought bubble hovering above her head: *This is the popular, athletic boyfriend I've always wanted for Mia. Can't let him get away.*

I'd said "maybe" in my bedroom, but Mom chose to hear "yes."

Dad continued. "I know you don't play football, but this is the only sports analogy I can think of. The first round of chemo switched the cancer from offense to defense. It's no longer attacking Mia's body. We've got control of the ball now and each consolidation round of chemo—like the one she's starting on Saturday—is a new first down. It keeps us in control. And when she's had enough . . ."

"Touchdown?" Ryan guessed.

"Something like that," Dad agreed. "When she's done the maintenance chemo, she'll be cancer free, hopefully for good."

He wasn't exaggerating, but it was an intimidating speech. Combined with Mom's over-the-top enthusiasm, I wouldn't have blamed Ryan if he fled. But he didn't. He paid attention and asked questions. He nodded and smiled at Mom's repetitive reassurances. He borrowed books from Dad's library of leukemia resources. He squeezed my knee under the table.

I started to doubt myself—to believe him. Could he possibly be serious?

"Can I pick you up tomorrow? Are you going to school?" he asked at the front door.

He looked nervous, like I'd never ridden in his car before, like I might say no. "Sure."

He kissed my forehead and we hovered close for a second before he stepped back. Apparently the time for casual kisses had ended. "It means a lot that you trusted me, even before you told the girls. I'm not going to screw this up."

"I know." And I meant it. There was something about seeing him vulnerable that made me feel protective. I'd done this to him, drained him of the confidence and carefree attitude—the things that made him Ryan.

I touched his cheek, smoothed over the skin where his dimples should be. "You're a good guy, Ryan Winters."

And they were back—the confidence, the charm, the dimples. "Then go out with me."

"Ryan—" It was a sigh-yawn hybrid. I'd slept all day, but tonight had depleted me and left me more exhausted than I'd been this morning.

"Fine, I'll stop asking, but let me try and change your mind. Every girl wants to be chased, right? Let me chase you and we'll see what happens."

I looked at him. Looked beyond him through the glass door to the shape of Gyver's Jeep in his driveway. "I really don't think I'll change my mind."

He pulled me closer. "I consider myself warned. All I'm asking for is a chance."

I could feel his breath across my cheeks. If I looked up, I knew he'd kiss me now. I wanted to.

Instead I squeezed his hand and stepped away. "As long as you understand I'm being honest when I say—"

"I understand." His smile was contagious. "I'd better go before you change your mind. See you in the morning."

I watched him walk to his car, saw the fist pump he made in the darkness. He pulled out of the driveway and his taillights were swallowed by the night, leaving me wondering what I'd agreed to.

I was still standing by the door when Mom's self-satisfied

voice drifted from the kitchen, catching my attention. "That went well."

"Think so?" asked Dad.

"Yes. No thanks to you. Hon, I can't believe you gave the boy homework! He wants to date our daughter, not write a research paper on the horrors of cancer." But she was laughing now.

"He asked for the books," Dad answered. Through the doorway I could see him take the dishtowel out of Mom's hands and put his arms around her. "And if he makes Mia happy . . ."

"Of course he does." She tipped her forehead against his chest. "I was so worried how he'd react. So worried. If he rejected her . . ."

"But he didn't. And remember, Gyver didn't either."

Mom shrugged this off. "She reminds me so much of me at her age—and Ryan's exactly the type of guy I dated."

"Hmm," Dad muttered into Mom's hair. "This was before you wised up and decided that geeks were far superior to jocks, right?"

"Far superior," she echoed, kissing him. "She's going to be okay."

"She's going to be okay," he repeated, sounding far more confident than she did.

Mom kissed him again.

I was spared from having to slink up the stairs or witness any more embarrassing moments because Dad whispered something in her ear and she laughed and followed him out the back door to his telescope shed. Some small part of me felt left out. I was missing something I hadn't thought of in years: the nights we had all spent watching Dad chart stars and show us things through his telescope: me truly interested and Mom pretending to be.

They'd left the sink half-full of plates, cups, and silverware. I hadn't done anything else productive today; I could handle rinsing them off and loading the dishwasher.

Maybe. It was such a small word, but it had made Ryan and Mom so happy. Maybe a smaller word, maybe *yes*, would make me happy too.

But everything seemed so fragile in this week before I went back to the hospital for more chemo—and it felt like if I changed too much, everything would collapse like a game of Jenga, or pop like the soap bubbles in the sink.

I slid the last plate into the dishwasher and shut it. Pressed the button to start the wash cycle and dried my hands on my pajama pants.

Just because Ryan had handled the news didn't mean everyone could. I wasn't willing to take that risk.

22

I thought Ally was driving me home, but when we crowded back into the locker room after practice, the plan changed with last-minute group momentum.

"The boys' soccer game is about to start," she said with a sly smile.

"And we haven't been to any of their games. It's not good if we just support the football team." Lauren grinned at Ally.

Hil rolled her eyes. I continued to sit on the locker-room bench, trying to gather the energy to object. "Didn't they just have a game yesterday?"

"It's a rain make-up," answered Ally.

"I'm tired. Can't we do this another day?" I asked.

"But I already told him you'd be there. Please? Pretty please?"

Hil came to stand next to me. "She said no."

"Boo." Ally pouted. "Don't be like that, it'll be fun."

Lauren nudged my shoulder. "You know you want to see Ryan all sweaty."

"Am I the only one noticing she looks exhausted?" asked Hil. To me, she said, "I'll take you home."

"No, it's fine. I'll go," I said. I didn't want to be that trans-parently ill. If I left now it would only raise questions, so I conceded. "Thanks though, Hil."

Hil slammed her locker but stayed quiet. Whatever Ally had said to her had worked; she hadn't given me crap about Ryan since the first day of school. Though if she'd known about our conversation last night, I'm sure she'd have plenty to say.

We hiked up the hill to the soccer field where a section of the bleachers was saved for us in the center of the front row—directly behind the bench.

His team was already huddled on the field, but Ryan broke away, jogged toward the bench, took a swig from a water bottle, and—just before he sprinted back to the group—winked at me.

Once the game started, it seemed safe to admire Ryan from afar . . . until he scored a goal. As the crowd cheered, Ryan turned my direction. Placing one hand on his chest—over his heart—he pointed the other at me. Or he did until Bill and Chris piled on his back with whoops and smacks. Any chance I'd remain unidentified as his target vanished when Lauren stood up and pointed at me too. The crowd awwww'd and a woman leaned forward to ask, "Is that your boyfriend, dear?"

"No," hissed Hil. "He's not."

I hunched my shoulders and wanted to disappear. My flushed cheeks were the only part of me that wasn't chilly in the cool September air.

The team celebrated Ryan's second goal without him. Because he kicked it in and continued running, straight to the bench, which he leaped onto. With one hand on the fence separating the bleachers from the field, he reached the other toward me. I took it tentatively and he pulled me to him.

And he kissed me. At first I was mortified; all I could think of was the "Ooh" of the crowd. Then all I could pay attention to were his lips on mine, parting mine, our tongues tangled and my hands woven through his damp hair. I wasn't cold—I was much too warm. And aware of every link of the fence that kept us apart.

My lips were suddenly chilled and lonely. I opened surprised eyes to see Bill tug Ryan off the bench by his jersey. "C'mon, Romeo, we've got a game to win."

As Ryan ran backward toward the kickoff, he caught my eye. "Go out with me!"

I remembered the crowd then—as they exploded with cheers and support for the handsome soccer star.

"Say yes!" Ally enthused from my left.

"That was like a movie. Things like that never happen to me," said Lauren.

I sank onto the bench and put my head down, trying to block out the crowd's encouragement and my own desire to agree. "Can we leave now?"

"You're not going to stick around and answer him?" asked Ally.

"He doesn't want to know my answer."

"Seriously? You're leaving? That's crazy. Like certifiable. Look at him!" Lauren pointed to the field.

"Enough!" snapped Hil. "Do you ever think about anything but boys? If she said she doesn't want to date him, why are you pushing it? *Mia* is your friend. Not Ryan, *Mia*. Shouldn't what she wants matter? And why is this so important to you? When I suggested we stay single, I thought we'd all hang out more. Like, do stuff *just us*, not have everything revolve around what the guys want to do. Is my company that boring? Because I think you all are a hell of a lot more interesting than them."

Ally and Lauren didn't move except to blink rapidly, then lower their heads. I put a hand on her arm—it was a gesture that I hoped communicated both "thank you" and "calm down."

"If you still want to leave, I'll take you home," offered Hil.

I stood. The motion broke through Ally's shamed silence. "I'm sorry."

"Yeah," Lauren echoed. "We're sorry. But he's—"

Ally elbowed her and she shut up.

I muttered, "It's okay," and Hil shrugged.

"I'll talk to you later," I called, then followed her off the bleachers.

Risking one glance at the field, I saw Ryan collide with an opponent as he passed the ball. He was helping up the Hamilton player and didn't see my exit. How would he feel when I wasn't here when the game ended? What if he scored again? I was tempted to turn around, but what if he asked again? I didn't need a crowd to pressure me; I wanted to say yes. I wanted his ability to erase Gyver from my thoughts. I wanted his smiles and kisses.

But I couldn't. Not because of Hil's pact, because of him.

Ryan wanted a girl to kiss in front of a crowd. He wanted a blonde to take to parties—wasn't that what Gyver said? If this was his idea of "proving he was serious" then he didn't get me at all.

I'd slunk away like a coward, yet when my phone rang later, I answered. "Hi."

"You left," he said.

"Sorry. I got cold."

"You must be my good-luck charm. I didn't score after you were gone."

"Me? Good luck?" I choked. My fingers sought my own lucky charm and twirled the chain. I searched my room for signs to indicate what those words could mean and found nothing.

"So, did I change your mind?" The laugh he tacked on sounded nervous.

"No," I whispered.

"No? Come on—that kiss didn't feel like a no to me."

I could feel the blush creeping up my neck. I was twisted into guilty knots. I needed Ryan's kisses and confidence boosting as much as I needed Gyver's friendship. And he was the guy Mom wanted for me, the guy my friends wanted for me, even Hil, once she got over this stupid pact. "Ryan, I like you. You know I do."

"But?"

"But I was flattered today—and also embarrassed. I don't want to play games. And right now I really don't want to be the center of attention."

"I wasn't playing games and I didn't mean to embarrass you, I was just showing you I mean it. I'm crazy about you—and I don't care who knows it. How about after you cheer at tomorrow's game, we go out, just you and me? No spectacle, I promise. Just us."

I wanted to believe him. One date. How much damage could that really cause? If I turned him down after that, at least I could say I'd tried.

I flipped my Magic 8 Ball over: *Signs point to yes.*

"One date," I agreed.

23

Gyver was quiet in the car on the way to school the next morning, so quiet I dozed lightly until we pulled into a parking space. We were both avoiding any conversation about what almost happened in my bedroom on Wednesday and the avoidance seemed to swallow all possible words.

Ryan was waiting for me, leaning against the trunk of his car and smiling. He stepped over and opened my door for me. "Good morning, gorgeous. 'Sup, Russo."

"Hey." His eyes flicked down to Ryan's hand around my waist and back to my face.

"Hi." I was clutching my necklace and trying to prioritize my last day in school before next week's chemo: I needed to smooth things over with Gyver, I had to talk to the girls, I needed to collect all my schoolwork for next week—hopefully I'd only be gone a week—and I had to figure out the right lies to cover my absence.

Gyver first. I smiled at him. "Thanks for the ride. Are you around tomorrow? Let's do breakfast before I check in."

"Check in?" His eyes narrowed. Ryan responded by pulling me closer. Neither was a good sign, but I didn't have the energy for their stupid macho competitiveness.

"I told Ryan about my cancer. He knows I'm going back to the hospital."

There was more than shock on Gyver's face. Was it confusion, betrayal, or pain?

Ryan was calm. He clapped his free hand on Gyver's shoulder—perhaps a little harder than necessary. "Thanks for being there this summer—when I couldn't be. I appreciate it, man."

"I didn't do it for you," Gyver snarled.

"I know, but still, thanks."

Gyver looked at me; I studied my shoes. "Breakfast sounds good. I'll see you in math class, Mia." He shoved his hands in his pockets and headed into the building.

"I think he liked being the only one who knew," Ryan said.

"He's just not a morning person." I watched Gyver's back disappear through the school doors.

"Apparently. Well, at least we can count on Ally for some OMGs about our date. What did the rest of them say? Do I need to stay away from Hil's claws?"

"I didn't tell them." It hadn't even occurred to me and now I felt like an idiot. A slightly panicked idiot.

"Really? Aren't you four psychically connected?"

The joke fell flat because it used to be true. Maybe if I

wasn't busy lying to them, debating whether to lie, and being exhausted by the reason for the lies, maybe then the Calendar Girls would know about the date.

"Did you tell anyone?" I asked.

"Yeah. Chris. Was I not supposed to?" We were at the top of the steps and Ryan opened the door. Chris was waiting for us—with Hillary and Lauren. "Shit," he said under his breath.

"Mia, do you have beer-flavored panties or something? Because I never thought I'd see this guy whipped!" Chris jumped on Ryan's back, and I stepped away to avoid being trampled.

"You mean it's true?" Hil latched onto my arm and shook me. "I told Chris he must be lying because I'd know."

Lauren watched the boys, but her words were for me. "You would've told us, right?"

"I didn't plan it, it just kinda happened. And then it was late."

"It was late? That's your excuse?" Hil's face was pinched with hurt. "I can't believe I had to find out from Chris."

"So it *is* true?" Ally's feet hadn't stopped sliding on the floor, but her arms were already around me—crashing me into Lauren, who laughed and joined in the hug.

She turned to Hil. "See? We weren't pressuring her into anything she didn't want to do."

Hil rolled her eyes and sighed. "So much for Single Senior Year. I guess if you're happy . . ."

"We'll do a toast tonight!" said Ally.

"Definitely! I can't remember the last time you came out," Lauren added. I could. Every detail. What I was wearing and the song that was playing when Gyver showed up and dragged me out.

"Wait. I'm still single." Wasn't I?

"See! I told you, Chris. You're full of bullshit."

Chris raised his palms in an I'm-innocent gesture. "Ryan said—"

"I said I was taking her out after the game." Ryan carefully extracted me from the crush of girls. "Give it a rest, Hil. Mia's a big girl and can make her own decisions. You'd know this if you'd quit bitching long enough to hear her."

When had people stopped listening when I spoke? It used to be I opened my mouth and had an audience, now they needed to be prompted to pay attention. And, ironically, Ryan used the same argument on Hil that she'd used on Ally and Laur yesterday: that what I wanted should matter more than what she wanted for me.

I finally had the floor, but I had nothing to say, so I repeated myself with an added dash of attitude. "I'm still officially single. Calm down."

"Not for long," quipped Chris, draping an arm around Hil's shoulders. "How 'bout you follow your brilliant friend's example and go out with me?"

She shrugged him off. "Shut up and go away."

The first bell rang.

"It's one date. I haven't broken the pact." I bit back the words "stupid," "idiotic," and "dictatorial," all of which threatened to sneak into the sentence.

Hil's eyes narrowed, like she'd heard them anyway. Or

maybe in response to it being five against one. "Yet," she growled, the heels of her boots clicking on the tile as she stormed down the hallway.

Hil was still angry at lunch. She was like fireworks: beautiful, volatile—and potentially dangerous. "So, you and Ryan," she mused as I sat down. "Well, since I slept with him freshman year, I guess I can't say you have bad taste."

I could play this game. "He could make a good boyfriend. He *really* wants this."

"By this, do you mean sex? You still haven't, right?" asked Lauren. I rolled my eyes and she added, "Just checking! I mean, you didn't tell us you were going to be absent Wednesday or your Ryan news. Who knows what else you're holding out on us?"

"Or what other promises you'll break," muttered Hil.

"It's one date, Hil. Drop it." She did, and the table became quiet, making the looks Hil and Ally were exchanging even more obvious.

"About tonight . . ." Ally played with her pretzels, lining them in rows on her lunch bag. "Coach Lindsey called a captains' meeting after school—I think she's going to suggest some changes."

"Like?" I asked.

Ally exchanged a do-I-have-to? look with Hil. "Like moving Emily up from the JV squad."

"Did someone get hurt?" I hadn't heard anything or seen lockers decorated with "Get Better" balloons.

Hil answered me. "We've given Emily your spot in lifts. It's only the third week of school and you've missed four practices. Just rest up until you can tumble again."

Shame colored my cheeks. I'd gone from our best tumbler to an afterthought: a girl who'd step aside and clap when flyer stunts were performed. A sign I was replaceable. "Oh."

Ally looked closer to tears than I was. "It's the best thing for the whole squad. It's Coach Lindsey's decision, but we thought it'd be better if you heard it from us."

"You okay?" asked Lauren.

"Clearly she's not. Mia, I'm not sure what's going on, but you've looked like crap since you got back from Connecticut." This was Hil's invitation to confide, but I couldn't accept it.

"I'm fine. Thanks for your concern and I'm sorry about cheerleading, but I don't need any more crap about Ryan, or being sick, or how awful I look!"

Ally flinched and Hil's scowl intensified, but Lauren spoke first, diffusing the anger by deflecting attention. "That is so unfair! Mia looks worse than usual—no offense—and she ends up with Ryan Winters. I lose three pounds and no one even notices." She frowned at her apple and waited for us all to compliment her, which we did.

"Do you think Bill's brother will be at the party tonight? He's . . . ," she continued.

I tuned her out and took stock of the past forty-eight hours: I'd agreed to a date but lost my spot on the squad. I'd confided in Ryan but alienated Gyver. If I were Dad, I'd create a T-chart with these facts, but what conclusions could I draw?

24

"I hate when they have captains' meetings," Lauren griped while driving me home after school. "It's like advertising: hey Lauren, you weren't picked to be captain, so you can just head out while the important people stay. And it sucks about your spot. If I were captain, I'd fight for you."

I didn't care at all—but I knew I should, and before cancer I cared quite a bit.

"Want to come in and hang out until the game?" I offered instead of agreement.

In the kitchen I hunted through the cabinets. "Want some hummus and crackers? Or we have ice cream, but it's made from tofu."

"That's okay, I probably shouldn't anyway." Lauren grabbed a water and headed to my room. I swallowed my meds and followed, hoping there wasn't anything incriminating lying around.

Except when I entered my room and found her sitting at

my desk paging through the magazine Gyver'd read, I was almost disappointed. It's not like I wanted her to be trying on a hospital bracelet or reading a chemo pamphlet, but a sign I should tell her or a situation where it was unavoidable—maybe that wouldn't be the worst thing ever. Ryan had handled it.

"You're staring at me. Is my hair huge and frizzy? I swear I look like a Chia Pet half the time."

"What?" I laughed. "You're ridiculous. I love your hair."

"Sure. Now sit and tell me all about Ryan. I want to hear everything."

My eyes drifted over the bed, pillows in clean cases since I'd sobbed all over the others. My throat tightened. I couldn't think of a plausible lie, and I didn't want to. I was sick, she was my friend; I deserved her support, she deserved the truth.

Lauren sat next to me on the bed. She put an arm around my shoulder and used her other hand to untangle mine from my necklace. "Hey, there's something going on, isn't there? You can tell me, you know."

So I did.

For the second time this week I turned my bedroom into a confessional. Lauren didn't sob or bolt, just turned so pale her freckles stood out like ink spatter. She hugged me tightly while I explained, then paced while asking questions.

"Who else knows? Did everyone but me?"

"No. Not at all. Just Ryan and Gyver."

"You didn't even tell Hil?" Lauren sounded shocked, then answered herself, "Well, duh you didn't. She wouldn't be acting so bitchy if she knew. Oh, Mia, I'm glad you told me. I can't imagine how hellish this summer must've been. I would've been an excellent hospital visitor, you know."

"You can prove it—I go back tomorrow for more chemo."

The color that had started to creep back into her cheeks faded. "More? It's not done?"

"Not even close. I've got a new round every six to eight weeks."

"Then I'll be there." She stooped to hug me again. "We'll do movies and manicures and I'll make it fun."

"Thanks." I exhaled this tension and inhaled the stress of my next challenge. "How do you think I should tell Ally and Hil?"

Lauren dropped onto my bed in a tangle of limbs only gymnasts and cheerleaders can accomplish. "Oh . . . so you are going to tell them?"

I was surprised by the sniff of disapproval in her voice. "Well, yeah. Shouldn't I?"

She exhaled slowly, motionless for once. "Honestly?" Even her voice was slow, like an idea was coming into focus and she couldn't quite make it out. "I don't think you should yet."

"What?"

"Not right away, at least." And then she was back up to manic speed. "It's just that Hil is still totally worked up over the Keith thing. She's about one stressor away from tearing someone's head off or locking herself in her room. Did she tell you he texted her again this weekend?"

I shook my head. I guess I wasn't the only one keeping secrets.

"All it said was: I miss you, which is totally unhelpful, since last week he posted all these pictures of him with other girls on Facebook. He's such a toolbox. She can't handle this right now. And if you tell Ally . . ."

"Everyone will know," I finished.

"Well, yeah." She unwound her arm from around her ankle. "It sucks. And, I mean, this is just my opinion; you do what you think . . ."

I grabbed a tissue to wipe my eyes. "No, I think you're right. Once Hil's in a better place, Keith-wise . . ."

"And I know we're not as close as you and Hil, and I can't replace her or anything, but I'm here for you."

That's when the real sobs came. Mine first, then Lauren's. Until I looked at the clock. "We need to be back at school in thirty minutes."

"Then we need some deep breaths and some serious cover-up if we don't want to show up looking like we spent the afternoon watching *The Notebook*."

I laughed.

"You know, that's exactly what we'll tell Hil if she says anything about puffy eyes. Then she'll be too disgusted by our sappiness to give it a second thought."

"I'm glad I told you, Laur. Thanks."

She handed me a tissue and squeezed my hand. "You're welcome, but no more sappy. We're done with sappy for today. Now it's dance music and get ready for the game time."

"Deal," I answered, sticking my iPod on its speakers and dialing up the volume.

25

That night I cheered with enthusiasm, fueled by the fact I'd be missing at least a week of practices for chemo and because I needed to prove I belonged. I loved this. In all my efforts to hide my cancer, I'd forgotten. I loved this: the camaraderie of the squad, the energy of the players, the excitement of the crowd, the thrill of feeding off that buzz.

When the game went into overtime and Hil grumbled about the party, I just rustled my purple-and-gold poms and began an impromptu cheer, encouraging the crowd to join my chant: "Let's go, East Lake!"

My cheer high floated me through the game and through Hil's postgame snark: "I can't believe you're blowing us off for Ryan. I don't want you devastated if you sleep with him and he dumps you."

"It's not like that, Hil."

"How do you know?" she demanded. "He's going to break your heart."

"He's not Keith, okay? He's Ryan. Thanks for worrying about me, but it'll be fine."

I gave her a hug; she returned it before adding, "But if he does, don't go the chocolate route or you'll look like crap at the Fall Ball."

I peeled the purple star stickers from the corners of my eyes and shoved my poms in my locker. Calling "Have fun tonight" back over my shoulder before heading to where Ryan waited by the gym door.

"Hey, you."

"Hi," I answered, feeling shy and nervous.

It was chilly now that I wasn't flitting around under the stadium lights, but Ryan responded before I had time to shiver. He stepped behind me, rubbing my arms. "Longest. Game. Ever." He took my hand and towed me to his car.

I felt twelve again, flush with the excitement of liking and being liked. Except when I was twelve, I hadn't felt quite this way about the still-hadn't-mastered-deodorant boys in my class.

He started the ignition before he shut his door. "You're freezing."

"I'm better already." I slipped cool hands beneath his shirt: warming them, kissing him.

He turned the heat on high and I leaned in again. Now that the car had heat, I was in no rush to leave our out-of-the-way space in the school parking lot.

"Oh, hang on a sec." Ryan reached into the backseat and grabbed a bottle of Listerine.

"Your breath is fine." I laughed.

"No, look, it kills germs—see?" He spun the label facing me. "I thought it might help. I know you can't be around germs."

It was a struggle not to laugh. Or cry. I'd forgotten I was sick—he hadn't.

He opened his door and spit the mouthwash on the cement. "Are you hungry? We missed our reservation."

Ryan's eyes were on my lips and I'd barely managed "not really," before his were on mine.

"Me either," he added as he kissed down my jawline.

I shivered and he froze. Pulled back and looked worried. "You're cold. I'm an idiot."

"What? No. That's not why—" I hadn't been cold, but now, with him looking at me like I might fall to pieces, reaching out to pull my shirt down so it covered instead of uncovered, I felt icy.

"You're headed to the hospital tomorrow, I should take you home." The look on his face was everything but desire.

I sighed. "I guess."

"Can I come visit? Are there rules?"

"Visiting hours are eight to eight. You don't have to come." I wrinkled my nose, trying to imagine healthy, handsome Ryan on a ward with sick kids.

"I'll be there."

"I told Lauren today." I figured I'd practice confessing to him before I told my mother.

"Lauren? Really?"

"Why are you laughing?" I asked.

"I don't know, I guess I always saw her as your fourth Musketeer—a spare in case one of you moved away or got fat or something."

"Cute."

"Don't get pissed. I know she's your friend and all, I just thought you'd start with Hil." He shrugged. "Now I'll have someone to drive with to Lakeside. How long will you be there?"

He asked me questions for the rest of the drive, and when he pulled into my driveway, I wasn't ready for The End.

"Want to come in?" My parents' light was on, so I told him to help himself to whatever in the fridge and went upstairs to say good night.

"How was the game?" Mom put down her magazine and pulled off her reading glasses.

"Good." I preempted her questions. "And I feel fine, I don't have a temp, I didn't get too cold, and I took my meds."

"Good girl." Mom's smile was sugary.

My father cleared his throat. "Is Ryan here? I didn't hear a car leave."

"We're going to watch some TV." I prayed they wouldn't decide to go downstairs and greet him in their pajamas. Dad's had "For Sale" signs all over them.

"Don't stay up too late. You've got a tough week ahead of you," Dad cautioned.

"Not long. I promise." I upped the wattage on my obedient-daughter smile.

"Tell Ryan we say hi. Sweet dreams."

When I came downstairs, I expected Ryan to be putting his hands all over me, like he'd always been at parties last spring, but he wasn't. He placed an arm around my shoulders and turned on *SNL* reruns. It would've been vindicating to know Hil was wrong if I wasn't panicked about why.

Was it Ryan who'd changed, or me? This seemed like the most important question in the world. Like I couldn't breathe until I'd heard his answer. "Do you, you know, want me? Even though I'm sick?"

"What?" He muted the TV and turned to me.

I stumbled over the words. "Now that you know. Do you still want me that way?"

"Mia, I'm eighteen. You're seriously hot. If your parents weren't upstairs . . ." He rested his hand on the back of the couch and leaned in. "I'd still go for it if I thought you wanted to. Do you?"

"It's not that simple. Leukemia's not a pretty disease. I'm probably going to lose my hair." I tucked my knees under my chin and played with the fringe on a throw pillow.

"If I shaved my head would you like me less?" He ran his fingers across his hair then placed his hand on my arm.

"No, but it's different." I leaned my cheek against his hand and wanted to believe him.

"Maybe. Or maybe you'll be faster getting ready and I won't have to make small talk with your dad. Do we have to worry about it now?" He shrugged and moved closer on the couch.

"I guess not."

"Do you want me to show you how sexy you are?" Ryan put a cool hand on either side of my face, leaned in, and kissed me until I relaxed out of my defensive ball. He erased my doubts with his lips and didn't stop until every thought but him had faded from my mind.

"There's no rush," he breathed against my collarbone, "but believe me, I want you."

But when he was gone—insisting this didn't count as a date and he wanted a raincheck—Mia-the-teenager vanished with him. I was back to leukemia-Mia, complete with her chemotherapy accessories: an IV pole, portacath, and barf bucket.

26

Ryan was more nervous about my tubes than Gyver had been. "Does that hurt?" He pointed to my port with a horrified expression.

I adjusted my pajama top self-consciously and tugged my necklace. "Not much. They have cream that numbs it before they stick needles in."

He looked green. "What's that?" he asked each time something was hung on my IV pole.

"Fluids." "Platelets." "Nutrients."

"And in there?" He pointed to the separate pole with its gray box and dials.

"That's the chemo."

It didn't take days for the nausea to catch me this time around. When they'd administered the first dose yesterday, I'd been sick within an hour.

"Can you explain it again—sorry—but they killed the cancer already, right?" It was a parody of "One of the These Things is Not Like the Other"—healthy, tan Ryan in my sterile hospital room with my stress-scruffy parents and chemo-weakened me.

I nodded; the motion made me queasy.

"Then why do you need more chemo?" He moved his chair closer and touched my cheek—a baby step that made me feel astronomically better.

Mary Poppins Nurse answered Ryan's question. "This is called consolidation therapy. We're giving Mia three days of chemo—this is day two—to make sure she stays in remission. We'll do this about every six weeks for six months."

"But she seems sicker."

"It's not the cancer, it's the treatment," the nurse explained.

"The treatment makes her sicker?"

"Chemo's rough, but I bet Mia's glad you're here." They looked to me for agreement.

"You should leave the room," I whispered.

"Why?" He looked around, confused.

"I'm—" I fought a wave of bitter saliva. "I'm going to be sick."

Ryan stiffened—fight or flight battling on his face.

Tears filled my eyes, the weak tears of knowing I was about to throw up, knowing I'd feel better afterward but I'd feel worse during. "Go," I said through my teeth.

Mom sighed and reached for the curved basin on the bed-side table. She was angry I'd told Lauren, and while I wasn't officially getting the silent treatment, her I-need-some-quiet-to-think-about-what-you've-done was pretty darn close.

Ryan looked at me again; his face was as pale as mine felt. "Sorry," he whispered as he fled.

Dad walked into the room at the end of my performance, carrying the ginger ale I'd sent him to fetch. "Oh, kiddo."

I wanted to tell him to go find Ryan so I could say I was sorry and embarrassed; I just didn't have the strength. Was it a sign? If he couldn't handle vomit without running, he couldn't handle this? I looked at my horseshoe above the door and traced the shape with my eyes.

Mom left instead, handing the basin to Mary Poppins Nurse on her way and pausing to ask, "Are you done or should I send Ryan on an errand?"

"Done," I croaked.

Dad handed me a tissue. I wiped my face and eyes and blew my nose. Then forced down a sip of ginger ale as Ryan returned—looking more flustered and terrified than when he'd left.

"Sorry," we said at the same time. My voice a gravelly whisper, his a guilty confession.

Ryan lifted my fingers to his lips. "I shouldn't have freaked. I've seen Matherson do worse after too many beers. I'll do better next time. Promise."

Lauren visited too, bringing "movies and manicures, just like I promised," but her fidgeting made me nervous. I kept waiting for her to snag an IV line or trip when she flitted around the tight confines of my hospital room.

Not that it wasn't good to see her. I was glad to hear news about school and the squad; relieved to hear Lauren had covered for me. "I told them you were too sick and contagious for visitors and implied you were puking your guts out." She learned the irony of this statement when she uncapped the nail polish and the scent had me groping for a basin.

Lauren left the room while I vomited, but managed a tight smile when she returned. "So, no nails. Got it."

"Sorry."

"Movie time? I brought Logan Lerman."

I vaguely remember watching previews before I fell into another one of my break-from-nausea naps.

⟨◇⟩

Gyver called that night. "Can I visit tomorrow?"

I shifted in bed, unable to find a position that wasn't achy. "Why would you even ask?"

"Ryan's been there a lot. I didn't want to intrude." He sounded frustrated, or angry.

"Don't be ridiculous. If you don't come tomorrow I'll be seriously offended."

"Right after school?" he asked.

"I'll be here."

Life continued outside my room, but my world was reduced to sleeping, vomiting, and bloody noses. Mom had decided that Lauren knowing wasn't a disaster after all, because Lauren listened to her complaints and added her own gripes.

"Ugh! I don't know how you can sit here all day without going crazy!" said Lauren. She was currently using the only free floor space to do yoga.

"Try staying overnight," added Mom.

I shut my eyes. Lauren's bouncing around wasn't helping my stomach.

"Mia, you've got to eat. Lauren, tell her to eat."

"Eat," ordered Lauren.

I kept my eyes shut and ignored them. When I wasn't actively throwing up, I felt like throwing up.

Mom sighed and continued, "We'll have to let Dr. Kevin know that these antinausea drugs aren't working. Skinny's a good look for you, but not heroin chic."

"I should be so lucky," grumbled Lauren, flipping upright. "Seriously, how do you not go crazy trapped in here all day?"

I was too defeated to do more than look at them.

Gyver came and held my hand. He made me a new playlist and explained the brilliance in song arrangements while I nodded like I understood.

"Do you need help with school? Calc's gotten pretty brutal, but I can try to explain it."

"I can't. Reading makes me sick. Everything makes me sick." I gave him a pity-me smile.

"You know, you were more fun as the patient when we played doctor in second grade," Gyver teased.

I returned a weak echo of his wicked grin, too tired to smack him. "You're awful."

"Speaking of awful, want me to read you *The Stranger?*"

I fell asleep soon after. When I woke, Ryan was the one holding my hand.

His phone was ringing. "Sorry," he said sheepishly, pressing a button to silence it.

"S'okay," I answered with a yawn.

"Can I get you anything?" He'd shifted his arm around my shoulder—cautious of the tubes dripping chemicals into my chest.

My mouth was covered with sores—another side effect of chemo that was worse this time. The idea of eating was repulsive, but the alternative was intravenous nutrients and a longer hospital stay. "Could you get me a milkshake from the cafeteria? Vanilla."

"Kitten, I can go," Mom stood.

Ryan stopped her. "I've got it." He was always asking to go get something: a cup of ice, coffee for Dad, herbal tea for Mom. And I'd recognized that he needed these breaks. But his visits had gotten progressively longer, and he no longer kept his hands in his pockets or flinched each time a nurse approached. Still, I wondered if he was proving something to me . . . or to himself.

"He's such a good boyfriend," Mom said proudly, like it was something she'd accomplished. One of the nurses had taught her to knit, and she churned out scarves like an adding-machine tape. Her needles clicked with anxious energy—a sound that intruded into my dreams and set my teeth on edge.

"He's not . . . ," I started, then decided it wasn't worth it to explain—again. I shut my eyes. If I pretended to sleep, she usually shut up.

There was a new nighttime nurse on the floor. His name was Mark, and I got to know him since I didn't sleep normal hours. It was totally sexist that I learned his real name, but the only nickname I could come up with was Hot Nurse. Plus, being the only male gave him an advantage. He was in his late twenties and very honest—he was a perk of insomnia. The only perk.

"It's good to see you do have female friends," he commented one night.

Dad slept in a chair; his loud snores overpowered the click of machinery. Southern Nurse was at the station in case anything came up. Mark and I played Go Fish.

"What? Of course." I laid down a pair of eights. Lauren had stopped by today, but she had plans with Ally and Hil, so the visit lasted just long enough for her to give me the play-by-play of how her lab partner was absent and she got to join hot Ben's group.

"How come this is the first time I've seen one visit? That's the gossip at the nurses' station: Mia Moore has two boyfriends who come visit her every day. Threes?"

"Go fish. I have zero boyfriends. Gyver's just a friend and Ryan's . . ." I finished the statement with a shrug. He'd called to tell me that he and Chris had plans in Summerset tonight—a party with some of the crew they'd guarded with this summer. Though it sounded more like asking than telling. It sounded like an apology. Like a test.

"Of course you should go. Have fun," I told him. What else could I say? We weren't dating—my choice—and he'd never be as comfortable in my hospital room as he was at the center of a party crowd. It was just one night, but I knew I'd be gripping my necklace a little tighter until the next time he visited or called to check in.

Mark gave me a dubious look and drew a card. "Okay, no boyfriends. But where's everyone else? Where are the cards and flowers? To hear your mom talk, you're Little Miss Popular Pompoms, so why doesn't your room have a waiting list for visitors?"

I frowned. "My mother exaggerates. Lauren knows, but I haven't told any of my other friends I'm here."

"Where do they think you are? Club Med? Well, I guess you could call this 'club meds,' but you know what I mean. Your turn."

"Fives? They think I'm home sick with something normal."

He handed me the five of spades. "That's bull. Why wouldn't you tell them?"

I put down my cards and crossed my arms. "Because I don't want to."

"That's a crap reason. If you're going to pout like a toddler, I'll go catch up with paperwork."

I picked up the cards and refanned them. "I'm not telling them. Not unless I absolutely have to. Don't you remember high school? You're not that old."

"Gee, thanks. Do you have any nines?"

I passed him a card. "High school sucks enough. I don't need to be 'leukemia girl.'"

Mark stared at me. "Mia, c'mon, you're not that naive, are you? This is cancer; it's not make-believe. You're not going to be able to hide this. I'm shocked it's worked so far."

"You don't know that! It could work."

He shook his head and placed his final pair of cards on the tray. "You lose. Better luck next time."

He left and I knew I'd been immature and bratty. I knew I should press the call button and apologize. Maybe Mark and I could have an adult conversation about this—what my rationale was, what I hoped, what I feared.

But giving those ideas a voice was scarier than answering Hil's increasingly impatient voice mails. Scarier than losing my hair. Scarier than any cancer fact on Dad's charts.

Just thinking about it gave me goose bumps, so I put down the call button and picked up my cell phone. A flurry of fib-filled texts later, I felt soothed. Mark was wrong, hiding this was easy. Too easy. Lies no longer paused on my lips, no longer felt weighted by conscience. Lies weren't naive—they were necessary.

27

It was five days before I could sit up without my room spinning and stomach lurching. A week and a half before I returned to school. I let calls go to voice mail. I didn't have enough energy to fake it, and Gyver, Ryan, and Lauren knew to come by.

My first day back, a Thursday, I only made it to lunch before the smell of food left me retching in the nurse's room. From there, I spent the day in my bed or on my bathroom floor.

I tried school again Friday with more success. Hil was withdrawn at lunch; Ally studied me as I picked at and threw away most of my food; Lauren chatted like she'd supersized her morning coffee. I was relieved when lunch ended and we headed out of the cafeteria to go to our separate classes.

I avoided the girls at dismissal—instead going from teacher to teacher to collect makeup work. They'd left by the time I finished, gone home to get ready for the night's game. I stopped by my locker, then hurried to Ryan, who was waiting by the front doors.

In his car, he leaned in for a kiss—then froze.

"What's the matter?" I asked. Ryan's eyes were panning my face with anxious sweeps.

"Do I have another bloody nose?" I flipped down his visor—no blood.

"That necklace you always wear, did you take it off?"

"Of course not." My hand went to my throat—it was naked. I continued searching my collar like it'd reappear. I gulped air, tried not to cry.

"I'll find it." His voice calmed into determination. "I'll take you home. You search your room. I'll come back and look."

I felt vulnerable without the weight of the charm against my neck: exposed and unprotected. And the necklace wasn't in my room, or the kitchen, or my bathroom. Dad checked the shower and sink drains. Mom went through the vacuum bags and searched my car. Ryan called to report he'd had no luck at the school—but he'd alerted the janitors and principal and left notes for all my teachers.

"Don't worry," he added. "I'll find it. I'm going to check my car and then the hospital. I'll meet you at the game."

I didn't want to go to the game anymore; I wanted to hide in bed until my necklace was found. Instead I called Hil for a ride so we'd have a chance to talk. I needed to fix us without telling her why we were broken.

"I like your new highlights," I said as I got in the car.

"Thanks." She turned on the radio.

I turned it off. "Lauren says one of the freshmen is becoming a great tumbler."

"Monica. You were better, but she'll do." Hil swore at a slow car in front of her and drummed sparkly nails on the steering wheel.

"Anything else new? I feel so out of it after missing all that school." I was embarrassed to be asking; I should know.

"Not really."

Maybe the direct route was best. "Are you mad at me?"

"No." The slow car turned into a driveway and Hillary accelerated with a jerk.

"Sorry I've missed so much practice."

"Whatever. It has nothing to do with that."

"Then what? Because of Ryan?" I instinctively grasped the empty air at my neck.

"What, you mean how you're supposedly not dating him, yet he's been your spokesperson for the past two weeks?"

"He has not."

"Really? He and Lauren are the only ones you bother to talk to anymore. Explain why I should tell you anything when you don't trust me enough to tell me what's going on?" She glowered at the yellow lines blurring ahead of us.

"I'm here now. Hil?"

"Forget it." She sucked in a breath and asked, "So, are your parents splitting up?"

"What? My parents? No. Why?"

"I thought—the whole Connecticut thing? My parents sent me away when they tried a last-ditch effort to fix their crap marriage." She sniffed once, her voice raw. "I thought maybe your parents—you've been totally non-Mia since you got back."

"No. They're fine."

"Oh. Forget I said anything."

"I'd tell you—if my parents were divorcing. I'd tell you that." That would be easy.

"Would you? You know Ally has all these theories about what's going on with you. Mia's depressed, Mia's anorexic, Mia's in rehab, Mia's got mono."

I tried to laugh but it came out mangled and fake. "Ally's so dramatic." Though mono would've been a great cover and part of me wished I'd thought of it.

"Is she? Where've you been? I stopped by your house more than once and there was never anyone home. Once I ran into Mac 'n' Cheese—he was coming out your front door and said he was feeding Jinx. Why did Gyver have to feed your cat if you were home sick?"

"You must be spending too much time with Ally—now you're being a drama queen too." I sounded like my mom—pacifying, belittling.

Hil flinched. "I'm worried about you. Don't you get it?"

I stared out the window and directed my lie to the row of mailboxes. "I'm fine."

Hil sighed. "Never mind. After the game we'll go to Lauren's party—thank God her parents are away. We'll talk there, okay? You can tell me how Winters is wonderful and I'll try to believe it." She gave me her pretty and persuasive smile and I wanted to nod, but I couldn't. "You are going, right? It's at Lauren's. You know, your new best friend's house? Wait . . . let me guess; you're busy with Ryan?" Her voice was acid and ice.

"You're still—" The rest of that sentence, "my best friend," felt awkward and forced. "I can't go, but he can if he wants."

"But he won't. He's like a puppy." She relented. "Please, Mia."

"Sorry."

"You two are so lame. He used to be hot and you used to be fun. He's just a guy. It's not worth it!" She pulled into the parking lot behind the field house.

"Is this the part where you explain to me how it's so different than what you and Keith did for a year and a half? You're such a hypocrite!" I snapped.

She got out without answering, but the parking lot lights reflected off tears on her cheeks.

I stayed curled in the passenger seat, knees to chin, bloomers visible to anyone who walked by, and tried to convince myself I hadn't just made things worse.

A knock on the window made me jump. Ally waved and mouthed, "You okay?" I nodded and uncurled my knees, wishing I'd stayed home, wishing Ally wasn't waiting with a what's-wrong? expression. Wishing I didn't have to smile and lie.

28

I should've been expecting it. Every morning there was more hair on the pillowcase and less on my head. I couldn't wear dark colors because the contrast with my blond hair drew attention to my excessive shedding. Still, I went down to breakfast on Saturday unprepared.

"Kitten, have you thought about when you'd like to go back to the hairdresser?" Mom looked at a box on the kitchen table.

"There's not much left to cut." I resembled one of those toddlers with stringy, wispy hair.

"I think it's time to accept the inevitable. The best thing would be to cut it off and wear this." She reached into the box and pulled out a wig packaged within some sort of netting. "It's real hair—*your* hair. Remember?"

"Oh." My hands strayed upward. "It's that bad?"

"It's not bad. You still look beautiful. It's just, if you want to pretend you have hair, we need to switch to the wig before what's left on your head is gone."

The wig looked like a shiny dead animal. "Today?"

"It doesn't have to be. Whenever you're ready—I've already talked to the salon. So, when you're ready . . ." Her eyes skipped by me and fixed on the telephone.

"I guess today works. There's no point in waiting, right?" I looked at my feet; my toes were clenched within my socks.

"Absolutely! I knew you'd make a mature decision. I'll reserve the salon so you have privacy. Don't worry, you're going to look just as pretty in the wig."

I ducked out the front door while she was on the phone. Mrs. Russo answered my knock. "Mia? What are you doing over here so early? And in your pajamas? Get in here before you freeze."

"Is Gyver up?" I asked.

"This early? I don't expect him to surface before noon. He was at a concert last night." She took a plate from the cabinet and piled it with fresh fruit and toasted raisin bread.

"Oh." I sat at the table and poured juice. "Thanks. Did you and Mr. Russo already eat?"

"Yes. Why don't I go wake lazy boy up to keep you company?"

"It's okay."

"Dearest, you would not be over here at nine in the morning on a Saturday—in your pajamas—if everything was okay."

I stared at the tablecloth. "Mom thinks I should shave my head and wear a wig."

Mrs. Russo refreshed her coffee and joined me at the table, leaning in and giving me her complete attention—the same way Gyver did. "How do you feel about that?"

I shrugged. "It makes sense. It's not like I have much choice, and my head's itchy."

"You wouldn't have to wear a wig."

"Walk around bald?"

She put a hand on my arm and waited me out.

"I don't want to be bald." Once I started to cry, I couldn't stop. Mrs. Russo bundled me in her arms and rubbed my back, rocking and cooing comforting words.

"I. Don't. Want. Any. Of. This." And finally the words I'd been fighting against since July came spewing out. "It's not fair. It's not fair. It's not fair."

"I know," she soothed.

"I just want—"

"Nancy? Is Mia here?"

At the sound of my mother's voice, I jerked upright, stifled a half-formed sob and wiped my cheeks on my sleeves.

Mrs. Russo pressed her lips together for a moment, then leaned over and touched them to my cheek. "We're in here. Eating some breakfast."

Mom walked in. "There you are, kitten! Good news, we're all set for ten thirty today."

I examined my raisin toast and hid my giveaway splotchy cheeks. "Great. Thanks, Mom."

"Would you like some fruit? Bread? Coffee? There's plenty." Mrs. Russo pointed to the mugs on the table and began assembling a plate.

Mom poured herself a cup of coffee. "When I can't fit in my pants, I'm blaming your raisin bread. It's sinfully good. Right, Mia?"

I um-hmmed, but my legs began to bob under the table. I couldn't fake it right now, and if I didn't leave soon, she'd notice. "Can I go wake Gyver?"

"Absolutely. Tell lazy boy it's time to join the living," Mrs. Russo said.

I knocked twice before I heard a noise that was half-groan and half-snarl. "It's early, Mom." His voice was muffled by the door and maybe a pillow.

"It's Mia," I said to the doorframe.

"Mi? What?" Less muffled; perhaps the pillow had been removed.

"Can I come in?" I waited five quiet seconds. "I'm coming in."

Gyver sat up and rubbed his face with the palm of his hand. His hair was an anarchy of black locks and the pillowcase had left creases on his cheek. He was shirtless. One foot and part of his calf were sticking out from under his blanket, making it clear he didn't wear pajama pants to bed either.

"Hi," I said shyly, sitting down in his desk chair.

"You're in my bedroom. In your pajamas." His words were sleep-slowed and rusty.

"Yeah," I agreed, waiting for his inevitable innuendo.

Gyver blinked. "And you've been crying. What's wrong, Mi?" He sat up straighter, alert.

"Nothing."

He tilted his head and raised an eyebrow.

"Nothing really. At least, nothing that matters. My mom wants me to get my hair cut today."

He raised the other eyebrow.

"Cut off," I clarified.

He nodded and waited. Were the Russos born with magical listening powers or did they cultivate them?

"It's superficial, but I like my hair. I don't want to wear a wig and I don't want to be sick." I was making trails in his carpet with my big toe. "Go ahead, tell me I'm being shallow."

"C'mere." He patted a spot next to him.

"Um . . . what do you have on under there?"

He grinned. "Would you like me to show you?"

When my cheeks lit up with blushes, he laughed and amended, "I'm joking, Mi. I've got boxers on. Come here, would you? I'll stay safely under the covers."

I sat on his bed—the way he'd sat on my hospital one. He gave me a sleep-warm hug. "You okay? You want to cry?"

"Did that already. I'm just so tired of it all, Gyver."

He leaned his cheek against the top of my head; I could feel the heat from his bare chest radiating through my pajamas. "I worry about you, Mi. It seems like you're more worried about people *finding out* you're sick than the fact that you *are* sick."

I heard him, but I didn't have an answer. I continued to

fidget: tracing lines with my fingertips on the inside of the arm he'd wrapped around me.

"Maybe you should give them a chance. If your friends aren't there for you when you need them, what good are they?" he asked.

I needed to push things back to safe waters—I should push away from him. I forced a laugh. "Maybe you just make it too easy; I don't need them when I've got you." I'd planned to add "and Ryan," but my voice betrayed me and I was suddenly nervous. "We should go downstairs. Mom's waiting in the kitchen."

"Yours or mine?"

"Both."

"So I guess I can't pull you under these blankets and take advantage of your fragile emotional state." Gyver laughed at my startled expression and rolled away from me to reach for something on the far side of the bed—revealing a pair of light-blue boxers decorated with purple musical notes. My cheeks burned again. I shifted my gaze and tried to shift my thoughts.

"Here." Something landed in my lap. I looked down at a black newsboy cap with a band logo on the front. "I got it last night, but it'll look better on you."

He gently brushed my hair back and placed it on my head. My "thanks" was breathless.

"No problem. Now, can you get out of my room so I can get dressed? If you're going to wake me up early to go to a salon, the least you can do is properly fortify me with caffeine first."

"What? You don't have to—"

"Go." Gyver nudged me through the blanket with his foot.

"You don't have to beg. I'll come with you—but most public places require pants. And I require coffee."

I forced myself to laugh, half-relieved and half-disappointed to be leaving his room. "I'll have a mug ready for you."

"Yes, please. And Mi?" I paused at the door and turned around. Gyver grinned. "I caught you checking out my boxers. Couldn't help yourself, huh?"

My face blazed again: embarrassment plus anger. I pulled the door shut—loudly—and headed downstairs to make him an overly sweet cup of coffee.

29

"Be honest." My posture was debutante perfect in the salon chair. "Do I look like an anorexic alien?" I hadn't seen myself yet, but I could imagine a huge, bald head on a too-skinny neck.

Mom was horrified. "No! Of course not. You look beautiful."

Gyver spun my chair toward the mirror. "Actually, you're kinda right—as usual."

Mom was more horrified. "MacGyver! My daughter certainly doesn't. You don't, kitten."

I looked at Gyver's reflection; he was making faces behind my back. I laughed nervously and lowered my eyes to my own face, sucking in a deep, loud breath.

"Your eyes look bigger," offered the optimistic stylist. "You've got killer blue eyes."

"Exactly!" Mom agreed emphatically. "Once you put on your wig, no one'll know."

She held it out, but I ignored her and continued to study the large-eyed, bareheaded girl in the mirror. I twisted the chain around my neck, pulling the charm out from under my smock so I could slide it back and forth while I processed.

"What's that?" Gyver frowned, reaching for the pendant.

"Is that new?" Mom also leaned in to inspect the gold heart.

"Ryan gave it to me last night." I pulled away from Gyver's grasp and tucked it self-consciously under my shirt. He'd surprised me with it after the game—when I'd bailed on Lauren's party and yet another of his rain check dates—pressing a small jewelry box in my hand while I was still making excuses. I knew I was probably supposed to respond with, "Yes, I'll go out with you," but I couldn't hide my disappointment that *my* necklace wasn't inside the green velvet case.

Ryan had looked disappointed too, saying, "I'm still here, Mia. I know you thought I'd run after seeing you in the hospital, but I'm still here. Trust me." I'd kissed his cheek and asked for help with the clasp, but it felt different on my neck. A heart wasn't good luck. What does it signify if you lose your lucky charm?

"Your boyfriend?" asked the stylist. "How pretty! You're lucky to have such a nice guy. I wish my boyfriend bought me jewelry."

Gyver snorted.

"She is lucky!" Mom gushed. "He's handsome, thoughtful, and last year's junior prom king. Now let's try the wig."

Instead I put on Gyver's hat. "I think my scalp needs to settle."

Mom blinked. "Oh. That's fine. It's not like anyone's going to see you in here." She scanned the empty salon. "Do you want to wait in the car while I pay?"

I nodded and yanked off the smock before the stylist could undo the snaps. Gyver took the keys from my mother and put a hand on my shoulder as we walked out.

With the doors shut, me in the backseat, Gyver in shotgun, and the radio tuned to one of his stations, I took the hat off. My head felt exposed and prickly. "Awful?"

Gyver leaned against the headrest, eyes closed and singing along with a song while he rolled a guitar pick between his fingers. "Are you compliment fishing? Because you couldn't look awful if you tried."

I put the hat back on. "I wish you'd be serious."

"You look fine."

"Fine? I hope Ryan's okay with 'fine.'" I was crushed. What did I want Gyver to say?

He opened his eyes and scanned me from the top of the hat down to the heart pendant. "So Ryan's your boyfriend now? It's official?"

"What?" I stopped fussing with the rim of the hat and looked at him. "No, Mom just refuses to listen, and I'm sick of correcting her."

"What kind of game are you playing, Mi?"

"Game?"

He turned around in his seat, searing me with intense eyes. "You're jerking the guy along. Either you like him enough to date him or you don't—so either go out with him or let him go while he's still got some dignity left."

I pulled the hat brim lower and stared at my fingernails. When I had I let them get so ragged? "You don't know what you're talking about. It's not like that."

Gyver nearly yelled his response. "I know exactly what I'm talking about—you're going to break his heart."

I scoffed. "I am not going to break Ryan's heart. He doesn't care that much."

Gyver paused for a second, his voice dropped to a deep whisper. "Well, if he doesn't care, why's he doing all this?"

Why was Ryan doing this? I could think about that later, right now I was too focused on Gyver and too unsettled. "He's hardly the only thing I'm worried about. Does it look real or will people guess? What if Ally and Hil find out? How do I keep a wig on while cheering?"

"Enough." He held up a hand—the pick held between pointer and middle finger—and shut his eyes again. "Didn't you hear? It makes your 'killer blue eyes look bigger.' Are you really going to make me tell you you're gorgeous, so you feel good about yourself for Ryan? You know I think so. I need a much bigger dose of caffeine if you're going to be whining about The Jock and the cheerbitches."

If his eyes had been open, he would've seen how much his words hurt, but he only sighed and rubbed his closed lids.

❖

I spent hours locked behind my bathroom door with the wig and the arsenal of products Mom bought to care for it. I ached to call Hil, have her come do hairstyling-goddess tricks and tell me honestly how I looked. She'd hug me and allow a five-minute cry if it was awful, then say "that's enough" and tell me her plan to make bald the newest trend. But after our fight yesterday, I couldn't convince myself to press the buttons to bring her to my dramafest. Probably because I was scared she wouldn't come.

I needed to believe that even withered, ashen, and bald, I didn't look too repulsive. I left the bathroom, trying to convince myself that I didn't need my clover necklace to keep me safe, but I paused again to check myself out in the foyer mirror.

It was gone. Replaced by a framed floral print. I stepped into the dining room; the decorative mirror in there was also missing. Ordering the wig hadn't been Mom's only preparation for today. How long had she been planning this?

Mom came in while I studied the dining room's new Monet print. Did she fake her smiles too? Her face looked falsely cheerful as she asked, "What are you up to tonight?"

"No plans." I shook my head, hyperaware of the whisper of the wig against my cheeks.

"No plans?" She frowned. "Call Hil, see what she's doing."

"They're all going over to Bill's house, and I don't feel like going out." I didn't want to leave the house until my hair grew back.

"Have them over here instead. I haven't seen anyone but Lauren in ages. What's everyone up to these days?"

I stared at the painting, a decoration to hide the ugly truth. My mouth tasted sour. "Lauren had a party last night. Other than that, I wouldn't know. I've barely seen them, I have no clue what's going on in their lives." My voice climbed octaves as I lost my battle with tears.

"That's not true, kitten." She patted my back. "You see them at school and practice."

"It is true! My whole life is illness and lies. I hate it!" I pulled the wig from my head and whipped it at the ground. "And that? It's just another lie—another thing to hide. I don't know my friends anymore, and I can't even tell them why!"

Mom retrieved the wig with trembling hands. I thought she was reaching to hug me, but instead she returned the wig to my head. I flinched away.

She rubbed her temples and looked at me—really seemed to see me—for the first time since my diagnosis. She winced. "It breaks my heart to see you so unhappy. When you decided not to tell your friends, I thought it'd make it easier on you. But it hasn't, has it? Maybe you've gone too far with the secrets—your father never thought it'd work."

Her change of heart stunned me like a slap. I grabbed the back of a chair. "I don't know how to tell them now," I whispered.

Mom looked exhausted. "It's been a long, emotional day. We don't need to decide anything right now. Wait and see if you still feel this way tomorrow."

Not lying anymore—the idea was liberating and terrifying.

It seemed too late to tell. I couldn't casually slip "By the way, I've got leukemia" into a conversation.

"I need to talk to Lauren."

Her smile was back, relieved. I let her fix my wig. "Good idea. Invite her over."

I nodded and wandered back to my room. Lauren wouldn't be honest and I wasn't in the mood for what she thought I wanted to hear. So I dialed Ryan. He looked at me more than anyone these days; his reaction would tell me everything and maybe give me the answer to Gyver's question: Why was he doing this?

I hoped to catch him before he went out, but from the sound of his "Hey. I knew you couldn't last a night without me" he was already a few beers in.

I tried anyway. "I need to talk to you."

Someone cranked the volume on a crappy rap song; I could barely hear his "What's up?"

"I got my hair cut today . . ."

Chris was yelling: "Winters, you've got to check this out, man."

"Yeah?" said Ryan. "Cool."

Was that for me, or Chris?

"I'm bald. They shaved my head," I snapped.

"Bald? What?" Ryan semicovered the phone with his hand, I heard a muffled "Be right back" and a door. It wasn't much quieter in whatever room he'd gone into. "Bald?"

"Bald," I repeated.

"Maybe we should talk later. It's loud and . . . bald? Shit."

He didn't really wait for me to answer. Or maybe it was so noisy he thought he'd missed my agreement. "I'll call you later."

A final burst of party noise, Ally's laughter, Lauren's half-whiny "Wait for me!" and the line was dead. It didn't sound like they missed me at all.

Damn it.

Gyver was right. I did need to know why Ryan was doing this—clearly it was all about the pursuit. And now that what he chased was broken, there was no reason for him to run after me.

Well, screw him. I didn't need Ryan Winters. I needed the one person who'd never have a run-and-hide reaction to me.

"You decided to go out?" Mom smiled as I passed her with my coat on.

"Just next door. I need to talk to Gyver."

"Oh." She didn't bother to hide her disappointment, so I didn't bother to stick around and finish the conversation.

Mrs. Russo answered my knock. "Mia, twice in one day."

"Is Gyver home?" I stepped into her kitchen—as usual, it smelled of cooking.

"He just left for a show. Do you want to call him?" She pointed to the phone I still clutched.

"No, it's okay. We got in a sort of fight earlier and I wanted to tell him he was right about Ryan." I didn't know why I was saying this, except the Russos radiated such comfort that I always felt compelled to go confessional around them.

"Ryan?" Mrs. Russo looked up from her cutting board. "Oh, that's right, the boyfriend. Your mother thinks he's quite the catch."

"He's not my boyfriend. He never was and now he's definitely not going to be." I was surprised by how raw I felt. How badly I hadn't wanted Gyver to be right. How far I'd allowed Ryan into my heart and how much damage he'd left behind.

"Hmm." She held up a piece of tomato and I let her feed it to me. "And this is what you came over to tell Gyver? Maybe you should call him."

I chewed and considered it. "Maybe I'll just show up and surprise him. I haven't seen Empty Orchestra in months."

"You should! It would make his night." She touched my cheek before adding, "Meagan's there, too, so you'll have someone to watch with."

I shrank away from her hand. "She is?" I had no problem admitting I was wrong to Gyver, but not in the middle of a date. I didn't want to see Meagan look at him or him look at her. Or both of them look at me with pity. The images wouldn't leave my head—him on stage and her an adoring fan. Would he play the M.A. song? Would he dedicate one to her? Would his electric eye contact, which always made me feel like I was the only girl in the room, be focused solely on *her*?

"It's all right. I'll talk to him tomorrow."

"You sure?" she asked.

"I'm sure." I pointed to the ingredients laid across the kitchen's island. "Can I help?"

"I'm just making sauce. The garlic's simmering, it's just chopping and stirring."

She looked at me. "The wig is good. You can't even tell. I knew and it took a few minutes to remember."

"Thanks." I fiddled with a green pepper and sighed.

"You don't want to go home." She placed a cutting board on the counter in front of me. "Why don't you stay and I'll teach you to make ravioli." She handed me a knife and nodded at the pepper.

"I'm sick of pretending all the time," I admitted. "It's exhausting, and I'm already exhausted. I can't do it tonight."

"Your mother loves you, but she doesn't give you much room to be human."

"She just wants me to be happy."

"You're allowed to be sad and scared. Cancer's a sad, scary thing. Experiencing those emotions isn't going to hurt you."

I nodded and let the truth of her words sink in as I sliced the pepper into irregular chunks.

It wasn't easy—even while mixing, kneading, and rolling the ravioli dough and listening to Mrs. Russo explain the secrets to making pasta—to forget that I was wearing a wig and teenage social life was going on without me.

"I'm going to tell my friends I'm sick," I announced.

"Good." Mrs. Russo wiped her hands on a towel and hugged me. "I'm proud of you. There are much better ways for you to be spending your energy."

Suddenly it all seemed possible. Standing in a kitchen that smelled of oregano and acceptance with Mrs. Russo stirring, humming to herself, and holding out spoons for me to taste, I felt hopeful. I felt relieved.

Mr. Russo wandered in from the family room where he'd been watching the History Channel. He took the lid off the saucepan and inhaled, then leaned in and kissed his wife on the cheek. "This is what I like to see: my two favorite ladies making my favorite foods."

He pinched my cheek and poured himself a glass of milk. Poured me one as well. "How are you doing, *mia piccola bambina?*"

He hadn't called me that in years, not since I'd kicked him in the shins and told him I wasn't "piccola," I was a "big girl." I smiled at the memory, at him.

"I'm fine," I said. For the first time in months, I meant it.

I was asleep, dreaming about ravioli and concerts, when those images were invaded. Replaced by Ryan's picture and ring tone. "Hello?"

"You sleeping?" There was alcohol heaviness in his voice.

"A little bit." I pulled myself upright and tucked a pillow between my head and the headboard. My bald head. The day began to trickle back into focus. I wasn't mad at Ryan, but I was disappointed. We were done with whatever it was we hadn't officially started.

"Go back to sleep. I'll come over tomorrow." He wasn't drunk, just buzzed-mellow.

"That's okay, you don't have to," I was too tired to give the words a this-isn't-a-suggestion cadence, but figured hanging up gave the same message.

A car pulled into Gyver's driveway. I cracked the window to hear Meagan's voice call good-bye and him whistling under his breath as he headed inside.

Things didn't seem as shiny anymore, or as easy. I didn't feel as resolved. I sent Lauren a text: Call me when you get up, then scrunched down under my covers and willed my brain to stop thinking and my eyes to shut.

30

I woke up wanting a lazy, kick-around Sunday. I pulled on my oldest cheerleading sweatshirt and a pair of yoga pants. I grabbed Gyver's hat—Mom had made it clear how she felt about me walking around bareheaded.

"Notice how I let you sleep in?" Gyver asked as I entered my kitchen. "Friends don't wake up friends before noon."

"What are you wearing?" Mom asked.

I shrugged. "It's my lucky sweatshirt. Hi, Gyver."

"You look homeless. People are going to think we can't afford to clothe you. That sweatshirt's going to disappear when it goes down to be washed—I'll buy you a new one."

"She looks fine," said Gyver. "I could lend her much worse if you want."

Mom ignored him. "What can I get you, kitten? Do you want breakfast or lunch?"

"I'll get it."

Mom hesitated, a hand on the refrigerator door.

"Didn't you want to rake out the flowerbeds?" I asked. She'd said something like that at dinner. "I can make myself a sandwich."

"I'll supervise," added Gyver.

Mom smiled and shut the fridge. "All right, I'll go. But retire the sweatshirt, m'kay?"

I busied myself with gathering plates and making PB&J sandwiches: two for Gyver and one for me. "How was the show? Did you have a good night?" I asked when his patient silence became torturous.

"Yeah. From the sounds of it, not as eventful as yours."

"Your mom told you?"

"Yeah. I was supposed to wait and bring you some ravioli, but"—he shrugged—"I wanted to see you."

I stared at my plate, not hungry for the sandwich or ravioli.

He leaned forward, sympathy radiating off him. "Are you okay? What happened?"

"You were right. When I thought about why Ryan was letting me 'jerk him around,'" I made weak air quotes and swallowed, "it was never about liking me—I was just a challenge. His reaction to my haircut made that clear."

Gyver shut his eyes for a second, rubbed their lids before looking at me with the Russo intensity. "He doesn't deserve you, but I can't believe he doesn't like you."

"I don't want to talk about it." I pinched crumbs off my crust and rolled them into balls.

He opened his mouth. Closed it. Pressed his lips tight.

Stood up. Leaned against the back of his chair. Opened his mouth again. Shut it. Sat down. Nodded.

I touched his knee. "Thanks for not saying 'I told you so.'"

He closed his hand over mine. "Let's get out of here, Mi. Go do something."

Escape sounded perfect. "Something from one of your lists? Can I see them yet?"

"Let's get them and go." He stood and held out a hand.

"You get them and I'll change."

"Why? You're fine." Gyver tilted his head and looked at me.

"I look like a grub. If I try and leave the house like this, Mom'll throw a fit."

"Suit yourself—but you look fine."

"Be right back."

When I returned to the kitchen in jeans, sweater, and wig, Gyver was bent over the fridge. "Hungry again?" I teased. "Or are you finding a place for my sympathy pasta?"

"Your mom said to help myself. What's sympathy pasta?" Ryan straightened and turned.

"What are you doing here?" I stepped back.

"You didn't answer your phone." Ryan shut the fridge. "What's going on?"

"That's a good question." Gyver stormed into the kitchen and stepped between Ryan and me. "What the hell are you doing here?"

"Back off. What's the matter?" Ryan looked from Gyver's glower to my lip chewing.

Gyver grabbed his arm. "I think you'd better go."

Ryan shook off his grip and turned to me with raised eyebrows. "Did I miss something?" He reached for me, but Gyver blocked his arm. Ryan snapped, "Chill out. What does this have to do with you?"

Gyver's voice came out as a growl. "She doesn't want you."

"Maybe," Ryan admitted with a shrug and a half grin, "but I'd still rather hear it from Mia."

They both looked at me. Ryan's eyes were lined with frustration. Gyver's flamed with protective anger, but as I extended our gaze, the corners of his mouth twitched with victory. My hand strayed to fiddle with my necklace and paused on the still-unfamiliar shape. Was it an unlucky charm? Or had I overreacted?

"I need to talk to Ryan. I'll call you in a little while, Gyver."

Gyver's half-formed smile faded. He left. He didn't say good-bye, didn't look back when I called his name.

Ryan took a step toward me and touched my crossed arms. "So . . . want to tell me what that was all about?"

"Look, I said I'd give you a chance, and I did. I don't really know what else to say."

"A chance? Is that what you call it when you cancel all my dates and hire Russo to play some messed-up version of bodyguard? I'm trying here—are you?"

Ryan's hand slipped off me and he slumped into a kitchen chair. "I give up. You've already made up your mind; it doesn't matter what I do."

The resignation in his voice made my stomach clench. I slid down the wall and sat on the floor, wrapping my arms around my knees so I wouldn't go wrap them around him. I had to remind myself: he'd disappointed me. He didn't want me.

"Why are you doing this? Is the chase that fun? What do you think's going to happen if I say yes?"

"Fun? Do I look like I'm having fun?" His laughter cut through me. "If I wanted a girl who'd get naked as soon as I winked at her, I'd go for Lauren or Hil. I want you. I thought you'd figured that out by now."

"Hil? Are you crazy? She'd rip your balls off before she'd let them near her."

Ryan shrugged and climbed out of his chair to sit across from me with his back against the refrigerator. "I wouldn't be so sure about that, but who cares—that's not the point. You're mad about something."

"Well, yeah." I tapped my head self-consciously.

"Because of how I reacted about your hair? What'd I do wrong? It looks good, by the way. Way better than I expected."

Now that he said it, I felt stupid. Especially since he was looking at me with unguarded appreciation. "'Bald? Shit!' wasn't really what I wanted to hear."

"You surprised me. I'm no good with stuff like that. I'm trying, but I'm no good with it. You've got to give me some warning." He stretched and touched my wig with a cautious finger. "I can't even tell. It looks like your hair and even feels real."

"It is my hair. It's just no longer attached." I wanted to lean into his palm or tuck my head under his chin, but didn't know how he'd react, or how the wig would. Or if I should even be thinking things like that.

"Will you take it off? Is that a weird thing to ask? I bet you're still beautiful without hair."

I stiffened. That I hadn't expected. The whole point of the wig was so no one would see me bald. And didn't Ryan only want a glossy, perfect version of me?

My fingers were clumsy as I pulled it off. I could feel my shoulders creeping up toward my ears and I kept my eyes glued to the bottom of Ryan's sneaker.

"Wow. I was right." I looked up. He still had that bedroom smile on. "You know that supersexy model with the shaved head, Syrena something? She's got nothing on you."

My exhale sounded like a sob and he crept over and put his arms around me, not at all tentative as he pressed his cheek against my head. "Sorry I hurt you yesterday."

"I'm sorry I hurt you today." I squeezed him tight and felt the same relief in his arms, his back muscles tensing as he pulled me closer. He reached down and lifted my chin, gently backing me up against the wall, as he held me in place with kisses and caresses.

◈

It was hours before Ryan left—not until Mom came in from gardening and invited him to stay for dinner. He'd learned his lesson last time and politely declined.

I went upstairs to fix my wig and to check my phone. I still hadn't heard from Lauren. I called and left her another voice mail, then called Gyver.

I could tell he was pissed from his "hello," but I couldn't tell how angry until he followed up with, "Are you done playing games with Ryan? Should I set up Monopoly for us now?"

"Don't be a jerk. I owed him a chance to explain."

"Oh. You owed *him*? Got it. Bye, Mia."

I redialed him, but got his voicemail. Left my apology after the beep. And I was left with a silent phone that didn't ring again that night, no matter how many texts I sent to Lauren.

31

I wanted to strategize my Big Reveal, but didn't stress too much about absentee Lauren. I figured she was busy cleaning up from Friday's party, hung over from Saturday, had dropped her phone in the hot tub again, or was totally busted and grounded. Before bed I texted her to meet me in the foyer Monday before school.

She did, with her face mottled with angry pink splotches that clashed with her hair.

But I didn't notice this right away, not until after she responded to my, "I was thinking I'd tell them after practice. We could all go to Iggy's. A public place would help control Ally's hysterics, right?"

"Whatever." The word was razor sharp and slashed through my good mood.

"What the hell, Lauren?"

"No!" She pointed a finger at me. "What the hell, Mia? Where were you Friday night?"

"After the game? I was tired, I went home." I was beginning to guess how Ryan had felt yesterday in my kitchen; I had no clue where this anger was coming from.

"Not too tired to hang out with Ryan," she accused.

"Please, he stayed for less than an hour. What's this about? Your party?"

"How many boring afternoons have I spent"—she lowered her voice to a hushed snarl—"at the hospital? Nice of you to let me know you weren't coming. Seems you had time to tell Hil you wouldn't be there, but you couldn't find two seconds to tell me." Lauren wasn't usually aggressive, but she kept stepping closer, one finger pointed at me and the rest of her hand clamped in a fist.

I stepped backward, but didn't back down. "I didn't know it was an RSVP event."

"It's always great fun when you throw someone a Welcome Back party and she doesn't bother coming." Her hand was shaking. She hid it by reaching up and twirling a curl around her finger.

"What?" I swallowed and felt my aggravation soften to guilt. "I didn't know."

"It's called 'a surprise.'"

"Laur, I'm sorry. I didn't know. I would've told you." I wanted to give her a hug or coax her fingers out of her hair. She was tugging so hard it looked like she was cutting off circulation, and she was making it frizz.

"Whatever. There's nothing you can do about it now." One last twirl and she wrenched her hand free, turned around, and stomped off to class.

"Laur. Lauren. Wait!" But she didn't wait and the late bell rang. I hurried to my locker, grabbed my books, and attempted to slam the door, but a notebook was in the way. My locker mirror slipped out and clattered on the floor. I kicked the notebook in and the door shut. Shoved the mirror inside the cover of a textbook, too overwhelmed and late to reopen my lock. Then I scrambled to French class feeling like I'd had a serving of battery acid and betrayal for breakfast.

During calc I tried to get Gyver's attention, finally poking him with my eraser when he refused to notice my waving pencil or the note I dropped on his desk. He gave me an expressionless nod, then turned back to his problem set with the note unread. Frowning, I opened my calc book and my mirror was lying there. It hadn't broken—it was safety plastic, not glass—but the bottom corner was chipped. What punishment did that earn me: seven days of bad luck, seven minutes?

Gyver would be annoyed if he knew my thoughts, and I wished he'd scold me . . . because to do so, he'd have to acknowledge me. I spent the rest of the period trying to catch his eye and apologize, but he didn't look at me once. When he left class without a good-bye, I glanced from his empty desk to the discarded note to my chipped mirror and felt lost.

Lauren hadn't gotten over it by lunch. And I'd apologized. Three times.

"Stop sulking, Lauren, it makes you look five. She said she was sorry, what do you want, blood?" Hil sipped her Diet Coke and rolled her eyes. She was hyper today, even a little bubbly, like a caffeinated Ally clone. It made me nervous.

Even if I hadn't decided the Big Reveal needed to wait until after Lauren removed the big stick from her butt, I'd still be uneasy around a Hil who greeted me with a hug and babbled, "Your hair looks cute. What'd you do different? We missed you at Lauren's and Bill's this weekend—you're turning into quite the nerdling homebody. I was telling Ryan on Saturday that we may need to do an intervention." She slipped an arm around my shoulders and pulled me into another hug.

Ally choked on a bite of apple and studied the table. I self-consciously touched my wig. Lauren gasped and practically stood up. "Are you kidding me, Hil? I don't believe you! Like you can talk—have you told your best friend what you tried to do with her boyfriend Saturday night?"

"I don't have a boyfriend." My answer was automatic, but then I paused and processed the words, pulling away from Hil to ask, "Wait. What?"

Ally packed her lunch away and looked like she wanted to

crawl under the table. Lauren's face was blotchy-mad again. Hil's was blank. The same blank it'd been right after her parents' divorce and Keith's breakup. "Nothing happened. Don't worry. Lauren's just pissy and trying to make us fight too."

"Nothing happened, but only because he rejected your ass," Lauren spat back.

I didn't need to hear any more. I shoved my uneaten lunch in my bag and stood, crossing the cafeteria with my head held high but legs that felt like they might collapse.

"Hey, you." Ryan gave me a questioning look when I sat down next to him.

"Hil," I muttered.

He nodded and opened his mouth to say something else, but looked at Chris and changed his mind. He bumped my knee with his. "We'll talk later."

I gave him a sincere smile, then turned to the rest of the table with a cheerleading grin. "You guys don't mind if I crash your table, right?"

Lauren apologized via text while I was in English and I replied with my own Really sorry. Neither of us mentioned leukemia, Hil, or telling.

But we weren't fine yet. I had to go to her locker at the end of the day for a hug. In all of our previous fights, she'd waited at mine.

The hug was brief, like she might break me or catch cancer.

"Ryan told me about your hair. It looks good. Can't tell."
These words were an afterthought, as she walked away, throwing a "See you at practice" back in my direction.

I had no intention of attending practice, but she didn't wait
long enough to hear my answer. Things were in flux. I'd known
that all my absences, lies, and limitations would change our
group dynamics, but I'd never stopped to consider *how.* My
spot in the high school pyramid was slipping. I was losing traction and Lauren was gaining it. I should care—I should be
storming down to the gym and confronting Hil, getting an apology from her and a pledge to throw me another party from Lauren. Resetting the power balance and reestablishing my place.
But I didn't.

I was supposed to be in the treatment stage when I'd feel my
best—enough postchemo that I wasn't vomiting. But I didn't
feel fine. I wanted each day to end so I could go back to bed.

Someone called my cell three times in a row Wednesday night.
I knew it was Hil without looking—this was her MO: calling
repeatedly because she couldn't be bothered with leaving messages and waiting for callbacks. I shut my phone off.

The house line rang. Mom came in my room holding it.
"Hil's on the phone—she says your cell's off. Did you forget to
charge it, kitten?" I was sitting at my desk, pretending to do
homework but really fighting waves of dizzying fatigue.

I pointed to Jinx in my lap, and Mom walked the phone

over. "It was good talking to you, Hil. I don't see you anymore! You'll have to schedule a girls' night soon. Here's Mia."

Mom glowed at me and left. I waited until the door shut, then asked, "What?"

Hillary responded with an equally cheery, "Are you going to be pissed forever or are you going to get over this?"

I didn't answer. I didn't know the answer. "I just can't believe you'd do that to me."

"I was testing him for you." Her voice was sweet as bubble bath and just as slippery.

"You told Ryan you'd sleep with him! That wasn't for my benefit. Don't lie to me—I'm not an idiot." I rubbed my forehead, trying to erase the tension and sweat that was beading there.

Her voice lost its silky persuasion. "Fine! I was an idiot. Is that what you want to hear? I'm the world's biggest idiot and it was a stupid, shitty thing to do. But I didn't say I'd *sleep* with him—just kiss him. Not that that's okay, it's not—but I would never—you know Lauren's lying." Her voice was panic spiked with apology. "I was drunk—so drunk Chris and I actually . . . I'm sorry. I don't know what else I can say."

"Tell me why."

"I don't even really remember. To see if I could? Because he was there. Because he was sad you weren't and wouldn't shut up about it. Because he's more important to you than we are. Because, apparently, I suck as a friend and it makes sense that you would choose him over me."

"Ryan's not more important than you guys! How can you

say that?" But as I spoke, I realized how much time I gave him and how little I had left for her. It wasn't that he was a higher priority; it was that I didn't have to lie to him. "I'm sorry I haven't been around, but really, Ryan hasn't replaced you. He couldn't."

"I miss you. And I made that mistake with Keith—I always chose him over you guys. Then he just left me. I feel like you're leaving too," confessed Hil. "And I'm so sorry. Please come back to practice. Don't let my being an idiot stop you from cheering at the East-Green game."

"We'll see." I was too tired to commit to anything. I left my desk and lay down on top of my comforter. I could put on pajamas and brush my teeth later.

"C'mon. It's East versus Green! After we'll all go to the party. I need some Mia time." Her voice became wistful. "Senior year has sucked so far. I wish we could go back to last year, you know?"

"Yeah." I had that wish on speed dial.

"Are we okay? There's not many people I care about hurting, but you're one of them."

I paused to gather my thoughts. They seemed so scattered and incoherent.

"Mia, I *need* us to be okay. I need to fix this. Date Ryan. *Please* date him if it will make you happy. But don't cut me out; I can't lose you too."

"We're okay." I surrendered, too drained to fight or feel relieved that we weren't fighting anymore. My whole body felt heavy and achy.

"You'll be at practice tomorrow and stop avoiding me and sit with us at lunch?"

"I'll be there," I conceded as sweat ran into my exhausted eyes, blurring the room. I dropped the phone and settled into an uneasy sleep, praying I would feel more like myself by morning.

32

"You know what I thought would be a great idea?" Mom asked as I entered the kitchen.

"Coffee?" I joked. Half joked. I felt like I'd need caffeine, a nap, and a body transplant to make it through the day.

"What? No! That's full of chemicals and toxins. You shouldn't mix caffeine with your medications—" She'd gone from chipper to panicked in two seconds.

"I'm kidding. Orange juice is perfect." I poured myself a glass. "What's your good idea?"

She gave a quick laugh. "Of course you were joking—you know better. I was thinking we should have a celebratory dinner."

"What are we celebrating?" I took a large sip of juice to swallow the pills she'd neatly arranged on a tea saucer.

"Your first round of consolidation chemo is over, and everything's going so well. I'll admit, Saturday was rough—it was hard to see you so upset. But you worked through it and everything is fine. I'm so glad you still get to be a normal teen."

I painted on a smile as I bit my lip to trap the swears I was mentally screaming. Normal teen? When? When I was lying to my friends, napping in the nurses' room, or dressing to avoid exposing my port? Or was it the wig, pallor, and nausea that made me normal?

Just thinking this made the room spin.

"Nothing elaborate—I don't want you overdoing it. Just me, Dad, you, and Ryan. You can invite Gyver if you want too."

"Ryan and Gyver don't really mix."

"That's too bad." Her sincerity was undermined by how quickly she moved on. "I'll make dinner reservations at Chez Bleu and we'll all dress up and go."

"When?"

"How about tonight? Tomorrow you're busy with East versus Green, and Saturday you're going to be recovering from East versus Green."

I looked at Mom's eager face. This was important to her, and the sooner we did the dinner the better, because if I gave her a week she'd rent a banquet hall and book a DJ. "Sounds fun. You can ask Ryan when he comes to pick me up."

"Do you have something to wear? If not, we can delay a few days and go shopping." Her eyes brightened at the prospect.

"No, I've got the perfect dress. I'm going to get in the shower."

"I'm excited about this—are you?" She hugged me and

touched the scarf I'd tied around my head. "You'll wear your wig, of course. You only wear these things in the house, right?"

I nodded and backed out of the room.

I fell asleep in the shower—something I hadn't realized was possible until I woke up sliding down the tile wall and had to make a slippery grab at the shower curtain. It tore free of two of the metal rings. I was too dizzy and disoriented to care. I wrapped up in a towel and lay on my bed, dripping and sudsy. It was eleven minutes before I could summon the energy to sit up and towel off, another two before my head cleared enough to stand and lurch to the dresser for clothing.

When I came downstairs, Ryan was in the kitchen eating oatmeal and nodding at Mom as she blathered. "Maybe there'll be a pianist at Chez Bleu. I love a good pianist, don't you?"

Ryan struggled to keep a straight face as he swallowed a scoop of oatmeal. "Absolutely."

I rolled my eyes behind Mom's back. His smile widened and she turned to see the cause. "Oh, kitten, Ryan's free tonight! I already called Chez Bleu and left a message to call me as soon as they open. I've got to pick up your father's blue suit from the cleaners and maybe buy him a new tie. I wonder if I'll have time to get a mani/pedi over lunch. How are your nails? Do you want me to wait and we can go together after school?"

"No, go at lunch. I may want a nap after practice." I meant it as a hint not to go overboard, to alert her that I wasn't feeling a hundred percent, but she barreled on.

"Okay. Maybe I'll call Christine's Bakery and reserve a

cake or pie. What types of pie do you like, Ryan? Mia, eat something."

I scooped oatmeal into a bowl, adding liberal amounts of raisins and honey, but even doctored up, it wasn't appealing. My stomach clamped around the first bites I forced down.

Mom prattled, Ryan smiled politely while poking me under the table, I pushed oatmeal around my bowl. Until I looked at the clock. "Ryan, we're going to be late."

Just as I was about to write her off as frivolous, Mom surprised me with her parting comments. "We need this, kitten. A reason to be excited, I mean. You've been gloomy and out of sorts this week—it's affecting us all. Could you get excited about this and perk up?"

My eyes widened at her observations, but years of practice summoned a smile to my lips. "Of course, Mom. You're right, this is a great idea—I can't wait!"

"Great. Now have a good day at school, both of you." She touched the tip of my nose with a finger. "Tonight's going to be perfect. Wait and see."

Climbing out of the car made the school parking lot tilt. I clung to Ryan as my vision spun.

He held me and laughed. "I'm usually the one convincing you it's worth it to be late. Not that I'm complaining . . ."

My forehead was beaded in sweat and my stomach churned,

but I felt steadier. I let go of his arm and took my book bag from his hand. "I just stood up too fast."

"Sure," he teased, his hand curling around my waist, thumb threading through a belt loop on my jeans. "We both know you find me irresistible."

I smiled and started up the steps. "Completely irresistible. Can you blame me?"

"Not at all." He opened the school door, then paused when he saw who was waiting on the other side. He'd taken a forget-about-it attitude with Hil, but they were awkward. "Oh, hey."

She nodded to him and turned to me. "Can I have a minute? I brought you a mocha."

Her question and caffeinated bribe conveyed her guilt; I needed my actions to speak as loudly. I unhooked Ryan's thumb from my waistband.

"Sure. I'll see you later, Ryan." I wobbled as I stepped away from his supportive arm and took the cup. "Thanks. I missed breakfast, so perfect timing."

She smiled tentatively. "We're still okay?"

"Yes." My voice was breathless and tired.

"Good. Come over before the game tomorrow? I need some us time. We can talk about everything *but* boys. And if you really want to talk about Ryan or Gyver too, I suppose I'll allow it."

"Gyver?" His name felt like a knife twist. He was still barely acknowledging me—but she couldn't know that.

Still, the look Hil gave me had some hidden significance. "I'll take that as a yes, you'll come," she said, then enveloped

me in a hug and her musky perfume. It made my stomach flip
and I splashed mocha all over the floor tiles.

I hugged her back with limp arms as the late bell rang.

"See you at lunch," Hil commanded, dashing down the
hallway.

I wanted to slump to the floor and rest my head on my
knees. The tile looked inviting and cool; the hallway was silent
in the moments after the late-bell scramble.

Fatigue and lethargy kept me planted for a minute before I
dropped the cup in the trash and shuffled into French. I mumbled, "*Je suis désolée,*" to Madame Simone. She nodded and I
stumbled clumsily against my desk.

"You okay?" Meagan leaned across the aisle to ask.

"Yeah." But I didn't feel okay. Hil's perfume had made me
queasy. I concentrated on the verbs Madame Simone wrote on
the board, but they spun. I focused on the corner of my book,
but it warped. My stomach lurched again, and so did I—out of
my desk and out of the classroom.

"Mia? Are you in here?" Meagan's concerned voice floated from
the bathroom doorway. I'd emptied my stomach into the toilet
and was gasping for breath.

My "here" was feeble. I closed my eyes and gathered the
strength to unlock the stall door.

She stood above me, horrified—her face the same color as
the off-white walls. "You need to go to the doctor."

I leaned my head back against the stall, too tired to support it unassisted.

"I'll go get Gyver—he's in study hall." She passed me a paper towel and used a shaking hand to brush my hair from my mouth.

"Can you get Ryan?" Gyver still wasn't talking to me; I didn't want him here if he was only doing it as a favor for *her*. "He's in history—Mr. Yusella."

An emotion passed over Meagan's face, but I'd closed my eyes before I could identify it. "I'll be right back. Hang in there."

I might have dozed or blacked out. Ryan's voice sounded far away, but when I opened my eyes he was kneeling beside me. "Hey, you. Tip your head back."

I complied. My face felt sticky and my lips tasted salty as well as sour.

Ryan cradled my head with one hand as he pinched a paper towel to my bloody nose with the other. "Are you going to be sick again?"

I spoke around the paper towel. "I don't think so."

Meagan hovered, wetting another paper towel and holding it out. "You probably can't get the blood out of your shirt without washing it, but this will help get it off your face."

I reached for it, but my arm dropped limply in my lap. Ryan shifted awkwardly so he could cradle my head and pinch my nose with one hand and use the other to wipe off my face.

"I can go get the nurse," Meagan offered, already fleeing for the door.

"No. Ryan, please just take me home," I protested. "Dad's there."

Meagan paused and wrung her hands. "What can I do?"

"Tell the office," Ryan said.

"And tell the girls I got sick. I don't want to start anything with Hil when we just made up." I tried to smile, but gagged instead.

Ryan shifted to hold my head over the toilet, but I protested, "I'm okay."

"Okay's not the word that comes to mind right now. Your nose stopped bleeding. Can you stand?" Ryan tossed the paper towels in the trash can attached to the stall.

"I'll try." He tightened his arms around my waist and helped me up. I sagged against him and struggled on legs that felt mushy.

"Can I do anything else?" asked Meagan. She was weaving her fingers into anxious knots.

"Could you go get my bag? I left it at my desk," I asked.

"I'll meet you in the foyer." She looked at her watch. "You should get going, class ends in ten minutes. You don't want to be in the hall when the bell rings."

"Thanks." Ryan offered a grim smile.

As Meagan reached for the bathroom door, it was opened from the outside, revealing a startled underclassman. She did a double-take then stepped out of the way to let us pass.

"Mia? You okay?"

I blinked at the girl; I knew her. A freshman on the squad. The good tumbler. Monica.

"Mia has the flu. Can you tell Hil or Ally she went home sick?" Ryan answered for me.

"That stinks! Feel better. Hopefully it's one of those twenty-four-hour things so you're better for tomorrow's game." She lowered her voice and added, "And the party! I can't wait."

I leaned against Ryan. He guided me forward and called "thanks" over his shoulder.

Meagan was in the front hall with my bag. "Just feel better, Mia. Please."

33

I fought Dad about the hospital, but only weakly. I hated ruining Mom's special dinner, but it was obvious something was very wrong.

"Oh, Mia, my dear, feel free to stop by and visit if you miss us. There was no need for you to catch the flu," Dr. Kevin said with a jovial pat on my shoulder.

I was too tired to even whimper. The medications, bed, the flu: I buckled under the stresses and demands of the past week and shut my eyes.

I slept eighteen hours and woke up on Friday feeling better-ish and also worse. Frustrated. I wasn't going home today; East vs. Green would proceed without me. I'd been foolish to mark it on my calendar; arrogant to assume I had any control over my life. Just recording the game on the tiny square marked October eleven was asking to be proven wrong. Hope can be the most dangerous emotion, because when it's destroyed, it's deadly.

I dozed most of the day, played cards with Dad—reminded him repeatedly to grab my horseshoe next time he went home—worried about how overwhelmed Ryan looked when he dropped me off yesterday, and the fact that Mom had run interference on calls from Ally and Hil but I hadn't heard from Lauren.

I didn't want to call her—she was right, the hospital was boring and I didn't want to be a burden. Plus, I was busy trying to calm an increasingly frazzled Mom. She'd "spent too much time in hospitals lately." I swallowed the words "less time than I have" and tacked on some mental swearing.

The nurses, and even patient Dr. Kevin, were starting to be annoyed by her endless questions. "How could she get sick? She was just here—did you release her too soon? Have you given her enough medication? The right medications? Do we need a second opinion? She's okay, right? She will be?"

"Mom, it's the flu. I'll be fine in a few days—they've explained," I said with my last ounce of patience. I was in pajamas and Gyver's cap; her eyes glossed over me without settling.

"Of course you'll be fine, kitten. I'm just making sure you're getting the best care possible."

"We're doing everything we can," soothed Nurse Hollywood.

"Well, what can I do?" Mom asked, breaking into loud sobs.

Dad was by her side in two steps. The nurse stepped up also, snagging the box of tissues from my bedside table. I tried to untuck myself from the blanket and untangle my IV lines and join them.

"No one has any idea how hard it is for me!" she cried.

I stopped struggling to get out of bed. "I have no idea how hard it is for *you*?"

Dad caught my eye. "She doesn't mean it like that. Let's go for a walk," he suggested to Mom.

She ignored us. "I never leave. I spend more time in the hospital than at work. I can't even plan a dinner without everything going to hell. No one understands."

Dad continued to try and calm Mom. I stared at the ceiling and locked my jaw to keep my mental f-bombs from escaping.

"It's not fair," she cried. "This isn't supposed to be my life."

That was my line. She wasn't allowed to steal it.

"Want to know what's not fair?" I demanded in a voice I didn't recognize. "That you think of my cancer as an inconvenience to your life. It's not fair you get to throw fits and I have to pretend everything's perfect."

"Kiddo . . ." Dad stepped to the middle of the room—an arm stretched in either direction, like he wanted to comfort us both. Or hold us apart. The nurses excused themselves.

Mom paled. "Why would you say such cruel, hurtful things to me?" She inserted herself in Dad's arms. "Did you hear that?"

"Because they're true! Your dinner was canceled and you had to miss work. Poor you! This is my life." I gestured to the wires, poles, and machinery. "I'm sorry it interferes with yours. Maybe you'll get lucky and I'll die. Then you won't have to worry about missing a dinner again."

The silence was a chasm filled with shock, anger, hurt, and disbelief. Dad bridged it first. "Um. Okay. Everyone calm down. Let's discuss this—"

"No. I don't want to talk or even see you right now. I need a break from Mom or we'll both regret the things I'll say. Just go home. We'll talk tomorrow; I need some space."

"You're sure?" asked Dad, but Mom was already packing her knitting. "I love you, kiddo," he said with a tight hug.

Mom was silent for a long time. Pacing the room with her purse on one arm and her coat draped over the other. Finally she paused and pointed a scolding finger at me.

"I know you only said those things because you're cranky about being sick and missing the big game, so I forgive you." She paused, but I didn't look at her or acknowledge her magnanimous gesture. She sighed. "I want you to think about this tonight. We'll see you tomorrow." I tried not to flinch when she kissed my forehead. I didn't exhale until the door shut behind them.

"Rough day?" Ryan asked.

"My mother is a self-centered bitch." I had no place to direct my anger, so it had only grown fiercer.

He squeezed my hand but judiciously changed the subject. "I got your shirt from Ally." He draped an East Lake spirit shirt over a chair—it was too fitted for me to wrangle over my pajamas and IV lines.

"Do you think I should tell them? I was going to, but then there was the thing with Lauren and the thing with Hil." I was weighted down with guilt and itchy with lies. Panic hovered an inch away, looking for a place to land.

"I've always thought you should," he confessed.

"You never said."

"I figured it was your decision and if you wanted my opinion, you'd ask."

Even Ryan thought I was wrong? If the only supporter of secrecy was Mom, what did that say about how rational the idea was? I nodded at the wall, seeing my idiocy written on its blank surface. It was illogical, but I was irritated—why hadn't he told me? What else did he disapprove of?

"What's going on in there?" Ryan traced a finger across my forehead.

"Nothing." Lots, but nothing I felt like sharing.

"You sure? You look pretty intimidating right now." Ryan's cell rang.

"Go ahead and answer." My words were clipped.

"Hello? Yeah, sure." Ryan gave me a puzzled look and covered the receiver. "It's Hil. For you."

I almost dropped the phone, I wasn't prepared for everything to happen this fast. "Hey. Why are you calling Ryan's phone?"

"Thought it might be the only way to actually get you. And it worked, didn't it? How are you?"

Despite my recent vow to tell, I offered a partial truth. "It's no big deal; I have the flu."

"Cut the crap, Mia. What's really going on?" Her concern morphed into frustration.

"Hillary . . ."

"No more lies—Monica said she saw Ryan carry you out of the bathroom and you were covered in blood. What the hell happened?"

I let go of the cover stories, excuses, lies, and pretending. I was done. "You're right. I'm not fine."

"I knew it! Why all the super secrecy?" Her voice was bright with triumph, then fizzled into concern. "What's going on? Why won't you tell me?"

I took a deep breath and looked at Ryan. I remembered the day I'd told him: the hours, tears, and questions. This wasn't something I could dump on her over the phone. "Can you get the girls together tomorrow? I'd rather tell you all at once."

"Just tell me now. I'm really worried. Do you want me to come over?"

"No. It can wait."

"Don't play martyr, Mia. If you're not okay, I'm coming. It's just a game. I can miss it."

I forced a smile into my voice. "Just a game? It's East-Green!" I needed time to plan this. After all the damage I'd done, I needed to get this perfect. Hil had apologized to me about Ryan, but wasn't what I'd done even worse?

"Promise you'll call tomorrow? No excuses?"

"Promise. Have fun tonight." I shut off the phone and sighed.

"Once you make up your mind, you don't mess around," Ryan said. "Want me to stay?"

"No, just go. You can tell me about it tomorrow." Irrational or not, I was annoyed with him. With life. My insides churned like a lava lamp, each new emotion burbling up and changing my outlook: rage, betrayal, remorse, irritation.

"I don't mind staying." Ryan reached over and took one of my hands, tracing the lines on my palm before threading his fingers through. "Maybe then you'll realize I'm serious and finally admit we're dating."

The lava lamp exploded and I was drowning in a kaleidoscope of feeling. "Please don't do this tonight. I really don't want to get into it right now." I tried to pull my fingers back, but Ryan tightened his grip.

"Then when? Tell me when's a good time because I've been patient. Whether or not you allow people to call me your boyfriend doesn't change the fact that I pretty much am."

He was studying me so intently I had to look away. I stared at our interlaced fingers, then at the other hand he put on top of our clasped ones.

"Why take that risk? I just don't want to lose you as a friend if we don't work."

"Don't give me that!" Ryan stood, pulling his hands away and leaving mine cold. He dragged them through his hair and grasped the back of his neck. "Goddamn it, Mia, that's bullshit! We may not work out, so don't even try? When did you turn into a coward?"

He sat on the edge of my bed so suddenly it startled me. My pulse jumped in surprise and then kept racing because he was so close. "Don't tell me you don't feel anything for me. I know you do."

His blue eyes were so close and I wanted to get lost in them like I had so many other times. Have him make me forget about medications and fights and everything but feeling beautiful and wanted. If I could have just a few moments of that, maybe the rest would make sense too.

I leaned forward to close the gap between our lips, but he dodged and kissed the side of my neck. Creating a blazing trail up to my ear, he breathed, "The nurses said no kissing till your numbers improve. Get better and we'll make up for lost time."

He gave me a devilish, dimpled grin, then pressed his lips to the V of my pajama top and traced a finger along my waistband. "Don't tell me it's not worth the risk—don't tell me we're not worth it."

I couldn't tell him those things without becoming a liar as well as a coward. So I pushed his hand away from my stomach and inched backward on the bed. "I think you should go."

He recoiled like I'd slapped him. "Fine. But I can't keep doing this. I'm not coming back until *you're* serious."

34

I wasn't going to answer my phone—until I saw who was calling. "Gyver?"

"Hey, Mi. Meagan told me you were sick. How are you?"

"I'm . . ." I couldn't think of an answer to that sentence that wouldn't require a lengthy explanation. "Will you come visit me?"

"You want me to?" He sounded surprised, like it hadn't been *him* avoiding *me* since last Sunday in my kitchen.

"Of course! Always." It was the simplest, truest thing I'd said all day.

"I'll be there soon."

While I waited for Gyver, I tried not to think about my fight with Mom. Or the tension with Hil. Or my frustration with Ryan. Or the enthusiasm of the crowd, the flip of my cheer skirt, the laughing pulse of the party. Now that I'd decided not to hide, the things I'd sacrificed crushed me with their absence.

Like she knew what I was thinking, Ally sent me a photo of them smiling in spirit shirts and cheer skirts. Wish u were here 2!

I was fidgety with emotion that thrummed just under my skin. Annoyed or not, I felt something for Ryan, but it was Gyver's company I needed right now. He'd help me figure out what to say to the girls and how to fix things with Mom.

"Hey, Mi."

"Hey!" I knelt up on the bed and held out my arms. "You're late!"

"Well, Impatient One, we stopped at Scoop's to get milkshakes and there was a line. I didn't know if you'd want strawberry or vanilla, so I got you both." He set them down on the bedside table and hugged me.

"Vanilla, please." I pulled away. "Wait, we?"

"Hi. It's okay I came, right?" Meagan stepped from behind Gyver and gave me a hug of her own.

No! I wanted Gyver to myself. I needed his perspective. I needed him to defuse everything in me that was about to combust.

I smiled plastically. "Of course."

"Meagan!" Doctors and nurses flooded my room and she was engulfed by hugs and questions of "How are you?" All my nurses, even Business Nurse, went out of their way to greet and pet her. I added bitterness and resentment to my internal cesspool—this was my hospital now, not hers.

While Meagan was treated like returning royalty, Gyver relaxed into his spot next to me. He reached over and tapped the IV line. "What good stuff are they feeding you today?"

"Just fluids. They're going to disconnect me for the night after this bag. My fever's down and I stopped puking."

"Not puking's good," he answered.

"You sure you don't mind babysitting me? I'd hate to inter-rupt." I looked at Meagan and held out my hand to him.

He took it. "There's nowhere else I'd rather be."

"I'm so glad you're here. It's been such a—"

"Your hair?" Meagan asked in surprise when her adoring horde had subsided.

"A wig," I pointed to the foam head on the windowsill.

"It's a good one; I didn't know." For someone who had seen this before, Meagan was edgy and twitchy. She stood awkwardly at the end of my bed and avoided looking at the IV tubes sprouting from my chest. The whole benefit of her friendship was supposed to be that she'd been through this before, yet she was the visitor who made me feel the most uncomfortable.

I tried small talk. "I can't believe Business Nurse hugged you. I've never even gotten a smile out of her."

"Who?" Meagan stared blankly at the wall above my head.

"Denise," Gyver translated.

"Oh," was her insightful response.

"Where are your parents?" Gyver asked.

"Probably at dinner."

Meagan surveyed the room, her gaze lingering on the door. She was twisting her hands in her lap, miming the process of lathering.

"I'll try and refrain from kidnapping you while they're gone." Gyver smiled and I felt some of my chaos dissolve.

"We'd have plenty of time to make a getaway. They're staying home tonight."

"They're not staying with you?" Meagan was appalled.

"Mom doesn't sleep well, then I don't sleep. And she had a major meltdown today." Gyver met my eyes with a knowing gaze and squeezed my knee through the blanket. I opened my mouth to confess the awful things I'd said—

"What about your dad?"

"He snores," Gyver and I answered simultaneously.

Meagan shook her head and began to twist her hands again. "I can't believe you want to be alone here."

"I'm never alone. Don't you remember? There's someone coming in every ten minutes." I laughed, but she didn't. I looked to Gyver, but he was also watching Meagan, concern cutting into the line of his jaw.

She chewed her lip, then said in a rush, "I'm sorry, Mia. I can't do this. I can't be here." Meagan was out the door before I could respond.

"What was that about?" I asked Gyver. A part of me, a small, guilty part, was glad to have him to myself.

Gyver tipped his head toward me, his eyebrows converging in a frown. "It's probably too familiar. Bad memories."

"Her brother." Realization began to gnaw at my insides. "You said Max had leukemia and I didn't need to worry. Did he . . ." I swallowed the last word.

"Yeah. He died."

"But you said . . ." I gagged on my guilt, shame, and blame. Terror.

"Mi, how could I tell you? It was a different kind. A worse kind. He had transplants. Radiation." Gyver's eyes and voice were desperate, but I was too furious to care.

"You lied to me!"

"I didn't want you reading into it. I was trying to protect you."

"You can't. No one can!" I dropped from a yell to a whisper. "You lied to me? *You*?"

"Mi, please understand." Gyver stood and swore. His conflict was clear, but he shook it off his face. "I've got to go. I drove."

I nodded, face blank. Inside I was collapsing.

"Say something," he begged.

I couldn't.

He sighed. "We need to talk, but Meagan lives across the lake; I can't get back before visiting hours end. I'll come first thing tomorrow."

He was leaving me. Alone. With my emotions from earlier. Adding a new layer of grief and fear.

"Don't go."

"I'm sorry, Mi." He bent to kiss my cheek. Impulsively, I turned so his lips brushed mine: stealing a little more of him before he went after Meagan. Maybe I thought he'd stay. Maybe I needed him to.

He didn't.

He just swore softly, touched my hand, and left.

I was shattering. Or being crushed. My last bit of strength was cracking and my lungs wouldn't cooperate. He'd left.

And I had no one left.

I was alone with nothing to do but stare at the vacant space where my horseshoe should be hanging and try to breathe despite the pressure that threatened to shred my heart and lungs. There were too many empty hours until morning and too many problems to face when it came.

I jammed the call button, and Mark stuck his head through my door. "How's my favorite patient?"

"Sleep meds. Can I have some?" The words quivered. My lower lip did too.

"It's only seven thirty—what's going on?" Mark disconnected the empty bag from my pole. He put a stopper in the line.

"I'm ruining everything I touch today!" This was a melodramatic Mom comment. I took a shaky breath and tried again. "I'm in a toxic mood and I started fights with everyone."

Mark picked up my phone from the bedside table. "So? You're a big girl. Call and apologize."

I drew my knees up and hugged them. "These are bigger than over-the-phone I'm sorrys."

"And?" Mark shrugged.

"But . . ." I searched for another excuse and tried to take a full breath. "Visiting hours are almost over."

Mark grinned. "Nice try, but I'll make an exception." He placed the phone in my hand and curled my fingers around it. "Call. Fix your fights and you'll sleep like a baby."

I nodded somberly and Mark patted my arm and left my room. I stared at the screen, blurred by tears that refused to stay out of my eyes. I'd made it clear to Gyver and he'd made a choice. He didn't choose me.

A shaky exhale became a sob and I dialed.

"Hey, you. What's up?"

"I'm sorry." I garbled the words.

"Is this a yes?"

If this was that important to him—if *I* was that important to him, then he deserved a chance. A real one. "Yes. Will you come?"

"Yeah, sure. But I'm, like, twenty minutes away. Will they let me in after eight?"

My eyes flooded and my throat tightened. I didn't deserve this guy who'd drop everything because I wanted him to hold my hand. "Yes," I whispered as the tears spilled onto my cheeks.

"Don't cry." Ryan sounded sympathetic, not triumphant. "Want me to stay on the phone?"

I shook my head, tears choking my breath. "No. I'm okay."

"All right. Soon."

Southern Nurse might have been waiting outside the door for me to say good-bye, or she might have uncanny timing, but she came in to check on me as I shut off the phone and surrendered to my desperation and tears.

"Mark said you were out of sorts. What's the matter, darlin'?"

I didn't answer, just sobbed. Panic was clawing me inside out with uncertainty. I sat up on my bed and broke: tears washing down my chin and over my knees. I couldn't find words or air.

"Breathe." Southern Nurse rubbed my back.

I tried to. Tried to make my lungs inhale and exhale with any sort of rhythm. To banish the dizzy spots forming in the corners of my vision. When I managed a half breath, Southern Nurse—no, I couldn't call her that anymore. I checked her name tag. When I managed a half breath, Polly said, "Good, that's better. Now you need to get some rest. We should call your parents."

"Please don't call my mom. I can't. I can't handle her tonight. We had a fight and she'll be a mess and I'll have to pull it together and reassure her. I just—I just can't. Ryan's coming."

Polly's eyes filled with sympathy. "I heard about this afternoon. Cancer's hard on everyone, darlin'; sometimes you need a little space. I won't call if you agree to this: when he gets here, you hug him tight, then you get some sleep. Your job right now is getting better. Nothing's more important than that."

I nodded, but didn't release her hand when she stood. She sat back down. "I'll wait with you until Ryan comes. It's all right. Sometimes you just need a good cry. You've been brave for so long, it's about time you cracked. Let it out."

When Ryan arrived my face was splotchy and tear stained; the shoulder of Polly's scrubs was damp and rumpled. After he'd stopped at the sink to scrub his hands, she turned me over to him, saying, "She's had quite the day. Try and get her to calm down."

Ryan climbed up beside me. "Mia?" My name was a question and the next move was mine to make. I fit myself into the U of his arm, buried my face in his chest, and spilled sobs and confessions in tangled gasps.

"I'm so tired of this, Ryan. All of it. I'm tired of fighting so hard to be healthy and trying to look brave. I'm not brave. I'm scared. Meagan's brother, Max, died. What if that's me? I don't know how to do this anymore. It's too hard. I'm so scared."

"Shh, baby, shh. It's okay." His arm around my shoulders tightened.

Polly came in with a sedative and I obediently sipped, swallowed, and blew my nose in the tissue she held out like I was a toddler. "Enough of that for today. Rest now. I'll be back to check on you."

"Rest," I echoed, already impatient for the sedative to fuzz my vision and words. But before they did, there were things I needed to say, gratitude I needed to express. He was trying so hard and being so much more than I ever imagined. I needed to give him credit, but lacked the words to say it right. "Ryan, I'm sorry about earlier. Thanks for coming. I really needed you."

"All you had to do was ask." He touched his forehead to mine and shut his eyes. "I'm not going anywhere.

"I'm here. Right here." It became a mantra. Ryan whispered it to me as he rubbed my back. I stopped fighting the sleeping pill and surrendered to its escape.

35

My temperature was edging above 103 when the nurses took it before seven the next morning. They hesitated a moment, eyes flickering to Ryan as he blinked himself alert. He wasn't used to waking up to an audience.

"He stays," I rasped. His presence meant yesterday's damages hadn't been part of my horrible fever dreams. Max had died; Hil had yelled; Gyver had left. Everything was blurry and surreal. I hiccupped.

"Is she okay?" asked Ryan as the nurses frowned and paged the doctor.

"No kissing," teased Mark, but his smile was flat. "This is more than the flu. We're going to need to do a full blood workup."

"I'll call her parents," said Business Nurse.

Mark drew blood, then the nurses were gone in a rush of rapid-fire medicalese.

"Is it always this crazy in the morning?" Ryan rubbed his eyes.

"Sometimes." My head felt so heavy; I rested against his chest and asked, "Will your mom freak out that you didn't go home?"

He shrugged. "She'll just think I stayed over at the party. No big deal."

Ryan leaned his chin against my forehead. Instantly he jerked away. "Baby, you're burning up. Your shirt is soaked."

"I'm too tired to change." I shut my eyes. "I just want to sleep."

The sunlight hit my room with stinging brightness. Everything looked pointed and sharp. I wanted the curves and buffer of unconsciousness.

"Two minutes. Change and wait for your meds, then you can sleep."

"You'll stay?"

"They'll have to pry me away."

I willed my eyes open and relaxed my fingers from Ryan's shirt. He opened the closet and unzipped my suitcase.

"Pick one that buttons. My IV." I made a weak gesture toward my port.

"Got it." Ryan selected a green paisley pajama top. "Do you need pants?" He held out a red-and-blue-striped pair.

"No."

He put an arm around my shoulders to help me sit up when my trembles made it clear I couldn't do it alone. I leaned against him and lifted shaky hands to my buttons. Why were they so hard to undo? Had the buttons grown and the holes shrunk? My fingers were clumsy.

Ryan gently pressed them out of the way. Shifting his arm on my back and sitting on the edge of the bed, his hands—most at home when shooting three-pointers—were soft as kisses as he unfastened the buttons on my sodden top. He held the cuff so I could pull my right hand out of the sleeve, then traded support arms and peeled it off my back, carefully freeing my left hand. The cool air hit my damp skin and I began to shiver, hugging my arms across my chest, too cold and weary to be embarrassed.

"This probably isn't how you imagined seeing me topless." I tried to joke, but my teeth chattered and mangled the words.

He helped thread my arms through new sleeves. "Plenty of time for that when you're better." He was being so careful and his fingers brushed like whispers, but still left aching pathways on my fevered skin.

Eyes shut, I leaned my throbbing head against his shoulder as he closed the buttons over my blue-white stomach.

"It's not the right time, not how I planned it, but I have to tell you—" His fingers stilled on my third button and he turned his lips toward my ear. "I think I'm falling in love with you."

I was trying to summon the energy to lift my head and look at him; the noise of the door opening barely registered.

"Hey—" The greeting crashed to a stop. "You're unbelievable, Winters. This is a hospital." Disdain dripped off each word. I twisted my head—still on Ryan's shoulder—to see Gyver at the door, his face darkened with contempt.

"God, what's wrong with you? She's sick. I would never—" Ryan's voice choked off and he turned his back on Gyver. Fastening my last three buttons, he eased me back against the pillow and tucked the blankets up. I shivered as the cool sheets replaced his body heat.

Gyver dismissed him. "It's nothing compared to this summer—not that you'd know."

"You're right. I wasn't here then. But I'm here now—so stop acting like you know everything." His voice was fierce, but the hand on my cheek was gentle and cool.

"It's just the flu," Gyver said.

"She's neutropenic—she has no immune system," corrected Ryan. "There's no 'just' about anything she catches. Do you know how bad her counts are? Or that her temp went up four degrees since yesterday?"

"Where'd you learn all that?" My voice was too thin to reflect my shock.

"The nurses just now. Internet. Books from your dad. And I listened when the doctor was talking to you." He sounded miserable. "I don't want you to end up in isolation."

"Isolation?" Gyver and I asked.

"My God, Mia. Were you in the same room when the doctor was talking? If you don't respond to antibiotics, you have to go in isolation. That's why there are hand-washing signs all over your door and why the nurses keep telling us 'no kissing.'"

"But they were saying I might go home today. Weren't they?" It was so hard to remember; it seemed so long ago.

"Yesterday it looked good, but now your fever's back up."
He reached for my hand, stroking it with his thumb.

Gyver had gasped "huh?" when Ryan mentioned kissing. I
shut my eyes. It was much more likely I was sicker via the stress
of last night than the barely-brushed-lips kiss I'd stolen from
him. Perhaps I should've reassured Gyver, but I couldn't. "Ryan
was helping me change. I sweated through my shirt," I offered
instead.

I peeked from beneath lowered lids; Gyver looked defeated,
wilted. "Mi, how'd you get so sick? You were fine. I would've
stayed." He took a step forward, then stopped. Ryan was in his
spot.

"I'm just tired," I mouthed.

" 'Course you're tired, you didn't sleep well last night. You
can as soon as your meds come. Promise."

"You stayed here?" There was a long pause before Gyver
continued in a detached voice, "I came to talk about yesterday,
but it looks like you don't need me."

The tears started as a whimper this time. They leaked from
under closed lids and felt icy on my fevered face.

"Don't cry, baby." Ryan's soft breath on my neck as his
hand wiped my face; Gyver's panicked, "Mi—"

I didn't open my eyes, couldn't look at either of them. Or
my parents, doctors, and nurses when they arrived.

"There's too many people in here," barked Business Nurse
over the melee of greetings, status updates, and my mother's
loud wailing. My hand instinctively closed on Ryan's.

"I guess I'll go," Gyver offered.

I didn't protest. Didn't open my eyes.

Couldn't bear to see him walk away from me for the second time in two days.

36

I spent two days at the mercy of feverish hallucinations. Voices alternated between whispering and yelling gibberish. Faces loomed clownishly large and then blurred behind the spots in my vision. In my delusions the nurses' needles morphed to guns, then transformed into my mother's knitting needles.

I woke up yelling something, my mouth coated with desperation, but I couldn't remember why. I'm sure there was a moment when my fever broke and danger passed, but I didn't notice it. Awareness came back gradually—being able to differentiate day from night. Sitting up without the room tilting. Realizing the only person who'd held my hand or called all week, besides my parents and Mr. and Mrs. Russo, was Ryan. That his summer tan was fading and being replaced by dark circles under his eyes and lines on his face. Lines that seemed to get deeper every time he rubbed his forehead.

His blue eyes filled the first time I opened mine and said, "Hi, Ryan."

He wiped them on his sleeve and climbed out of his chair so he could pull me against his chest in an urgent hug. "Hey, you. How are you feeling?"

"Tired."

He sniffle-laughed and rocked me gently. "Tired? How's that even possible?"

I wanted to answer him, but my eyes were sliding shut and my lips wouldn't cooperate.

Mrs. Russo walked through the door carrying a plate of biscotti. Mr. Russo was behind her with a cardboard tray holding four cups of coffee. I didn't care about either of those things. I cared about Gyver, and when he didn't appear behind them, my stomach sank.

"Where is he?" I asked, still staring at the door like I could will him into appearing just by wishing hard enough.

Mrs. Russo handed the biscotti to Dad and washed her hands before answering. Then she came to stand beside me and put a warm hand on my arm. "Gyver's at home." There was sadness in her voice and eyes, I didn't want to think about what it meant.

"He didn't . . . He hasn't . . ." Finishing those thoughts meant acknowledging his continued absence out loud and I couldn't do it.

"Is there a message we can give him for you?"

I shook my head. *Always*. When he'd asked if I wanted him to come, I'd told him *always*. It hadn't occurred to me that his answer might not be the same.

After four more days I was discharged and sent home, where Dr. Kevin ordered me to spend three more days resting before I attempted school. I was still borderline neutropenic—I didn't have enough white blood cells to fight off an infection. There were rules about visitors: one at a time and I had to wear a surgical mask. Not that it mattered. Ryan was the only one who came.

I knew the lack of messages from Lauren was a bad sign. The fact that Hil hadn't stormed my house demanding explanations was an awful omen. I wouldn't let myself think about what Gyver's absence meant.

I wanted numb back. I wanted the hospital drugs that had made it possible to sleep and pretend I wasn't terrified. Instead, the skin around my eyes and nose were raw from tissues and tears. I sometimes woke up and caught Mom standing in my doorway like she was guarding my sleeping body. Dad was constantly on the phone with doctors and on the Internet. He'd started making charts of experimental treatments and new drugs in development.

"We won't need them," he told me. "But I feel better knowing what's out there."

Mom hovered now. Fingertips always reaching for my forehead, searching for a fever. She fussed with the thermostat and fretted about germs. Her manic kitchen cleaning surpassed Mrs. Russo's; she vacuumed my room and changed my sheets daily.

That night apart had changed her—I wasn't sure if it was our fight or my fever. She didn't ask questions or intrude on my silence; she gave me so much space it started to feel like a barrier. Stuck in my own thoughts, or in my struggles not to think, I didn't know how to reach out and give her the reassurance she needed. We revolved around each other in careful orbits.

"Kitten, you have a visitor." She gave the germ masks a pointed look, patted my arm, and disappeared into the laundry room.

I was filling a glass from the dispenser on the fridge door, wishing I could convince myself it was only the metallic distortion that gave my reflection such an ethereal look.

"Hey." Gyver's voice was hesitant and soft. He was leaning against the kitchen door, one hand grasping the opposite elbow, his feet crossed at the ankles. It was a casual pose, but his posture was stiff and he was staring at the tile floor.

"Hi. Water?" I lifted my glass, then fumbled like an idiot putting it on the counter. "Want some?"

"No, I'm good."

I looked at him, waiting for him to look back. He should wash his hands and I should put on a surgical mask, but those reminders seemed less important than bridging the distance between us.

"Can we?" I pointed to the family room behind him. I wanted to leave the kitchen—Mom would be bustling back in to unload the dishwasher and wipe down counters. He let me lead him through the doorway, then chose a recliner across the room from my spot on the couch. Not a good sign. I pulled my knees up to my chest and hugged them.

"Gyver, at the hospital—" I began.

"Ryan said you wanted to see me," he interrupted.

"He did?"

"Yeah. If you wanted to see me, *you* should've called."

"I didn't ask him to say anything." I leaned my cheek on my knees. "But I did want to see you. Why haven't you called or visited? I know the hospital's a pain, but I've been home for days. I miss you. I don't get what's going on with us." I pulled my knees in closer, knotting my fingers in front of my shins.

Gyver shut his eyes and groaned, a hurt-animal sound in the back of his throat. "That makes two of us, Mi. I don't know what's going on either."

"Is this because of what happened at the hospital?"

"We need to talk about that." He leaned forward and rubbed his face with tired palms.

"It didn't mean anything." I could still picture his anger when he'd seen Ryan help button my pajamas.

Gyver flushed, leaned back in the chair, and pressed his hands flat to his knees. "Got it."

"He's a good boyfriend." I wanted to continue, but words felt too heavy.

"Did I come here so you could tell me about The Jock?"

His words were cold and slick as marbles. His eyes were scorching a spot on the wall behind my head.

"No, that's not why I wanted to see you; I wanted to make sure you're not mad at me." It hurt I needed a reason to see him, and he had to be asked to come.

"I'm not," his voice softened to exhaustion.

"Good." I wasn't sure I believed him, and I had so much I needed to tell him. "Thanks for coming to check on me that morning, I never got to say that."

He raked his hair into unruly points. "Mi, I didn't sleep that night. All I could think was: you were alone and upset. I didn't want to leave you and I drove like a maniac to get back." A riptide of accusation tainted his words. "But you weren't alone."

"Would you rather I was? That was the worst night of my life. Yeah, Ryan stayed over. So what? Why do you even care?"

My voice was climbing as I clutched my calves and tried to hold myself together. "You've got Meagan—you were so quick to run after her when she was upset. Why do you care if Ryan does the same for me?"

He looked at me—eyes dark and hopeless. I couldn't stomach the intensity without crying. All I'd done lately was cry. This time, however, I didn't know whom the tears were for.

"You're right. I shouldn't care." His sigh echoed with resignation and reverberated in my chest. "But what does Meagan have to do with this? I don't know what you want from me. Now I'm not allowed to have any female friends but you?"

I lowered my chin to the hollow between my chest and legs

and peeked over my knees at him. "There's a big difference between female friends and girlfriends."

"Exactly." He stood and paced the room, picking up a throw pillow and mashing it between his hands. "And Meagan will never be anything but a friend to me."

"What?" I recoiled from his outburst. No. Gyver couldn't be single. He couldn't. Because if he was . . . I'd just said yes to Ryan, after "jerking him along" for a month. And he was a good guy. A great guy.

"Mi, don't you get it?" He was gripping the pillow so tight his fingers disappeared to the second white knuckle.

I shook my head. I didn't get it. Nothing made sense.

"I know you have your perfect boyfriend and don't need me anymore, but wake up! Can't you see?"

"I didn't mean—" The words clumped and clogged my throat. "And Ryan—" I shook my head again.

"I've got to go."

"Gyver! Wait. Please?" I stood and ran to him, grabbing his arm with both hands. I tugged on his shirt until he turned around. "Please."

There was so much I needed to say, but only one thing I'd rehearsed. The idea I'd been battling and gagging on all week. The words it only felt safe to tell him and the words I needed to get out. "At the hospital that night, it was the first time . . ." I sucked in a raspy breath. "The first time . . ."

"Mia, you've made yourself clear. I really don't want to hear any more." He pulled me into the briefest of hugs, then pushed me away. "Rest up. I'm glad you're feeling better. I'll see you soon."

Soon wasn't tomorrow. It wasn't I'll call you later. Soon was vague. I watched him walk away, wishing I knew the words to call him back—not just to my house, but back to August.

He hadn't listened; he hadn't let me finish my thought: At the hospital, it was the first time I realized I might not beat this. I might die.

37

Monday night we got the call that my white blood count had rebounded. My parents reluctantly agreed to let me return to school on Tuesday. After refusing Dad's offer to drive me, Mom's "are you sure you don't want to stay home just one more day?" and armed with extra anti-bac gel and strict instructions to call and check in, they sent me off with anxious first-day-of-kindergarten smiles.

Underneath my oh-Mom-I'll-be-fine facade, I was a mess. Hil wouldn't call back and Ryan wouldn't meet my eyes when I asked about the Calendar Girls. I'd promised Hil the truth but hadn't had a chance to deliver. It wasn't my fault this time, but the cumulative weight of my past lies marked me as guilty and slowed down my getting-ready routine so I was thirty minutes late.

"Hey, stranger. I didn't know you were back."

I shut my locker to see Chris standing there with a sheepish grin. "Hi."

"Do you have a sec?" He juggled his bathroom pass from one hand to the other, then shoved his free hand in the pocket of his jeans.

"Sure. What's up? Is Ryan okay?" He was shifting one foot to the other and staring at my legs below my skirt, but not in his typical I'm-checking-you-out way. This was in a I'm-nervous-and-you're-in-my-line-of-vision way.

"That's kinda what I want to know. Are you guys okay? I know he doesn't have a lot of extra money with the car and saving for college." He looked from my legs to my face as if I was supposed to have a clue what he meant. When I quirked an eyebrow and shrugged, he continued, "I want you to know, if you and Ryan need money or anything, I'll help."

"Money?"

"For, you know, diapers and shit. Babies are expensive as hell. At least that's what Dr. Phil's always saying." Now he was holding the bathroom pass with both hands, staring at the Sharpied paint stirrer like it held a hidden message.

"Babies?" The word was a hissed whisper. "Chris, I'm not pregnant!"

"It's okay," he reassured me. "We're gonna be here for you guys. I hope it looks more like you than Ryan or it's going to be an ugly bastard . . . er, baby."

"We're not. Why would you even think that?"

"You don't drink or come to parties anymore. You're

eating like a crunchy hippie—all those weird natural foods. You're always absent. Isn't that morning sickness and pregnancy shit? And—" As he got worked up, he grew louder. A few of the late arrivers and hallway wanderers looked over.

"Enough! I'm not pregnant." My voice was low and nearly a snarl. I wanted to be angry with him, but then I remembered why he'd sought me out. Not to spread gossip or mock me, but to offer help. "But thanks. It's nice to know that if we did need help—make no mistake, we don't—that we'd have friends we could count on."

Chris shrugged. "It's no big deal," but his pink ears and aw-shucks smile betrayed him.

He started to rock back on his heels, ready to turn and leave, but I wasn't done. "Wait, who said we were?"

He looked down. "No one."

"Hil?"

He cleared his throat. "A lot of people have been saying stuff. I mean, something's going on. You're a zombie this year. And I've known Ryan his whole life and I've never seen him like this. Not even when his dad left."

I flinched and looked down.

"Has she seen you yet?" Even Chris sounded nervous.

"So she's really mad?" I wanted to put down my French and math books and wipe my sweaty hands on my skirt.

Chris shrugged. "Yeah, but she won't tell me why. Is this still because of that stupid thing with Ryan? She's not into Winters. I swear to God, she's not."

I leaned against my locker; it used to be the girls would've decorated it to welcome me back after any sort of absence. But that was back when the Calendar Girls were the jealousy standard at East Lake—they still were. I, apparently, wasn't a part of that anymore. "No. It's not that. Besides, Ryan loves me, he'd never—"

Chris whistled. "Whoa. I knew you'd gone all rebel and started dating, but love? You and Winters are using the L-word?"

"I'm not." My mind was still on Hil, and my answer was automatic and careless.

"Wait, Ryan—Ryan Winters—says he loves you and you don't say it back?"

"I like him a lot." I hadn't thought about it, but hearing Chris laugh made it seem awful.

"God, you have him whipped."

"Like Hil doesn't have you on a short leash?" I shot back, praying my accusation was accurate.

Chris grinned. "I don't know what you're talking about."

"You need to work on your poker face."

He tried, and failed, to stop smiling. "Anyway, I'd better get back before Mrs. Fryer sends out a search party. Good luck at lunch. I'm glad I'm a dude; girls are too much drama."

I'd need more than luck, but I didn't know what. Maybe I wasn't ready for school yet. Maybe I should get back in my car and head home. Climb back in my bed and hide for just a few more days. Instead, I headed down the hall to French, dreading every minute that brought me closer to the cafeteria and my best friends.

38

At lunch I saw Ryan waiting at my locker before he saw me. He looked anxious, exhausted, then relieved—all of this before his dimples appeared. He asked, "How are you?"

"Hanging in. Can I have a hug?" I wanted to stay like that, with my cheek against his chest and his arms tight and warm around me. Just a few more seconds, minutes, and I'd have the courage to go to the cafeteria and face the girls.

"Do a guy a favor—it's lunchtime and I'd rather not feel sick before I eat the school pizza." I heard Chris's voice and footsteps as he walked the five lockers between us, but I didn't pick up my head and look.

I felt Ryan shift as he responded with a hand gesture, but I didn't look then either.

Chris laughed. Ryan squeezed me tighter for a beat and I knew that was my cue.

Lunchtime.

Showtime.

Showdown.

Neither of us encouraged Chris's stupid jokes on the walk to lunch, but that had never stopped him from having a conversation with himself. Today, however, even he was quiet as we approached the cheerleading table. Everyone stopped eating and regarded us silently.

Chris coughed. "Hey, Hil, look who I found."

"I wish you hadn't," she said icily, and resumed dismantling a bunch of grapes. Ally dropped her bagel. She was the only one who returned my "Hey, guys," with a quiet, guilty "Hi, Mia," before Hil shot her a look that made her drop her bagel again.

I kissed Ryan on the cheek and told him I'd see him later. I wanted him to stay and sit beside me and hold my hand, but he and Chris didn't sit at our table on a normal day, and I wanted to pretend this was normal.

It was lunchtime, where the main event was everyone watching Hil ignore me; Ally and Lauren following her lead.

This wasn't where or how I'd planned it, but after my third lame question about cheerleading was met with silence, I couldn't take the tension anymore. "Can we talk?"

"No," Hil said and stood.

I turned to Ally, who was too busy chewing her lip and watching Hil to notice. Lauren wouldn't meet my eye, which made no sense. She knew, so how could she possibly feel betrayed or left out or whatever was fueling Hil's pissy mood?

I tried for faux sternness, but only managed desperate. "Hillary, sit down and listen to me. I know you're mad I didn't call, but I really had a good excuse."

She whirled, her burgundy fingernail pointed a few inches from my nose. "I don't want more excuses. I don't even care anymore—why should I? It's been eleven days since you *promised* to call. I'm obviously not important to you." Her hand dropped back to her side, clenched in a fist as she began to walk away.

This stupid secret seemed the only card left to play, and even more than I hated telling, I hated telling her this way. "Of course I care. Hil, wait!"

She didn't. Kept widening the gap between us. Two lunch tables. Three. Tables full of students watching us with open fascination and hope for a scandal.

"I have cancer!" I yelled the words across a five-table chasm and hurried to where she'd finally stopped, two-thirds of the way across a room that was lined with gawkers. Her back was still to me, so I took a deep breath and plunged on. "Leukemia."

With shaky fingers I reached up and removed my wig. It was like the world had a mute button. Some of the students shifted uncomfortably and others leaned forward—the rustling of lunch wrappers and a whispered echo of *leukemia* were the only sounds.

"Hil? Did you hear me?"

She turned, revealing a face of wet eyes and trembling lips.

And hands in fists, as she crossed her arms in an angry self-hug. "I heard."

The cafeteria resounded with *shh* and buzzed with the giddy energy of eavesdroppers. "I also heard it from Lauren a week ago. I can't believe you didn't tell me. I kept waiting for my turn—God knows I gave you plenty of opportunities. How could you not tell *me*?"

"Hil, it wasn't like that . . ." I felt more people join us, but my words weren't for Ally or Lauren or Chris. Ryan put a hand on my shoulder, but I shook him off.

"Wasn't like what?" she asked. "Like you told Gyver, Ryan, and Lauren? God, Lauren! But you didn't tell me?"

"Hey, what's that supposed to mean?"

"Shut up, Lauren," snapped Hil, at the same time as I said, "Stay out of this."

Lauren retreated to stand next to Ally, who looked at my bald head and began to cry, quiet at first, but with the great gulping breaths that heralded sobs.

I didn't know what to say. The cafeteria was noisy now, filled with unconcealed gossip: *I would've bet it was anorexia. My money was on drugs. Can you believe he's dating her? Why?*

Hil was clenching and unclenching her fists and my heart was beating much too fast. My throat tightened, so even if I'd known what to say, I couldn't have spoken.

Hil broke our staring contest with a voice that quavered. "I'm supposed to be your best friend. Best friend! And you hide something like this from me for months?"

"I'm sorry. I just didn't want your pity or—"

"I'm sorry too. Sorry I wasted so long worrying what I'd done to offend you and make you shut me out. For as much time as you spend complaining about your mom, you're turning into a fabulous mini-her. Congratulations, you don't have my pity. You don't have my friendship either. I'm done."

When she stormed away this time I didn't follow, but Lauren did. Ryan was engrossed in a conversation with Chris, a hand on his shoulder. Ally was wailing. I felt like the epicenter of a disaster.

"Why didn't you tell me?"

I looked at our Spring Girl, but she wasn't sunny or optimistic right now; her normally impeccable hair twisted in a sloppy knot, splotches on her cheeks, tear-smudged mascara.

"I didn't really tell anyone. It wasn't personal."

Her eyes hardened and her voice lost its dreamy edge. "Wasn't it? Lauren says you didn't tell me on purpose. You didn't trust me to keep it a secret, right?"

I took a deep breath to offer denials, but she wasn't done talking. "I thought we were friends," she whispered. Hurt radiated through her tears. She looked so breakable right now and we'd always gone out of our way to protect Ally, but I was exhausted. Everyone wanted something from me and I didn't have the energy to satisfy even my most basic needs—like breathing. My chest was so tight.

"We are friends."

"Really? Doesn't seem like it. Mia, you might *die*—how could you not tell us this?"

Her words awoke the fear that lay coiled in my stomach. Fed by Dad's manic research and Mom's new worries, the fear hissed of my own frailty. It wasn't something I needed reminding of, or something I could control.

I sucked in a breath and blinked back tears. "You're right. I might." The words were bitter in my mouth, toxic enough to make me nauseated. My voice was flat and expressionless, my mind shutting down and detaching from this hellish situation.

She wailed. "Don't you . . . Don't you even care?"

What did caring have to do with it? It was beyond my control—and all my focus needed to be on standing upright, breathing. I didn't even have the energy to look her in the face, so I watched her jeans.

They turned and walked away from me, breaking into a run when she was a few steps from the door. I wanted to chase her, to apologize and tell her everything—starting with *I'm sorry* and *I'm so scared* but I couldn't move.

What had I done? Ryan and Chris had stopped talking and were watching me with matching horrified expressions.

Ryan recovered first. "Mia, sit. You're shaking so hard I don't know how you're standing." He led me toward a chair at my empty table.

I sat, but then stood back up. "I need to go get Ally."

"Sit. I'll go. Chris, stay with Mia?" Ryan waited for his nod, then headed across the room.

"He won't know where to find her," I babbled toward Lauren's abandoned banana. "She's probably in the girls' locker room. He won't look there."

"What the hell, Mia?" He wasn't looking at me, but also studying the lunches strewn across the table. He began to stack the yogurt cups and Diet Cokes on an empty lunch tray. "Can you at least put your hair back on?"

"It's a wig." It was tangled from being balled in my fist, but I more or less settled it on my head.

"No shit, it's a wig. You didn't think to tell me any of this this morning when we had our little locker talk?"

"I hadn't even told Hil yet. I wanted to tell her first. And not like this." I rested my forehead on the lunch table, not caring if it was germy or sticky. I didn't have the energy to face another round of accusations.

"So, you're using Ryan, you made Hil cry, and you've got cancer. Anything else?"

"Using Ryan?" I forced my chin up so I could look at him. "It's not like that. He knows I'm sick, he's always known I was sick. He's been to the hospital."

"Hospital? You've got a deadly illness and you'll date him, but you don't love him? Damn."

"I like him a lot. And I might love him someday. I just don't yet." I realized I was rationalizing, but couldn't stop. "People don't have to like each other equal amounts. If you and Hil started dating right now, you'd like her more. Would that make her evil?"

"That's different." He stood and I followed; I couldn't be in this room of stares and whispers any longer.

"Why?"

"Because she's not dying!" he thundered. "Are you? Do you know what that'd to do to him? To Hil? She can't handle that."

Part of me respected Chris's reaction—at least he was honest and hadn't responded with false optimism.

"I didn't ask to be sick."

"What am I supposed to do now?" He threw the lunches in the trash, tray and all. "He's my best friend and she used to be yours. Shit! Where does that put me?"

I shut my eyes and answered his question along with all the ones stomping through my head. "I don't know. I don't know. I don't know."

39

I packed up my cheerleading uniform that night. There was no sense in keeping up that charade anymore. Now my performances took place off field, where I pretended to be untouched by the scrutiny and whispers of my classmates. Dodging their questions and teacher concern was a specialized skill set, and I was a black belt. I sat in class, I stared down the gossipers and shrugged off the attention-seeking sycophants, and I alienated anyone who was sincerely sympathetic.

Ryan didn't do big shows of sympathy. At least not when it came down to choosing between his friends—my former friends—and me. If I wanted condolences about Gyver's continued distance, I bet he'd have found plenty to say about that, but about everyone else he was pretty quiet. I'd wanted him to come running, to hold me and tell me everything would be okay, to offer to skip the rest of the day and take me home so I could hide beneath my covers.

Instead he squeezed my hand and walked me to class. "Okay, that was bad yesterday, but how'd you expect them to react? They're hurt."

I hurt too. And my cell stayed silent, like I'd never been a girl whose phone seemed alive with buzzes and chirps. The shopping bag containing my uniform still sat in my locker, taunting me each time I retrieved books: *you used to be this girl; you used to be happy.*

"Good. I thought I'd have to call and tell you to turn these in and I already deleted your number from my phone," Hil said when I finally worked up the strength to hand it to her on Thursday.

"I know you're mad, but don't be like this. Just because I'm not on the squad doesn't mean we can't be friends."

"Newsflash, you and I haven't been friends for a while. All you did today was turn in the uniform that marked you as a person worth noticing." She shook the bag, then shoved it in the bottom of her locker.

"Hil—" I pleaded.

"No! You've always acted like you were better than us: with your perfect grades and perfect parents. You thought you were smarter and kinder and prettier."

"Not prettier—" I clasped a hand to my mouth, realizing what I'd implied.

Hillary narrowed her eyes. "One of these days Ryan's going to dump you, and Gyver's going to stop looking like he wants to jump in front of a train for you. Then what will you be left with?"

"Apparently, *not* my best friend," I retorted.

She wilted. "How could you not tell me?" She slammed her locker and ran down the hall before I could answer.

What would I be left with? Her words haunted me as I drove the sleepy streets of East Lake, circling the body of water the town was named after. I didn't want to go home and deal with Mom's anxious energy. Ryan was stuck at soccer practice.

What would I be left with? Gyver had judged, Ryan was distracted, but it was Hil's question that made me pause. Cancer had cost me so much: friendships, grades, cheerleading, my whole sense of who I was. I needed to know: Would I beat this and have time to fix things?

Press gas. Pump brakes. Turn wheel. Flip turn signal. Pause at stop signs. These things were automatic. I could do them without thinking, which was good because my mind was spinning too fast for thoughts to develop into coherence. My eyes stared out the windshield, seeing other cars and keeping appropriate distances but not registering anything. Not until long after my gas light was on and beeping persistently. Then I looked around and didn't immediately recognize where I was. I wasn't in East Lake. I was probably pushing the boundaries of Green Lake too. Edging closer to Hamilton and the bigger highways. There was a gas station within sight on my left, attached to a run-down strip mall that I studied while the numbers next to the dollar sign spun upward and the pump glugged gas into my car. An insurance agency. A cash for gold place. A dollar store. And a psychic's sign.

The pump beneath my hand jerked to a stop, and I had to force my eyes away from the gold lettering on a teal background so I could unhook the nozzle and close the gas cap on my car.

I'd been searching for a way to know the outcome, and this was a clear sign: a four-leaf clover found under a lucky horseshoe. Or a black cat walking under a ladder on Friday the thirteenth. I wouldn't know which until I went inside.

I expected scarves and crystal balls, like I'd pass through the modern glass door and face the flaps of an ancient gypsy tent. Not so. It resembled my dentist's waiting room. There were potted plants, generic landscapes on beige walls, industrial carpeting, and a TV tuned to Lifetime. A large L-shaped desk sat in the center of the room; one arm covered with a computer and printouts, the other with tea things, crystals, and a stack of worn tarot cards. A large woman with frizzy gray hair was seated behind the desk. She smiled and turned off the TV.

"Are you here for a reading, dear?" Her soothing voice sounded too young for her wrinkled face and knobby knuckles.

"I guess." My hand wouldn't release the door despite the heat whooshing past me into the cool, late October afternoon.

"Ah, first timer. Don't worry, I don't bite." With effort, she pushed herself out of her chair, plugged in an electric teakettle, dimmed the lights, and pressed Play on a stereo. Exotic music filled the air—Gyver would know the instruments and origins; I found it distracting.

"Come. Sit. Let's do a tarot and tea leaf reading; that's a good start."

I let the door slip from my fingers. It banged closed and

I startled forward. A printout of prices was displayed in an ornate frame on the corner of the desk. I fumbled in my purse and pulled out a twenty. She hummed as she slid it off the desktop, then began to shuffle and organize her deck of tarot.

"You need to keep in mind that each new card affects the others. The meaning won't be clear until all cards are laid out. Their order, orientation . . ."

She continued her explanation, but I found it hard to hear her over the pulse hammering in my ears. After this, I'd know. I'd be able to breathe and relax and maybe start processing all of the thoughts I kept forcing aside. I'd know if we should have the college conversations Dad began and Mom terminated. I'd sit Ally and Hillary down, explain why I'd been so horrible, but tell them not to worry because soon . . .

"Do you understand?" she asked, gripping my hand with hers. The deep purple-black of her nail polish was disturbing against my pale skin.

I nodded. Soon I would understand everything.

"Good. I need to center myself before we begin." She closed her eyes and breathed deeply, audibly.

I looked at the deck and my anticipation decayed into terror. The longer she kept her eyes shut, the more ominous the tarot cards appeared. My lip found its way between my teeth.

"I am ready." She opened her eyes and stared at me. "Let's begin."

She flipped the first card with a flourish. It showed a couple in an Adam and Eve posture. "Ah, the Lovers," she intoned, caressing a dark nail across the title written at the bottom.

I leaned in, curling my hands around the desk. I could feel my heartbeat in my fingertips.

She turned the next card: the Tower—a building struck by lightning, people falling. I shivered as I searched the alarming illustration for symbolism.

The third card didn't need a label. As soon as she'd moved her hand and revealed a skeleton mounted on a white horse, I knew. The letters D-E-A-T-H at the bottom were superfluous.

I didn't want to know anymore.

I didn't notice my trembling until I parked my car in the empty lot at East Lake's beach. The moments between fleeing from the third card and turning off the ignition were a blur. I had no memory of the turns or decisions that took me to this deserted location. Or if I'd answered her calls of "Wait! I'm not finished," as I'd bolted out the door.

I stumbled out of my car and vomited on the cracked pavement. The car beeped incessantly to let me know the door was open, but I turned away. My shoes crunched on the frozen sand coating the parking lot as I crossed to the picnic tables where we used to be organized into grade school swim-lesson groups. The same one where I'd first told Gyver I was sick.

We'd had birthday parties and picnics here, back before we turned ten and it became uncool to go to East Lake's small beach. Chris's house was across the lake; the Jet Skis pulled up on his dock until the spring. I'd been to so many parties there.

I could see my memories on the surface of the water, rippling with the wind or when an autumn leaf gave up its hold on an oak tree and spiraled down to drift on the lake. Nights of giggles and smiles and dances and kisses. Sleepovers at Ally's house, where she and I tiptoed downstairs so we could surprise Hil and Lauren with banana pancakes in bed. So many hours of Hil's hairbrush dance routines, Lauren's homemade facials and crazy beauty regimens, Ally's mom's brownies as we studied and watched musicals. Why hadn't I appreciated these things when I was healthy? Why had I hidden away from them all fall?

I wouldn't have a second chance. I cried all the time, yet I couldn't right now. Maybe I'd used all my tears. And, really, what was I giving up at this point? There wasn't anything left of the giggling girl I used to be. I'd killed Mia Moore the first time I'd decided to hide my illness.

I wasn't going to beat leukemia; I was going to die. I'd been dying all along—it had just taken me this long to realize it. I expected the knowledge to burn, but I felt frozen. Defeated. I didn't care. No, I did care—but caring wouldn't make a difference.

I laughed; the bitterness in it ricocheted off the empty landscape. My car continued to chirp for my attention.

Blinking, I took deep breaths, retraced my steps, started the car, and drove home. I went into the house, not bothering to bring in my school bag from the backseat. I wouldn't be doing homework; it wasn't important anymore.

40

My life had a time limit. It was becoming an obsession. Would my funeral be well attended? Would my name echo in the hallways and inspire tears from the classmates I was busy alienating? Would the yearbook be dedicated to the girl who hadn't survived senior year?

I twined my fingers more tightly with Ryan's, trying to cling to the here, the now, the present. And when it was just us, it was easy to be distracted by his hands and lips—thank God the kissing ban had been lifted. To almost forget I was a living dead girl. But right now I wasn't going to think about anything medical.

I flipped his hand over, pulled loose my fingers, and began to trace them across the lines of his palm. "Does that tickle?"

"A little. You've been in a good mood lately."

We were sitting on my bed; it was the Monday after my

psychic shake-up. I hadn't told him. Hadn't told anyone. I hadn't slept much and hadn't been able to overcome the feeling I was running a sprint while others faced a marathon. But at least I was back in the race. After the numbness of the hospital, I finally felt things again. I'd reclaimed what remained of my life and began to make decisions about how to spend it.

"I just decided it was time to do some things I want. Right now, I want you." I pulled him back on the pillows with me. One thing I'd decided: I wasn't going to die a virgin.

"You're feeling okay? You're up for it?" Ryan asked in quick words as I reached for his belt. His breath was hot against my neck as I nodded and unfastened the buckle. "And your parents?"

"At a party for my mom's company. They won't be home till late." They rarely let me out of their sight, and I wasn't going to waste this chance. But he was moving slowly, feathering kisses along my neck. I pulled my sweater over my head. "Do you have . . . ?"

"Yeah, of course." He removed the condom from his wallet and tucked it half in the front pocket of my jeans while unbuttoning them. Mirroring my grin, he pulled my lips back to his. I slid my hands over the warm skin of his back beneath the blue-and-yellow stripes of his rugby shirt. I wanted to bottle the feel of this moment and label it "life."

Ryan's hands had just traveled from my face to the clasp of my bra when Jinx decided to live up to her name. She jumped from the desk to the bed.

We rolled apart, laughing. "I didn't even realize the cat was in here," Ryan said.

"Me either." I scooped her up. "I'll be right back—I'm going to open a can of food to keep her preoccupied—ninety seconds."

He smiled enticingly from my pillow, face flushed, hair disheveled. "One, two, three . . ."

I resisted the urge to shove the cat in the hall and crash back against Ryan. My bare skin prickled with goose bumps, but Ryan would warm me up soon enough. I put Jinx down in the kitchen, humming as I grabbed cat food out of the cabinet. She did her best to trip me, twining through my legs as I carried the can to the electric opener.

The motor whirred, the can spun, I turned to grab Jinx's bowl. And screamed. The front door was opening.

I dropped the can. It landed on my toe and I yelped as wet chunks sprayed the floor and lower cabinets.

"Mia?" "Mi?" Both boys said my name simultaneously. Ryan from where he was tearing down the stairs in a panic, buttoning his jeans as he ran. Gyver from the kitchen floor; he'd knelt to take the sharp-edged can away from Jinx and dump the remaining contents in her bowl.

Ryan reached me, arms outstretched. "What's wrong, baby? You okay?" My heart was still in my throat, blocking explanation. He turned from me with wide eyes, which darkened when he saw Gyver. Ryan stepped in front of me and tugged off his shirt.

The motion broke my panic trance. I zipped my jeans and shoved the all-but-fallen condom deep in the pocket. Tugging Ryan's shirt over my head, I fought the urge to hide my blushing face against his back.

Gyver was calm. I wanted to go over and shake him. He had barely looked at me, barely spoken to me since that afternoon in my living room. How could he show up *now*? And how could he be so composed?

He took a rag from the sink and wiped up the spilled cat food. "Sorry. Didn't mean to scare you. Mom wanted me to invite you for dinner. I knocked. The door was unlocked. I didn't realize you were . . . busy."

I looked between Gyver's patient cleaning and Ryan's restless energy. The muscles in his bare back tensed all the way down to his fists. "You're okay?" he asked, taking deep breaths.

"Mostly. I dropped the can on my toe." I forced my voice into a laugh. Ryan's reaction made sense. Gyver? I prepared for his judgment.

But he didn't seem upset. He finished wiping the floor, hung the rag on the sink, scratched Jinx, then headed for the door. A week ago he'd confessed to feeling something for me. But maybe it was *felt* now: past tense. Over.

"I'll tell Mom you've got other plans. If you're hungry later, stop over. She made lasagna and there's plenty. Mi—tell Ryan how good it is." I could hear him whistling through the closed door, the tune growing fainter as he walked to his house.

Ryan slid his hand down my arm and clasped mine. He tried to laugh. "Well . . . that was longer than ninety seconds."

"Sorry for giving you a heart attack."

"Let's lock the door."

I grumbled as we headed back into my room. "My jeans reek of cat food."

"I know how to fix that." His eyes were smiling again as he unbuttoned, unzipped, and tugged them off. "Let's see that toe." Kneeling beside the bed, he picked up my foot, caressed a hand up the back of my calf, and brushed his lips across the inside of my knee. "Does it still hurt?"

"No." I beckoned him to me.

"Mmm. You look better in my shirt than I do." Ryan joined me on the pillows.

"I like you better shirtless, so that works." I felt nervous now, wanting to joke and delay. Gyver's lack of reaction shocked me. He'd flipped at the hospital over something innocent, but us—clearly mid-something—hadn't made him blink. It made no sense. Unless he didn't care anymore. I bit my lip and held my breath, willing myself to ignore the ache in my chest.

Ryan's hand stilled on my stomach and his lips left my neck. "You're on another planet."

"Sorry." I crinkled my nose and sat up. Shaking my head to clear the maybes and focus on my reality—a guy I'd initially given so little credit and who exceeded my expectations daily. A guy who loved me.

Ryan groaned. "You know, this really doesn't make me like Gyver more."

I kissed him softly. "It's my fault—and he did offer lasagna.

I just keep picturing what would've happened if his mom had come instead . . ."

"The police chief? Okay, yeah, the moment's pretty ruined for me too."

"Sorry. Soon?"

"Please." He pulled me into his arms and lay down. I nestled against him, inhaled his sunshine scent; relaxed into his fingertips rubbing my back and his warm skin against my cheek.

I woke to an empty pillow beside me and my parents' voices in the hall.

"Kitten, are you asleep?" Mom leaned in my room and asked.

"Yes," I mumbled.

"Did you eat, take your meds, and do your homework?"

"Yes," I lied.

"Sweet dreams." She kissed my cheek and felt my forehead.

But when she shut the door, I got out of bed. My restlessness had returned and sleep had fled. I didn't have enough time and I couldn't waste any of it.

"I don't want to go to school today," I told Ryan as I climbed in his car the next morning.

Ryan frowned. "Because of the girls? It's been a week; maybe they've calmed down. Apologize. Talk to—"

"No." I didn't want to discuss it: Hil was hostile; Ally was teary-eyed polite; Lauren avoided me with obvious discomfort. At least Chris had more or less gotten over it. "Not because of them. I want you to take me to the shore, since I never made it this summer." I reached over and turned his keys in the ignition.

"Really? You want to skip?" He gave me a disbelieving half grin. I traced his left dimple, making him smile wider and reveal its twin.

"Yes, really! Can we?" Making up for my stolen summer with a trip to the shore would be the first thing I could cross off my before list.

"Let's do it."

Ryan talked the whole two-hour drive. Anecdotes about the people he'd worked with, the places they'd hung out at night—clubs where the bouncers didn't check IDs; beach houses of the week-long renters; the homes of year-rounders who were equal parts distrustful of and intrigued by the summer workers.

"Chris always threw the best parties. His mom was gone half the time, and his house is insane. If I'd known we were skipping today, I would've gotten him to give me the key."

"It's okay, we'll only be there a few hours."

Ryan ticked off the things he needed to show me on his fingers. "We've got to go to Spud McGee's. They make these french fries—but it's a whole potato that they cut into a long spiral, and then they serve it on a stick. And Hot

Diggity—stupid name, I know, but they've got the best hot dogs. I practically lived on them this summer. And there's a smoothie place, where, if the right person's behind the counter, they'll pour some vodka in your cup as they take it off the blender. We'll skip the coaster, the thing rattles like a mofo, but maybe the Ferris wheel and definitely a funnel cake."

"You ate like that all summer?" I laughed and tugged the hem of his shirt free from his seat belt so I could slip my fingers under and onto his hard abs. "Where do you put it?"

He grinned and came to a stop at a traffic light, leaning over to press his lips to the shoulder of my sweatshirt. Well, it was one of *his* sweatshirts, but I was wearing it. "I can't wait to show you everything. I really wished you were here this summer."

And for the last few streets of the beachside town, I thought this was a good idea, one of the best I'd had in a while. After a week of causing nothing but fights, I was making someone happy. Making *Ryan* happy—hopefully as happy as he made me.

The center of town had some traffic, but not much. The farther we got from the main street, and the closer to the boardwalk and sand, the more the cars dwindled. Ryan pulled into a parking lot with a ten-dollar bill in his hand, but the attendant's booth stood empty. He idled there, his window half-lowered.

"Park anyway," I told him. "We can leave the money under a wiper blade in case anyone comes—they're not going to tow you."

I should've told him to turn around. There was unease

growing in my stomach. Maybe this wasn't such a good idea. Maybe it was a horrible one.

Ryan looked disoriented the moment he stepped out of his car—he surveyed the empty lot, and the empty lot next door, with a look of confusion.

On our walk to the beach we passed Spud McGee's. It was shuttered. Hot Diggity had a sign taped to the window: SEE YOU IN THE SPRING.

When our shoes touched the sand, his grip on my hand tightened. He looked up and down the beach, taking in the choppy water, the same dull gray as school trash cans, and the vacant sand. I could see the pier from here. The roller coaster and Ferris wheel that glowed so brightly in his stories were unlit and unmoving. The track of the coaster stripped bare of its cars and stark against the mottled gray of the cloudy sky.

I pulled him forward a few steps, leaning into him and out of the wind. It was cutting through my clothes and raising goose bumps, which rasped against the fabric of my jeans.

The wind ruffled the ocean's surface too. Making it look like it was being prodded with a million paint brushes—nothing like the smooth, easy, blue-green waves from the photos I'd seen of Ryan, Chris, and the girls spread out on crowded sun-drenched sand.

"This is it." Ryan finally spoke, pulling me to stand in front of him as he did so. Wrapping his arms around me and rubbing his hands up and down my arms. I was grateful, not just for the warmth, but because I didn't want to have to see the lost expression on his face. "But it doesn't look anything like it did. I guess I just thought . . . I don't know what I was thinking. I know half the staff weren't local and it's hardly beach weather. Even the guard stands are gone. I guess they pull them in for the winter. I can't even tell where mine was anymore."

The wind turned wet. Spitting a fine mist of spray that made my lips taste salty and the flyaway strands of my wig frizz.

I felt cold. Colder than the temperature really warranted. Even this, even this good thing I'd tried to do, was just more ruin.

I couldn't reclaim my summer any more than I could prevent my future. All I'd done today was taint the memory of a place Ryan loved.

"Let's just go home," he said.

My teeth were chattering too hard to agree, so I just nodded and slipped my hand in his.

Trips to Iggy's made my before list too, and the next day when Mr. Bonura questioned me about making up a calc test, I told him I needed to go to the nurse. Instead, I got Ryan out of his class and we went for midmorning, midweek pie. He didn't hesitate or deny me anything now, but asked often, "Are you happy, baby? Are you feeling okay?" I remembered Chris's comments about Ryan never smiling, how he'd never seen him like this, and I was scared to turn these questions around and ask them back. Ryan wasn't happy; he wasn't okay.

I was doing the best I could to change this, doing the best

I could to prove that I cared for and appreciated him more than I could express. And needed him. There was a constant tugging in the back of my mind, saying that if I just tried harder, I could fall in love with him. I could just never quite reach it—and the night of our beach trip I spent half the hours until morning trying to convince myself I could. The other half I spent trying to sleep and trying to ignore the Gyver-shaped hole in my life.

I suggested we didn't need to go to homeroom the next morning—it was Thursday, exactly one week since the tarot cards spelled out my future in five grim letters. Instead we went for coffee at Bean Haven, a chic bakery in Cross Pointe I'd always wanted to try. I ordered the largest size and drained the pink cardboard cup and—despite Mom's warnings of its chemical poisons—it didn't make me keel over. It did give me enough energy to make it to all of my afternoon classes and paste a placid smile on my face while I doodled in my notebook and ignored my classmates and whatever the teachers wrote on the board.

41

"Mi, wait up."

I ignored Gyver and kept walking. I didn't want to be in the building. I didn't want to think about school. I didn't want to discuss what he'd walked in on Monday night either.

He caught up with me outside the school's double doors, wrapping his fingers gently around my arm and pulling me to a stop. "Mi, I was calling you all down the hall. Didn't you hear me?"

I shook my head.

"Don't you need a ride home? I thought The Jock—sorry, Ryan—drove you, and it doesn't look like you want to wait around for soccer practice to end."

"Thanks." I headed down the stairs to his Jeep.

"Wait a minute. You okay? I heard you had a big academic meeting."

"Not so big." I tapped my foot, anxious to keep walking. Standing still took effort.

"Mr. Bonura asked if I'd tutor you. Why didn't you tell me you needed help?"

"I don't. It's not a big deal." I was in danger of failing history and calculus. My English and science grades weren't much better. "Can we go?"

The progress report from Principal Baker was wrinkling in the bottom of my bag. I'd already forged Mom's name and would turn it in on Monday.

Gyver froze, oblivious to the roadblock he created at the stop of the stairs.

"Home? Us? Now?" I prompted.

He followed me down the steps, then tugged me over to the wall. "What do you mean it's not a big deal? Last year you obsessed over hundredths of GPA points. Don't tell me you're giving up and handing me the valedictorianship. Did something happen?"

I shrugged. "It's just not a big deal. Not so important anymore."

"Why not?" His eyes narrowed. My fingers were drumming restlessly against my thighs until he trapped them in his cool hands. "What happened? Tell me."

It seemed pointless to resist; he wasn't going to give up. "I went to see a psychic."

"You what?" His voice was loud and angry; people turned, then turned away when there wasn't anything to see. He lowered it to a growl. "Let me guess, she gave you a dire prediction and now you think you're not going to get better."

I pulled my hands free and met his eyes. "At least now I know."

"You believed her? So what? You're giving up and waiting to die?" He stepped closer, shaking his head in anger and disbelief.

"I'm going to enjoy however long I have. Do what I want to do, make sure I don't miss out on anything. What choice do I have?" My voice quivered; the rest of me shook. I'd fought so hard to make peace with this idea, leaving all second-guessing in the parking lot at the lake.

"You fight! You stay healthy . . . you try! Are you seriously giving this crazy person more credit than your doctors?" He put his hands on my shoulders and shook me lightly.

"There's no point." He wouldn't understand.

"Mi—how many times do I have to tell you, you create your own luck. Look at me. You're not going to self-destruct. I'm not going to let you. You're not going to die."

I ducked my head and he pulled me toward him, capturing me in an iron hug. "I won't let you," he repeated.

"Maybe I deserve this." I hadn't meant to say it; the words escaped through the crack he'd chiseled in my composure.

"No! Don't ever say that. Ever." Gyver rocked me in his embrace.

I was still shaking, only now it was with fear, not frenzied energy. It'd been easier to just know, even if it was bad news; at least I wasn't wondering. I needed to escape from him and the conclusions he wanted me to question.

"Leave me alone, Gyver. Just let me—"

"Isn't this adorable. And in-ter-est-ting!" The voice was loud, high, and syrupy-sweet. "Mia, are you double-dipping? I thought Ryan'd be enough."

"What?" I stepped out of Gyver's hug. His intimidating stare was back, aimed at Hillary.

But Hil wasn't intimidated. She was furious. Probably, she'd expected me to track her down and grovel by now, but I hadn't. I wouldn't. There was no point.

She pointed a dark-purple nail at us, waving it between Gyver and me in a sideways tsk-tsk. "I always thought you guys were hooking up, but I didn't expect you to look so cozy right outside the gym where Ryan's practicing."

She wasn't alone—I hadn't noticed at first, but Lauren, Emily, Monica, and most of the squad were behind her.

"I wasn't . . . We weren't . . . We're just friends," I stammered.

"You don't need to justify yourself," Gyver said. "Especially not to the queen bitch."

"Of course not," Hil simpered. "Because we all know what we saw. Soon Ryan'll know too. But that's okay, right?"

The two people who used to be my best friends—attacking each other, attacking me. I was used to playing mediator between them, but I couldn't handle that today, and what was the point anymore? The panic from my conversation with Gyver spilled over. "We're friends. Neighbors. Gyver doesn't think of me that way . . . He couldn't.'"

"Mi—" Gyver warned.

"Couldn't? Why couldn't he? Ohhh. Wow. I get it now." Hil's face lit up like she'd just solved a complex choreography dilemma. It made me nervous. "God, it finally makes sense why you two never got together." She laughed and adopted a faux whisper. "Gyver likes guys."

"What?" I squeaked. I hadn't stopped shaking; Gyver's "I won't let you" rolled through my mind like a threat.

"Not that I'm judging," she continued. "I think that's great, Gyver. I should've known. All Mia's unrequited, angsty pining. And her insistence that you were 'just friends.' But you're gay! That is what you were saying, right, Mia?"

"I . . ." The cheerleaders were watching expectantly; Hillary standing in the front with hands propped on her hips. Escape! Every part of my mind demanded it. Instead I stared her down. "First, you're wrong. Second, stalker much? You've made it clear we're not friends anymore, so why do you even care?"

She blinked, and for a moment her glare slipped to a wince.

I slid my gaze from her to Gyver, offering my next words to both of them. "My life is none of your business. Leave me alone."

And then I walked away.

Gyver followed. Hil did not. Even if she'd wanted to, her pride would never let her chase me in front of the other cheerleaders.

"Mi." His voice was soft but condemning. "You don't mean that. Don't be an idiot; think about what you're doing."

I'm letting go! I cried inside. *And you make that too hard.* "Just leave me alone. Please. I just want you to leave me alone," I whispered.

His face transformed into a stony fury I'd never seen before. "Fine. I'm done, Mia. Done. You're not who I thought you were." I watched him walk away from me, then turned and stumbled in the opposite direction.

I entered the first door I came to: the gym. Something about my face stopped Ryan in mid-drill. He froze with his hand extended toward the baseline, then stood and jogged to me. "You okay?" he asked, ignoring his coach's whistle and calls.

I constructed a smile from the scraps of my self-preservation. "I missed you."

"That's all? Nothing's wrong? 'Cause Coach'll have my ass if I don't get back to practice."

"Can I have your keys? I don't want to wait. My parents are out to dinner with the Russos. Have someone drop you after practice; we'll have the house to ourselves. No interruptions today, I promise." My manic sentences without breathing were more crazed than sexy, but I couldn't pause. If I did, I'd think about what Gyver'd said. What I'd said . . . "How long till practice is over?"

Ryan inhaled. "Maybe I'll fake an injury and come with you now."

I laughed, but Coach Burne didn't. "Winters! If you don't

stop flirting and get back to work, your ass won't leave the bench till basketball season. Now, five extra."

Ryan grinned. "I'll do ten extra, but I've got to get my keys out of my gym bag first."

I threw up in the parking lot. Gagged on the taste of my words—of the words said and those that remained unsaid. I woke up every morning with the intention of fixing things—but got into bed every night with the knowledge that I'd only made them worse. I couldn't see any way to come back from what had happened today—I'd pushed Hil even further away. And Gyver.

I'm done.

I pulled Ryan's car over and vomited again on the side of the road. My chest felt tight; it was hard to breathe. Maybe I was getting sick. I couldn't think about it. I couldn't think about any of it. I got back in the car and drove home at a reckless speed.

I showered, smearing on lavender lotion and plying eye makeup with a hand so shaky, a smudged-smoky look was inevitable. Only, instead of looking bedroom-sexy, it made me hollow eyed and haunted. I ransacked my pajama drawer—looking for something that didn't emphasize my jutting ribs and collarbones—and settling on Ryan's rugby shirt and ruffled boyshorts Hil had dared me to buy last spring.

I hated the idea of losing it bald, but decided that was better than my wig falling off during, which had almost happened last time. I knotted a pink scarf over my spotty fuzz.

Then I paced. And flipped through college catalogs—Dad had removed last year's sticky notes and retabbed them with schools close to home. I paced more. Tried to prevent guilty Gyver thoughts from invading. Paced to the kitchen and unlocked the door. Tried to coax Jinx upstairs to keep me company. When I'd first gotten sick, she'd shadowed my every move. Lately she'd stayed downstairs and avoided me. Even my cat was judgmental. I gave up and paced back to my bedroom. Lit candles.

Midstride I was winded. I sat at my desk and tried to catch my breath. Then curled up on my bed when it wouldn't be caught. I gasped and wheezed. Then fell asleep.

When I woke the candles were cold. Ryan's car was gone.

Flipping on my lights, I blinked at a note on my pillow.

Wouldn't let myself wake you—even though
I wanted to. God, you're sexy.
Call me when you get up.
I love you,
Ryan

I dug my phone from the bottom of my school bag. "Hey."

"Hey," he answered. "You know, you're going to give me a complex. Or drive me crazy."

"Where are you?" I could hear voices in the background.

"Chris's. We're doing a guys' night. Poker and guy movies."

"Porno?" I asked, not even trying to hide my disgust.

He laughed. "Um, no. That's not really a group thing. I meant blood-and-guts movies. The kind you hate."

"Oh. Oops. Will you come back over?"

"Not tonight. I'm going to hang with Chris."

"Really?" I was used to *be right there.*

"Not tonight," he repeated. "I just . . . I need a break. Things have been a little . . . intense. Sorry."

"It's okay." My voice was small. If I lost Ryan, I'd have nothing. Whatever he needed, he could have, because I needed *him.* "It's no big deal. Say hi to Chris. Have fun."

42

"Kitten, it's been great to see you so energetic lately," Mom said as I walked in from a "study date" with Ryan on Sunday. Really we'd been the annoying couple groping in the back of the movie theater, but she didn't need to know that.

Right now my energy was of the caffeinated variety. I'd made Ryan stop for a large espresso post-film. She didn't need to know that either.

"Thanks, Mom." I hugged her and went upstairs, leaving her complaining to Dad about how Jinx kept peeing outside her litter box and Dad responding with the results of my latest kidney function tests.

I'd always played the role of obedient daughter, but now I'd taken the charade to a new level. They didn't know how often I was breathless and exhausted, or see that my smiles only extended to the edges of my lips.

I was a puppet, strung up with panic, yet still performing

when I had an audience. Gyver saw straight through it, or he had back when he was looking at me, before he let my apologies land in unanswered voice mails, e-mails, and knocks on his door. Ryan knew. How could my parents be so oblivious?

Even Principal Baker recognized something was wrong, stopping me in the hallway on Tuesday afternoon when I was wandering during English. "Miss Moore?"

"Yes?"

"I'm concerned with what your teachers are telling me. They're still not seeing the types of changes we discussed at our meeting on Friday. Is everything all right? Would you like to meet with Ms. Piper?"

I cursed at my shoes. "I'm working on it. I just get so tired."

"I think it's time to have your parents in to sit down with all the teachers and reevaluate your needs. Mia, you're going to need these grades for college."

"Just give me a little time," I begged. "Then, if I don't fix things, you can call."

"You have until next Friday. That's nine school days to show me some improvements," he said. "But if you don't get it together by the Fall Ball, I'm calling and we're having a meeting."

The week blurred by in a flurry of motion. Gyver refused to acknowledge me. He didn't even look in my direction—as if he were already getting used to the idea of sitting next to an empty desk. He pretended I didn't exist; I pretended not to notice I was weaker or that my heart sprinted and my lungs clenched.

I was tired. All the time. Racing pulse and tight chest hadn't been symptoms before, but they were constant now. These had to be signs I was sicker. Did it show in my blood counts? Would they be able to tell I was a lost cause when I went in for my second round of consolidation chemo in two weeks? Was that why Dad shut himself in his makeshift planetarium after long phone calls with Dr. Kevin?

I couldn't ask. I couldn't sit still. I couldn't sleep. When I tried, I choked on the things I wouldn't live to experience or woke up sweaty and breathless.

Only once did I lose post-psychic detachment—when I unearthed last year's Halloween costume during a two a.m. cleaning binge. I stared at the sequined honeybee tube dress and wondered what happened to the costumes Lauren picked for this year. I couldn't remember what they were or if I'd been school/hospital/home on Autumn Girl's favorite holiday.

I sobbed as I threw the costume in the trash and covered its yellow-and-black stripes with the ratty cheerleading sweatshirt Mom hated. All my pictures of the Calendar Girls were boxed and hidden; the costume had been an emotional ambush. I'd be more prepared next time.

"Don't you miss them?" Ryan asked on our way to lunch

on Friday, his head tilted to the side, his fingers woven through mine. I clung to him; he was the only thing grounding me to this school, where I drifted through the halls like a ghost already. People's eyes slid over and around me, uncomfortable with my pallor, too-thin body, and vacant eyes.

"Why do I need them? I have you." I offered this with a smile and a peck, but they were empty words and a hollow kiss. He pretended to believe me, but his eyes tightened with recognition.

I did miss them, especially as the hallways filled with talk about the Fall Ball. Their names were on the ballot. Mine wasn't.

"Do we have to go?" I asked Ryan at lunch.

"I kinda have to—I'm on the court. You don't want to? You used to live for this sort of thing."

"You go; I'll stay home." I poked holes in my sandwich.

"Don't be like that. We'll have fun." He put a hand on my knee. "Promise."

"What's he promising now?" Chris interjected. "The moon, stars, and everlasting bliss?"

"Something like that," I answered, a fake smile forming automatically on my lips, though it was hard to maintain because my chest hurt, my lungs felt flattened.

"But Ryan, you promised me those same things last week— you man-whore!" Chris grinned and swiped my apple.

"Tell Mia Fall Ball will be fun," Ryan prompted.

"Of course it will," Chris scoffed. "Just picture me in the crown and dancing like this."

I laughed at his robot and running man and when he moved

behind Bill and began to grind. Laughed because it was expected. I tangled my fingers in my necklace: under the table I was tapping a pulse with my foot.

Ryan joined in, but there was desperation in his laugh and on his lips when he pressed them against mine and whispered in my ear, "We'll have fun. Promise."

I squeezed his fingers and tried to believe him. We all had our coping methods. Gyver had his anger. Mom had her obsession with finding me the perfect dress for the Fall Ball. Dad had his star maps and phone calls to doctors. I had Ryan.

I still needed him, but did he still want me? By the end of the day, my hand ached from how tightly I gripped his, but it was getting harder to convince myself that we still worked.

"Promise," Ryan repeated. His coping method: self-deception.

43

Gyver's desk was empty on Monday. I'd decided the night before to ask him for calc help. He might be furious, but I couldn't imagine he'd say no. In my plans, he'd help me and, more importantly, forgive me. Getting Mr. Bonura and Principal Baker off my case would just be a bonus. But Gyver wasn't in any of our classes.

On Tuesday, dizzy panic compelled me to ask Meagan.

"He'll be home this afternoon. He's visiting colleges." Her face was a blend of judgment and pity. "I know it's none of my business, but fix things with him, okay?"

"I tried, but he won't talk to me," I mumbled.

"Keep trying, then. Hillary managed to apologize to him, and it's not like they're friendly. You know how much he cares for you."

Hil apologized? He'd accepted her apology but not mine?

I swallowed past the tightening in my throat. "Did he tell you I didn't know about Max? I feel awful about the hospital."

"It's okay," Meagan answered, but she was suddenly engrossed in her calc notes.

I excused myself to go to the bathroom and went home instead. Gyver'd left on college tours. Last year we'd planned our route together. We'd spent afternoons with Dad making spreadsheets and sending away for catalogs.

He'd gone without me. It was a sign he'd accepted next fall I wouldn't be around to matriculate with him.

There was a note in the kitchen when I got home. I read it out loud as I pulled off my itchy wig. " 'Mia, I've got a house showing at 4:30. I'll pick up dinner on the way home. Love, Dad.' " I grabbed a can of cat food.

"I guess it's just you and me, Jinx." But despite the humming can opener, she wasn't twining between my legs.

"Jinx?" I carried the can over to her bowl. It was full with food from the morning. Maybe she'd gotten shut in my room. It'd happened before; I'd come home from practice to find her yowling. She'd also shredded a shirt out of boredom. I hoped I hadn't left anything on my bed.

But my door was open. "Jinx? Jinxsy?" She was curled up on the spare pillow. When I nudged her, she raised a lethargic paw toward me.

"Hey, bud, aren't you hungry?" She sneezed in my face. "Gross! Jinx!" Instead of stretching or leaping from the bed, she shut her eyes. I stopped wiping off cat snot and looked at her: nose and eyes streaming green mucus.

"Jinx?" I picked her up; she didn't curl closer or fight to get down. She lay limp. I called Dad. No answer. Mom's cell was off. Gyver didn't pick up, but his car was back in his driveway.

"Hang on, Jinx." I tucked my sweatshirt around her before walking out my door and across my driveway to the Russos'.

I pounded and pounded before he answered. I could see my mess of a reflection in the door's window; tears had painted my cheeks three tints of splotchy sadness. Jinx hadn't reacted to the cold or the noise of my banging.

Gyver had been mid-workout. His black T-shirt was adhered to his chest with sweat, but I launched myself at him anyway. Or tried to; he held me off with one hand. "What do you want?"

My breath seized in my lungs, caught on his physical and verbal rejection.

I pulled back a flap of sweatshirt sleeve to expose Jinx's oozy face. "She's sick. No one's home. I don't know what to do."

Gyver looked from her pathetic furry face to my pathetic sobbing one and pulled me into his kitchen. He told me to "sit," took Jinx in one arm, looked up the vet's number, and picked up his phone. He spoke assuredly in the receiver, pausing to ask me, "Has she eaten?"

"Not today. Dad gave her dinner last night; I don't know if she ate."

"We'll be right in." Gyver hung up the phone, grabbed his

keys and a sweatshirt, and headed out. He didn't look back, but paused on the porch to shut and lock the door behind me.

I opened the passenger door. Gyver handed me his sweatshirt. "Put this on. It's too cold."

"You're wear—" I started to protest, but agreement was faster. I pulled on his sweatshirt. It pooled around me in piles of excess fabric. I shoved the sleeves up my arms, and Gyver handed me the bundle containing Jinx. She opened an eye and yowled.

"Do you want to go get a hat or your wig?" he asked, his hand paused on the ignition.

I shook my head. "We need to go. Please, please be okay, Jinx."

Gyver fastened his seat belt and looked at mine. As soon as I'd buckled it, he pulled out of the driveway and tore through the streets to the animal clinic.

I attempted one conversation. "Do you think she'll be okay?"

Gyver looked over—made eye contact for the first fractional second since he'd opened his door—then turned back to the road with a clenched jaw and white-knuckled grip. "I don't know. God, she's thin. How long's she been sick?"

"She hasn't. I didn't . . ." Guilt kept me mute for the rest of the drive.

44

The guilt grew to tremors as the vet examined Jinx and gave me options: put her down humanely or try and manage her pain with medications that would make her groggy and disoriented.

"Maybe you should wait until your parents are here before you make any decisions."

"But she was fine yesterday," I protested.

The vet's eyes examined me as well: my stubbly, patchy head, circled eyes, tiny frame drowning in Gyver's sweatshirt. His voice was full of pity. "Jinx is a very sick cat, Mia. She's in the final stages of kidney failure. Maybe if you'd caught this sooner, but a lot of cats don't have outward manifestations. We have no way of knowing, and unfortunately, there's nothing I can do at this stage."

I hadn't noticed. When was the last time I'd made time for Jinx? Done more than complain about her shedding? She used to sit on my lap while I did homework, but I hadn't done any in a while. I saw her when she slept on the pillow next to mine, but Jinx had become impatient with my nighttime mania and started sleeping downstairs.

She'd been suffering and I hadn't noticed. The thought made me gag. My legs faltered. Gyver pointed to a chair and blocked my view of the exam table where Jinx shivered and vomited.

"Why don't I give you a few minutes to make your decision?" the vet said while mopping up the mess. "I'll go try your parents again. Come find me when you're ready." He gingerly picked up Jinx and set her on a clean blanket on the table.

It was impossible not to make the connection between my dying cat and me. She was sick. She was in pain. And there was no way I could help her. She stared at me through barely open eyes. Did I have enough courage to be merciful?

"Do you want to wait for your parents? Your dad might be home soon," Gyver said.

I didn't answer, but went to stand beside her at the table. I was too busy memorizing the whirl of hair on her nose and the contrast between her eraser-pink tongue and midnight fur.

"We could bring her home now, and you could come back later with your parents. Or you could try the drugs," he suggested.

Jinx yawned, crying out again from the motion. Her eyes, rimmed with gummy discharge, were full of trust and agony. One of her paws batted against my arm. I touched it softly and she flinched.

"I can't." I turned my head away and muffled the rest of the words in the shoulder of the sweatshirt. "We have to do this now. I can't make her suffer anymore."

"I'll get the vet." He paused to trace a finger around the edge of Jinx's ear. She tried to purr, a reflex reaction, but the sound was stuttery. Gyver rushed out of the room, and I kissed her nose and wiped my eyes on her fur.

The vet entered, followed by a stone-faced version of my best friend. He crossed the room and stood with his back toward me, engrossed in the pet medication flyers tacked to a bulletin board, his arms tight around his chest, gripping handfuls of shirt.

The doctor began to explain how Jinx wouldn't feel a thing. "It's like falling asleep. You can even hold her while I administer it." Tears flooded my cheeks, and I tightened my grip on the nearly motionless bundle on the table, clutching at the last moments I'd have with her.

"This is an emotional decision. I spoke with your father while I was out of the room. He and your mother can't get here before we close tonight. I'll understand if you want to go home and come back with one of them tomorrow. Or I can recommend a twenty-four-hour vet." I shook my head. "I don't want you to have any regrets, Mia. If you'd prefer, you can wait in the lobby."

"No!" The word was knotted in a sob and shaken from my chest. Gyver turned and it was spelled in the set of his jaw and the shroud of his eyes: his heart was equally broken. "She has to know I'm here."

And Gyver was there too. At my side in four strides, arm around me and supporting me as I stood at the exam table. I was trembling, but he was steady. I gave Jinx a last kiss, whispered in her ear, and Gyver did too. Then I gave her a last, last kiss. With the dregs of my courage I turned to the doctor. "Ready."

If Gyver's hands hadn't been under mine, I would've sagged to the floor. I would've run from the room.

When it was over, he had to nearly carry me to the lobby. He filled out the paperwork while I sobbed in the corner, pulling the hood up over my face. Turning to lean my forehead against the wall when an eight-year-old and his mom came skipping in with their calico kitten.

By the time he said, "We're done. Let's go home," my eyes were swollen to slits. He put an arm around my shoulders and led me to the car.

I pulled my feet onto the seat. With my face lowered onto my knees and the hood obscuring everything, I'd built my own fortress of grief. If I could keep my arms around my knees, keep holding myself together, I might make it home in one piece.

"We're here." Gyver turned off the engine. His hand stretching to fold back the fabric around my face. "I'm sorry about Jinx. I'll get you a new kitten."

"Don't," I moaned.

"It doesn't have to be right away. When you're ready. I'll let you name this one." He tried to smile, but it faltered and faded.

"I don't want a new cat." I buried my head in my knees again. "She didn't look like she was in pain, did she?"

Gyver shook his head. "No, she looked peaceful."

I peered out the windshield, focusing on the clouds above his garage. "That's what I want—when it's my time. I want to go to sleep and have everyone I love holding my hand."

Gyver's eyes went flat—like Jinx's had at her final moments. He pressed his lips together, shook his head, and got out of the car. I mirrored his movements; using my puffy eyes to decipher his face and stiff body language. It wasn't a difficult read: the walls had been reconstructed between us. His mask of detachment was firmly in place, and I was lost in my grief all alone.

"Can I come over? I don't want to go in." Jinx's toys and bowls flash-bulbed in my mind.

He didn't bother with an excuse. "No."

"But . . . I thought you'd forgiven me."

He shut his eyes and shook his head. "It's not a matter of forgiving; I'm choosing not to hang out with you. I can't do this to myself, Mi. I can't."

"Am I that awful?"

"You were someone incredible. You were my best friend. And now?" He shoved his hands in his pockets and closed his eyes again. "The way you've handled your cancer . . . Who are you?"

"I don't know if you've noticed, but I'm just trying to survive." Hillary's acid voice had nothing on mine. "If I'm not the perfect person while dying from cancer, that's okay with me."

"If I've noticed? I was there every day this summer! Did you forget? I was the only one there. I've seen how awful and painful this is, and how terrified you are. But when this is over—because you *will* beat this—who are you going to be? Regardless of whether or not you have cancer, you're not someone I want to know anymore. My Mia Moore wouldn't just give up."

"Well, lucky for you, you won't have to know me much longer."

His eyes sparked with fury, then glazed with tears. He walked into his house without looking back. It felt like Jinx had been the last link between us, and now that was severed.

I sat on the front porch and curled into myself, trying to breathe.

I was still there when Mom drove up. "Oh, kitten, I'm so sorry . . . ," she began.

At the sound of my nickname, I began to wail.

If I couldn't hold Jinx, I wanted to be held, so I called Ryan.

"Where were you? I called your phone and your parents and the hospital." His voice was a tangle of panic, anger, and relief.

I gulped a breath and tried to answer.

"Do you know how freaked I was when you were gone at the end of the day? I thought you were . . ."

"Will you come over?" I sounded five years old.

"I need some space." His panic and relief had faded, leaving frustration-coated anger. "Now that I know you're okay, I need to, I don't know, breathe and calm down."

"Later?" I asked.

"Let me take a drive, clear my head, then I'll come."

But he didn't. He called later, but I was already two hours into a sleeping pill. Apologies, explanations, and kisses waited until the morning. Exchanged with forced smiles. My chest ached, my pulse pounded in my temples, and the hallway focused and unfocused as I blinked past tears.

"We're okay, right?" Ryan asked, raising our intertwined hands and brushing his lips across my knuckles.

I swallowed and coughed before I could answer. "We're fine."

We had to be.

45

I sat in the kitchen and stared out the window. Tapping my nails on the counter while I pretended to listen to Mom's pre-dance blather. Gyver came out of his house carrying a trash bag; I bolted out the door and cornered him on the driveway.

"Gyver!" I paused and caught my breath. "Wait. Please?"

He replaced the trash can lid and turned toward me with an impassive face.

"Can we talk?"

"Talk." He gave me a palms-up, go-ahead gesture.

"I'm sorry! I'm so sorry! I miss you." So much so I'd found myself sobbing at three a.m. when I discovered Mom washed his sweatshirt and it no longer smelled like him. It had been three awful days since Jinx died. Three days of Gyver acting like I didn't exist.

"I miss you too, but it doesn't change things." He raked his hair into chaos and hooked his thumb in his pocket.

"Will you forgive me?" I ached to reach for him, so I clasped my hands behind my back.

"It's not forgiveness. It's self-preservation. God, Mi—don't you get it?" He hesitated, then walked over to his car. He reached in the driver's door and fumbled in the console before pulling out a battered envelope. "I've been carrying this for weeks. It's a mix for you."

"Thanks." I tried to sigh, but my chest was too tight, my lungs crowded by the hammering of my heart. I didn't want a CD; I wanted him back in my life.

"Listen to it." And he left.

I flipped the CD around in my hands. I could more or less decipher the title. He'd written it in all caps: it was "MUSIC FOR . . ." and a scrawl of my name.

I slipped the CD in my car as I pulled out of the driveway to go to the nail salon. The first song was an oldie. I twisted the volume, and the lyrics to a Stevie Wonder song filled the car:

Very superstitious, the writing's on the wall.
I frowned but continued listening:
When you believe in things you don't understand, you suffer. Superstition ain't the way.

I punched the advance button; the next song was familiar; we listened to it every year at cheer camp. It was the "I'm sexy,

I'm cute," song from the beginning of *Bring it On*—a movie Gyver loved to hate.

Was this whole CD songs that mocked me? I shut it off and pulled into a spot in front of the salon. The door was open and I could see the customers inside. All girls from my school in chatty, smiley groups.

Predance preparation had always been a Calendar Girls gossipfest. We rotated whose house we got ready at and brought in nail and hair stylists so we could nibble and giggle as we were pampered. Fall Ball meant I should be at Lauren's right now.

My chest tightened. I coughed and punched the steering wheel, clipping the horn. The girls inside turned. I flushed as they gave puzzled looks, half waves, then turned back to each other and laughed. It wasn't worth it. Why did it matter what my nails looked like?

I put the car in reverse and drove home.

Gyver was waiting on his driveway when I pulled into mine. After spending so many nights wishing he'd acknowledge me, I cursed as he sauntered over and opened my door. "Did you listen to it?" There was an unnerving intensity in his voice.

"I listened."

"And?" He leaned down and offered me a hand.

"I don't know. Is there an answer you're looking for?" I ignored his hand and stood.

"That's your whole reaction?" He hadn't stepped back; I was squeezed between the open door and him. I fought the urge to hug him and inhale his familiar scent—the smell of my childhood and seventeen years of Saturdays.

I rubbed my throbbing forehead and closed my eyes. I wasn't going to cry. "What do you want me to say? Yes, I'm superstitious. Yes, I like cheerleading. Great."

"How much did you listen to?" His voice tightened.

"Enough. Thanks. I have to go get ready." I put a hand to his chest and pushed gently. I needed space and air before I choked.

He stepped out of the way but caught my arm. "Listen to all of it, Mi."

I masked pain as annoyance. "I will. God."

"You know, for someone who's always looking for signs, you're pretty blind to the ones I've been giving you for years." His thumb caressed the inside of my arm before letting go. "You see what you want to. Maybe you're looking for signs you won't get better because it's easier to give up."

He was walking away. "So is this it?" I called. "You're back to ignoring me because I didn't like the mix. Friendship over again?"

He spun and walked back. "You've made your priorities clear over and over. I knew we were done the day you switched your lucky necklace for one The Jock gave you. If he was more important to you than your superstitions, more important than . . ." He locked his jaw, looked at the ground, and gave his head an angry shake.

"I lost my necklace! I would never have taken it off. Ryan bought me a replacement because I was so upset. What was I supposed to do? Not wear it? What is this really about? You feel threatened by *him*?" I scoffed on the last word.

It was a minor lifetime before he lifted his eyes from the crack in the driveway to drill them into mine. "I won't watch you self-destruct. You can't ask me to do that."

This time he didn't stop when I called after him. The door banged shut and I was alone. I wasn't going to cry, but I couldn't stop the choking coughs.

"Let me see." Mom held out her hand for one of mine when I entered the kitchen.

"I didn't like any of the colors," I lied.

"Well, we have polish. If you can't find one you like, I'll run out to the store."

I wanted to get upstairs and give myself room to think. And breathe. I forced words around gasps and hid shaking fists in my pockets. "I've got something."

I sank to the bathroom floor with a bottle of Merlot Mission polish and smeared some on my unsteady hands.

Ryan. It couldn't go on this way. I clung to his hand, clung to him, because I was scared. But it wasn't fair; I couldn't keep pretending to feel more than I did. And I wasn't the only one pretending; he knew we didn't work. The question was: Which of us was brave enough to say it? My lungs and heart clenched: more good-byes. I bent over, bracing my hands on my knees, and tried to take deep, slow breaths. All I accomplished was convulsive coughs.

Blowing on my nails caused another coughing fit—I needed

to calm down. I gulped air and stood up. Too fast. The room spun and I steadied myself on the towel rack.

I yanked my dress from the closet, spilling memories from the shopping trip I'd had with Mom. Finding a formal dress that covered a port wasn't easy. Mom had vetoed anything in black or white—saying both colors made me look "washed out and sickly." I'd bitten back a laugh and let her choose. She'd settled on a mint one-shouldered dress. It was important to her, so despite the amount of fluff and tulle in the skirt, I'd agreed.

I tugged it on and zipped it up. Stuck a rhinestone clip on my wig, painted on some makeup, and headed downstairs, pausing a moment on the landing to clench and unclench my hands until my pulse calmed.

"Hey, beautiful." Ryan greeted me with a kiss. I frowned at the scent on his breath and the flush in his cheeks; turned away from a second beer-flavored kiss. Mom was too busy with the requisite *ooh*ing and *aah*ing to notice.

She waved a thermometer at me, but I shook her off with unveiled annoyance. "I'm not messing up my makeup. I'm fine. We need to go."

"Just a few photos." I forced smiles through the dizziness of camera flashes.

"Where's Dad?" I asked.

Mom frowned. "He's been on the phone for an hour. I knocked a few minutes ago to tell him you were almost ready, and he snapped at me that he didn't want to be disturbed."

"*Dad* did?" I'd never heard him yell at Mom. Ever.

"I know!" She seemed less upset than surprised. "I'm sorry, kitten. I know he wanted to see you—it's got to be a very important phone call. Maybe it's that doctor in Boston he's been trying to get in touch with? I don't want you to be late; I'll just show him the pictures when he gets off the phone. Have fun, you two."

Then she was shooing us out the door, and all my worries about his odd behavior were forgotten as I inhaled outside air. It had gotten colder in the last few hours. There was a feeling of snow in the air, and it burned like icy fire when I breathed.

46

"Aren't I driving?" Ryan asked when I stopped at my car and opened the door.

"Are you kidding? You've been drinking—I can't believe you drove here. Get in the car."

"Sure." He shrugged. "Let me just grab my bag—we're still staying over at Chris's, right?"

I ignored his question and the accompanying raised-eyebrow grin, waiting until he'd shut his door to demand, "What were you thinking?"

"You look great." Ryan reached over and touched my knee, trying to slide his hand across the endless tulle until I swatted him.

"Thanks." There wasn't any enthusiasm in the word. "But that wasn't what I meant."

"I like your dress. You look hot. Sometimes I forget . . ." His words and caresses bypassed playful and seductive and escalated to turmoil. He sighed and pulled his hands back into his lap.

I turned into the Scoops parking lot. It was closed for the season, the picnic benches coated with a lace of frost and the neon ice cream cone turned off. "What's going on?"

"Do we have to do this now?" he asked, not looking at me. "Can't we just go to the dance and the party and not do this?" Instead of waiting for my answer, he got out of the car.

I followed. The icy air of the parking lot sawed at my lungs, providing some clarity but cutting into my breathing. I choked my way from the car to the picnic bench.

"You okay?" Ryan asked, his concern shooting through multiple levels as my inability to catch my breath continued.

"Fine," I gasped. "It'll pass." I dabbed my eyes and shrugged farther into my coat, taking slow, shallow breaths until the choking stopped.

We sat on the bench closest to the building. Ryan wasn't filling the silence or trying to overpower my raspy breaths with compliments and reassurances. Not a good sign.

"Ryan? Talk to me."

"I can't do this anymore." His head was in his hands. His voice was shaking.

"Do what?" Although I knew, and knew I couldn't do it either.

"This isn't what I thought. I'm scared shitless all the time. What if Mia gets a cold? What if I kiss her and get her sick? Can I touch her without bruising her? What if you don't get better?"

He turned toward me, his eyes wet and face crumpled. "I shouldn't say that—I shouldn't even think it, but it's all I think about. Mia, I love you, but I can't handle the idea of—I can't handle that." He dropped his head into his palms.

"I know."

I put a hand on his arm, and he covered it with his own. "I just wanted to get through high school and get away to college. And you . . . shit! I thought I could handle this, but I can't. I just can't. I'm sorry."

He kissed me and it felt nice, but no longer necessary. He tasted of tears, longing, and farewell. "I'm sorry."

I remembered when his blue eyes had laughed instead of worried and his hand had tickled instead of clamped. "Don't be sorry. You were the best part of this year. The only good part."

His face collapsed under my sincerity. "Maybe I . . ."

"Ryan, why don't I drop you at the school? We can talk tomorrow." The cold was creeping through my coat; each icy inhale burned my lungs.

"What about you? You could still come."

"I just want to go home and put on pajamas." My head was heavy, cloudy—sleep would help. "Go with Chris and everyone; you'll have fun."

"Fun? You really think anything that happens tonight could be fun? Mia—"

I wanted to think through how Ryan must be feeling, but more than that, I wanted to go home. I tried to swallow through my tightening lungs, and choked out a sputtering cough.

He exhaled and deflated. "It doesn't matter anymore. C'mon, drop me off and then get to bed."

The drive to the school was tense. My fingers wouldn't stop trembling, even after Ryan redirected all the heat vents at me. He'd sent a few texts, then slumped against his window, fists in his lap. The only time he spoke was to comment on the music.

"This is Coldplay, right? Can we turn it off? It's depressing as shit."

I nodded.

Ejected Gyver's CD.

Gulped air, then forgot how to exhale.

My head spun as pieces clicked.

Coldplay. Gyver. Oh God! "Surrender" song.

Gyver?

I bit my lip to keep myself from sobbing. Clenched the wheel to prevent myself from pulling a U-turn and speeding home. What would that accomplish? What would I do? He'd said . . . And I'd said . . . My head was too busy tilting and blurring to focus. It took all of my concentration to see the dotted street lines and navigate the roads to East Lake High.

Hillary, like a shark, scented the blood from Ryan's broken heart. She hurried to my car seconds after he exited. Ryan dropped his bag in the back of Chris's SUV and entered the school. He didn't look back. Hil leaned against my driver's door, tapping the window with her manicure until I lowered the glass. She looked like petite perfection in a skimpy golden dress and three-inch heels.

"You broke up," she stated.

Her words distracted me from my task: breathing.

"You know," she said, a smile tugging at the corner of her lip gloss, "I *did* tell you it'd happen before Fall Ball. You should've listened to me."

My mind wanted to say: stop being such a hardass and admit you care. But my body was too tired. "At least I didn't OD on chocolate."

"True, you did follow my advice about that." She tilted her head and studied me. "Though you still look like crap. Since when do you let your mom pick your dresses? Don't even try and deny it; you would never pick out something that pageanty, and your mom loves that color." Her tone wasn't caustic, it was teasing. She reached through the window and plucked at a layer of the tulle.

"It's bad, isn't it? Good thing I'm not going in." I managed a few seconds of laughter before it turned to choking.

Hil didn't ask if I was okay, but the question was written in the lines marring her forehead. When I stopped coughing, she asked, "Does this mean you'll be abandoning the soccer players and rejoining our lunch table?"

"Am I welcome?" My voice was quiet and raspy, masking how desperately I wanted her to answer yes.

"I don't know. My best friend wouldn't be skipping the dance because she's all pouty about a guy. Even if she *does* look like a contestant from *Toddlers and Tiaras*." There was a challenge in her words.

But I was too tired to play friendship games or jump through hoops. Every weary cell in my body demanded an end to tonight's drama. "Well, when you decide, let me know."

She opened my door, adding the car's key-in-ignition beeping to the percussion of my coughing. Leaning forward, she hugged me. A fierce, almost painfully tight Hil hug. She pulled back, eyes wide and sad. "I miss you."

Then she turned, her heels clicked on the pavement, and the fabric of her dress looked like molten gold as she practically ran for the school entrance.

And I was left in silence. Even my coughing momentarily ceased as I shut my door and tried to sort through my scrambled thoughts to make sense of what had happened.

My head and palms were sweating. I pulled off my wig and reached to direct the heat vents away—I must've already turned them off—there was no air coming out.

Hil had extended an invitation to open my car door and rejoin the group. It was tempting. So tempting. But the parking lot looked huge; the school looked impossibly far away.

I needed a sign.

I pressed the Power button on the radio. Nothing happened. I reached for the ignition.

It was empty.

My keys—I knew with sudden, many-years-of-friendship clarity—were being held hostage in the dance. Hil *had* made the decision for me, just like I'd asked.

47

The gym was full of students, music, and hot, sticky air. I slipped through the crowd, who nodded greetings, then left me alone. The pulse of the bass made my heart throb, the movement of the dancers made me dizzy, the strobe lights were disorienting.

They were at the center of the crowd. Of course they were; they were the ones people wanted to watch. I was a watcher now. Chris was dancing like he demonstrated in the cafeteria, making Hil laugh so hard she teetered on her heels. He put a hand around her waist; she leaned against his shoulder and smiled up at him. Ally was here with Bill. Whether it was a date of convenience or more, I didn't know—but I wanted to. Lauren's hair glowed like flames under the lights; it was styled and tiara-ready. I scanned for Ryan—found him, found the Ryan of last year: all dimples and charm as he chatted with a pretty junior. But it looked forced. When she turned to whisper something to a friend, his mask slipped, his dimples dimmed.

The air felt too thick, like breathing through a wet towel that smelled of perfume, deodorant, and sweat. I wanted to slump and sneak out, but I couldn't without my keys, and I wouldn't let myself. I'd stay, keep my head high, and watch them crowned. Then I'd head over to congratulate and apologize.

"Mia! Look at your dress—it's beautiful." I turned and found Meagan standing with a tall guy with neat brown hair and a kind smile. "This is my boyfriend, Craig. He goes to Cross Pointe."

"Hey, Mia. Megs talks about you a lot. You're pretty much her hero. I can see why; it's really brave of you to come here without a wig or anything."

"Hi. Oh—" I put a hand to my head, surprised to touch stubble and sweat. Screw it, everyone knew I was sick; I didn't need to hide behind an itchy wig. "It's nice to meet you."

Craig was easy to talk with. He filled my bewildered silences, and Meagan's sincerity quashed my third-wheel worries. "I heard about Ryan. I'm sorry."

"It's okay. I'm okay," I answered, surprised that it was more or less true.

The longer I stood talking with them, the more people came to join our group, offering hugs and praise for my courage. Courageous? Me?

Emily linked an arm through mine and leaned her curly head on my shoulder. "Please say you'll come back to the squad for the winter season. It's not the same without you there. Ally cried when she told us you were off the squad; Hil and Coach Lindsey are still barely speaking because of Coach's decision."

"It wasn't Hil's choice?"

Emily laughed. "Wait? You're serious? No. She threatened to quit over it. It was major squad drama. Summary: you're missed and loved and I'm glad you're here tonight." She squeezed me, then let go. "I should probably find my date."

I waved good-bye and Meagan stepped closer. "You okay? You look confused."

I moved my head. Just enough to indicate a nod. More than enough to make me feel dizzy. I shut my eyes to block out the spotlights. "Tired. It's so loud and hot in here."

"Where's Gyver tonight?"

Gyver. Coldplay. I needed to talk to him. I needed to go home.

The door looked so far away. All the way across an out-of-focus, sequined, gossiping crowd. The opposite direction from the Calendar Girls.

The music stopped. All eyes in the room automatically flicked to the stage.

Mr. Bonura picked up the mic and tapped it. "Good evening, East Lakers. You all look nice tonight—what have you done with my students?" He paused for laughter that didn't come. "It's time to announce Fall Ball king and queen. Could I have the royal court on stage?"

It was a bitter Wonderland nostalgia—watching Hillary, Ally, Lauren, and Molly Cohen weave through students who parted to create a path. I could almost see myself behind Lauren; her seeking last-minute reassurances as I tucked one of her escapee red curls back into place. I blinked and they were at the stage. Ryan was paired with Molly; I was in the audience.

Hil was squinting into the lights—studying the crowd with a frown. It disappeared when she caught my eye, replaced by a smile and a wink. And a flash of my keys as she struck a model pose and dangled them from a finger.

I lifted a hand to wave back, but the motion knocked me off balance. I shut my eyes and swayed. An arm slid around my shoulders.

"It's got to be hard watching Ryan up there. But he's really not the guy for you," Meagan soothed.

I leaned against her, grateful for the support. If she wanted to blame it on my breakup, I was okay with that.

I could hear Mr. Bonura fumbling with the mic and a piece of paper. Ally's chipper voice: "Can I hold that for you?" Laughter from the audience.

"Thanks, Ally. Let's see here: East Lake's Fall Ball king is . . . Ryan Winters." Clapping. I kept my eyes shut. I could picture Ryan stepping forward and bending for the plastic crown better with my eyes closed; when I opened them colors blurred and spun. Was I crying? I felt like crying, but I didn't feel like I *was* crying.

"And his queen is . . ." There was the inevitable clumsy-envelope dramatic pause. I stared at the room with eyes that wouldn't focus.

"Lauren Connors!" Applause as she sauntered forward and ducked for the rhinestone tiara.

Mr. Bonura announced, "Now the king and queen will share their royal dance. Please clear them a spot on the floor." Between blinks the crowd closer to the stage melded into an indistinct blob; they pulsed and a space appeared. A space with Ryan and Lauren in it. I hadn't seen them leave the stage or heard the music start.

Meagan's hand felt cold and heavy on my arm; when she stepped backward, I stumbled and fell.

There was a localized *whoosh* of gasps and curses. Craig carefully helped me up, but now two spots had been cleared on the dance floor: the one where Lauren twirled, tiara'd and oblivious, and the one of concerned attention around me.

"I'm okay." I'd said that so many times tonight the words tasted worn out. I needed to go. I needed space. And quiet.

"I'm fine. I just need air." I held out a "stay there" palm to Meagan and Craig, moving it to cover my mouth as I coughed, the sound overpowering the song's instrumental interlude.

"Mia? Is that—?"

"Ryan, the song's not over. Where are you going? Get back here." Lauren's anger was ill-concealed in her pretty-me voice.

"Mia, baby, wait up!"

All of my strength was directed at making progress through the gym. I passed through the doors and into the foyer before pausing. "What?"

Ryan looked smaller, like the events of the night had shrunken him. He removed the crown from his head and dropped it on a bench. "I wanted to see if you're okay. To drive you home if you want. I'm sober now, I swear. I had no idea you were in there."

"I'm okay, and thanks, but I just need to be alone right now."

Ryan nodded again, eyes tortured. He turned to leave me, then turned back. "Drive safe. I'll call tomorrow. We'll talk." He gave me a long look before stepping back through the doors.

They shut, closing in the gossip, music, and teenage normalcy. I wanted to slump against the wall and put my head on my knees. I ached. Today had been draining—breakfast to breakup—I wanted it over.

I shook as I tried to take my coat off the rack. I used both hands; it took four tries to unfasten the top button and get it off the hanger. Draping it over my arm, I pulled my cell phone out of the pocket, waiting impatiently for it to load and pull up Gyver's number. It was so hot in the foyer. The air was oppressive. The hall seemed to throb with a pulse, contracting and expanding with the beat from the gym. I started for the door and the frosty air of the parking lot. My arm spasmed under the weight of my jacket. I let it slip through my fingers and used one hand to steady the other as I held the phone to my face.

The ringing sounded far away, but I couldn't remember how to turn it up. "Hi. You've reached Gyver. I'm not here. You know—"

I heard the clatter of its impact on the tile floor before I realized I'd dropped my phone. Picking it up was impossible. It was so far away. I leaned forward, but the world leaned more—the walls and doors at odd angles. I shut my eyes so I wouldn't have to see them.

"Get the hell out of my way." I knew that voice. "Mia? Your idiot ex-boyfriend wouldn't let me through the door. Mia?" Hil's voice was echoing off the walls. It hurt my ears. "Mia! Are you okay? Ryan! *Ryan!*" Something icy touched my cheek, jolted my eyes open. She was right next to me, kneeling on the floor in her formal dress. I was on the floor. When had that happened?

"Mia!" Ryan's feet appeared, then the rest of him. "What happened?"

I shut my eyes to block out their anxious faces.

"Should we take her to the hospital?"

"Mia?"

"Her face feels so hot."

"Call an ambulance."

48

My head hurt.

I tried opening my eyes, but everything was too bright and too white. It was noisy: hushed conversations and rhythmic beeping. The talking stopped when I blinked, but the beeping continued. I was in Lakeside Hospital. In pajamas from the just-in-case suitcase Mom kept in the front hall closet.

"Kitten? Are you awake?"

"Mom?" I coughed and forced my eyes open, looking around the room until I located her: Hil, Ryan, doctor-I-didn't-know, Gyver, Mom, Dad. I panned the room, but went back to the face that mattered most. "Hi."

"Mia Moore—you get passed over for Fall Ball queen and react by collapsing?" Gyver said. He'd been leaning against the wall playing with a pick, but stepped forward and placed his hands on the bed rails. "A little melodramatic, don't you think?"

I smiled. My brain felt fogged. "Hi," I repeated.

"Hi." His voice was soft, almost shy.

"How are you feeling?" Dad startled me—I'd forgotten there were other people in the room.

"I feel . . . lousy." My throat clenched in coughs to punctuate my statement.

The doctor cleared his throat. "I'd imagine you do. You have pneumonia. In fact, now you've all seen she's okay, the best thing we can do for Mia is to let her get some rest. Then no more than three visitors at a time."

Mom kissed my forehead. "I'm going to go call Dr. Kevin. Say good-bye to your friends, then get some sleep. We'll be back." Dad squeezed my hand and followed.

"Five minutes, then go," the doctor ordered. "I'll be back to check on you."

Ryan, Hil, and Gyver hesitated. They each had an agenda; I owed each an explanation. Ryan stepped forward first. He touched my cheek. "You scared me."

"I'm sorry." The words grated against my throat and I coughed to clear them.

If possible, he paled further. "Don't apologize; just get better."

Hil stepped forward and pushed Ryan out of the way. He looked like he might argue, then didn't. Simply drifted back to lean against the wall. She opened and shut her mouth three times before she could get the words out. "I thought it'd be easier to be mad at you than scared. It wasn't." Her eyes were anguished; they flitted between my bare head and the needle in my arm. "Don't *ever* lie to me like that again."

"I won't. I'm sorry," I rasped.

"I'm sorry too." She hugged me, wary of my tubes. "I thought you didn't need me anymore." She was tearing up and I was too.

"Not possible, Hil. I was stupid."

That was the limit of Gyver's patience. He pressed past Hil and sat on the side of the bed—claiming his spot and my attention. "Not stupid. Scared."

Over his shoulder, Hil gave me an amused smile. "I'll visit soon—I've got some questions and want answers." She rolled her eyes in the direction of Gyver's back, then propelled Ryan out the door.

I leaned close to Gyver, inhaled a painful breath, and began. "You were right. I was selfish. And really, really hurtful. I'm so sorry. I need you to forgive me. I need you." Tears again.

Gyver waited until I was done coughing. "As much as I'm convinced you're perfect, the doctors keep telling me you're only human . . . Though there's nothing *only* about you. You were scared. Sorry I was so judgmental."

"I didn't get your CD before, but I do now."

"Do you?"

"I think so. I hope so. I listened to more of it. 'Fix You,' by Coldplay. That's a 'surrender' song. Isn't it?"

"That's why I picked it. What do you think?"

"I think—" There was so much I needed to say, but my head was clouded with fever and fatigue. I reached for his hand. "I think you've given me another reason to prove the psychic wrong."

"Time's up," the doctor said from the door. "Let her rest. You can come back tomorrow."

Why couldn't it be Dr. Kevin, who knew it was Gyver's right to be by my side now and whenever?

"I didn't get to listen to all of it yet. And my car's at the school." Alarm tightened my grip on his hand.

Gyver removed his iPod from the pocket of his jacket and scrolled through its screens. "It's on here too. I'd tell you to sleep now and listen later, but you've got a history of falling asleep to my music." He gently tucked the earbuds in my ears.

I blinked at the small screen. "You spelled my name wrong."

"No, I didn't."

I gave him a dubious look. "I know how to spell my name."

"I didn't. Your name has never been awesome because it's alliterative. Remember, Mi, I'm Italian."

"What does that mean?" I yawned.

"You're a smart girl; you'll figure it out." Gyver squeezed my hand, then released it to cup my face. Slowly, making intense eye contact the whole time, he leaned in and brushed his lips down my cheek. "You sleep. I'm not going anywhere."

"Doctor?" I called as he held the door open for Gyver. "Can I talk to you?"

"Sure." The doctor looked young and driven. Four pens spaced evenly in his pocket, short hair gelled into perfection. His face was focused determination versus Dr. Kevin's endless cheer.

"How sick am I? Did you say pneumonia?"

"You're sick. You'll be in here for about a week while we get your fever down and lungs clear. Maybe longer."

"No, I mean, other than that: the cancer?"

He frowned. "That hasn't changed—you're doing well. Responding to treatment. I checked your records and your last counts were excellent. I know you're supposed to begin your next round of consolidation chemo next week—we'll have to push that back until you're better. But it won't be a problem."

"But I've been getting these pains. My heart races and it feels like I've forgotten how to breathe. It feels like I'm dying."

The doctor appraised me. "Rapid pulse? Shallow breathing? It sounds like anxiety."

"Aren't I sick?"

"Yes, but that sounds like anxiety." He reached out and put a calming hand on mine, which was so twisted in my necklace it was cutting trails in my fingers.

"I'm not dying?"

"Not today. But you need to take better care of yourself— you shouldn't have let yourself get this sick before telling anyone. Have you been sleeping? Eating well?"

"No." I plucked at the sheet, pulling my knees up toward my chin. "I can't. It got so . . . It just seemed like too much." My heart was starting to throb and something began to beep.

"Take a deep breath."

I did, but it made me cough. I tried again with more success.

The doctor nodded encouragingly as my pulse slowed and the beeping stopped. "You are responding to treatment, but there's a mental toll as well as a physical one. I'm going to have a counselor visit you."

Yesterday I would've scoffed and rejected his advice. But yesterday I'd been ready to give up and accept death. I wasn't anymore. "Okay."

"Cancer's part of your life; it isn't your whole life. You need some long-term perspective, and we need to get that anxiety under control."

"Thanks."

"Now get some sleep," he insisted.

Like I had a choice. My eyelids were already sealing out his words and the world. Anxiety? I fumbled closed-eyed until I found the Play button on Gyver's iPod.

"Mark, do you speak Italian?" I asked drowsily. I'd been fading in and out of sleep as I tried to focus on the songs Gyver'd chosen. I'd fall asleep in one song and wake up coughing in the next. Fall asleep and wake up during the same song—did that mean I'd slept only seconds, or through a whole repetition of the playlist? The fever wasn't helping either. Not much was making sense.

My parents—thinking I was asleep—had exited at Mark's entrance.

"Are you worried about school? You know it's 3:30 a.m., right? I guarantee your teacher will give you an extension."

"I'm just trying to figure something out." I rubbed a sleepy hand across my eyes and tried to focus. "Gyver made me this.

Does this mean what I think?" I tapped the dial to illuminate the screen.

Mark chuckled. "Clever boy; great play on your name."

"Humor me. I'm not sure I believe it," I said, wider awake now.

Mark grinned. "Yup, 'Mi Amore' means 'my love.' Like I said, pretty clever."

"Oh. I thought so, maybe. I hoped . . ."

Mark laughed at the blush creeping up my neck. "Should I send him in? He's in the waiting room. You can have a quick visit as long as you remember the infection rule . . ." He looked at me expectantly, but I stared blankly. "No kissing," he reminded.

"Mark said you wanted Gyver, but I asked to see you first." Ryan's eyes were red and his suit was rumpled. His blue tie was crushed half in his pocket.

"Hi." I failed my weak attempt to sit up. "You didn't go home?"

"Chris came. He took Hil home and me to get my car, but I came right back." His words had the flavor of confession.

"You didn't have to. You should get some sleep."

"Gyver stayed." Ryan's posture went rigid, then slumped in resignation. "I wanted to make sure you're okay. How're you feeling?" He sat in the chair beside my bed.

"Better. Tired. Sick. It sounds like I'll be here a while."

"Yeah." Ryan swallowed and fidgeted with the pockets of his suit coat. "I'd take back all the crap I said last night, but . . ."

I reached for the hand that had been my lifeline, and he crushed my fingers one last time. "No, you were right, I just wasn't brave enough to say it first. We weren't happy."

"God, this sucks." He extracted his fingers from mine and stared out the window. "What happens now?"

"I hope we can be friends."

"Yeah . . ." He sighed. "I should let you sleep. Or see Gyver." The second sentence was harder for him to say.

I thought about denying it, but I was done lying. "Thanks, for everything. Will you send him in?"

Ryan nodded; it was a quick, tight motion. "Mia, I'm not going to visit for a while. I need some time."

I swallowed a lump in my throat. "I'll miss you."

He smiled, but it was a small, sad, dimple-free smile. "Ditto," he said, and backed out of the room.

49

"I keep asking for Gyver and getting everyone else." I held out my arms for parental hugs, expecting coos of "Kitten, how are you?" and offers to hunt down Popsicles. Instead, Mom sat in a chair and Dad frowned from the end of my bed.

"You knew," Mom said simply. "You knew you were sick and you didn't tell us."

It wasn't a question; it was an accusation.

"Yes."

"Why?" Dad's voice was a thunderstorm, crashing and making me tremble. My throat began to constrict. "Why would you take risks with your health? You're smarter than this."

My mother reached for a tissue. My father turned his back to me.

"And your grades? I spent an hour on the phone with Principal Baker this afternoon." Dad's voice rebounded off the wall but didn't lose any of its anger.

This surprised me, but it shouldn't have. Fall Ball was the deadline I'd agreed to, and I'd ceased pretending to catch up after Jinx died.

Dad stomped to my side. "Goddamn it, Mia! What have you been doing? It's like you've given up."

"I had," I whispered.

"What?" The emotion drained from Dad's face as he uncurled his fingers from the bed rail and sank into a chair.

"I had given up," I explained, trying to fight off the chest tightening and continue. "I was so tired, and I didn't think I'd make it. It didn't seem worth it to keep trying so hard."

"How could you do that to me? You can't give up." Mom sobbed and held her arms out to Dad, but he stayed frozen on the other side of my bed.

"How could you expect me to handle all of this? Mom, you put so much pressure on me. My life was hard before—it was impossible once I got sick. It got so bad; giving up seemed like my only option."

"You should have told us," she countered. "How are we supposed to help if we don't know what's wrong?"

"It's always been so hard to make you proud and so easy to let you down; I don't know how to flat-out fail at something. I didn't want to disappoint you."

I watched the tissue flutter from Mom's hand as she reached out to squeeze my fingers. Tears flowed down her cheeks undabbed.

Dad looked lost, his mouth gaped.

"I was just so scared." I let the tears salt my cheeks; I shook with months of fear, coughing convulsively.

Dad reacted first, coming to rub my back and offer me water as I choked. Mom stayed still: confusion, then something else, passing over her face. She picked up the box of tissues and murmured, "It's okay."

"It's not okay! I can't do it all." I continued crying, alternating sobs with coughing fits that hurt enough to make me cry more and left me woozy. "I . . . I can't worry about being your perfect daughter with the 4.0 and pretty friends and popular boyfriend and fight cancer at the same time."

I wiped my cheek on my sleeve and took a few deep breaths. "I don't want to do it all." Paused to cough. "And I need it to be okay if I don't always do what you want." Paused again to catch my breath. "Or live your dream for my life."

Mom handed me tissue after tissue. She wasn't saying anything, but she was listening. That was a start.

Between gasps, I managed to convey the conclusions I'd reached. "I was focused on the wrong things. Everything I gave up and couldn't have. I stopped realizing how lucky I am. I mean, treatment is going well, right, Dad?"

"Very well. Your latest platelet count—" Mom held up a hand and he nodded and let me continue.

"If I can't go to college far away, or can't go full time, or even can't go right after graduation—it's not the end of the world. Neither is not cheering or not having hair."

"I can make a list of colleges near hospitals with good oncology programs," mused Dad.

I nodded; list making was his form of comfort. It was the Dad version of superstition, but I needed more than that. "I want to have conversations where you hear me, not just compile facts and make mental graphs. Do you get the difference?"

Mom shot him an I-told-you-so look, but I took one last shaky breath and finished. "What I'm saying is, I'm sorry I lied to you. I get it now." I wiped my face.

"Feel better?" Mom asked, her voice hopeful.

I would have nodded and smiled yesterday. Today I shook my head. "No. But can I see Gyver?"

"Now?" Dad asked.

I lost my battle with a yawn. "I need to talk to him. I've been waiting all morning."

"All morning? It's four thirty. You need some sleep, kitten."

"After I see Gyver, I promise."

Dad spoke up, "No. No more promises or bargains. I listened, I heard you, but you've got to earn back our trust. Right now, your top priority has to be your health. You need to sleep, not socialize."

"But . . ." My voice rose in pitch as my eyes filled again.

"But nothing. Sleep and eat breakfast; then you can see him." Dad's voice was firm.

Mom looked between Dad and me. She nodded. "Get some sleep and then he can visit. It's just Gyver; he'll wait."

"I don't want to sleep," I whined like a toddler protesting

bedtime, my argument undermined by a second traitorous yawn.

"Then I guess you don't want to see your friends," Dad countered.

"Fine." If it's possible to slam your eyes shut, that's what I did. Of course, all it did was jar tears loose and send them disloyally down my cheeks.

Mom wiped them. "He can visit after ten. I'll send him home to get some sleep too."

50

Since I slept until eleven, my parents compromised and allowed Gyver to visit while I ate breakfast. They even allowed me to see him alone—after a stern "Make sure she eats"—because they were speaking with the counselor I'd soon be meeting. Mom still wasn't keen on the counselor idea. "What are you going to tell her about me?" Gyver rolled his eyes, and Dad shooed her out of the room.

"If I eat the toast, will you eat the rest so they get off my case?" I bargained when the door shut.

"Nope." Gyver smiled and sat on the edge of my bed. I didn't like the table with my breakfast tray between us, but my parents would be peeking in, so it stayed.

"I've been asking for you since three thirty," I confessed.

"I know." He grinned wider.

"I did some translating." I reached under the table for his hand and blushed. "How do you say 'kiss me' in Italian?"

Gyver's forehead wrinkled, and as the seconds stretched silent, my smile melted. My eyes itched with the tears of the rejected. I wrestled for composure, but my heart sprinted and my irregular breath caused a coughing fit. Gyver's fingers had tightened when I'd asked, but now he released my hand and passed me a cup of apple juice.

I fought for control of my breathing, fought the tears blurring my eyes. I sipped, sending stinging juice down my raw throat.

"Forget I said anything," I whispered, studying the banana browning on my tray. I wanted to shove it all aside and pull my knees to my chest.

"No, Mi—"

The door opened and we turned toward my father. "You okay? I could hear you coughing down the hall."

I nodded and held up my juice, hoping he wouldn't look too closely at my stricken face.

"I've got her, Mr. Moore. I'd come get you if anything . . ."

Dad smiled at Gyver. "I know you would. Just checking." He pointed to the tray. "Eat," and backed out of the room.

I crumbled some toast and peeked at Gyver with a hummingbird's heart thrumming in my chest. "I assumed . . . Forget it."

"I'm thinking. I know mostly kitchen Italian. If you want to know how to say something food related, I'm your guy. 'Kiss me' doesn't come up at the dinner table." He laughed and I raised my eyes to him.

"So you do . . . ?" I trailed off. "The playlist wasn't so subtle by the end."

"I tried subtle, Mi. You didn't get it."

"And the last song? It's you singing; you wrote it for me?"

"I could make you a whole playlist with the songs I've written you," he confessed.

"Please do." I put down my juice and leaned forward. "Gyver, I believe I'm going to get better—I do—but I've got lots of this left. Are you sure it's what you want?"

"Lots of you—in bed? It'll be torture, but I think I can manage."

I frowned. "Be serious."

"Mi, I've waited years for you already. I know what you're saying, but I'm in love with you. Did you really not know? It's going to take something worse than cancer to scare me."

I shook my head. "You've called me 'Mi' forever. How long have I been oblivious?"

"Only since I was ten. Don't you remember? You caught me repeating your name in the backyard."

"You told me you liked alliteration. You were lying?"

Anyone else would have blushed; Gyver smiled and handed me a slice of toast. "Eat or I'm gonna get kicked out."

I took a hasty bite. "All these years I've been collecting alliterative names for you—"

"*Baciami!*" Gyver interrupted, satisfaction settling on his face.

"Ba-cha-me?" I repeated slowly, my initial grin falling to a pout. "It's not fair. I want to kiss you and can't."

"I don't know; last time I initiated a kiss, you dropped ice cream on me."

I laughed. "I didn't do it on purpose! Is that what you thought?"

Gyver shrugged and nodded.

"Seriously? You think I'd waste perfectly good ice cream? That was a poorly timed clumsy moment, which I interpreted as a very bad omen."

Gyver groaned. "You and your signs."

"I'm done. I promise. I'll cancel my horoscopes and throw away the Magic 8 Ball."

"Keep the Magic 8 Ball. I gave you that." He picked up and rubbed my hand. It was a gesture that should've been familiar and comforting, but it felt new and electric.

"Gyver, just so you know, Ryan and I didn't . . ." I blushed and stumbled over words. "That day in the kitchen it looked like— But we never."

He cupped my face, thumb stroking my cheek; there was a smile in his voice. "I didn't think so. At least not that day."

"How were you so maddeningly calm? I can't believe you invited Ryan over for lasagna while we were standing there half-naked."

"Rest assured, I went home and lifted till I threw up, but I didn't think you'd . . . I knew you'd interpret my interruption as a *very bad sign* and cancel your plans." His smile was smug. "But I don't want to hear the words 'Ryan,' 'you,' and 'naked' in the same sentence again."

The door opened too soon. My parents and the counselor entered the room. Far too soon for me to tell Gyver everything I needed to. "Come back later?"

"Tomorrow," Dad corrected.

I opened my mouth to protest, but Dad repeated himself.

Gyver squeezed my hand under the tray. "I'll see you tomorrow, Mia Moore."

I twisted my hand in his, tracing the guitar-string calluses on his fingertips. In a voice as steady as a statue and only slightly raspy, I answered, "I love you too, Gyver."

"Did she say . . . to Gyver?" Mom looked from the door where Gyver exited to my father.

"Dear, let's go," said Dad.

"But what about Ryan?" she asked.

"We broke up."

"You and Ryan broke up?" Her voice climbed from confused to baffled.

"Mom." My voice was stern. She stopped fussing and turned to me. "You've got to start trusting me to make my own decisions about what makes me happy."

"Of course, kitten. I do." She smoothed her already smooth hair and laughed nervously. "Gyver Russo, really?" It wasn't criticism, it was curiosity.

"Really."

"Well then, it looks like I've got some catching up to do . . . that is, if you want to tell me." She looked almost timid, adjusting and readjusting the shoulder strap of her purse.

"I'd like that." We exchanged smiles, and Dad patted my hand before taking her arm and leading her out of the room.

That left me facing the counselor. She looked at me from behind thick lenses with an expression both patient and compassionate. I thought about Mrs. Russo's comments. "Are you going to tell me it'll help to talk? Because I have a lot to say . . ."

51

I woke Tuesday afternoon to a gentle but persistent poking in my shoulder.

"I'm up, I'm up," I grumbled, swatting away someone's hand.

"Finally," Hil answered. "I've been sitting here for almost two hours, and I have to go soon."

I scooted over on the bed and she climbed up next to me. We leaned against each other, hip to hip, shoulder to shoulder, and stared at the wall in front of us.

"It wasn't supposed to be like this," she reflected with a wry laugh. "Remember all our plans for a perfect senior year?"

"Do you get why I couldn't tell you?" I asked.

"No."

"You wouldn't have let me mope. You would've gotten the whole squad to—I don't know—shave their heads in solidarity. You would've been there for me. Right?"

"I don't see the problem."

"I didn't want to be held accountable. Lauren let me wal-low in self-pity and hide from this—at least at first she did. And if she had a bad reaction when I told her and she rejected me, oh well. I didn't think I could handle that from you."

"I'm here now, and I'm not going anywhere."

"I'm going to be fine." Each time I said it, I was more con-fident it was true.

"Promise?" Hil turned to look at me, her face overwhelmed by her large, worried eyes.

"I can't promise, but everything looks good and I believe I'll get better."

She gave me a smile. "That's good enough for me—I've never seen you not meet a goal. I mean, you even got Ryan Winters to beg to be your boyfriend."

"Is he okay?" He had kept his word and hadn't visited. My fingers traced the chain around my neck. It didn't feel right to wear Ryan's heart post-breakup, but I needed to fidget, so the chain stayed. I'd punched a hole in one of Gyver's picks and wore that instead.

Hil rolled her eyes. "He's Ryan Winters; there are already new hook-up rumors. Though I think they're more girls' wish-ful thinking than truth. I'm sure he'll be fine. Mostly, he and Chris have been locked away doing 'guy stuff.' What do you think that even means?"

"We watch musicals and eat chocolate; maybe they eat wings and watch war movies?" I suggested, then giggled. "But seriously, how awesome would it be if they're at Chris's watching *Annie* or *Grease*?"

She threw her arms around my neck; I hugged back just as greedily. "God, you're not allowed to go AWOL again, Summer Girl. Okay? Whatever happens, you tell me!"

"Deal," I agreed.

She let go. "Welcome back. Also, I expect you to come out for winter cheerleading. We can figure out how to deal with missed practices. We can't figure out how to miss you."

Before I could respond or tear up, she added, "Though it totally sucks you can't tumble, because the new recruits are hopeless at it."

I laughed and shook my head. Hil would always be Hil. From the hallway I heard Mary Poppins Nurse—Mariah—call, "Hello, handsome."

My favorite voice responded, "How's our girl today?"

I turned to Hil. "Gyver's coming. You have to be nice. Gyver's my . . ." I trailed off. Boyfriend didn't seem right, not strong enough. "Gyver's mine."

Hil laughed, her throaty, haughty laugh. "Gyver's *always* been yours. Why do you think I wanted-slash-hated him so much?"

"Can you be satisfied with every other male? What about Chris?"

"Am I the biggest hypocrite for hiding him all fall and giving you grief about dating?"

"Yes, but it really wasn't so hidden—we all knew. Play nice

with him; he's crazy about you." I would've said more but Gyver knocked and entered.

I smiled like a fool; I couldn't help it. "Hey." My voice was whispery, girly, ridiculous.

"Hey, Mi." He answered with a matching smile and extended eye contact before acknowledging the impatient girl beside me. "Hi, Hillary."

"Hey, Mac 'n' Cheese." She wiped her cheeks, smoothed her hair, and stood.

"You know, I don't actually like that name," he said, but his voice was amused, so I relaxed back against my pillow.

"I know." She gave me, then Gyver, impromptu hugs and walked to the door, turning around and grinning at our shocked expressions. "I'll call you later, Mia."

Gyver claimed his spot and my hand. "Hi."

"Speaking of calls, I called you from the dance."

"I know. I called back, and Hillary answered from the ambulance. I drove here like a maniac."

"I thought you didn't pick up because you were mad."

"No. That's not why." Gyver took my hand in both of his. I could see a flush creeping up his cheeks.

"Why?"

"It's embarrassing. You know, this is what I always thought your hospital room should look like." He pointed to the cards, flowers, and stuffed animals, sent by classmates and crowding all flat surfaces.

"Nice try, but I'm not that easily distracted. You, embarrassed? This I've got to hear." I tugged on his hand.

"I didn't answer because I was out in my backyard."

"Why? It was freezing."

When he didn't continue, I snuggled closer and pouted. He kissed me on the nose. "Your necklace. You told me you'd lost it, and the jewelers were closed."

"I'm pretty sure I didn't lose my necklace in your backyard."

Gyver studied our entwined hands. "I was looking for four-leaf clovers."

"What? You're not serious. In the dark?"

"I had a flashlight."

I tried not to laugh and failed. "Why? Why in the world?"

"I thought maybe if I found one for you, you'd cheer up and feel less hopeless."

"Gyver Russo! I believe someone's always telling me I put too much faith in superstitions. And"—I deepened my voice in a poor imitation—"I make my own luck."

His grin was full of mischief. "I can't wait to get lucky with you."

"Gyver." I groaned. "You're ridiculous!"

He started to retort, but I cut him off with a finger to his lips. A finger I began to trace around his mouth with a feather-light touch.

His puzzled look turned to concern as I began to lean in. He put a hand on either side of my face and warred with impulses to pull me close and push me away. "Mi, we can't."

I smiled and leaned still closer, fitting myself into the space between his arms, the space that felt like sanctuary. These were the words I'd been waiting all day to tell him. "I asked. My counts are good."

This time there were no ice cream accidents and no fevers. If I had been attached to a heart monitor, I'm sure it would have set off every racing-pulse alarm.

But I wasn't.

There was nothing to interrupt, nothing to interfere, and nothing between Gyver's and my lips but a few inches of empty air.

And then there wasn't even that.

There were Gyver's hands sliding up my neck, his thumb caressing my jawline and his fingers sliding around the back of my head, tilting up my chin and lowering his mouth to mine.

We didn't bump noses, or grind teeth, or mash lips. There wasn't that period of awkward learning—because it was Gyver and it was me, and there was no one who knew me better, no one I'd ever know so well.

It was sweet and fierce and many things my mind and body couldn't name. The type of kissing that eclipsed all prior kisses—the type of kissing I hoped to be doing for a very long time.

And when Gyver and I finally pulled apart, his face was flushed and we were both the best kind of breathless. I knew exactly how he felt and what he was thinking: *more.* We both leaned in for a second kiss at the same instant—and this, I decided, was the very best sign.

ACKNOWLEDGMENTS

I've always daydreamed of writing an acknowledgments page, much in the way that actors dream of giving Oscar acceptance speeches. And now here's my chance! Even better, I get to type this while wearing pajamas instead of an uncomfortable gown and heels. Lucky for me there's neither a live audience nor aren't-you-done-yet? music because I'm overwhelmed with gratitude for the many, many people who have helped me reach this stage, and it's making me a little teary eyed.

Huge, from-the-bottom-of-my-heart-accompanied-by-hugs-and-baked-goods thank-yous to the following people:

My team at Walker—Emily Easton, Mary Kate Castellani, Laura Whitaker, Patricia McHugh, Jill Amack, and everyone else there who worked to bring Mia's story to the shelves.

The dreamiest of dream agents, Joe Monti, as well as Barry Goldblatt, Tricia Ready, and the rest of the BG Literary family. *Regina Forever.*

Jenny Southard, my go-to person for all things medical, and Kari Olson, whose patience with my radiology questions was truly impressive. Any mistakes are my fault. All medical brilliance is theirs.

My friends who forgave me when I canceled plans to stay in and write and were waiting to hang out when I needed to get away from my computer. And my fellow writers who read these pages and pushed me to be my best: Jonathan Maberry, Nancy Keim Comley, Kerry Gans, Katie Foucart, Leah Clifford, Tiffany Emerick, and Stacey Yiengst.

Team Sparkle—a.k.a. Scott Tracey, Courtney Summers, Victoria Schwab, Emily Hainsworth, Linda Grimes, and Susan Adrian—I owe them my sanity. Especially Emily, who read this manuscript more times than I can count and never lost her enthusiasm for Mia, Gyver, and co—have I told you how pretty you are?

The Apocalypsies—I couldn't imagine sharing this publication adventure with a better group.

Andrew McMahon—for being an inspiration with his music and his leukemia survivorship and for permission to use his lyrics—as well as to Ellie Waite for doing all the permissions paperwork! For those who are interested in more information on Andrew's story and his work promoting awareness about cancer in young adults, please look into his charity, the Dear Jack Foundation. (www.DearJackFoundation.com)

The Mysza family. You are my superheroes. Not a day goes by that I don't think of you, miss Morgan, and send you all love.

And, finally, for my family. To my parents and siblings for putting up with my endless princess and puppy stories as a child. To my Schmidtlets, who were nappers when I needed to revise and snugglers when I needed to pace and brainstorm. And St. Matt, thank you for being so . . . *saintly* and putting up with me through this whole crazy process. I love you.

Read on for an update from Gyver

Mid-December, four weeks after the end of *Send Me a Sign*

The downside of being the nurses' favorite visitor—the boyfriend of their favorite patient—is there's no getting by their station unnoticed. They want to chat. To show me pictures of their babies, grandbabies, and fur babies. They want to ask about my band and college applications.

"Hi, Gyver! What are you and Mia going to be up to today?" asks Polly.

Mariah looks up from her paperwork and beams at me. "We were wondering when you'd come in. Any fun plans to make our girl smile?"

"Hey!" I say, but I keep walking. Normally, I'm all for letting them tell me how devoted and awesome I am. Normally, I'd listen to and join in their complaints about the weather and having to track down ice scrapers for windshields this morning.

There are perks to being the favorite. Unlimited ice pops whenever I want them. And Mi hasn't had to eat off the hospital menu once during this round of chemo. She hasn't managed to keep a whole lot down, and every time her face turns gray it kills me that all I can do is hold her hand, get her wet washcloths, and pray her stomach stops revolting. If vanilla milk shakes from Scoops or soup from Iggy's makes her even slightly more willing to eat, then thank God the nurses like me and are willing to ignore the cups and bowls that fill Mi's trashcan.

Another bonus of being their favorite: I've never once heard the words "visiting hours" directed at me.

But right now, I'm just hoping they don't notice my guitar case is starting to drip.

I'm not going to let a stupid thing like leukemia stand between Mi and me and our unofficial start of winter tradition.

"More serenading?" Polly winks. "That Mia is a lucky girl."

"She knows it too," says a hoarse voice from the doorway of room 317, and I spin to catch my favorite smile on my favorite lips.

She looks beautiful—always—and pale, tired, too thin. But not as pale or tired as yesterday, and her smile reaches all the way to her eyes—all the way to my heart, making it clench the way it does every time she looks at me like that.

"Hey, Mi. Get back in bed or at least put some slippers on. The floor's cold."

"Yeah. Yeah," she says. I follow her into the room, grabbing a pair of fuzzy socks off a chair and tossing them to her. She rolls her eyes as she sits on the bed and puts them on, then points at what I'm carrying. "Isn't that your old guitar? You're not going to try and teach me to play again, are you? Gyver, I will happily be your eternal audience, but I can't even clap to a beat."

"Wait and see." I trace a line around her wrist inside the band of her hospital bracelet and love the way her breath catches in response. I tap on her fingernails—they're painted with daisies—and tilt my head in question.

"Ally," she says. Then holds up her other hand. On these nails the flowers look more like Rorschach blobs. "And Hil . . ." Mi shrugs. "She tried. And she went off on Mom when she was whining about the heat in here, so that was kinda awesome."

Yeah, the heat. It's pretty atrocious and is likely ruining my surprise, but if Mi's not feeling up to it . . .

"What's today?" I've promised never to ask, "How are you feeling?" because she gets that too often. Instead, we agreed upon a rating scale; it's nothing superoriginal, but it works.

"Eh, somewhere between a C+ and a B–. "

Yesterday was a C, so that's progress, but I still have to grit my teeth. She deserves a lifetime of A+ days, without blood tests or being caged in by hospital walls.

She gives me a look that says *I know what you're thinking* and pats the space beside her. "Now get up here and play me a song. I can forget just about anything when you're singing."

I tuck the blankets up around her before I plop the case next to her and flip open the latches. But not the lid. Not yet. It makes sense to lean in for a kiss now, because it's possible she'll be too annoyed to let me kiss her afterward.

I love how she curls her fingers through the hair at the back of my neck and clutches the front of my shirt, right over my heart, which seems to beat out the words *I love you, I love you, I love only you* over and over.

It's so easy to get lost in this that I don't notice she's opened the case.

Not until the lid bumps my chest. Before I can react, there's something icy dripping down the back of my shirt. She giggles against my mouth.

I gasp against hers. "Cold. Cold! So. Cold."

"You're lucky I didn't drop it down your pants." She raises her eyebrows and shrieks when I sprinkle a handful of snow over her head. Retaliates with double fistfuls to my cheeks before pulling up her blanket like a shield.

The snow's not lasting long in a room this hot, but it's melting into her laughter, into drops of water I'm shaking from my hair and slush she's flicking with daisy-painted nails.

"Truce! Truce!" Mia's always the one who gives up first. And it always occurs when I'm holding something above her head.

I raise an eyebrow. "Already? I was just getting started." The slush in my hand drips onto her neck. I watch it slide over her collarbone and underneath the collar of her candy-cane-print pajama shirt.

She shrieks and shivers, holds up two empty hands in surrender. "Remember: you love me."

"That's a cheap trick, Mi Amore."

"Did I mention I love you too?" She peeks up at me with those blue-blue eyes and I've got no choice: I dump the slush back in the case and drop it on the floor. There's the thermos my mom filled with hot chocolate and extra marshmallows inside, but that can wait. I need to be next to her. Even if that means sitting in a puddle.

"Good surprise?" I ask, picking up her hands and warming them between mine.

"The best. I can't believe I missed the first snow." She licks a clump of snowflakes off my neck, and now I'm the one who's shivering. "Except, I guess I *didn't*. Thank you."

Instead of saying "you're welcome," I kiss the melting flakes off her eyelids, the drops of water off her cheeks; I follow the path of the slush that slid over the hollow of her collarbones. It doesn't matter that I've got handfuls melting in my hair and beneath my shirt. I am miles away from feeling cold.

"We've got a lifetime of snowstorms ahead of us, Mi," I whisper against her neck, pulling back to study her face and add, "unless you decide to go to college somewhere warm. Then we'll have to make do with snow-cone fights or something. Maybe sand castle competitions."

"What would I do without you?" she says with a smile. *That* smile. My smile.

"Good thing you'll never have to find out."

One night can change how you see the world.

One night can change how you see yourself.

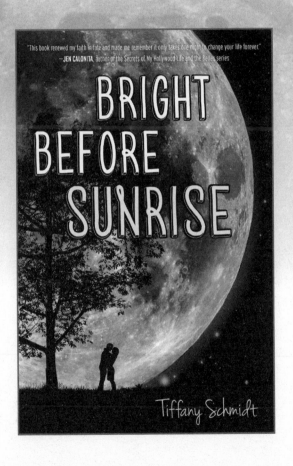

Read on for a sneak peek of Tiffany Schmidt's
new novel, *Bright Before Sunrise*

JONAH

☀ 12:57 P.M. ☽

TIME MOVES SLOWER ON FRIDAY AFTERNOONS

"You dropped something."

I totally miss that the girl is talking to me. She's sat next to me in English for five months and other than her falsely sweet "Welcome to Cross Pointe" on my first day, the only interactions we've had are her *indulge-me* smiles when she leans across my desk to talk to the girl who sits on the other side of me. One is Jordan and the other is Juliana—I'm not sure who's who. Both have long, light brown hair and toothpaste-commercial smiles.

She clears her throat and taps my desk with her pencil. Then points to the pink baby sock at my feet. It must have fallen out of my sleeve or the leg of my jeans. Even though all of Sophia's laundry is washed separately in her organic, hypoallergenic, dye-and-fragrance-free, all-natural, probably-promises-extra-IQ-points detergent, it seems to get everywhere. Especially her socks. She's just found her feet, and her favorite pastime is freeing them.

It drives my stepfather, Paul, into panics about her

catching cold. Even when it's eighty degrees out. What can I say; the baby is cute *and* crafty.

I reach down and grab the sock—that little monkey must have managed to kick it into my pocket or stick it down my shirt while I was holding her this morning.

"Thanks," I say to Jordan/Juliana.

"Is it your daughter's? It's so cute." She's smiling, but there's something off about the question. Besides the fact that it's none of her business, she looks too eager, almost hungry for my answer. "You're from Hamilton, right?"

"What's that mean?" I ask, crushing the sock in my hand. I already know the answer. I'm the new kid from *Hamilton*. And because I didn't grow up in Cross Pointe, with nannies and beach homes, I must be a teenage father.

At least she has enough decency to blush when she stammers something about, "Well, it's just—I've heard that in Hamilton . . ."

"It's my sister's." I hate myself for answering. For caring even a little what my Cross Pointe classmates think of me.

"Oh." She looks me up and down again, like I'm a new person now that I'm not someone's baby daddy. "But it *is* true about Hamilton, right? Did a lot of your old classmates have kids? I heard they even have a program where you can bring your babies to class. I can't even imagine a *baby* in a classroom."

She draws out "imagine" into three syllables: im-mag-gine. And ends her statement with this absurd giggle.

I bite my tongue so hard.

She leans over and takes the sock from my hand. I could've held on to it, but I'm too shocked by her complete disregard for my personal space. "This is so little! I can't believe you have a sister who's a *baby*."

I wonder what part of my body language or expression makes her think I want to continue this conversation. Does she think I've been waiting all semester for her to wake up and notice me? Or maybe she's just bored because the other half of Jordan/Juliana is absent.

"I just can't get over it—that's *so* much younger than you. Talk about an *oops*—I bet your parents were shocked." She's turning her whole body in her seat, leaning toward me; like she's starving and will feed off whatever information I'll share about myself. "Whole sister, or half?"

"When I left for school this morning she was in one piece. I hope no one's halved her by the time I get home," I say, taking the sock back and shoving it into my pocket. Then I turn around and continue filling out the I-don't-feel-like-teaching-on-Friday busywork sheet on the themes in the fussy Gothic novel we're reading.

I hear her exhale in a huff. I'm sure she's rolling her eyes and getting ready to make some insulting comment about me to someone nearby, but I don't care.

I am not providing fuel for their gossip. I am not playing any of their Cross Pointe games.

I'm surviving.

Counting down the days until graduation. Eleven.

Then I'm out of here.

Brighton

☀ 1:16 P.M. ☽

23 HOURS, 44 MINUTES LEFT

"Brighton! Why weren't you at lunch?"

I freeze at the familiar voice. I'd been hoping—just this once, just today—I could make it from my locker to class without been seen, but Jordan latches on to my arm as I walk by the door of Mrs. Watson's room.

"I had to do something for yearbook." The "something" had been to take a moment just to breathe. The yearbook room had been a convenient place to hide out and do it.

"Why didn't you tell anyone?" She tsks like I'm being silly and gives my arm a playful shake. "Everyone was looking for you."

Which is why I hid.

I thought I'd be fine. Until the moment this morning when we were getting ready to broadcast morning announcements and I glanced at the first story I was supposed to read and almost burst into tears. I don't know what I would've done if Amelia hadn't noticed and stepped in with a quick lie: "Oh, Brighton, your mascara is smudged! Go, I'll take your spot—" so I could run off to the bathroom, pull myself together, and lecture myself on being ridiculous. So the captain of the baseball team is named Ethan—same name as my dad. This isn't news to me. It certainly isn't a valid reason to cry like an idiot during a live broadcast.

Since then, I'd done a fairly decent imitation of *fine* during my morning classes, but skipping lunch had been necessary.

"Sorry." I pluck off my headband, smooth my dark brown hair, then put the band back, using the motions as an excuse to extract my arm from her grip. "What did I miss? Do you need something?"

"Not really." Jordan shrugs, leans toward me with a conspiratorial smile. "But since you weren't there, you didn't hear how Natalie wants to have her graduation party the same day as mine! And we both want the yacht club; so one of us will have to use the clubroom instead of the ballroom. I'm sure Natalie is going to have a fit if it's her—which isn't fair, why should I have to be the one to settle? Regardless, you'll come to *my* party, right?"

I stare at her for a moment; she's serious. "Why don't you two just throw your parties together? You'll be inviting all the same people, and that way no one has to choose."

She squeezes my arm again. "B, you're brilliant! This is why you need to be at lunch! I'll go find Natalie and tell her it was your idea."

She dashes down the hall, and I fight the urge to lean against the lockers and shut my eyes. Not just because I hadn't slept well last night. Or any of the nights this week. Or because seniors do not need party planning advice from juniors—especially not advice that's so obvious they should've thought of it themselves instead of creating drama or asking people to pick sides.

Except now I'm just being rude. I'm sure they're already combining their guest lists and moving on to debating invitations, colors, and food—

"Oh, I almost forgot to tell you—" Jordan is back, standing in front of me and trying so hard to fight a grin. I force myself to look engaged and interested in whatever the new gossip is. "Since you weren't at lunch today, you also missed my big announcement: I got off the Brown waiting list! I'm in!"

"That's amazing! I'm so proud of you. Congrats!" My last word gets buried in her shoulder as I grab her into a hug. For a few moments I can shake off my exhaustion and be happy for her. "Oh my gosh! How could you possibly not tell me that *first thing?* You've got to be so excited."

"Next time come to lunch and you'll be in the know!" She fake-pouts at me. "Seriously, I only have two weeks of school left—get underlings to do your yearbook tasks; I don't want you missing any more lunches."

"I promise." And I can do that. It's only today. Today and tomorrow. If I can just survive the next thirty-six hours, I'll be able to breathe again. But just thinking about them deflates me, drains all the enthusiasm from my voice. "Brown! Wow. I hope Rhode Island is ready for you."

She doesn't even notice, just laughs and says, "Of course they're not! Okay, gotta get to class, but I'm sure I'll see you tonight. Later, gator."

I call another weak "Congrats" after her and head toward my own class.

"Hey, Brighton!"

"Hi, B."

"What's up, Brighton?"

The hall seems so crowded. All the people passing by, throwing smiles and greetings at me—each one feels like a minor assault of friendliness. Each one makes me more aware of how many sets of eyes are watching—and how big an audience I'll have if I let myself fall to pieces.

I twist the ring on my finger. I expected it to provide some comfort today, but mostly it just feels heavy, foreign—a constant reminder of what's happening tomorrow.

I need to shake this off.

Dad had two favorite sayings: *Everything looks better when you're wearing a smile* and *Eighty percent of any achievement is making the decision to achieve.*

So I'll pull on a smile and be okay. If I can't quite achieve *okay,* at least I'm 80 percent closer to it.

I can fake the rest.

Rebecca J. Romero

TIFFANY SCHMIDT

is the author of *Send Me a Sign* and *Bright Before Sunrise*. She lives in Pennsylvania with her saintly husband, impish twin boys, and a pair of mischievous puggles. She's not at all superstitious . . . at least that's what she tells herself every Friday the thirteenth.

www.tiffanyschmidt.com
@TiffanySchmidt